The Eye of the Storm

By

Tara Fox Hall

Published by
Melange Books, LLC
White Bear Lake, MN 55110
www.melange-books.com

The Eye of the Storm ~ Copyright © 2014 by Tara Fox Hall

ISBN: 978-1-61235-969-4

Cover Art by Caroline Andrus

The Eye of the Storm
Tara Fox Hall

Sar and Theo move on from Sar's affair with Lash, struggling to build a new life with their werecougar son, Devon. Rebuffed, Lash resumes his solitary existence, biding his time. Ulysses lurks in the shadows launching repeated attacks on his enemy Devlin, whose darker side emerges rampant in an effort to protect those he loves. The vampire Danial prepares his dhamphir son, Theoron, for manhood, even as Ulysses delivers a last crippling blow to Devlin in his relentless quest for revenge.

*To my friends, family, and fans. Thank you for helping me realize my dreams!
I love you very much.*

Chapter One

I snuggled close to Theo. While both of us were silent, neither of us was asleep.

Only a few hours ago, my werecougar husband, Theo, had come to blows with the weresnake, Lash, on our front lawn. Theo had come to my defense when he saw me struggling with Lash, and had gotten stabbed for his trouble. In the aftermath of patching up his wound, we'd had makeup sex, I'd gone to pieces, and he'd forgiven me my indiscretion with Lash more than a month before.

Indiscretion. If only that was all it had been. Lash had been dying, and I'd given him a lot of my blood to save his life. In the painful process, he had also regained his youth...and we'd had sex. That might have been bad enough, in some people's book. But I'd gone ahead and compounded the error by throwing the gates wide open, welcoming Lash into my arms again and again, afterwards. We'd been friends for some time already, but somewhere along the line we'd ended up more...or, at least, those were my feelings. Lash's were unknown to me. Sometimes he seemed thoughtful and caring; then, like today, he'd turn violent and nasty. And his language and crudity...appalling was the only word to describe the things he'd said to me in his anger.

Why had I welcomed such a man into my body and heart? A question I couldn't answer. Sure, we liked the same entertainment, and I'd been going through more than a little angst with the vampire brothers, Devlin and Danial, clamoring for a re-Oathing with me by Christmas, enduring my second paranormal pregnancy—and The Lust that always accompanied it— and my husband Theo's ever-present jealousy over having to share me at all.

It doesn't matter why it happened. It's over. Stop thinking about it and move on already, Sar.

"We should get ready," Theo said abruptly, standing up. "I should have been at Danial's hours ago."

"Let's get dressed then," I said with a satisfied sigh. "I'll grab Devon from the living room."

"He's sleeping in front of the TV," Theo said, handing me my clothes. "Here."

After dressing hurriedly and throwing a new change of clothes and my hairbrush in a bag, I went into the living room to get Devon. As Theo had stated, our little cub was curled up asleep on the couch, snoring softly with his left paw over his eyes, his tawny tail twitching ever so slightly as he dreamed. The TV was still on, the last few minutes of the old animated version of *The Return of the King* playing. As I moved to turn it off, an ominous feeling came over me as the dramatic music swelled louder, freezing me in my steps.

...If you win then you will lose. Choice of evils yours to choose....

It was the scene at the end of the movie, where Aragorn confronts Sauron's emissary with his small army at the Black Gate, knowing that he cannot win until Frodo destroys the One Ring. That same sense of utter despair had also been present in the same scene from the later movie with real life actors, sans, of course, the song. While I'd always thought the music perfectly suited to the scene, there was some edge to it today that caused an involuntary shiver to go up my spine.

You are standing in the eye of the storm. Move an inch...and you'll be dead...

Of the many themes from my most beloved childhood story, this was the one message that I had hated: that sometimes there was no way to triumph without a terrible loss. I always wanted to believe if I worked hard enough, was good enough to others, and tried my best that I could win out over the odds against me, whatever they might be. And hadn't I? Wasn't all I'd gone through in the last few years proof enough of that?

Win the battle, lose the war...choice of evils lie before your feet...retreat, retreat, retreat!

"Not this day," I said harshly, clicking off the TV. I woke up Devon by stroking his tawny head, then handed him to Theo, who had just come up behind me. He slung our yawning sleepy-eyed son up onto his shoulder, then grabbed my hand with his free one. I teleported us to Danial's home in an instant. Devon reacted as usual to the magical transport, sinking his claws into Theo and hissing, even though Theo reminded him to relax. We arrived in the great room to find Danial on the couch with Theoron, waiting for us.

Danial gave me a nod, his gaze unreadable. "Theo, come into the office with me for a moment."

Theo handed Devon to me, and followed Danial upstairs.

"Mom, can I talk to you?" Theoron asked.

To my shock, his voice had deepened to that of an older teen. My son who had been a toddler less than a year previous was well on his way to becoming a man. I was instantly ill at ease, not knowing if I should treat him differently. He already seemed so different to me, so changed from the little boy he had been. While I was relieved that he would be safer now that he was older, I missed the child wearing horns and a tail who had played at being a devil only a few months ago.

"Mom?"

Pull it together, Sar. He needs you now, and you need to be there for him.

"Sure, what about?" I responded, sitting down next to him on the couch.

"We need to go for a walk," he said cryptically.

Curious, I followed him into the mudroom. "Do you mind if Devon comes?"

"No."

Devon ran around making little cries as we dressed in jackets and shoes, so excited and eager to be going for a walk. He loved to play in the snow and wasn't often allowed outside at night. This would be a special treat for him.

When we were a hundred yards from the house, with Devon running back and forth looking for snow mice, Theoron finally spoke. "I want self defense lessons," he said hesitantly. "Dad's okay with the idea, but he is a little hesitant about me actually getting physical."

"Why?" I gave Theoron a look that said I didn't get what he was saying. "I'd think he would be glad to teach you—"

"I don't want to learn from Dad," Theoron said, looking into the forest. "He can shoot, and defend himself okay, but he's not really into fighting. He told me with a little disdain he has bodyguards for that, and then began talking about teaching me sword fighting. I'll take those lessons, but that's not really practical in today's world. I need real-life lessons."

"I'm sure Theo would be glad to—" I began.

Theoron quickly took my hand in his, squeezing. "I want to learn from the best," he whispered.

Now I understood why we'd come out here. Theo and Danial would not only be angry, they would be hurt, too, that Theoron wanted lessons from Lash instead of either of them.

"Have you asked him to teach you?" I said pointedly.

Theoron shook his head. "I finally told Dad that I wanted Lash to train me. He said to ask you first, because maybe you could convince him to teach me," he said hopefully. "Dad says Lash has never taught anyone. Dad wanted Lash to teach Theo back when Dad first hired him years ago, and Lash refused. You go to Hayden regularly and you've gotten to know Lash this past year. If you asked for me, he might agree—"

I didn't think Lash would be in any mood to be doing me any favors after my rebuff this afternoon, but I couldn't say that to Theoron. "I'll ask him to consider it," I said haltingly. "But I can't say that he'll make an exception for you, if he's never taught anyone."

"Lash loves you, Mom. Dad told Theo he did," Theoron said, making me flush. "Doesn't a man who loves a woman want to please her?"

Ah, if only it was so easy, Theoron. "Even if that is true—which I don't know if it is—that doesn't mean he'll teach you," I said, giving him a raise of my eyebrows. "Lash can be very stubborn about some things. He separates his emotions from his reason easily."

Well, maybe not today, but most of the time.

"But you'll ask him, next time you see him?" Theoron pressed charmingly, smiling at me.

"Yes, I'll ask," I conceded. "Next you'll be wanting lessons from Dev in his specialty, too—"

"Since you're bringing it up, yes, I do," Theoron said quickly.

Gaping, I blinked stupidly, then blushed from my face to my toes. "Theoron!"

"Dad said I'm old enough for that," Theoron said hesitantly. "And I've...I want to know what to do about that, too. I know Devlin's renowned for his skills in the bedroom. I've never even kissed a girl, and I want to be confident that if I wanted to be with a woman, that I'd know what to do, so it would be...good for both of us."

What had Danial said to that request? I couldn't bring myself to ask. I was woefully unprepared. Where was Danial with his smooth words when I needed him? "I'll talk to your father about it," I said quickly. "But when it comes to this subject, I think you are too young, Theoron. Not to mention that your sister will be saying she's ready for sex, too, if she hears you have permission from your father—"

"Elle's still looks only thirteen at most. I'm a man."

"You are a boy who is becoming a young man," I corrected him. "You are not a man, not by a long shot. It takes more to be a man than looking a certain age."

Theoron opened his mouth to protest, his green eyes spitting fire.

I held up my hand. "But I allow that this is your father's territory. He was raised a certain way—as was Devlin—and you are his son. He wants a lot for you, and I trust his judgment. So if he tells me that he believes you should learn from Dev, I'm not going to stand in the way. He would never allow you to do something that might hurt you. He loves you too much for that."

4

"Really?" Theoron said, eagerness on his face. "You'll let Devlin teach me?"

Had I ever been so young, so hopeful? A long, long time ago. "Yes. But you'll have to ask him yourself, or have your father arrange it," I said flatly. "I'm not asking Dev for that."

"I wouldn't expect you to ask him, Mom," Theoron said a trifle arrogantly. "I'll ask Dad whether he wants to talk to Dev or he wants me to."

We began walking back to the house.

"Anything else?" I hoped not. I was still coming to terms with the little we'd discussed.

Theoron shot a look at me and smiled. "No."

He was so much like Danial, so handsome. He was right that it was time for him to start becoming a man, as he certainly was going to get female attention the moment he stepped off this estate. But that also meant it was time for another big talk. And even though I was sure Danial had mentioned this subject to him, it was my place as well to bring it up now.

"What do you think you want to do, when it's time for you to work?" I asked. "I know that you read well, and can do some math and sciences on a high school level, Theoron. You are very intelligent, even though you have had only a little time to learn schooling—"

"I want to try going into business with Dad," Theoron said, kicking at a few visible rocks. "I know how much he wants that. I can answer most of the e-mail already, and Dad has been teaching me some of the computer programming, and code writing he knows. I have a gift for it, he says."

I'd gratefully thought that the business was slowing down. Instead, unknowingly, I'd had help. Still, this was a good first step. If Theoron wanted so badly to learn to be a man, the first thing he needed to learn was how to work long hours. Because no matter what career he decided on, he would need concentration, drive, and more than a little ambition to make his dreams happen.

"Good. Has he taken you to meet clients yet?"

"Not until I look eighteen, at least, he said," Theoron said grumpily. "He is having some contacts of his make up some valid ID for me, and he said he is going to have one of the foxes, probably Hans, teach me to drive starting tomorrow. But he doesn't want me to go on jobs until I have some defensive training. He told me about Ulysses—everything. I know even if Devlin or Lash kills him eventually, there will always be someone else out there wanting to hurt me, to get to either him or you—"

I sighed. "That's true. I wish you could get your sister to understand that."

"Some of that is because Dad is too protective of her," Theoron said, kicking a clump of frozen grass. "He wants me to grow up, to be a man, but he wants her to stay a little girl forever. And she wants to be a woman, not a girl."

I could understand that, even if I didn't know what to do about it. "Some of that is that Elle was your dad and mine's first child, Theoron—"

"Can you call me "T" please, Mom?" he said interrupting.

I stopped walking and turned to him. "Danial and I called you Theoron for a reason, *Theoron*," I said, irked. "For Theo."

"But I can't be called Theo," Theoron said with a sigh. "People are always getting us confused, especially now that my voice is deeper. Theoron is too long to say all the time. Please, call me T."

I didn't like it, not at all, but he had a point. And I myself had a shortened nickname I preferred to use, so what could I say? "Fine, T," I said reluctantly. "Elle was the first one to call him Dad, and to hug him, and in part, she brought your dad and I back together. It was our shared joy in raising her that made me tell your dad I wanted a child of our own. Elle is a girl, too, and your dad is protective of her just for that. And some of it is that she will need to leave the state, probably the whole east, to seek out a werecougar mate, and your father is afraid to let her go off on her own. I'm afraid too, because I worry about her."

"Can't she just change someone, or just mate with a human? You're married to Theo, and you had a werecougar for a baby," Theoron stated, as if that was the obvious solution.

"Technically, she could be with anyone she wanted," I said slowly, realizing Theoron had brought up a good point. "She doesn't have to choose another cougar to be with. But then there is the worry that she'll pick a human who isn't accepting enough, and he'll either 'out' her or try to hurt her. And I wonder if she wouldn't feel more comfortable looking for love without both of her dads and me peering over her shoulder."

"You're good parents," Theoron said softly. "Besides, Elle needs someone looking over her shoulder. If Terian wasn't shadowing her, I know for a fact it wouldn't be Violet she was meeting at the mall."

"What do you mean?" I said sharply, putting my hand on his arm.

Theoron looked at me and blushed. I waited, crossing my arms over my chest.

"I mean that Elle likes men. She may not know a lot, or even be shy around them, but she wants to be around men. She hangs out a lot at the werecompound now, and spends a lot of time with Warren, Hans, and some of the other single weres."

Nice. Something else to mention to Danial tonight.

"Let's go back to the house," I said, my good mood deflated. "C'mon, Devon!"

As we walked back towards the house with Devon bounding in front of us, I noticed with a start that Theoron was taller than I was now. He was nearly Danial's height. I wiped away a few unshed tears discreetly. He really would be a man shortly. I would be finding out very soon if Danial and I had done a good job of raising him.

* * * *

Theo and Danial were waiting for us when we returned. Devon ran in and jumped on Theo, who smiled at him. But then he pushed his son away gently, and walked over to Theoron. "T, Danial wants me to take you to the armory, and set you up with your own gun, and armor," Theo said, his tone all business.

Theoron nodded. Theo turned to me, then gave me a hug and kiss. I made it last longer, clinging to him when he went to pull away. Theo hugged me extra tight before finally letting me go. The door shut behind them, leaving me alone with Danial.

I turned to face him. Danial leaned against the wall, watching me with his arms crossed over his chest, his dark eyes a little reserved.

What to say? I assumed since he'd asked me to stay the night that I was supposed to sleep with him. But it was too awkward after his distant behavior for the last weeks to just walk into his bedroom as if everything was fine between us. Instead, I picked up the cups that Theo and Theoron—no, T—had used and took them to the kitchen. I'd seen no sign of Mary. From the general disarray in the various rooms, she hadn't been in today again. She hadn't been in all last week, either. Her daughter Jenny was very close to dying. Last I knew, Danial had told Mary he would turn her daughter to vampire if Jenny agreed to his conditions. But Theo hadn't mentioned anything lately. Had Danial talked to her yet?

As I tried to think of ways to bring up the subject, Danial touched my shoulder, rubbing gently. I went still under his fingers.

"I have to finish up some things in the office," Danial said cordially. "Please come back by nine or so, Sar."

What? I turned and followed him back towards the study. "Where am I going?" I said in confusion.

"Terian said he needed to talk to you as soon as you got here tonight," Danial said as he went upstairs. "He's in his lab. I figured you knew what it was about."

Talk to me? About what? I'd gone to see him two days ago, and he hadn't mentioned anything then. But we'd only said a quick hello, as he'd been on the way to teleport Theo and himself to a last-minute client meeting. Terian had just shot me a smile, and said he would see me later. What could be so urgent now that he had to see me first thing? Maybe he was finally going to ask Sundown to marry him? He might be looking for some support. God knew I hadn't been very supportive lately. If it hadn't been for Titus asking me to watch him and report on his moods, I probably would have avoided him, worried about the wrong words falling out of my mouth.

I went back towards the sink, and began washing the cups, planning on how to play this. Terian didn't know about Lash and I, just as most of the other weres at Danial's didn't. They didn't know about my saving him, or what I'd had to do to make that happen. Everyone had bought the story of my finding him at the last moment at death's door, but Devlin and I had heaped the credit for his miraculous recovery on Titus. Trouble was I had no idea what Titus had told his son about the potion he'd supposedly made that had saved Lash. What if I innocuously let something slip? Terian was naturally suspicious, and he could often tell if I was lying.

Calling Hayden for pointers was also out. Titus had been absent from Hayden whenever I'd visited, spending most of his off-duty time now with Leri at their house on Devlin's land instead of his basement workshop. There was nothing else to do but plead ignorance, and vague everything up.

I rinsed the cups, stuck them in the dish rack to dry, and then teleported quickly to Terian's lab. He was there, studiously working on a concoction on one of his tables. All lights were off except for one near the door. Used glassware and spilled liquid and powder surrounded him. A heap of scrolls lay on the table, some badly aged and stained.

I'd never seen the lab such a mess. Something was up. "Hi, Tears."

"Hey, Sar-baby," Terian said, not looking up from the vial into which he was pouring powder.

I recoiled from his tone, a strange mix of anger and lust. "Danial said you had to see me? What's so urgent—?"

Terian didn't reply, concentrating hard on adding more ingredients to the vial. Smoke issued forth, along with a sultry sweet smell.

Something was very wrong. My nerves were screaming that I was in danger, telling me to run or teleport now. I tried to teleport and couldn't. Fear coursed through me like a bolt of lightning, and I ran for the door. Terian exploded, hurling the tiny vial of red liquid at me. I ducked instinctively, and it hit the wall behind me, splattering and smoking as it ate away at the wall and door, the paint and wood oozing together.

"What the hell?" I screamed, pulling at the immobile door handle. "What's wrong with you?"

Terian spun me around to face him. Heat and anger came off him in waves. His eyes were red with flames, and his teeth had changed. Now he had

8

the pointed teeth of Titus, row upon row of them.

Oh shit. Terian's become full demon, just as Titus had feared. I backed away as he advanced, my eyes wide and scared.

"You fucking slut," Terian snarled, reaching one taloned hand up into my hair, his nails raking my skull. With the other, he motioned to the door. The knob melted into a twisted lump of metal, some of it dripping down to puddle on the floor.

"Terian, let me go!" I said loudly, furiously struggling. "Right now!"

"You cunt," Terian hissed in my ear. "All the years I protected you, fought for you, rescued you! You knew I had feelings for you, you knew I wanted you! You were always so happy to come to me when you needed something, and as soon as I helped you, you were off again, fucking someone else!"

Titus had been right to worry all those months ago. Terian had succumbed to the demon side of himself in the space of a day or less. How could I get to help without teleporting?

"I love Sundown because she looks like you, and she doesn't mind if I hurt her a little sometimes, or make her pretend to be you. But it was always you I really wanted, just like I want you now."

Terian kissed me on my neck, his lips so hot my flesh sizzled under their touch. I let out another scream, fighting to free myself, the scent of burning flesh strong in my nostrils.

"Scream all you want, Sar-baby!" Terian laughed. "No one will hear you! There's a dampening spell around the room that I just finished. We won't be disturbed."

He kissed me again. Fresh pain lanced through my nerve endings, acrid smoke rising from my flesh.

"Stop it, please! Please!"

"I should've given in that day you grabbed my ass in the kitchen years ago. I was an idiot to take you to Danial and play the fucking saint." Terian ran his hand down the wall, his sharp talons making long digs in the blistered drywall. "A waste of hours of work." He touched my cheek, pressing the tip of one talon into my soft skin. "It would have recreated the lust you had, Sar. This would be so much more fun if you wanted to play."

"Stop it!"

Terian laughed with brittleness. "Stop what? Don't try to play the virgin princess. You fucked Lash when you saved him with your blood. That story of my father making a potion was all a lie! He lied to me, his own son, for you! He's my father, and he lied to me for you!"

How did he know that? "You're crazy! Let me go!"

Terian shoved me so hard I fell into one of his chairs, hitting my knee on the wooden leg.

"Ow!" I yelled, rubbing my knee, even as I maneuvered fast to put the chair between Terian and I. He was coming for me again, his burning eyes fixed on mine, filled with repulsion. The very air around him shimmered with heat, forcing me to retreat.

"You willingly fucked a vicious snake that ate people to live, who has killed hundreds of people for money, who broke your husband's neck, and who gave you an STD the first time you had sex! You let his boss fuck you last night, the same villain who would have drained your blood until he killed you, who raped you repeatedly until you almost couldn't move, and forced you to bear him a child! I heard Danial tell Theo you loved Lash! I heard you yourself tell Devlin you loved him! They are monsters, both of them, and you *love* them! But you couldn't love *me*, me who loved you best of all! Me, who was *always* there for you, who saved your *life*, saved your lovers' lives, saved your marriage, and protected your children!"

"I don't love you like that, Tears," I said, slowly and calmly as I could manage. "I'm sorry, but I just don't. I never pretended to. I always told you the truth about how I felt. I'm sorry if I wasn't more appreciative of you, if I wasn't there for you when you needed me, if I made you feel that you were anything less than a treasured friend—"

"Save the treasured friend crap," Terian rasped hatefully, his left hand twisted in my hair. "I don't want your poor excuse for friendship, Babe. But I do want something else. I'm getting it tonight from you, right now, whether you want to give it to me or not." His right hand retracted its talons, then unzipped his fly. "Get on your knees, Sar."

God, no! I struggled as Terian's burning hand reached under my clothes, then in a last ditch effort tried once more to teleport. The walls of the lab fell away to be replaced by the kitchen walls of Hayden. Startled, I fell backward and went down, Terian on top of me still fumbling with his pants.

Dear God, let Lash still be here! "Lash! Titus! Dev!" I screamed, trying to fend of Terian's hands. "Help! Help me!"

"Go ahead and call for them!" Terian hissed, grasping my wrist. He rose to his feet, a ball of blue fire in his other hand. "They aren't a match for me, none of them—"

"Get away from her now." Lash was before us, infuriated, his knife in his hand. His fangs were bared, venom steadily dripping.

Relief washed through me. Terian had seen that knife kill one of his kind this year. He'd back off now.

"Come and get her, you vile snake!" Terian dared. "This fire can reduce you to nothing in an instant."

"I'm not afraid of you, you fucking Hellspawn!" Lash hissed back. "Let her go and fight me."

"No," Terian sneered. He tightened his hand in my hair, making a fist at the top of my head, and began forcing me down. I pushed back and held a second, then went down on all fours.

"You can watch."

I put my hands up, trying to unclasp his hand, but he was too strong, and his hand was broiling. His skin was so hot I couldn't grasp him. I turned desperate eyes to Lash. "Do something!"

"He's afraid," Terian sneered. "He knows his knife and his poison, even combined, can't kill me now that I'm pure demon." He unbuttoned his pants. "Get to it, Sar."

"Stop, Terian, this isn't you."

He jerked my hair hard, so I let out a cry of pain. "Unbutton my pants and open your mouth or I'll set your beautiful hair on fire. It's already smoking."

With shaking hands, I reached for the front of his pants, and folded back the denim. Terian looked down at me, his hot, lustful gaze savoring, then gestured with the ball of fire. It left his hand and hung in the air beside him, burning steadily.

"I'll cool my flesh so I don't burn your throat, Sar-Baby. I'll be nice to you, if you're nice to me. Theo says you can be very nice when you want to be—"

I threw myself backward in a last ditch effort. Terian's hand tightened, pulling me back upright, my face inches from his groin. I swayed, shaking, as he took my right hand and slid it in into his underwear and onto to his rigid flesh. Terian let out a groan, then made my hand stroke his erection as he flexed under my fingers.

"Enough foreplay. Take me in your mouth, now, or I'll burn you again," Terian hissed. "And you're going to swallow it all—"

I shuddered, even as he pushed my head closer to his groin.

Chapter Two

Terian's angry words abruptly cut off as he sank to his knees, screaming. I lurched backward, sprawling on my back. Devlin, eyes red and furiously determined, shoved again with the full weight of his body, both hands twisting the twin of Lash's long serrated knife in Terian's back. With a wet ripping sound, the bloody point came out of Terian's chest beneath his heart. The ball of blue fire dissolved into nothing as Terian sank to the floor, sulfurous smoke and black blood pouring from his chest wound.

Thank God for blessed weaponry.

"Get her!" Devlin levered his weight onto Terian, keeping the knife buried as he twisted it over and over to stop the flesh healing around it. Terian kept screaming, his taloned hands flailing in the slick blood as he tried to grab the blade.

I pushed backward, kicking at him. Terian swore and reached for me, refocused.

A dark fist smashed into the side of his face, knocking him back to the floor. Then hands were pulling at me, getting me away.

Lash pushed me behind him, sheathed his knife, and then drew his gun in a smooth practiced motion, aiming it at Terian's heart.

About fucking time! Why the hell hadn't he done that sooner?

"Are you okay, Sar?" Lash said softly, his eyes riveted on Devlin and the still-struggling Terian.

"Yes," I whispered, my voice trembling. "Do it."

"Let me shoot that bastard at least once, Dev," Lash hissed, his fury white hot. "You saw what he was planning."

"I told you no shooting, Lash. Titus is on his way," Devlin said with effort, still twisting the knife as Terian struggled to his knees. "Terian needs to be no more damaged than he already is. Titus is coming."

Practicality explained Lash's actions, or more accurately, his lack of action. Still, one well-placed bullet was deserved, in my opinion.

Titus appeared near Lash. When he saw Terian's black blood and rows of teeth, all the energy seemed to go out of him. Murmuring words, he went to his son, catching him in his arms as Terian suddenly slumped, motionless. Devlin pulled the knife out in a practiced smooth motion. Terian and Titus disappeared. As they vanished, my vision went grey about the edges, then black.

* * * *

I came to on the couch, Devlin holding me in his arms. Lash watched us with hooded eyes from his position against the nearest wall.

"Are you hurt?" Devlin said softly, his golden eyes concerned. "I see the burns, Sar, but was there anything else?"

"You were prepped for this to happen," I said, hating the sound of my wavering words. "You had that knife blessed. How did you know he'd turned demon?"

"I saw Sundown, Terian's woman," Devlin said darkly. "Her close resemblance to you wasn't the fluke Danial fluffed it off as. And I knew Titus was worried about Terian. It made sense if he was going to snap, it would be over the object of his unrequited affection."

I cracked a smile. "So you know a lot about unrequited love, do you?"

Devlin didn't smile. "He's been carrying this torch for you since you saved his life years ago."

"How many men's lives has Sar saved, besides mine and Danial's?" Lash said with a roll of his eyes. "I'm not feeling very special anymore."

I ignored Lash. He'd been a royal pain in the ass today, and I hadn't forgiven him for making that scene with Theo earlier. Plus, he should have fucking shot Terian at least once, no matter what Devlin told him to do. Dev could have stabbed Tears later, when he was healing the gunshot wound. "What will happen to Tears?" I asked Devlin.

"Titus took him to his home. He and Leri will do what they can to get Terian back to normal. But it's going to take a while. Its good Theoron's older, as he's going to have to be more responsible for his own safety. Titus is going to have his hands full with his son."

"Now that we're all sure that Terian's safe, why the hell didn't you do more to stop him sooner?" I said bluntly, trying hard not to give into hysteria. "I was scared, Dev! He almost—"

Devlin didn't flinch or look away from my accusation. "Because we need Terian back as he was, the sooner the better," Devlin soothed. "He is Danial's most powerful protector. Titus's brother will fill in to help protect Danial, when he's not helping Titus and Leri with Terian, in exchange for my help tonight in containing Terian. You'll like him, Sar. He's much like Titus, though a little bigger."

Titus was the size of a linebacker, and at least seven feet tall. Demons seemed to run to the big and tall side of the spectrum, at least male ones, anyway. "Dev, I was still—"

"You were not at risk, not really," Devlin assured. "Lash would've shot Terian if it had gone any further."

"I say we still should have fucked him up a little," Lash hissed meaningfully. "You can bet your ass when he's well, he'll be taking a bullet or five from me on general principle—"

"Hush up, and stop posturing," Devlin said sharply, darting a look at Lash. "Sar is not going to forgive you for that scene today at her house because you say you'll shoot Terian someday."

Lash hissed at him, then looked away.

My adrenaline was slowing down, though relaxing was still not an option. But Dev was right; it was over now, and I was safe. "Thank you both," I said, cautiously running my hands across my scalp to check for talon scratches. "I'm just glad you were all here and came as quick as you did."

"I called Titus as soon as I felt blackness, and heard you screaming," Devlin replied. "Lash heard you, too, and came down here to distract Terian while I got into position behind him." He gave me a gentle kiss, and got up from the couch. "Let me get you a glass of wine, and I'll call Danial to tell him what happened. He'll need to have to arrange for another bodyguard for the next month at least. Rip can't guard him twenty-four hours a day—"

"That long?" I said, aghast.

Devlin nodded. "Titus will do his best, Sar, but Terian is going to be spending some time under house arrest. I don't envy Titus or Leri. It's going to be a sort of exorcism, trying to get the human half of Terian back in control. But Titus will do it, if it's possible that it can be done."

Devlin went into the kitchen. I leaned back into the couch, closing my eyes and trying to fathom one good scenario in which a demon had ended up with the nickname Rip. Within seconds, a rush of air from movement brought the scent of musk, leaves, leather, and earth as Lash settled beside me.

He leaned over me, close enough to hug. "I'm sorry for how I acted today," Lash hissed softly, his warm breath on my face. "I was angry about your change of heart."

"There hasn't been any change," I said tiredly, keeping my eyes closed. "But I can't be with you, Lash. Can you accept that?"

"I get it," Lash hissed, obviously upset. "And I'll respect it. It hurt a lot to hear you say…what you did. I let my emotions get the better of me. I'm sorry for the things I said. And I won't touch you again like that, unless you ask me to."

I opened my eyes. Lash instantly moved back and away, crouching beside the couch on his haunches. His remorseful expression softened my anger, but I resisted touching him, even though I wanted to take him in my arms more than anything.

"Please tell me that your threats…that what you suggested by your truck was just a bluff?"

Lash grinned widely. "If you asked me to do that, sure," he said easily. "But just forget it, okay? I said it to shock you. This is not the time of year to be performing outdoors in the raw. If you want to frolic together naked outside with me, you'll have to wait for next summer."

I rolled my eyes. "Thanks for your honesty."

Devlin returned with the wine. I took it eagerly, then downed half of it in one gulp. Both men looked surprised, but didn't comment. I downed the rest of it, then handed the glass back to Devlin. "Can I have another?"

Devlin nodded, then went to get it.

The alcohol had the opposite effect I was looking for. Instead of calming me, my head spun, images of Terian replaying again and again as the full horror of what he had tried to do hit me like a sharp slap. I clutched the couch arm, my breathing rapid and shallow.

Lash got up from the floor and sat down on the couch beside me. He put his arms around me hesitantly. "Come here."

I snuggled close, clutching him tightly. *Screw Theo.* I was scared, I wanted to be held, and he wasn't here to do it.

"You're safe," he whispered. "Anyone coming for you has to go through me first. Got it?"

"I got it," I said, my words muffled by his shirt.

"Are you hurt anywhere else?" Lash hissed urgently, worried. "Did he do anything to you before you were able to teleport him here? I thought I scented burnt flesh, but all I smell now is that demon stink of sulfur and brimstone."

Devlin came back in and sat down on my free side. I took the wine from him gratefully, and sipped it, still sheltered in Lash's embrace, then handed it back. "Thanks."

"What happened?" Devlin asked.

"He called me some names," I said hollowly, shame coloring my face. "Things Terian would never say to me. He knew the truth about what happened with Lash in the Everglades. He said it was his turn, basically. You saw the rest."

"That fucking demon," Lash hissed angrily, tightening his arms around me protectively. "I'm going to fuck him up when he comes back. I don't care who—"

"That's not the most pressing issue," Devlin said pensively. "We need to know how he found out at once. Neither Danial nor Theo would have slipped and told him."

"It had to be Titus," Lash hissed angrily. "Who else knows?"

"I'll find out who it was," Devlin said resolutely. "Titus wouldn't have risked Sar being hurt. It can't be him. Someone may have heard Danial and I arguing that night. I'll have to find out who, then have Titus do a mind wipe on them to take the memory so they won't tell anyone else—"

"It wasn't Titus," I interjected, downing another half-glass. "Terian was angry Titus had lied to him about what really happened."

"I'll call Danial. He'll account for his people that night," Devlin said, taking my wine from me and downing the rest of it in one swallow. "I'll find out who it was. What a cluster fuck!"

"Some of what he said was true, though," I said sadly. "I should have been a better friend to him. I only saw him when I needed something for the last year. I kept telling myself I was too busy."

"You had a lot going on," Devlin soothed, taking me from Lash's arms into his own. "Don't blame yourself for this, Love."

"I'm not to blame for Terian losing himself in his demon nature," I admitted, putting my arms around his cool shoulders. "But I am to blame for not being a better friend. Maybe I could have done something—"

"Hush. You should stay here for a while, until you recover," Devlin said firmly. "Stay the night, if you want." He kissed me gently on the forehead.

God, it would be so easy to stay here with them both, watch a movie and eat popcorn, and later go to bed with Devlin. But I didn't need Carol here to tell me that Lash wouldn't leave my side tonight if I stayed over at Hayden. I didn't want him to; I was feeling both fragile and needy. How long would it be before I was in his arms doing more than hugging? Devlin obviously wasn't going to protest. Lash and I would be lovers again before the night was through.

I couldn't do that. Lash had to make his appointment tonight with Gina, his would-be lover. It was a first step for him to move on, something I needed to encourage. And Danial was expecting me, though there weren't going to be any intimate moments for us tonight. He wouldn't expect any now. Instead of his distant and cold manner, he would likely be his charming, attentive, and much-preferred normal self. Bitterly, I thanked Terian for his part in smoothing things over with Danial.

I got up reluctantly and faced Lash and Devlin. "I need to get back," I said, trying to keep out of my voice how much I wanted to stay. "Danial and Theo must both be worried, and I'm exhausted."

"Go and get some rest," Lash said with concern, his dark eyes disturbed.

"I'll call Danial and tell him what happened," Devlin added. There was a grim set to his gorgeous face, and his golden eyes were fixed on me. "Call if you need me, even just to talk, Sar. Let us know if there is anything we can do."

Blinking, it registered that there was something Lash could do, just not for me. "This is awkward, but I might as well get it out there. Lash, Theoron wants to learn to fight. Will you teach him?"

Lash narrowed his eyes. "Why doesn't he learn from Theo, his namesake?" he hissed sarcastically. "Or how about his real father?"

"He said he wanted to learn from you because you're the best. Danial told him you would refuse to teach him."

"I don't teach anyone," Lash replied, giving me a considering look. "I never have."

I nodded. "It's fine if you'd prefer not to. He wanted me to ask you, and I said I would. I'll tell him your answer. He can learn from Theo."

Maybe this would be better anyway. Maybe Theo and Theoron could bond...

"Why don't you teach him?" Devlin asked suddenly, looking over at Lash. "He's the closest thing I have to a son. The closest thing I'll probably ever have. I'll expect you to teach Venus when she's older, enough to make sure she can protect herself if she's ever cornered. Why not perfect lessons on Theoron first?"

Lash sighed dramatically, then gave a self-incriminating grin. "Okay, I'll teach him the basics," he said finally. "But unless I find him extremely talented, he'll have to learn the rest from Theo. I'm surmising that Theoron only needs to be able to hold his own in a fight, to learn to take a little pain, and how to escape if he's taken prisoner. He's not going to be fighting any bad guys. He'll be shooting them instead, and then only rarely. Is that sufficient?"

Hopefully, Theoron would think it was. "That's more than fair."

Thinking about Lash's response, I debated asking for escape lessons myself. If I'd had the know how, maybe there was something I could've done when I was Ulysses's prisoner to get myself free. But that wasn't a favor I felt comfortable asking tonight. Then there was the other one that Theoron wanted me to ask of Devlin. *No, don't mention that.*

"Bring your son with you next time you visit Dev," Lash hissed to me. "I'll talk to him. Besides, if he's man enough to want to learn to fight, he needs to have the balls to ask me himself, and not have his mother do it for him—"

I smiled at Devlin, then let go of my verbal inhibitions. "Be warned:

Theoron wants you to teach him your skills too, Dev."

Devlin gaped at me, appalled.

Lash laughed uproariously. Devlin shoved him off the couch in irritation. Lash sprawled on the floor, still guffawing. "I'm teaching him to fight, and Dev's going to teach him to fuck!" Lash finally got out. "This is too much! What's left for Theo to teach him? How to flee?"

"Shut up, Lash," I said sweetly with dagger eyes.

Lash flashed me a smile, then got up and flopped back onto the couch.

"He's too young for that," Devlin said in a tightly controlled voice. "He needs to be sixteen at least."

"He looks sixteen now," I countered with a shrug. "Danial said it was time."

"Sure enough, he's your bloodline!" Lash put in snidely, still laughing. "You said you wanted a son. You seem to have gotten one with *all* your interests, Dev."

"And just who am I supposed to have him practice with?" Devlin said, furrowing his brow. "Serena?"

"That's for you and Danial to work out," I said quickly. "I just thought I'd mention it to you, so you knew. I don't want to know any more about it than I do already. What I know now is TMI. But you might as well know tonight that T's expectation is looming on the horizon, even if the exact moment isn't here yet."

Devlin looked at me, gritting his fangs together. I didn't need him to tell me that he was self-conscious about being the master sex educator with his own new sensitivity; it was all over his face he was worried about his ability to demonstrate and perform. But he would have to work out that problem on his own.

Devlin rolled his eyes. "I'll handle it, then. But before you leave, we need to check over your wounds, Sar." He beckoned to me. "Come here and sit, please."

I carefully felt my neck burns, pulling down my shirt's neckline to expose the blistered welts. "It's where Terian kissed me. I could hear it sizzling."

Lash hissed immediately, then got to his feet, angrily glaring at my seared flesh. "I'm going to hurt him bad. Next time I see him."

"Why is it not healing?" Devlin said, anxious. "It should be healed by now, but it isn't."

I shrugged. "My bites from Venus healed okay. Maybe because it's a demon-inflicted wound? I don't know."

"Is there any pain?"

"Only when I touch it...Ow!"

"Call Camlyn tomorrow," Devlin instructed, drawing his hand back. "I don't want to give you my blood to heal, because I want you to have Danial check the burns for you tomorrow, and see if they've improved. If you feel like you need an infusion, just ask Danial. We never checked your virus levels after what you did for Lash. I'm hesitant to either drink or donate to you—"

"Don't you know if it's safe for me?" I asked, suddenly worried.

"My desire for you and your blood is ever-present," Devlin answered lovingly, embracing me. "It's how you act subconsciously and consciously that let's me know if you're close to turning. Right now, nothing is giving me any clues. Odds are it's safe, but I'd rather not risk it without more data."

He'd always been so sure before that he knew exactly what to do. Has Devlin's insecurity over his sexual prowess affected his other judgment? Only time will tell. I nodded.

When Devlin let me go, Lash leaned in and gave me a careful hug. "Dev's right. Put some dressing on it when you get to Danial's. It shouldn't get infected, but—"

"I'll put some salve on it," I interrupted, nodding. "Have a good night."

"Make the appointment with Camlyn for tomorrow," Devlin put in quickly. "Call me when you're about to leave. I'll either have Lash go in my stead, or have Titus teleport me if he's able. Something about you has changed, Sar. We need to find out what."

I pushed down my unease, nodding. "I should get back."

Devlin gave me a kiss. "Take care."

I teleported to Danial's home, arriving in the great room. No one was around. Relieved, I went into Danial's bathroom, and took a long, hot shower. The burns hurt under the warm spray, but after I emerged and put some salve on them, the pain eased to a dull, persistent ache.

It was only a little before nine, but screw it, I was ready for bed now. I slipped on a nightgown and lay down in Danial's bed, drifting off immediately.

I was awoken a moment later by the door opening, and a bright, intrusive light going on overhead. "Sar!" Danial exclaimed in relief, Theo echoing him. They came to either side of the bed, and both tried to embrace me at once.

I hugged them both back gingerly, hyper aware of my neck burns. But it was good to feel their strong arms around me. Danial inspected my neck. His worried eyes met mine.

"It's true that her burns are not healing as they should," he said. "Sar, call the doctor tomorrow. Get the earliest appointment, whatever opening Stephen has. We need to know what is wrong."

Theo nodded agreement, worry in his blue-gray eyes.

"You should stay the night here with us, Theo," Danial said.

Theo shook his head, his expression anxious. "I need to get back to the dogs. They need to be walked, and let out, and Devon likes it better there, anyway—"

"Go on home, then," Danial said dismissively.

Theo gave me a hug and a kiss, and then left.

"I'll be back soon," Danial said lovingly. "Rest, Sar."

* * * *

When Danial eased into bed sometime later, I awoke, yawning, then rolled on my side to face him. "I'm glad you didn't press," I said finally.

Danial watched me with his dark eyes, the only illumination the very faint nightlight from the bathroom. He was breathtaking in the dimness, his lustrous skin shining with a glow of its own. Had he been feeding downstairs earlier? He must have been, to look this good.

"I turned on the nightlight for you," he said. "So if you woke it wouldn't be in total darkness."

That light was reassuring, a reminder of a less complicated time when I'd lived here with him. "Do you not want to touch me, or are you waiting for permission?" I whispered.

"An invitation," Danial answered. "Though I'll understand if you don't want to give one after what happened to you tonight."

I did not want to talk about that now. "Why did you suddenly forgive me?" I said, staring at him. "Nothing between us had changed. Yet you asked me to come to you tonight like everything was okay between us."

"Because Theo forgave you," Danial said. "It had to be this way, because I did not want to rush him, but to have him come to it on his own."

I looked over at him in bewilderment. "What?"

"I didn't want him to be the only one who didn't forgive you," Danial explained. "And the truth is that I needed some time to forgive you, too, for what you did."

So we were going to talk after all. Might as well get it over with. "Have you?"

"I'm not happy you saved Lash with your blood, but I understand your reasons," Danial said quietly. "I suspect you love him, so it's not hard to conclude you might desire him, or risk your life to save him. But you need to understand something, Sar."

I waited, apprehension building.

"You asked me once what I would do if you were Oathed to me and broke the Oath to be with someone else. At the time you were thinking of Devlin, and your guilt over him, but I answered you honestly."

I went still as death under the covers.

"You were not technically Oathed to me when you let Lash have you," Danial said quietly. "But you were wearing my choker. Yet, you still were willing to open your legs to him. I want to remind you what I said to you a year ago, Sar. Because a life hangs in the balance, even if it is not your own."

Chapter Three

"I told you I'd kill a human, or a were, anyone except Dev," Danial stated sharply. "I meant that. If you had told me your choker had fallen off and wouldn't refasten, I'd have hired some men to go after Lash—as many as it took, for as long as it took, until they killed him."

"You would have started a war," I whispered, aghast. "Devlin wouldn't have stood for you killing Lash. And Lash himself—"

Danial snarled loudly, drowning out my words. "I would merely be protecting my Oathed One from an interloper! Samuel, and the other Rulers would approve, and Devlin would have no law he could call on to save Lash."

"We were not Oathed," I said, my anger overriding my shock. "You told me so yourself, with all your talk of a gray area! I didn't go there to have sex with him, Danial! I let him have me, because I thought he was dying! I was in pain! You have no idea how much it hurt!"

"When you were healed and lying in his arms in the hotel, there was no pain on either side, only your wanting of each other," Danial retorted angrily. "I am not blaming you for the first times, Sar. But later on, you made a willing choice to be with him. Don't lie to me."

That was true, and there was no point sugarcoating it. "You're right. I'm sorry."

"Lash saw the choker at your neck, and he didn't care you belonged to me. All he cared about was that you agreed. All you cared about was that you wanted him. And I am reminding you now that you should have thought about who you belonged to, and you should have said no—"

The same, old possessive Danial. My fury engulfed me like a sudden wave. "Maybe I should have," I hissed, turning my back to him. "But I didn't. And if I had it to do over, I would do it again, Danial! You don't own me!"

Utter rage emanated off him, but I was too angry to care.

"I know you would," Danial hissed at me. "I know you, Sar. I know you're

22

in love with him, no matter how much you deny it to yourself, and everyone else. Theo is in denial about it too. He thinks you and he are fine, that your attraction for Lash is in the past." He grabbed my wrist and squeezed. "I'm telling you right now, you ever give yourself to Lash again without Devlin's express permission and approval, and I'll have Lash killed, if it takes years and all of my resources to do it!"

"I already have Dev's permission," I said with relish in the darkness, letting the words fall from my lips one by one like sharp knives. "If I wanted to, I could have been with Lash today, Danial. All it would have taken was three words from me to Lash telling him I wanted him."

Danial didn't answer.

"Call Dev if you don't believe me," I added triumphantly. "How do you know all of this, anyway?"

"Lash told Devlin all of it when Devlin found the two of you together," Danial said, his tone now resigned. "Devlin related it all to me." He paused. "He would have killed anyone else you had done that with, Sar, anyone but Lash, Oath or no Oath. You need to remember that, too."

"He made it very clear to me, Danial," I interjected. "Don't worry about another bed partner in the mix. I have too many as it is. The last thing I want to do is add another dick to my growing pile."

Danial didn't answer.

Embarrassed at my crudeness, I began again. "Danial, if it had been anyone else but Lash, I wouldn't have gone to save them. I mean, I would have done it for you, the children, Dev or for Theo, but I wouldn't have risked my life for anyone else. Not Terian, or any of the foxes—"

"What is there between you and him?" Danial said with irritation. "There is something, Sar. I hear it in your loyal words, just as I hear your love for him. You are grateful to him for something; there is something you think you owe him for—"

This was getting dangerous. I needed to remember who I was talking to. Danial would be guessing about Lash's deal with me soon, if I didn't take back control of the conversation in the next breath. He could not know my return to Devlin's side had been at Lash's behest—that Lash had saved Theo's life from a gang of bounty hunters that would have surely killed him as the price, or that Lash's dying had been precipitated by a wound he'd sustained in the process.

"He's my friend," I said flatly. "I don't owe him anything. But the truth is, right or wrong, I do wish I was allowed to spend time with him. I miss him."

"Be that as it may, I have just as much claim to you as Devlin does now, if not more," Danial said firmly. "I'm telling you, Sar, you are not to be with him again, unless Devlin either asks you to be, according to his preferences, or you take a new Oath to Dev that includes him as one of your lovers. Is that understood?"

Try to restrain yourself, Sar. Don't tell him to go fuck himself. "Completely and utterly," I said wearily. "I am trying hard to make it work with Theo. As for the proposed new Oath, I don't want to give Devlin any more power over me than he already has. So nothing is going to happen between Lash and me, because wanting is one thing, and acting on that want is something else. Is that sufficient for you?"

"Yes," he said quietly. "More than sufficient."

I lay there in silence for a while, feeling uncomfortable, and wishing I could just get up and leave.

"Sar, may I touch you?" Danial said. "I've missed you very much, these past weeks."

I thought about not answering, but he knew I was awake. There was no point pretending I hadn't heard him.

"I'd rather you not," I answered finally. "Not after your threats, and all that happened with Terian earlier, and Lash and Theo before that. It's been a day from hell. I don't want anyone to touch me right now."

"I understand," he said gently. "Sleep. Know you're safe, and that I won't touch you until you say it's okay."

I lay there for a long time in the darkness before I fell asleep, thinking I didn't want to be there. I wanted to be somewhere safe, where no one was telling me what was expected of me. But there was nowhere like that for me now. Danial, at least, would leave me alone tonight.

* * * *

In the morning, I woke up to find myself in Danial's arms. He'd not broken his word; he'd unconsciously pulled me close as he slept, just as he always had. He was spooning me, his arms around me, his head in back of mine. I just had to move the slightest bit, and I'd wake him. He had always been the lightest sleeper I'd ever known, at least after he got used to sleeping again with someone after four hundred years of sleeping alone.

I shifted. Danial woke, then immediately moved to let me go.

I stopped him. "It's okay."

Danial pulled me closer to him, and hugged me to his chest, his body cool next to mine. "Did you sleep well?" he said tenderly. "No nightmares?"

"None I remember. No dreams either."

"I dreamed of you," Danial whispered in my ear. "Of us dancing, you in your red dress, that night Elle sketched our picture, years ago."

Better times. Times that had been less confusing, at least.

"Will you wear a red dress for me again this weekend, Sar?" Danial said temptingly. "I want you to come to the Hallows party. Devlin is hosting it with me this year—"

I thought about griping at him that he had waited long enough to ask me, but decided there was no point. I had known when it was, and that he would want me to go. This was just Danial being Danial, expecting me to jump when he asked me to.

"I know," I said, turning to him slightly. "Elle has been talking about it nonstop."

"She's excited, too excited," Danial said darkly. "I assume she showed you the dress?"

"She said Tatiana had made it. It's too low cut, Danial."

"Tatiana made it, but Elle altered it, Sar. You taught her to sew, remember?"

His tone was sarcasm mixed with blame. *Jerk.* "She was supposed to mend things and make blankets and pajamas, not turn herself into a soiled dove. I suppose you tried to change her mind?"

"Of course, to no avail," Danial said grumpily. "But she'll be wearing the choker, so at least no vampire should bother her."

"Look," I said, letting out a breath. "Maybe we shouldn't let her attend, Danial. What if something happens? There are sure to be men at your party who might take advantage—"

"She has to start growing up," Danial interrupted. "As it is, Terian can't watch her anymore, not for at least a month or two, until he is back to his old self. She's either going to have to go with one of the weres to the mall as a tail, or not go. Theoron is going to have to look out for himself more, too. But he's handling responsibility well so far. He, at least, will be fine."

"Did you know Theoron wants to be called T now?"

Danial nodded, flashing a smile. I didn't smile back, making my annoyance plain.

"He is right, Sar. Some clients got him and Theo confused. It's easier calling him T."

I didn't like it, but it was clear Danial wasn't going to be my ally in this, so that was moot. *Time to move on to the multitude of other subjects needing discussion.* "Lash agreed to teach him, at Dev's insistence. But I'm worried about Devlin teaching Theoron his skills."

"Why?" Danial said in surprise. "It's—"

"Don't you think he's too young?" I said flatly. "Sixteen is pretty young, Danial."

"Maybe in today's world," Danial said with a ghost of a smile. "There was less playing around a few hundred years ago, Sar. Boys were expected to work, and by the time they were sixteen, they were either married, betrothed, or thinking about being betrothed. Some of that was that there weren't so many options for safe sex. If a boy got a girl pregnant back then, he usually had to marry her. T talked about it with me honestly. He has the urges of an adult. His body is that of an adult now, not a boy. And I would rather he be safe, and have his first time under the watchful eyes of my brother than in some back alley whorehouse, or with some girl he picked up in a bar. I'm sure you wouldn't be too happy if he got some girl pregnant when he was so young. He's very handsome, and as my son, he's a very eligible bachelor. As soon as he begins meeting clients, there are going to be women coming on to him, and not one or two either, Sar."

I said nothing, considering his words.

"Theoron is probably not infertile, as I naturally am as vampire," Danial said seriously. "He could probably father a child easily. I don't want him becoming a father until he's older, and ready for the responsibility. But I'm not going to tell him to abstain from sex, if he wants to have it, and he's careful. We already had 'the talk' about respecting women, and being honest with them, and not leading them on…"

There were so many issues here I wasn't sure which one to address first. I made myself be calm, and listened to what he was saying. Danial loved Theoron more than anything. I would trust that even though I thought this was strange, he most likely knew what he was doing. Maybe this was the best way to handle T's first time. My personal views didn't agree, but to be utterly truthful, I wasn't sure that held any real insight: my own first sexual encounter had been terrible. Sure, I'd had the talk with my mother, and told her that I would be safe and wait until marriage. But when my boyfriend of the time had pressured me to have sex, I'd given in, not just because I knew he wanted to, but because I'd wanted to very much myself. We'd been safe, but neither one of us had known what we were doing. When he pulled out of me after, the condom had broken. Then had come days of worry. I'd been lucky, and not gotten pregnant. When he'd broken up with me a week later, leaving me devastated, I'd gone through the rest of high school without a boyfriend, not trusting that the boys who showed me interest weren't going to hurt me as he had.

I didn't want fear or worry or any kind of bad feelings for my son. Strange and unemotional as I found Danial's proposal, maybe I'd have been better off myself with an instructor standing by and a partner who not only knew what they were doing, but was there to ensure the experience was a positive one. In any case, I'd let Danial try it his way with T.

Danial was still talking.

"—and besides, it is far better for Dev to instruct him than what I told you my father did for me, showing me those horses."

"Was it really your father who did that?" I said searchingly.

Danial let out a long breath. "It was the man I thought of as my father, my uncle Theoron," he said finally.

"I thought it might have been," I said tenderly, and then gave him a gentle kiss on his cheek.

"I am glad Lash will teach him, despite how I loathe that reptile," Danial said flatly, changing the subject as fast as he could. "He is the best. When Lash is done with him, Theoron will be able to handle himself in a fight. As for Devlin, don't worry about it. Theoron doesn't just need sex instruction; he needs the complete package, Sar. He needs to know how to woo a woman—"

I stifled a snort, hearing him use the word "woo."

"—how to kiss, and the rest, before even getting to bedroom skills. So don't worry. Devlin won't have him running when he's just ready to take his first tiny step. Dev will probably take longer to teach T his skills than Lash's defense lessons will take."

That made me feel a little better, if not a lot better. "I'll leave overseeing that to you."

"Theo clearly didn't want to be here with us tonight." Danial chuckled softly. "He's worried now that you've had the baby that I'll want a threesome. He's very, very careful not to bring it up, ever, Sar."

I smiled, but didn't comment. The uncomfortable note in Theo's tone had been a clear indication that he wasn't ready for a threesome. I wasn't sure I was, either. We had too many other problems to solve. At least he and I had made a huge step toward getting our relationship back on solid ground.

"Will you come to the Hallow's party?" Danial asked.

"I'll come to the party," I said gently. "Do I need to shop for a new red dress, or have you taken care of it?"

I knew the answer, of course. I just wanted to hear details.

"I have your dress, of course," Danial said arrogantly, just as I knew he would. "Tatiana has completed her replica of your original red gown. I would like you to wear that with your fox earrings, and Devlin's choker."

The fox set would be better. But Samuel and the rest would expect Dev's symbol. Worse, they would be expecting to see something else, too. "You or Dev are going to have to mark me again. The bite mark Dev gave me last Christmas is almost fully healed. There's just a faint scar."

"I noticed that it had faded significantly," Danial said carefully. "I will be the one to mark you this time. I'll ask Titus to do what he did for you last time, so there is as little pain for you as possible. His brother, Rip, could also do it—"

"What is his real name?" I said. "It can't really be Rip."

"Rip is a nickname, for Rest In Peace," Danial said. "There's some story behind it, but I don't know it. His real name is Darius, but he hates that, so he goes by Rip."

Fair enough. Back to more important things. "What are we going to do about Elle being a target at the party?"

"I'll get one of the foxes to tail her to the mall, and also at the party," Danial replied. "You should also know that Lash will not be at the party, as he is going to be guarding Venus and Devon at Hayden or here that night. Theo will be guarding you and I, and Titus or his brother will be on hand for Devlin."

Was he telling me so I wouldn't be disappointed, or to reassure me that the kids were safe that night with all their parents partying? "That's best. I don't want him fighting with Theo."

"You do know that he is banned from my parties anyway?" Danial said mildly. "I have never let him come to them, not since the time he broke Theo's neck."

He was doing this to be nasty. "Over Neoline, I know. Lash told me one night."

"Did he tell you it all?" Danial said seductively.

His tone said he knew something I didn't, and he was really going to relish informing me.

"Danial, I'll tell you this once, like I told Dev: don't tell me lies about Lash, thinking you'll make me hate him. I don't work that way."

"I'm only telling you the truth," Danial whispered innocently. "Lash didn't start it, it's true. Theo mouthed off to him, told him to go fuck himself. Lash went for Neoline, to grab hold of her, and Theo got in front of him with a knife. They fought. Lash broke his neck, after he stabbed Theo several times. The wounds weren't serious, but they bled a lot.. Lash did it on purpose."

"For what reason?"

"He knew that it would get the scent of blood in the air," Danial hissed angrily, remembering. "He knew with a broken neck, Theo wouldn't be able to defend himself, or even move."

I went still with horror, because I understood what Danial was saying. "The blood—"

"It only took me a few seconds to notice," Danial said, his eyes glinting red. "But it took me another few minutes to reach Theo's side, and began pulling vampires off him. By the time I had, Theo was almost dead from blood loss. The vampires had scented his blood, and were feeding on him. Werecougar is not a common type of were. There are some vampires that relish

28

his type of blood, though not as much as they would relish yours. They drank him down like a savored bottle of vintage wine."

Tears formed in my eyes.

"Lash was watching and laughing," Danial hissed. "Devlin was as well, but when he saw my utter rage, he helped me get the feeding vampires off Theo, and he took control of the vampires at the party, while I got Theo to safety. Theo recovered, but it took him a week before he was back to his old self."

Now the rage Theo felt for Lash made complete sense. Worse, I believed Danial. Lash was cold enough to do something like that, particularly to anyone who insulted him, especially Theo.

"This is the man you care for," Danial said with disgust. "Most of the other things he's done through the years were much worse."

"Please, don't tell me any more," I whispered.

Danial fell silent.

As the minutes passed, a bigger picture suddenly snapped into focus. I got mad in an instant. "Why didn't *you* stop the vampires that were feeding on Theo?" I said angrily. "You were the Ruler of New York, weren't you?"

Danial took an intake of breath, and then released it. "I had just beaten Garrett a few days before the party. I didn't have the foxes then. I was just building my home here. Theo was the only guard I had—"

"Then I'd say you were woefully unprepared!" I snapped at him. "Didn't you know the kind of vampires you were going to have to control? That something like that might happen?"

Danial pushed me from him with enough force that I rolled over to the far side of the bed, ending up on my stomach. I caught myself before I fell off the bed, and looked over at him angrily.

"I cannot believe you are taking his side!" he shouted. "How can you—?"

"He was wrong to do what he did then," I said flatly. "He was wrong to do what he did yesterday. But you were the one who should have been in control of the vampires at that party! You should have had the power to get them to back off!"

"They were younger vampires, Sar, newly made by Devlin," Danial hissed at me. "I had no control over them!"

"Devlin did," I shot back at him. "And did they just happen to be right there, waiting for blood to flow, or did Dev summon them over, because he knew Lash would do what he did? Or did Lash do what he did because Devlin asked him to do it? Because Devlin knew you wouldn't be able to control them once Theo had started to bleed?"

Danial looked floored. The great detective had never put two and two together, or thought of the possibility. He had always just blamed Lash for what happened.

Danial's eyes narrowed, his words biting. "You are just saying this to defend him, because you can't face what he is."

Time to take off the gloves. "Terian was going to force me to fellate him last night."

Danial's eyes went completely blood red in a split second. "What?"

"Lash wanted to shoot him, but he held off. Devlin had ordered him not to. Things got pretty far before Devlin stopped Terian, Danial. Far enough that I was badly scared Terian was going to have his way. If Lash wouldn't act against Dev's orders to save me, he probably wouldn't have done what he did to Theo at your party without permission. Lash might be a killer, but I don't think he enjoys inflicting pain as Devlin does. From what I've seen of him, he doesn't. It's a job, not a hobby."

Danial reached over for me, but I scooted away from him, and got out of bed.

"Please come back," Danial said quietly. "I will not say anymore about him. For all I know you are right, that Devlin was behind what happened to Theo." He moved closer. "I didn't know that had happened to you, darling, please let me—"

"I need to take a shower anyway, and call Dr. Camlyn," I said, gathering some fresh clothes. "I've spent enough time in bed."

Danial didn't reply. I left him there alone, and went to take a shower. When I came out of the bathroom, he was gone.

Chapter Four

Dr. Camlyn said he could see me after five p.m. today if I would be willing to wait. He was booked solid until then.

"That sounds fine," Theo said, when I called and told him. "I'll be at Danial's in an hour. I should be able to rearrange my day to go with you."

I wasn't sure seeing him so soon was a good idea. I was still upset over fighting with Danial. "Sure."

"Is something wrong?" Theo asked sternly. "Don't you want me there?"

I closed my eyes and swallowed hard, blinking back tears. *Get control, damn it.* "Danial and I fought last night. We haven't really talked for weeks. He had some things he had to say. I said some things, too. That's what you hear in my voice."

"He'll forgive you, as I have," Theo said reassuringly. "That's all over, in the past."

It wasn't, not really. Danial had seen the truth. Still Theo sounded so sure, so hopeful. More tears formed at the corner of my eyes, then ran down my cheeks.

"Are you going to Devlin's today, to work? It's Wednesday."

Shit, I'd forgotten. "I'd better call him and ask. Probably not, though. I don't feel so good."

For a moment, I wondered why I had said those words, and then realized I meant them. I felt kind of...sick.

"Why?" Theo said with a trace of panic. "What's wrong?"

"I'm achy, my throat's sore, and my head feels stuffed," I said slowly, shocked at the prospect. "My healing powers must be on the fritz—"

"You've never been sick since I've known you. Not once."

"I got sick often enough before I met Danial," I reassured him. "I haven't been for a long time. I'm probably overdue."

"Rest, and go back to bed. I'll be there soon, to take care of you."

31

"I'm not that sick," I said with a laugh, but then my laugh turned into a cough, a deep hacking one. *What the hell?*

"Get off the phone, and stop talking," Theo commanded. "I'll see you soon."

Replacing the phone in the headset, I debated what to do. I knew I should probably eat, even though I wasn't hungry.

Equipped several minutes later with ginger ale, chicken noodle soup, a bagel, and the phone, I settled myself onto the great room couch to eat, pulling a few blankets over my lap and around my shoulders. After I finished the meal, I called Devlin. It was picked up on the first ring by one of the bears.

"Hayden."

Was it Keith? I wasn't sure. "Is Devlin there? It's Sarelle."

"Hold on," the werebear said. There was some talking, then a light clunk.

"Sar?" a hissing voice suddenly said in my ear.

"Lash, is Dev there?" *Why had he picked up? Was he hissing because something had happened?*

"He's sleeping. Are you coming today?" he asked hopefully.

I was going to have to disappoint him. "I'm not coming today, Lash. I'm sick."

"You shouldn't be able to get sick," Lash hissed, worried. "You are part vampire, and the virus should fend off all diseases. Have you called the doctor?"

"I have an appointment at five today."

"Dev and I will be there," Lash hissed reassuringly. "I'll wake him immediately—"

Say it now, coward. "You shouldn't come, Lash."

There was utter silence for two seconds. "If you don't want me to come, I won't!" Lash hissed angrily. "I—"

Do NOT say you want him to come. Elaborate quick, then ring off. "Theo will be bringing me. I don't want another fight between the two of you. Besides, Stephen isn't dumb. He is going to see how young you are, and that even after a month, my body clearly isn't back to normal. He'll put it together. We can't have that."

"You're right," Lash hissed regretfully. "Devlin can tell me what Camlyn says when he gets back. I'll go tell him now about the appointment, so he'll meet you there. Please rest, Sar."

"Thanks," I said softly, and hung up. Settling back, I drifted off to sleep.

* * * *

When I awoke, Theo was sitting across from me reading the latest issue of

America's First Freedom. He put it aside when he saw me wake, and came over to sit beside me. "Are you feeling better?" he asked with concern, his blue grey eyes troubled.

I blinked bleary eyes at him. "No. I have a headache now, too. I must have the flu. At least I'm not throwing up."

Theo looked at me cautiously, as if I might have jinxed myself by saying that. But when nothing happened, he relaxed.

Danial came down the stairs. "Do you feel better?"

"No," I echoed. "I feel weak, tired, and sick."

Danial turned to Theo. "You had better get ready to go to your meeting. I'll watch over her until it's time for her to go to Camlyn's."

"I told you to cancel it," Theo growled. "I need to go with Sar."

"You need to do it, or we'll lose the client," Danial said sharply. "Terian's loss right now is almost crippling. As it is, T and Warren are going to go with you, because there's no one else who can! I can't go, because it's day."

Theo slowly got up and faced Danial, his expression irate. "Look, I realize you want to have this dynasty now for T. But Sar and Devon come first with me. I have to put them before anything else."

"Theo, I need you now more than I ever have," Danial said in exasperation, his eyes tinged red. "Sar has a cold. As much as that upsets me, it isn't life threatening. I can have Brian take her to the doctor's, or she may be able to teleport herself—"

"I'm not talking about her needing transport! She needs me with her," Theo growled. "I'm not going to any meeting! You know as well as I do something is very wrong with her!"

"Something may be wrong, but your presence there with her isn't necessary," Danial snapped. "Devlin will be teleporting in to meet her there. He should be there alone with her anyway. He is going to say that he bit her, and took most of her blood. Camlyn may not believe that, when he sees you there and that you aren't trying to put a stake through Dev's heart."

Theo curled his fists at his sides, and glared at Danial. "And you wonder why she left you," he growled in a low voice. "She got tired of always being second."

Danial's eyes bled to red again as he bared his teeth at Theo. Theo stalked to the door and left, slamming out of the house. Outside, the wheels of the SUV spun, then drove off.

Danial sat down beside me as another wracking cough hit me. He grabbed the box of tissues and passed it to me. My eyes teared up at the force of the coughing. When it subsided, I wiped my face with tissues, then lay back on the couch heavily, exhausted.

"Do you want anything more to eat?" he asked quietly. "I could heat some soup up for you."

"No," I replied. "As bad as I feel, you're right. It's just a bad cold. I just haven't been sick for a long time, really sick. I forgot how awful it feels."

The silence stretched between us. *What was there to say?* What Theo had said in anger had been the truth, and we both knew it.

"Do you want me to stay here with you, or leave you alone?" Danial said finally. "Elle is at her lessons, Devon is being watched by Cia, and Mary won't be in today—"

"It's almost time, isn't it?" I asked sadly.

Danial nodded. "Next week, probably." He sighed. "Jennie is coming to meet me this weekend on Saturday afternoon, before the party. By Monday, I'll have her decision."

"Are you worried that it won't work?" I said hesitantly.

Danial shook his head. "I have gone over what to do with Devlin a dozen times now, so I'm confident that I can do it. But I worry when it's done, she'll regret it, or want me to change her back. And there's no going back, once it's done. There's only final death, or blood and darkness forever."

Danial's grim description surprised me. I chalked it up to him being on edge. "I can be there with you when you tell her, if you want."

He looked over at me, surprised. "I'd appreciate that, Sar."

"Will you stay and read to me? It doesn't matter what. Just until I fall asleep?"

Danial went and got my *Vampire Hunter D* book that lay beside his bed, and opened it to my bookmark. Then he settled onto the couch beside me, putting my head on his lap, with a pillow under my head. He got through only a paragraph before I was asleep.

* * * *

Danial awakened me at four thirty. "Do you want to try teleporting?" he said as he helped me put on my jacket. "Brian can take you by car, but it will take much longer to drive there."

I felt worse now than I had. I desperately wanted some aspirin, but was afraid to take anything until I saw Stephen. Speed was of the essence. "I'll try it."

With a moment's concentration, I made it to Dr. Camlyn's office outside the doors. Glad Danial hadn't come—and been burned in the sunlight streaming down—I pushed open the door. Devlin was waiting for me in an office chair, his expression an instant grimace.

He hugged me loosely, and helped me sit down in one of the waiting room chairs. "How do you feel? You look terrible."

"Thanks," I said, rolling my eyes. "I feel that way too."

"Not to worry," Devlin said reassuringly, as he patted my back. "We'll get you some good drugs."

I wanted to laugh, but I knew I'd cough, instead. I settled for flashing a quick smile.

About five-fifteen, a nurse showed us into exam room one. I wondered to myself why Stephen always put me in the same room each visit. *Maybe this one had the most equipment, and he wanted to be ready for anything?*

My humorous snort brought up phlegm, making me choke. Pushing down the urge to throw up, I swallowed the awful sickly taste and plopped my behind down on the exam table. I just had to keep breathing. Stephen would help me. Besides, at least my cough wasn't any worse.

Devlin stood beside me while Stephen checked me over, and I related my symptoms. He made me take several deep breaths. All of them ended in me coughing hard and choking.

"It looks like bronchitis, Sarelle," Stephen said calmly. "Not too bad of a case. Just take care of yourself and rest."

"Give her some drugs," Devlin said commandingly. "Something for the cough at least, if not for the headache and fever. She feels badly."

"How long has it been since you took blood from her, or Danial did?" Stephen said flatly.

"About a month," Devlin lied. "But when I did, it was a lot, Stephen—"

"How much is 'a lot'?" Stephen said angrily.

"Over half," Devlin said, glaring at Stephen. "We used blood replenishing packets, to keep it flowing."

"I should throw you out of my office right now!" Stephen said angrily. "You must have almost killed her!"

"Titus healed her with his blood," Devlin replied. "Sar recovered, and has been fine since then, with no ill effects—"

"Sar, did you do this with him willingly, give him permission?" Stephen said quickly. "By vampire law, if he didn't have your permission and you were Oathed to him, I have grounds as your doctor to notify the nearest vampire hunter for Breach of Oath—"

It was on the tip of my tongue to tell him Dev and I weren't Oathed anymore, but I stopped myself in time. Stephen—as well as anyone outside my inner circle—needed to think the Oath still stood.

"Shut up, Camlyn," Devlin answered harshly. "You know well that any Vampire Ruler is above that law, and also that exsanguination is a favorite punishment. Even if we weren't untouchable, no vampire hunter would go after a Ruler by themselves—"

"There are some hunters that are banding together now," Stephen said mildly, writing in my file. "Working in teams to take on the more powerful vampires, the ones over a hundred years old."

"Yes, I know," Devlin spat angrily. "And it's not for any justice, either. They're after our blood to sell to the highest bidder and any loot they can steal from us in the process."

Time to speak up. "He had my permission," I interjected as forcefully as I could.

Stephen looked at me incredulously. "Why?"

"I wanted to feed him," I said simply, deciding that was the easiest lie. "I wanted to recreate that moment when Danial and he drank from me years ago. But this time, I didn't want him to stop until he had taken all he wanted from me—"

Devlin's eyes were hot with lust, his breathing more rapid with each word. This was turning him on.

"Sarelle, you are lucky you didn't die," Stephen said in exasperation. "How many packets did you take?"

"I lost count," I said, hoping he wouldn't suddenly recall that some had been taken from this very room a month ago. He'd know I was lying, as the ones I'd ignorantly taken had been vampire victim packets, ones that added a bitter taste to human blood. *Ones that Devlin could not have stomached a taste of, much less pints worth.*

"Let me draw a blood sample," Stephen said grumpily, brandishing a needle.

I offered my arm, wincing as the needle slid in.

* * * *

When Stephen returned a half-hour later, he glared at us both. "Does one of you want to tell me what really happened?"

I didn't know where to look or what lie to tell. So I looked at the floor and stayed quiet.

"Sar told you what happened," Devlin said calmly. "What is the matter? Is there something wrong?"

"Sar's human again," Stephen said flatly. "There is a faint, faint trace of the vampire virus in her system, but for all intents, it's gone. She's mortal. But there is demon DNA in her now, enough in her blood for the computer to pick it up. It's doubled from what it was."

Devlin's mouth dropped open, mirroring mine.

"You didn't take her blood," Stephen said, fixing Devlin with his eyes.

"You would have gotten some of the virus into her from your saliva as you drank from her, which would have raised her virus levels, not decreased them. Tell me what happened—"

I was thinking furiously, but I'd used up my one best idea. *Shit...*

"I didn't bite her and drink from the wound," Devlin interrupted smoothly. "I bit her deeply, then withdrew. Her blood flowed out like sweet, pure water."

I went crimson, remembering how Dev had done that very thing to me during The Lust.

Stephen saw my embarrassment, and took it for proof we were telling the truth.

"You are a sadist," he said, looking at Devlin in disgust. "It's not my business what you do in your own bedroom if your lover is willing. But you shouldn't do this again, Devlin, at least not the amount you took."

"I haven't tasted her blood since that night," Devlin offered. "May I now, as you confirmed there is no danger?"

"Her blood readings say that she's okay, but not great," Stephen said. "Some of that is probably her illness. I'd advise only a small taste. Also, don't give her any of your blood to heal, Devlin. You might turn her."

"I'm not going to turn her," Devlin barked back, his eyes red. "You always think you know more about that than me. I have centuries more experience than you do on who is turning, and who is not—"

"Her blood is not the same now as it was," Stephen shot back, not giving an inch. "You took too much. I think whatever made her resistant to you is gone. As for whether it is temporary or not, I can't say."

"No," Devlin growled. "I don't believe that."

"Taste her then," Stephen said flatly, his angry eyes boring into Devlin. "You think you know it all, go ahead. See if her blood tastes the same."

Devlin looked down at me. I nodded to go ahead. He sank one fang tip into the side of my throat, making a small, deep scratch, and then put his mouth over the cut. There was a gentle sucking sensation. Abruptly, Devlin broke contact, grasped me by the shoulders, then sank both his fangs in. I jerked back, hissing in pain. Devlin withdrew, swallowed, then put his mouth over the wound. I relaxed, my pain easing. Stephen saw he was healing me and tried to intervene, yelling at Devlin to stop.

Devlin gave him a shove, sending Stephen back against his cabinets, even as he moved his mouth to my burns, ripping the bandages off. Stephen crashed to the floor, then began to get up, calling for help.

Devlin drew back from me. "Take her blood again, right now," he challenged Stephen, looking into my green eyes with his golden ones. "We'll see if what I just did made any difference in the virus levels."

Stephen took another sample of my blood, then went out of the room, glaring at Devlin.

Dev hugged me to him. "You're all healed up, Love."

"Thank you. Those burns hurt a lot."

"Did you have pain at my bite?" he asked. "I felt you jerk."

I nodded. "Like always."

"If you did, you must still be resistant to the virus. A normal woman would feel only a rush of pleasure. The same would be felt by a woman who was turning."

"I know. But what are we going to do now?"

"I'll have fun making you as you were," Devlin teased. "We'll both enjoy it, Love."

"I meant about Stephen," I retorted wryly.

"We'll wait to see what he says."

Stephen came back about ten minutes later, his face grim. "What you did elevated the virus in her system enough to put her in the area of a turning human."

"But she is not turning," Devlin said, triumphant. "She is still resistant to the virus, though it's true, she doesn't taste of summer—"

"What do I taste like?" I said quickly.

"Like the first thaw of winter, before the spring. In time, you'll taste of summer again, Love."

Whew. I'd been worried he'd say I had demon flavor.

"Why did you come here when you only argue with me about my diagnosis?" Stephen said irritably. "Why bother, if you aren't going to take my advice on your lover's health?"

"I needed to check the virus levels in her blood, and for you to do that for me," Devlin said flatly. "She also needs something to kill the disease in her system that's making her sick. The rest of your observations and ideas you can keep to yourself, Camlyn."

"She needs rest, a lot of fluids, and to be kept warm," Stephen said sternly. "And for you not to take any more pints of her blood."

"I'm beginning to think you have something against vampires, Camlyn," Devlin said mildly.

"Only ones who abuse their positions," Stephen said nastily. "Or their lovers."

Devlin glared at him. "Give her the meds."

"Here is some cough medicine, Sar," Stephen said gently, handing me a bottle. "Any over-the-counter medication will do for the fever, or the headache—"

"Give her something to heal her quickly," Devlin growled. "The Hallows party is Saturday night."

Stephen gave him incredulous eyes. "Sarelle is sick. She can't attend any party."

"She *has* to be there, at least for the end of it," Devlin said, red glints in his golden eyes. "The other Rulers will be there with Harriet—"

"Who is Harriet?" Stephen asked.

"A woman like Sar. She's pregnant right now with a vampire child, a dhamphir."

Stephen's eyes widened in shock. "There is another woman who has been able to—?"

"Get moving, Camlyn!" Devlin shouted, his calm veneer vanishing. "There has been enough talk!"

Stephen shook his head and began rummaging through his cabinets. He handed some plastic packets of pills to me. "Sar, you can take some of these blue pills, they'll help your immune system to fight off the sickness. You'll still be sick, but you should recover faster. Come back in a month or so, and I'll test your blood again, to see if the levels of virus are changing at all. You should be very careful of how much blood you give Devlin or Danial, and about them giving you their bodily fluids—"

"Enough, Camlyn," Devlin growled. "I'll tell Danial what you said about her blood. We'll both be careful of her, though I don't think there is any real danger of turning her."

"Thank you. I will," I said to Stephen. "'Bye."

Stephen left. Devlin followed, saying he would settle the bill. I took some of the medicine—both pills and cough syrup—then got up and put my jacket on.

Devlin was waiting for me in the lobby. "Thanks for coming, and for your quick thinking," I said, giving him a hug.

"It was you who thought quickly," Devlin said, his look calculating. "I hadn't known you were that good of a liar, Sar. I almost believed you myself."

"I learned from you, Sweetheart," I said in a sugar-filled tone.

Devlin glared at me a second, then burst out laughing, hugging me. "Do you want to come home with me?" he offered hesitantly. "It's supposed to be cold the next few days. I don't like to think of you at your drafty home, with only your wood fire to keep you warm."

I was slightly offended, my pride hurt, but he wasn't saying anything that wasn't true. "Theo will be there with me and Devon," I reassured him. "Besides, you know he'd be irritated if I went with you. We are finally making some progress toward repairing our relationship—"

"I know," Devlin said emptily, his eyes averted. "Danial told me you made up with Theo yesterday."

He was worried he was going to lose me.

I took his face in my hands, and made him look at me. There was worry and fear in his beautiful eyes.

"We did," I said gently. "But I'll still come to you this weekend. Saturday's the party, but I could come Friday night?"

Relief welled in his eyes, and he gave me one of his dazzling smiles. "Friday night it is," Devlin said, kissing my forehead. "If you aren't well yet, you can just come for a mini vacation. I'll take care of you, like you took care of me when I was hurt."

He was trying hard to be the man I wanted him to be. *The question was, could that last?*

When I teleported back to Danial's, a large shadowy figure was waiting in the great room.

Chapter Five

The man stood when I appeared, looming over me, easily seven and a half feet tall. This had to be Rip, Titus's brother. His hair was the same reddish-black color as Titus's—though longer by a few inches—and also waving a little from the heat coming off him. His eyes were red and reserved, his skin that odd dark demon red-pink flushed color that I'd never been able to discern the source of, though I'd narrowed it down to either the heat of his blood or the natural pigment in his skin. The air around him seemed to shimmer with the heat of him, and I basked in it, still feeling a chill from my cold.

I held out my hand to him. "You must be Rip."

He nodded, baring rows of sharp teeth. Still unnerved after seeing Terian's teeth last night, I controlled myself enough to let him kiss my hand. His lips were hot, but not uncomfortably so.

"Titus speaks highly of you, Sarelle," Rip rumbled, inclining his head.

His voice was as deep and reverberating as Titus's was. *Maybe all demons are like that.*

"Sar, you are back," Danial called out. He rushed down the stairs from his study, grabbing me as soon as I was within reach, crushing my body to his. "What did the doctor say?"

He already knew—it was in the desperateness of his actions. "I'm mortal again."

Danial hugged me tighter. "Devlin said your blood would change back in time, that you already taste of the first thaw of spring," Danial murmured frantically. "It will change back very soon, Love. Then he and I will give you our blood again. You aren't going to die, don't worry, darling, you will be as you were, we will be together always—"

"Shh," I said softly in his ear. "I'm right here. I'm not going anywhere, Danial."

41

He was afraid that now I was mortal again, now that I no longer needed vampire blood to survive, I would reconsider giving an Oath to him and Devlin. He was right in that I did have that choice now. What I needed to know is if he had told Theo about this yet.

"There is a good part of her being mortal, no matter how briefly," Rip rumbled. "The mark you are going to give her tonight will stay, and not heal. While you might enjoy doing this to her every year, it can't be much fun for Sarelle, even with someone taking most of the pain away."

"That's true," Danial assented. "Come, Darling. Let's finish this, so you can rest."

He led me to the couch, lay down, then settled me atop him. I didn't protest; whatever else happened, I needed to be marked Saturday night.

"Ready?" Danial said to Rip. I felt the gentle prick of his fangs, as he put them into position.

"When I tell you, bite and then withdraw completely," Rip instructed, as he finished mixing up some of the glowing blue healing paste. With a knife, he cut himself, then eased a drop of his blood into the mixture.

I tensed, then tried to relax, knowing it would hurt less that way.

"Now," Rip said abruptly.

Danial bit me deeply, shuddering in pleasure as he sank his fangs all the way in. I shrieked loudly in pain. Danial withdrew, and Rip quickly smeared paste on my wounds, taking away the pain. I went limp, resting on Danial as he began to lick the blood off me with long strokes of his tongue. Rip's expression as he watched said he would have been happy to join in, but he didn't ask. Soon, most of the blood was gone.

Rip wiped away the paste. "You are healed," he rumbled, getting to his feet. "It was good to meet you, Sarelle. Danial, I'll see you tomorrow night." With that, he was gone, his smiling face fading into nothingness in a blink.

Danial took my hand, helped me stand, then led me into the bathroom. "I'll help you shower, Love. It's time you went to bed."

* * * *

As I dressed in fleece pajamas, I looked in the mirror at the new mark. It was as it should be, almost a twin of the other one Devlin had made. Danial's teeth were just a touch closer together, so the bites didn't completely match. That was a good thing. I was supposed to be both Danial's and Devlin's Oathed One. I had been marked by only Devlin for too long. It was better this way.

Danial entered. "Our clothes are washing. I put stain remover on the blood. It should come out." He touched the new mark lightly. "Your new mark shows up well."

I nodded, then coughed. "The meds are wearing off."

He handed me some pills, then helped me take some cough medicine. After, he brought me close to his woodstove, and sat me down on the floor, putting a down comforter about my shoulders.

I looked through the glass front at the flames dancing inside and was warmed just watching them. Then I wondered again if Theo knew about my diagnosis, and shivered.

"Are you cold?" Danial asked, carrying in a tray of soup, and a toasted bagel.

I took it from him gratefully, and shook my head. "No."

He sat down behind me, running his hands over my skin and hair as I ate. "You should stay here tonight. You shouldn't go out in the cold, when you're sick. Your hair will take a while to dry."

I nodded. He was right. I was warm here, and comfortable. I didn't want to risk going back outside where it was cold, even to go home.

"Theo should be back soon," Danial said with an authoritative tone. "He can stay here or go to your house, whichever he chooses—"

Danial was forgetting the dogs. I ate in silence, too tired to argue with him or think about Theo. The warm soup was doing wonders for me, my aching body soothed by the warmth of the fire.

"I have missed you so much these past weeks," Danial said lovingly.

I could have spent every night in his arms, if he had only asked me to come to him. *He'd been too busy being prickly about Lash to want me to even touch him.*

"Why are you scowling?" Danial said with concern. "Is the soup not to your liking? I could make you another kind—"

"It's wonderful, more than wonderful," I said, giving him a grateful smile and pushing my unkind thoughts away. "I'm just thinking of what to do now."

"What do you mean?" Danial said tersely, a lot of meaning in those four short words.

It was better to get it all out, right now. "Does Theo know?" I asked him.

As I knew he would, he understood instantly. "No," Danial answered. "Do you want me to tell him?"

"No," I said tiredly. "If he asks, I'm going to say I'm sick because saving Lash weakened me. That's true; it's just not the whole truth. Will you back me up?"

"If that's what you want," he answered.

He wasn't doing it for me, but because it fit with his plans for me. "Will the other vampires at the party be able to tell that I'm mortal now? I'm worried they'll try something—"

"Hush," Danial said, pulling me close, his voice radiating strength. "Everything will go fine on Saturday. Afterwards, things will go back the way they were. You'll come to me, and see Devlin at Hayden. We'll see your parents again, I know your mom has called here several times asking for you—"

She had, and I hadn't returned her calls, because I'd been too worried she'd ask us over. She would see right away there was trouble between Theo and me.

"—they want to know when you are bringing Devon again."

The week before I'd saved Lash, Theo and I had taken Devon to see my parents for the first time. My mother had been apprehensive when I told her that her grandson would be in his other form, but she'd loved Devon on sight. He'd purred for her almost at once, which was rare. He wasn't usually very friendly to people he didn't know. We'd gone every day that week. It had been wonderful to see my parents accepting my son, how much they loved him...

"We'll go out with Theo and the kids to the movies like we did before, at least while Elle and Theoron are still young enough to tolerate our presence—"

"What about Venus and Devon?"

"Devon will come with us in a month or so, when he wears his human form," Danial conceded with a smile. "Venus is close to saying her first word now, and outings aren't far behind. Devlin has talked to me about the four of us getting together here every week: he, Theo, you and I, and the four children. Venus does need to meet her siblings, especially her twin—"

Danial was right in one respect; it was time to stop acting like a child. This was my life, and I needed to play my parental, adult role in it. So what if it hadn't been my choice to be with three men? I'd made a choice just for myself that night in the Everglades and what had it gotten me? More problems.

I wouldn't take back what I had done with Lash. But it was time to let it go, and stop romanticizing him. He was a killer. No matter how much I liked him, there was no place for him in my life. Not as my lover, and maybe not even as my friend. He hated Theo too much to ever be included in any kind of family gathering, and Theo and Danial didn't want him there anyway, because they hated him in return. That wasn't going to change, no matter what else happened.

I'd see Lash at Hayden in passing, probably, and that would have to be that. That would probably be best for both of us. He needed to find someone else that could love him back, someone who didn't have more men than she could handle already. I didn't want him to carry a torch for me as Terian had, or to keep hoping that when I Oathed to Dev I'd be his lover again. I could never be his lover again and still hold on to Theo. That was crystal clear. But Lash was alive and young, and I knew he loved me, even if he'd never told me the words. That and the memories I had of him in my arms would have to be enough, even though I wanted more.

Because fuck it, there was more than just friendship, or good sex between that erstwhile snake and me: Danial was right, I was in love with Lash. I'd loved him from the moment he'd told me he wanted nothing more than to be in my arms as he took his last breath. I loved his nasty sense of humor, his cackling laugh, and the quiet way he had about him, that he could reach inside and caress my heart so easily with just a look, or the touch of his hand on my face.

"I feel your love," Danial murmured. "I love you, Sar."

"I love you, too," I said quickly, then relaxed back into him, and let my thoughts of Lash go.

* * * *

In the morning, I felt a little better, but still sick. My eyes even hurt, prompting me to hold a washcloth over them.

"Stay here in bed today," Danial said firmly, holding out some pills. "Theo can take you home tonight, if you feel better. He should arrive soon for his shift."

I took them. "Thanks."

"Theoron asked to go with you to Hayden on your next trip. Is that all right?"

I nodded, watching him pour the cough medicine. "Tell him Friday afternoon."

Danial nodded, offering me the spoonful. I was asleep again seconds after he had given me the dose.

* * * *

When I awoke next, it was Friday morning. I got up and showered, thrilled that my coughing had lessened. It was so good to feel better, to draw a breath without worrying if I was going to wheeze or if there was going to be a sharp pain. My appetite had also returned with a vengeance.

Theo came in as I was finishing my second peanut butter sandwich.

I gave him a radiant smile. "How are you?"

"You look a lot better," he said, happily hugging me.

"I feel like it's been days since I last saw you—"

"It has been days," Theo grumbled. "Every time I came to see you, Danial said you were sleeping, and he didn't want to wake you."

45

"I pretty much slept since my doctor's appointment," I said, shrugging. "I was in a medicine-induced haze most of the time, so you didn't miss anything. How was your meeting?"

"It went okay," Theo said, irritated. "I should have been there with you."

"Really, it's okay," I responded quickly, relieved that he hadn't been present for the news of my mortality. "Danial does need you more than ever now with Tears out of commission, especially with Ulysses back in town."

"Devlin said he told you," Theo said, his eyes determined and harried. "I've given a description to all guards. If they see him—even just out in town—they are to let me know about it. Danial doesn't think Ulysses will attack us, but I'm still glad Rip is guarding him."

"Is there any word from Titus on Terian?"

Theo nodded. "Titus said he thinks it will take a few weeks to a month at most. He was able to break through the demon part of Terian that is controlling him to find the Terian we know and love. His human—well, actually it's his faerie side—wants to be back in control. Titus said it's good that Terian is half-faerie, and not human. The chances of humanity fighting demonity aren't good. The demon side almost always wins in the end. But faeries are both resilient and powerful. Titus thinks that Terian can wrest control back and keep it, it will just take a while to accomplish. But once he does it, it should be permanent. He should never lose control again to his demon half."

"That's really good news," I said happily, feeling some hope for the first time in days.

"So you're mortal now," Theo said abruptly.

Damn you, Danial. "Devlin said my blood doesn't taste like summer, but that the resiliency is still there."

"He told Danial not to take more than a tiny bit at the Hallow's party. They're waiting until your blood becomes like spring, whatever that means—"

"I know what it means," I said irritably.

"Did you get tested?" Theo interjected.

I'd forgotten all about that. "I'll need to go back next week for a recheck. Let me wait until then. Stephen already suspects that it wasn't Devlin who took my blood. Asking about STD tests will only make him more suspicious. But I will do it. I'm sorry—"

Theo nodded, and kissed my hand. "That's fine. Don't worry about it. I just wanted to know."

I looked at the clock. "I should get moving—"

"You shouldn't go to him tonight. You're still sick," Theo said.

I gave him a weary glance. How to tell him that Theoron was coming with me to meet with Lash for training? I couldn't. "You know I need to go."

Theo carefully removed my hand from his. "You don't need them anymore, Sar."

I began to answer, then closed my mouth. I was tired of trying so hard with him. He knew Dev. No matter that Devlin had been willing for me to not come when I was sick, now I was better it was going to be a different story...

As I finished my bitter thought, it occurred to me that Titus had to have broken at least one layer of the bond between Theo and me. I'd almost always put Theo's wants and needs above my own. Now, I couldn't see why that had been so important to me. I had feelings too, damn it. But I would be asking Theoron tonight to come clean with Theo about the lessons from Lash. "I need to go. Please take care of Devon—"

"Just like I did last night," Theo said snidely. "See you, Sar." He left, shutting the kitchen door behind him.

I sat for a while in the empty kitchen, thinking about my life, and all that had happened to get me to this moment. Then I got up, and started getting ready.

* * * *

That afternoon, instead of teleporting, I let T drive us, figuring he could practice his driving. He went through two stop signs before I made him pull over.

"You said Hans gave you lessons," I accused. "You just missed that tree!"

"He did," T said defensively. "But we just started today. I keep mixing up the brake and the gas—"

At that point, I took the keys. "No more driving, until you learn which pedal is which."

He grumbled, then exchanged seats with me. A minute later, he had forgotten he was ever irritated. "What should I say to him, Mom?" he said excitedly. "I want him to teach me so badly. I don't want to say the wrong thing, and offend him. Dad said he's touchy—"

I rolled my eyes at the hero worship in his tone. Part of me wondered if T was really ready for this. We'd find out soon enough.

As I pulled into the garage, I glimpsed Devlin there waiting, leaning against the door. This was a surprise. I'd expected Lash, as he knew we were coming. It was only late afternoon. *What was Devlin doing up and around this early?*

We both got out, Theoron trailing behind me.

Devlin looked his usual gorgeous self, dressed in some jeans and a shirt of black silk. It was open a little in the front, baring his golden chest hair.

"Dressing to impress?" I teased.

47

Dev gave me a welcoming hug and a kiss, then turned to T. "Welcome to Hayden, Theoron," Devlin purred. "Come upstairs and see your half sister, Venus."

Apparently, he hadn't gotten the memo about Theoron's new nickname. Or maybe he had, and was trying to score points with me.

T nodded, then followed us upstairs.

I had to admit, I was wondering what Venus would think of her half brother. So far, they were still the only two dhamphirs in existence, though perhaps not for long. I was leery of seeing Harriet tomorrow at the party, though I wasn't sure why. Maybe because I couldn't guess if the baby she was carrying was Perseus's or Samuel's child. Possibly it was even Zane's. Poor woman.

Devlin showed us both into the nursery. Venus smiled at me from her crib, but gave an unsure look to Theoron. As he walked toward her, she scented the air, her eyes rapidly widening.

"Me," she whispered.

T nodded. "Yes. I'm like you—"

"She spoke!" I said excitedly, turning to a beaming Devlin.

"She said 'Daddy' today," Devlin gushed. "I'm working on getting her to say 'Mommy,' but it may be a while, Sar."

"I'd be happy to just hear her say 'Daddy'," I said, hugging him around the waist. "Our baby's growing up fast."

"I'm your half brother, Theo," T said to Venus. She reached for him, and he picked her up and hugged her. "We're the same. You are like me, a dhamphir."

"Damn pier," Venus said slowly, her golden eyes wide and thoughtful. I was afraid for a split second that she would bite him, but she didn't.

"I'm so happy to see this," Devlin whispered longingly. "I didn't want her to feel alone."

"She'll never be alone, she has you," I consoled. "And she has me, Danial, and Theoron."

"But she misses her twin," Devlin said, agitated. "Please ask Theo if he would allow Devon to come visit her here, just for a few hours."

"I've asked him repeatedly, and so has Danial. He keeps refusing, because he's so protective of Devon."

Dev looked at me skeptically, his expression saying that he knew most of the reason was Theo didn't want Lash anywhere near Devon.

"We need to teleport in mass one night to Danial's, and let them visit together there."

"It's too risky," Devlin said flatly. "No one would attack Hayden, ever. I built it to be strong. Venus is staying here until she's older."

Enough was enough. Someone had to bend. "You can't keep her here like Rapunzel in a tower. Danial said that you mentioned Theo, me, you, and he getting together with the kids at his house. Did you, or didn't you? I'm not saying Venus should go out shopping with us or anything, Dev. But Danial's house is safe enough. And if we teleport, there isn't even the danger of traveling."

I expected Devlin to blow up, or tell me I didn't know what I was talking about, that no way in hell was he risking his only child. Instead, he looked at me and nodded. "You're right, Sar," he conceded. "I did mention it to Danial, though I meant when Venus was older. But you're right, that it's going to have to be that, or nothing. Theo's not going to relent. And Danial's house is safe enough. I'll make arrangements for next week."

Well, at least that had gone well. Now I had only to get my parents there to see Venus, and one more of my ongoing problems would be solved.

We stayed in the nursery for a while visiting, while I marveled that my child who was less than six months old already resembled a two-year-old toddler in size. Devlin took Venus from Theo when she began to doze, gave her a kiss, and laid her in her crib. "Come with me," he said.

We followed him downstairs, T trailing behind as before.

Lash was waiting for us on the couch, his feet up, watching TV. I knew he was aware of us, though he paid us no visible attention.

T shot me a questioning look. I motioned to him to get on with it. He squared his shoulders, and walked over by Lash, who ignored him.

"Excuse me, Lash?" Theoron said softly, yet with conviction.

"What the fuck do you want?" Lash hissed at him, pausing the episode of South Park he was watching, his snake eyes flat and cold.

"For you to teach me to defend myself, please," T said replied. "I want—"

"I don't teach anyone my secrets," Lash hissed. "So why should I teach you, boy?"

"I can't give you a reason, besides I want to learn from you," T said. "Theo has taught me a little bit, and so has my father. But they—"

"Are you going to do what I tell you, when I tell you?" Lash hissed.

T nodded eagerly.

Lash stopped the DVD, and got to his feet. He was dressed in black jeans like usual, his black T-shirt and shirt the cotton he usually preferred to wear. He moved closer to T, so he was right in front of him.

"You're going to hurt like you haven't before," he hissed, flicking his forked tongue at T. "Your daddy's kept your ass safe till now, and you've probably never felt a knife slide in to tickle your heart, or your bones breaking inside you. But you're going to feel both of those, if you train with me. And you're going to bleed, Theo. In a real fight, you are going to get hurt, sometimes badly. I'll beat you within an inch of your life and expect you to get up and still take more. Can you do that?"

T looked a little scared, but he nodded.

"I'm not teaching you any candy-ass honorable stuff like your father, or Theopolis's pathetic tricks, or even special mythical moves," Lash hissed. "This is not an after-school special, and you aren't suddenly going to be able to take on armies. I'm teaching you dirty fighting, bar fighting, and only enough to handle yourself, so you can get away, if you are cornered sometime without your gun. And when I say we're done, that's the end of it, and you go home. Got it?"

"I got it," T said, looking pale but determined. "Will you call me T, please?"

"When you earn it. Come with me," Lash said, changing in an instant back to full human, and striding off. T went after him, Dev and me following.

We went towards the bear quarters, and down a flight of stairs to a basement room that was wide as a basketball court. It was outfitted like an upscale gym: there were various weight machines, treadmills, racks of free weights, and some mats in an area with heavily padded walls for practice fighting. It was also completely empty.

This is where Dev's bears trained. I'd figured something like this existed. I knew Devlin too well to think he would risk his beloved grand piano to any accidental falling bodies, and the ballroom was the only room I'd seen so far in Hayden that was big enough.

"What other mysteries are down here in the basement?" I asked Dev.

He gave me a slow smile.

Lash walked onto one of the mats, and faced Theoron.

Was it obvious to my son that his teacher's reluctant speech had been a farce? Lash had obviously arranged for the gym to be empty so he could pass on his trade secrets with a measure of privacy.

T faced Lash and adopted a stance I'd seen Theo use when he fought; legs bent, arms up and out, fingers splayed a little. Lash unsnapped his whip from his belt and tossed it down beside the mat, drawing his survival knife from his belt sheathe. I shot Dev a look. *How was this fair?* T was unarmed…

To my horror, T drew a wicked looking knife from a hidden leg sheath. He faced Lash, knife in hand, their circling figures reminiscent of Danial facing Terian years before.

"Come and get me, boy."

T went for him silently. Lash sidestepped easily at the last second. As T lunged past him, Lash struck a powerful blow to his shoulders with his arm, knocking him sprawling. T got up, his eyes angry, but he again relaxed into the stance, breathing and circling. This time he didn't attack when Lash gave him an opening.

Lash nodded, then immediately attacked T. He slashed in from the side, moving so fast he was almost a blur, opening up T's side in a gush of blood. T cried out, holding his side with his free hand, staggering around to face Lash's knife. Lash cut him again, blood fountaining up from T's slashed arm. The knife dropped from T's hand, his eyes wide and pain filled. Lash came in for the kill, wrestling T's struggling form to the mat, his knife stabbing down into T's chest near his heart, the tip of the blade pinning him to the mat. T screamed and writhed, pinned like a bug.

Lash eased him up into his arms, gripping the knife in one hand, and T's shoulder in the other. He pulled the knife out of T's chest in a smooth motion. T screamed again in agony as the knife came free in a gush of blood. Lash laid the knife aside, and pulled back T's head by the hair, his clenched fist making T look him in the eyes. "Stop screaming," Lash hissed.

T gritted his teeth, and held it in, hate flashing from his eyes, his body shaking in shock and pain. He didn't cry out again. His blood slowly dripped to the mat, spreading out into a pool beneath him as his wounds healed.

"You are your father's son," Lash hissed with approval. "Your first lesson is this: sooner or later, you will have to take pain at someone's hands. Numbers can always overwhelm you, even if the fighters aren't that good. So take it as best you can, and try not to scream or cry unless you have to. And it's truth that sometimes you have to, because the pain's too bad not to—"

What the hell was this, Torture 101? This wasn't what I'd envisioned. But T was learning to fight, really fight. That meant getting cut, bleeding, and doing your damnedest not to be killed while trying to kill your opponent, not just disarm him.

Being Danial's son, T needed this education and instruction. Lash was right, sooner or later in his long life to come, there would be a time when T would be at someone's mercy. It was better he got some experience with it now. Lash might hurt him badly, but he wouldn't hurt him in a permanent way, or kill him.

T's wounds were fully healed in a few minutes.

Lash let him up. "Again," he hissed, facing T with his knife.

Again, the scene played out: T went for him and Lash opened him up, the swift fight ending with Lash on top of T, his knife in T's chest, telling T to hold it in as T tried not to utter a sound. There was a heavy spattering of blood over the mats, the smell permeating the air.

"I can't watch much more of this," I whispered to Dev.

"Lash is almost done with this part. Relax, Love."

Easy for him to say. It wasn't his son there on the ground, blood leaking out of him.

When the wounds had healed, Lash let T up again. This time he put his knife to the side and faced T with no weapons. "Again."

T circled him for a while, Lash lunging at him every so often and T sidestepping at the last minute. Lash was fast, but T was equally fast. It was the greater skill that made the difference.

T finally darted in, hoping to gouge Lash's side. Lash grabbed Theoron, both kneeing him in the groin and punching him hard in the jaw. Theoron went to his knees, stunned. Lash stomped on T's hand. The knife dropped from T's smashed fingers, even as he strained to hold onto it. His ever quick weresnake adversary dropped onto T, wrapping his hands around T's neck and squeezing. Theoron fought, kicking and snarling, his eyes red, his fangs extended. While Lash was strong, T was a near match for him, managing several times to break the weresnake's grip. But Lash did not relent, his hands snaking in again to grip and twist. T attempted to punch Lash, but Lash moved out of the way of T's flailing arms, then delivered a right hook that must have loosened a few teeth. T snarled, still fighting. Again and again, Lash's fist connected, until Theoron's face was a mask of blood. Finally, my beaten son collapsed back on the mat, his eyes and face so bloody it was hard to recognize him.

The victor crouched beside his fallen opponent. "You've got balls, I'll give you that. Can you get up by yourself?"

T rolled slowly on his side, and got to his feet, swaying a little. But he didn't fall.

Lash stood, looking him over, his snake eyes going back to their normal dark brown. "Go take a shower," he hissed finally. "Rinse off the blood, and change into the clothes that you brought with you. I'll wait here. We aren't done yet."

T shuffled off, and went through a door at the side of the gym, his bag of clothes in his hands. Lash grabbed a towel at the side of the mat, and wiped off some of the blood on his face and hands, then cleaned his knife, setting it beside the bloody mats.

"He's got spirit," Lash said, shooting me an appreciative look, "And your determination."

"Will you beat him before you teach him, each time?" I said carefully, trying not to sound horrified.

Lash didn't hesitate. "Yes. More than knowing how to fight, Theoron has to learn how to take pain. Sooner or later, he'll be in a situation where it may mean his life; whether he can get up and move when he's left for dead, or whether he'll just lie there and let himself die."

His words horrified me. I didn't want my son to ever be in a situation where someone would want to kill him, or even try to. Lash saw my repugnance, and took it for me questioning his methods. His eyes narrowed.

"You remember the night I saved you and Dev?" he hissed, his eyes flattening back to snake. "I was hurt, but I still got the job done."

"Titus said a were had bitten you on a job," I said pointedly, asking with my tone if it had been Satar who had hurt him, the night he'd saved Theo.

"One did, on a job," Lash hissed vaguely, shooting a look at me to watch my words. "Because I was stupid just for a moment and looking away. It got infected. The pain from it was like a knife in my side that whole night saving you two. When I got shot down carrying Dev, the bullet impacted the armor over the wound. It was agony—"

"You should not have come for us by yourself that night," Devlin interjected, putting his hand on Lash's shoulder. "I never asked you to give your life for me."

"My point is that I got up and finished what I had to do, even though it hurt just to breathe," Lash hissed stubbornly. "Theoron needs to learn to get up, even when he thinks he can't. This will teach him how far he can push his body when he has to."

Devlin nodded, and removed his hand. "Yes, it will."

Lash's eyes glanced to me. "I learned this way. I will teach him as I learned."

"It's between you and him," I replied, shrugging. "I'm not going to interfere. He asked for this. If he wants to stop, he and you can work that out."

"Good," Lash hissed. "You both need to leave now. We need to practice punches, both giving them, and taking them."

The door to the showers was flung open. T plodded through it towards us, his hair wet and his body healed, a stubborn cast to his face. He handed me his bloody clothes. After I took them gingerly, he went back to the mat and faced Lash. Devlin took my arm. I went with him, and didn't look back, even when I heard the sound of a body hitting the mat and a cry of pain. T had wanted this. He was man enough to stay the course. Or, at least by the time Lash was done with him, he would be.

As we climbed the stairs, Devlin said in an off-hand manner "What were bit Lash?"

I made myself keep walking. "Titus said that was what happened the night he told me Lash was dying—"

Devlin turned me to face him, his golden eyes boring into mine. "I used to think you were a bad liar, Sar. But I think you are much better than I realized."

To say anything would mean spilling my deal with Lash. I stared at him, silent.

"You know what were bit him, don't you?" Devlin growled. "Tell me."

"I don't know," I said with a shrug. "Lash never told me, and Titus didn't say—"

"But you suspect a particular one, Sar," Devlin growled. "Who?"

"If you want to know so badly, ask Lash. He'll tell you. I can't say, not for sure."

"I will ask him," Devlin snarled. "And I'll see if his lies match yours, Sar." He extended his hand to me. "Come."

* * * *

I lay that night in bed, Devlin in my arms. He was sleeping soundly. I stroked his hair as he slept, thinking of Lash, and what Danial had said to me about him.

Did I think I still owed him, down deep? I'd paid that bill last month, when I'd given Devlin another chance with me, but had I marked the bill paid in full? Yes, but not then. I hadn't marked it paid until I'd saved his life, as he'd saved Theo's.

Lash hadn't known that Theo had told me it was okay to go back to Devlin, that he thought it was the best course of action. That had made me feel a little like a cheat. Theo's life was worth so much to me, and Lash had gotten the wound that would've spelled his doom saving that life. And what had I given him in exchange? Something I'd known on some level that I was going to do it anyway. Part of the reason I'd gone to find Lash was that I felt he deserved to be paid in more meaningful currency for what he'd done for Theo and me. So I'd paid him with my blood, and my body...

Oh, knock it off, Sar. Just admit the truth, and stop rationalizing. You went to him because you loved him even then. You would have done it in any case, because he needed you, and you just plain loved him too much to let him die. Now let it go, and go to sleep. Thinking about this again isn't going to make anything different.

I sighed to myself, and stroked Devlin's hair. He'd talked to Lash before coming to bed, but hadn't broached the subject again to me. I hadn't expected him to. I knew Lash would back me up.

The Eye of the Storm

I let my eyes feast on Devlin, lying asleep in my arms. He was always so lovable when he was asleep. It was the only time he was quiet. "I'm happy to be here with you," I whispered. "I love you, Dev. We'll work out our problems. In time, you'll be as you were."

He was trying to be a good father and partner. Most of all, I was glad that those feelings originated solely in me; that it wasn't just his blood influencing me. I felt in control of my life again, as if I was making decisions, good ones. Now there was only the Hallow's party to face.

Chapter Six

I yawned, and gave Devlin a kiss to wake him. He opened one golden eye groggily, and peered at me.

"I need to get up," I said teasingly. "That requires you to move."

"No, you need to sleep all today," Devlin said, yawning widely. "You're going to be up all night, and I don't want you getting sick again."

"I told Danial I'd help him tell Jenny about what he is this afternoon," I said, trying to move him off me. "I need to be there when she arrives at noon."

"Why did you offer to help?" Dev said, looking at me in puzzlement. "You don't know her."

"Because I'm the only mortal handy to help. Danial's nervous enough as it is."

"I don't know why he's so nervous," Devlin said, rolling his eyes. "He only has to take most of her blood, and give her a little of his. How easy is that?"

"It's because he hasn't done it as much as you have," I snapped, glaring daggers at him. "He's worried he won't give her enough." Giving him a shove, I rolled him off me.

He rolled over on his back to watch me, uttering a long-suffering sigh. Then he shrugged. "Five swallows is plenty. Tell him that. I told him once, but he might have forgotten."

Nodding that I would, I left to shower, Devlin declining to follow me. After, I dressed in jeans and a feminine pink silk blouse Devlin had bought me for a present. I wanted to look credible, so Jenny wouldn't think I was some type of vampire groupie. I wanted her to believe what I was going to tell her. If she didn't, there was no point in me missing my sleep today. I kissed Devlin good-bye. "See you later."

As I turned to leave, he purred "Sar?"

Turning back, I saw my choker dangling from his fingers. Stifling a groan,

I went back and let him fasten it around my throat, above Danial's.

"Have Danial remove his, when you get to his house. No doubt he's hoping for you to wear both, but he's going to have to settle for your ankle or your wrist for his. Mine needs to be the one on display tonight."

I nodded, irritated that my new mortality now barred me from removing either choker by myself. "I will."

Walking downstairs, I passed Titus just coming upstairs from the basement. "Hi," I said, concerned. "How is Terian?"

Titus looked worn out, his eyes sunken a little in his skull, but when he saw me, he smiled. "Terian's recovering slowly," he rumbled. "Rip's helped me a lot with him, and Leri's helped too, channeling magic to block his demon half from breaking free of us. But it's hard going, Sar."

I gave him a hug, bracing myself for his heat. "You can do it. Will it still be a month, or do you think it will take longer?" I asked hopefully.

"I think another three weeks should be enough," Titus answered with a reluctant sigh. "But he's going to have to stay away from the darker magic for a while, if not for the rest of his life. Doing that is going to put a limit on his power."

"I'm sorry," I said automatically, lacking a better answer.

"I'm sorry for what he did to you," Titus said, hugging me again. "Devlin told me the whole story a few days ago, though I had to drag it out of him. Terian would never have done what he did, if he'd been himself."

"I know that. When he is himself, please tell him I know that it wasn't him, I mean, it wasn't the Tears I know and care about. I don't blame him for it."

"He'll blame himself anyway," Titus said heavily, his burly arms still around me. "It's going to be one of the hardest things for him to have to face. But I will tell him you don't blame him. It will make a difference for him to know that."

"Titus, how is Sundown?" I said, pushing back from him so I could cool off a little. I'd have to take another shower, otherwise. "Theo told me that she was keeping to herself at Danial's, and staying in her room since Terian's, um…possession. Is she okay?"

"I've been to see her," Titus said, letting out a deep breath. "Terian hurt her too, Sar. He had her as a demon, before he went after you."

I went still, my mind conjuring graphic images that made me cringe. *What should I say?* Expressing outrage wasn't good, as Titus must have Leri as a demon all the time. *I mean, how could he not?* As bad as that might sound to me, Leri clearly enjoyed being his woman. Everything she'd done to Terian had been to keep from losing Titus. Leri must have a way—something magical probably—to keep cool being naked with him...I flushed, imagining them together.

"I healed her burns from where he touched her," Titus continued, oblivious to my discomfort. "But she's scared of him now. She said she still loves him, but I don't know that she'll take him back when he's better."

God, why was I so into sex lately? That wasn't important; my friends were. "She'll forgive him," I comforted, laying my hand on Titus's shoulder. "She loves him."

"She might be pregnant," Titus said. "That complicates things."

"That can't be," I said slowly, shocked. "Tears was afraid to father a child because of what he thought happened to his mother. He always used protection."

"Sundown insisted that they always did," Titus agreed, nodding. "But she went off the pill for a while on her doctor's orders, to give her body a break. Terian succumbed to his demon side during sex with her. The moment his demon half took over, his body heated up. His semen when he came was hot enough to melt the protection, and get into her—"

Jesus...if he was that hot, his whole body must have been broiling. No wonder Sundown was traumatized. To be naked, and suddenly feel your lover was hot enough to literally burn your skin, to not be able to get away, or get him out of you..."What happened to make him change?"

"Sundown said they were role playing," Titus said, clearly uncomfortable. "She didn't want to admit it to me, but I gathered it was some kind of damsel in distress scenario, where Terian had just saved her from an evil vampire that had kidnapped her."

I looked at Titus with horror, then closed my eyes, not wanting to hear anything else. "This is because of me—"

"Don't think about it," Titus said sternly. "Terian wouldn't have wanted you to ever know most of what his demon side admitted to you."

"I know that. But I still feel bad for him, that I don't have those kinds of feelings for him."

"You can't help that," Titus said gently. "Don't feel badly for something you can't control. He'll need you as a friend more than ever, when he's well."

"I'll be there for him."

"Good. I've got to get back," Titus said, looking at his watch. Oddly enough, it was a Rolex. "I'll see you tonight at the party. I'll be guarding Dev. Rip will be there too, on and off, just in case."

"Will you tell me the story behind his nickname?" I asked, offering a smile.

"Ask him tonight," Titus said in his bass tones, a smile gracing his features for the first time. "He loves to tell the story."

"I will," I said, my expression turning serious. "I've been meaning to ask, did you break any of the bond? I thought I felt a little differently towards Theo lately."

Titus looked at me with sad eyes. "Yes. The last two layers, Sar, from the second and third times you dreamed with him. The first one is going to be the most difficult one to break. It should've broken already, really, but for some reason it's remarkably resilient. I've still got a lot of things to try though, so please be patient."

That was a relief. "Take your time. I'm grateful to you for taking the time to work on it, when you have so much going on with Terian."

"I told you I would," Titus rumbled. "You're like my daughter now, Sar. I want you to be happy."

"I was going to ask you about that, too," I whispered. "Are you sure I don't have to eat any other—?"

"No," Titus rumbled. "You don't need to eat flesh or blood. My blood repaired your body, but it shouldn't have any lasting effects on you. It might have, if you were mortally wounded, or if you were closer to death when I gave it to you. But blood loss is one of the easiest things to heal."

Not according to Stephen, but then he wasn't a thousand years old. Titus had no doubt seen the full range of wounds possible for a human to sustain; maybe he had even inflicted most of them himself.

"—and you were healthy to begin with, not like Lash was when he first began to drink demon blood. You must be asking because of him. Someone must have told you what he needed to do when he was taking the potion these last few years."

I looked at him and bit my lip, saying nothing. Finally, I nodded.

Titus gazed at me, his red eyes troubled, his reluctance obvious. "Is it true you care for him, Sar?" he asked, his tone carefully neutral.

I love him. "I've told him we have to be friends. He agreed."

"Good," Titus said in relief. "I was worried that you were getting too close to him. I don't want you to be hurt. He's not a good man, not the kind I'd want any daughter of mine with."

Lash would never hurt me. But even if he would've, he would never get the chance now.

"Take care until tonight," Titus said, stepping away. He disappeared with a last smile.

I went into the kitchen, and made myself some cereal and toast, belatedly wondering where Lash was. *Was he avoiding me?* He'd often waited to have brunch with me in the morning when he knew I stayed overnight with Devlin. I gave a mental shrug, and ate my breakfast.

Serena came in as I was finishing, and nodded hello, though she otherwise didn't speak. She began to make some coffee. It wasn't until I went to leave that she blocked my way.

"Sar, can I talk to you?"

She was upset. "What is it?" I said, coming over to her.

"I think I might be falling for one of my lovers. I've never been in love, and I need to know if that's what I'm feeling."

This was sure to complicate things. At least there was one upside: her love couldn't be Lash. "What do you feel for him?" I said searchingly.

"I miss him when he's not with me," she said, sighing. "I think about him when I'm with other men. I wonder what he's doing when I'm alone. I want him to be thinking of me, but when I see him, I can't think of anything to say. And when he makes love to me, it's better than it's ever been with anyone else. I feel like I'm so alive, when he touches me, Sar. I've stopped taking pleasure in my other lovers. I try to pretend that they're him."

"It's love," I said, nodding. "At least, the first stages of love."

"I thought it might be," she said brokenly, and then began to cry.

I hugged her. She began to wail, tears coursing down her face. I led her into the living room, and sat her on the couch, hugging her as she sobbed. "It's okay," I comforted. "It's good to love someone, Serena. Don't be sad about it—"

"But he doesn't love me!" she said, sniffling.

I handed her a tissue. "How do you know he doesn't?" I said gently. "Did you tell him how you feel?"

"I can't tell him," she said hopelessly. "I'm just a warm body to him, Sar. He's never treated me as anything but someone to have sex with. And if I tell him I have feelings for him, he might stop coming to me for sex."

"Why wouldn't he want to be with you, if he knew you cared for him?" I countered. "Even if he didn't want more from you than what you already give him, he must enjoy being with you—"

"Sar, you were with men you didn't love. But once you loved them, could you be with them, knowing they didn't want anything more from you than to have sex with you, and then leave?"

I had no real basis for comparison. Those first times with Lash, he'd distanced himself from me as soon as the sex was over. Devlin had been the same way when he'd seduced me. But I'd been fine with that; the lack of any emotion had been mutual. The last time I'd been with a lover who didn't love me was that jerk in high school that had loved and then left me. That memory was so faded with time I possessed only remnants of my hurt and anger. There was no regret, only relief that I hadn't stayed any longer with such an asshole. I was too happy now with who I was to care much about how I'd felt back then.

"You either have to tell him how you feel and risk he'll stop seeing you for sex, or keep your feelings silent," I said finally. "I know it's not much of a choice, but it's always scary, when you realize you love someone, and don't know if they love you."

"What did you do, when you knew you loved someone? I want to tell him, but I can't bring myself to say the words."

Her eyes had that hunted look, the one they'd had when I first met her. I hadn't seen it in months. It was back in her eyes again as if it had never left.

"I usually always waited for the man to tell me how he felt, before I said anything," I said sheepishly. "But men are sometimes shy about baring their hearts. Sometimes they need to hear you say it first."

"Was Devlin like that?"

"No," I said, smiling ruefully. "He told me he loved me first. I didn't truly love him until much later. But my first husband Brennan was like that. He'd been hurt badly by a woman he loved very much, so much that he couldn't love me at first, because of it. He was too afraid of being hurt. But him not being able to say it didn't matter. When I knew I loved him, I told him. Once he knew how I felt, he was eventually able to tell me he loved me back, though it wasn't right away. But I was willing to wait."

"Would you tell him, if you were me?" she asked, biting her lip.

"No," I said frankly. "Do little things for him first, like mend his clothes, or make him some baked goods, or offer to take a walk with him—"

I went crimson, realizing I was describing things I had done with Lash. But I pressed on, rationalizing that I had done those things with Brennan and Theo, too.

"—see how he reacts, if he takes you up on the offers, or seems pleased that you want to do things for him. See if he offers to do things with you so he can spend time with you, or take you out to eat, or wants to take you someplace special to him—"

I flushed again, thinking about how Lash had done all those things with me.

Stop it, Sar. Focus on Serena.

"—and you'll know, if he does, that he loves you, or could come to love you," I finished.

"I already know he likes me to make him things to eat. I can try the others this week," she said with a sigh. She hugged me. "Thanks. Have a good time at the Hallows party tonight. It must be so fun to dress formally and dance the night away."

61

I thought about telling her I'd be really grateful to send her in my place. "I'm sure it's going to be perfectly horrible," I said, grimacing.

Serena laughed. "Have the best time you can. I'll be wanting to hear all about it afterwards."

"Sure," I said, standing. "Have you seen Theoron?"

Serena flushed scarlet. "No. Devlin told me about what he needed me to do, though. I wanted to ask you if it was okay with you, but I couldn't think of how to talk to you about it."

Now I was flushing, too, remembering Devlin's proposed "lessons" for T. "It's okay with me. Theoron's going to be an adult soon, and it's his decision. I only meant to ask if you've seen him this morning. I need to know if he needs a ride with me, or if he's going to come later with Devlin."

"I think he and Lash are training again in the basement," Serena replied. "I thought I heard them in the kitchen very early getting breakfast, though it might have just been Lash."

I hadn't known he got up early regularly. But then we hadn't woken up together often enough for me to know. Now I'd never again be in a position to find out...

Knock it off, Sar. Get a grip. "I'd better go find out, then," I said quickly. "See you."

I went the route I had gone last night, reaching the gym door easily. As I opened the door, Lash's raucous voice billowed out, echoing.

"I had your mother on a pool table, and she loved every minute of it!"

"You bastard!" T hissed. "Shut your mouth!"

I was going to kill that snake. Then I was going to skin him.

I burst through the door, just in time to see Lash knock T off his feet and onto his back. Lash went to stab him. T evaded him at the last minute, the knife sinking deep into the mat.

"You know I'm not lying! It's true!" Lash hissed, grinning.

T went for him again.

Lash evaded him. "Eight times! And she begged me for more!" he hissed, laughing.

T sliced at him. Lash sidestepped, and knocked him to his knees, putting the knife against his throat. T went still, then swore.

"What was the second lesson?" Lash hissed angrily, cuffing Theoron upside his head. "If you're not going to pay close attention and do what I tell you, I'm sending you home now! You won't heal someone cutting your head off, idiot!"

"To not let my anger get control of me," Theoron said with a sigh. "To let my enemy's words run off me like water, because all that matters is my weapon, and the first opening he gives me to use it."

"That's right," Lash hissed, stepping back. "I could tell you I fucked your sister, and you need to give it no more notice than a passing bullet. You have to keep all your attention on your enemy. Words can't kill you in a fight. But they can get you killed very quickly."

Hearing the reasoning behind his words calmed me somewhat, but I was still appalled. "I'm sorry to interrupt. I just wanted to make sure T doesn't need a ride home."

"Go get your other clothes on," Lash said, sheathing his knife. "Your mother's ready to go, and your father is no doubt waiting, too. You need to get ready for the party tonight."

T got up gracefully, and stood in front of Lash for a moment. "I'm very grateful that you're teaching me," he said respectfully. "If you need my help sometime, it's yours. I know that might not mean much, but I'm offering it anyway."

Lash nodded once. "It means something," he hissed thoughtfully. "I may need it someday quite badly. Thank you, T."

Theoron turned to me. "I'll just be a minute, Mom," T said, jogging quickly into the shower room.

Lash turned to me, smirking. "Are you over your anger?" he hissed teasingly. "I saw your face as you came through the doors."

"I'm over it," I said in a clipped tone, looking at him with narrowed eyes.

Lash came close, stopping just in front of me. "He needs to not have Theo's weakness," he hissed very quietly. "It's one of the hardest lessons to master, at least it was for me. But I'll cure him of it, before we're done."

"I'm glad," I said, softening. "He'll be a better fighter that way."

Lash stepped closer to me, his arms going around me.

"Don't, please," I said softly, my weak words so rife with need that I flushed.

"I'm not going to do anything but hug you," Lash hissed in my ear. "I need to breathe in the scent of you to calm myself. I'm worried about tonight, about letting you go to that damn Hallows party with only Theo to protect you."

I inhaled his familiar scent, closing my eyes. There came the gentle touch of his hand on the back of my head, gently pushing it against his shoulder as he stroked my hair.

"But there's no way I can go with you. Danial would shit a brick."

"I'll be fine," I said confidently, trying to step back. "Rip will be there—"

"Fucking demons can't be trusted!" Lash hissed angrily. "Rip is not a fighter; he's a sorcerer, like Titus. He's not fast at all! You're mortal, Sar! All it would take to kill you is one well-placed bullet!"

"Nothing's going to happen," I reiterated. "Devlin will be with me, Lash."

"That's the only reason I'm not crashing the party," Lash hissed meaningfully. "I know he'll stay close to you at all times, and he'll keep you safe. Plus, I have to watch Venus and Devon while you're all out in your finest."

I looked up into his flat eyes, their coldness giving nothing away. "Change back for me."

Lash's eyes reverted to their dark black-brown color in a split second, his fangs disappearing. "Why did you ask me to change back?" he said, tilting his head with a faint smile. "Are you remembering that night we—?"

Desire rose in me, mingled with sadness and longing. "I like to see your eyes. I like to look into them. I can see what you're feeling in your human eyes the way I can't in your snake ones."

Lash's dark brown eyes darkened, his expression changing from curiosity to abject craving. "Tell me I can kiss you," he said sensuously, taking my face in his hands. "Just one kiss, Sar—"

I looked down at his lips inches away from mine, and ached to taste him, to feel his body against mine as he devoured me…

Stop. Right. Now.

"Can you stop with just one?" I asked, reaching up and removing his hands from my face. "I can't. Worse, I know I won't and I still want to."

Lash leaned in close, rubbing his cheek on mine. "No, I wouldn't stop, not 'til I was spent—"

"There you go," I said, stepping back from him. "I'd miss the party. It would be another eight times before I let you go again."

"Actually, it was only seven," Lash hissed, a wide grin splitting his face. "I kept count that morning. I didn't want T to hear too much truth in my words, to suspect I was telling secrets."

I gave him a smile, though my eyes were sad. "No telling secrets to T, okay?"

"Okay. You'd better go," he said, looking away. "Danial is sure to be throwing a fit. These Hallows parties of his are the highlight of his immortal life. He'll be furious if you're late."

"I know. I'm going to have to leave my truck here, and drive it home later, or we'll be late—"

"I could drive it back for you to your house later today," Lash offered. "If you leave me the keys."

"You're sure?" I said hesitantly. "It's a pain for you to go out of your way."

"I'm seeing Gina again this afternoon," Lash said casually. "I can ask

Titus to teleport me back, once your truck is at your house. Her place of business is not too far from your house. It's in the small town just east of you, Edgefield."

I was both glad he wasn't pining for me, and upset he was seeing another woman for sex. Telling myself to grow up, I handed him the keys. "Thanks."

He put them in the back pocket of his jeans as T came in with the bags. "Be safe tonight, both of you."

I teleported us to Danial's great room. Theo was there, playing with Elle and Devon. He looked up and smiled at me, then gaped at Theoron.

"T, you went with Sar?"

Theoron looked at me. I gave him a look back that said it was past time he came clean.

T gave a sigh, then he went over and sat down on the couch across from Theo. "I was there getting self defense lessons from Lash. He agreed to teach me."

Theo's eyes widened, then narrowed as he rounded on me. "He's doing it for you," he growled. "He's never taught anyone. He refused to teach me—"

"It means a lot to Theoron," I interjected.

"If T gets to do all that, I want some more freedom!" Elle said loudly. "I want to be able to go to the mall by myself! Violet gets to do it."

"Violet is not my daughter," Danial said, coming out of his bedroom, and striding into the middle of the room to stand in front of her. "But you are, and you will not be going anywhere unchaperoned."

"I'm not a child!" Elle screamed, jumping to her feet. "I'm tired of being treated like a little girl!"

"Go to your room, Elle!" Danial thundered. "Not another word! Or you'll be spending tonight at home, and missing the party!"

Elle looked at Danial defiantly, her eyes yellow. She stalked off to her room, slamming the door.

"Did your first lesson go well?" Danial said to Theoron, as if nothing unpleasant had happened.

"Yes," Theoron said, nodding eagerly. "Lash is a good teacher."

"Good. I expect you to make the most of your time with him. Please go prepare yourself. We need to leave in a few hours for the party. Remember, you will need to perform like your mother and I, as we discussed yesterday morning."

Theoron nodded, and left.

Devon was still playing with a stuffed squeaky toy, biting it repeatedly. I picked him up and cuddled him. "And how are you, Sweetheart?" I said, kissing him. "Were you being good for Daddy?"

"No," Theo said in a mock scolding tone, giving me a brief smile. "He's been clawing up his other toys. He's torn apart three just this morning—"

"I'll sew them up," I said, giving Devon a hug. He purred loudly in my arms as I stroked him. "Does he need to eat?"

He shook his head. "We shared some chicken. He's got a huge appetite."

"Just like his Dad," I said lovingly.

Theo's gruff exterior melted a little, giving me a loving smile back, his blue eyes happy.

Danial was pacing back and forth now. "Jenny should be here any moment," he said nervously. He turned to Theo, who was getting up to leave. "Theo, maybe you should stay too."

"Me? Why?" Theo said, sounding nervous, too. "I'm not ever going to be vampire. What good could I possibly do?"

"But your life changed completely when you were turned," Danial said. "Maybe you can tell her it's something she can manage, something she can get used to. There isn't anyone else I can ask. All the current other guards were born were, including Brian and his wife. They aren't going to be any help."

Theo looked dubious, but he sat back down on the couch. The doorbell rang. Danial gave me a nervous look.

It was past time I took control of this situation. "Stay here," I said calmly. "I'll get it."

I went to the door, and opened it. A young woman stood there in her early twenties. She looked haggard, her thin body and pain filled eyes showing her sickness. She was pretty, in a delicate way; her light brown eyes kind, her hair a beautiful chestnut color. Looking closer, I saw it was a wig. That made sense: she'd been having chemotherapy.

"Please come in," I said politely, resolving the next time I got my hair cut to send the clippings to Locks of Love. I shut the door behind her, and took her coat. "You must be Jenny," I said, giving her a warm smile.

"I am she," she said, laughing.

I liked her at once. "I'm Sarelle. Please come in. Danial is waiting for you."

She followed me to the great room. Danial came over to us to greet her. "Danial, this is Jenny," I said, playing the hostess. "Jenny, this is Danial."

"I'm pleased to meet you," he said charmingly.

Instantly, Jenny was captivated by him, a little in awe, and a little in lust. "Thank you for seeing me. My mom said you had something to tell me that might help me?"

She sounded so hopeful, yet so afraid to hope at the same time.

"Yes. Please sit down," Danial said

66

They all sat.

"Would anyone like anything to drink?" I said.

"A glass of water," Jenny said.

I brought one for her, and myself then sat down.

"Jenny," Danial said, clearing his throat. "Your mother had been a trusted employee of mine for most of her life. She asked me to speak with you. I asked you here today to make you an offer."

"What kind of offer?" Jenny said curiously.

"I don't know how to say this, so I'll just say it," Danial said, sounding nervous for the first time. "I'm a vampire. Your mother asked me to offer to give you some of my blood, to make you vampire, too. I only consider it because I know you are dying and your mother has been a trusted employee of mine for her whole life, and never asked me for any kind of favor. So when she asked for this, I told her I'd be willing to do it to save your life."

Jenny looked at him in shock. She didn't burst out laughing, but it was obvious she didn't believe him.

"Danial, show her your fangs," I said.

Danial bared his teeth, revealing his upper and lower fangs. Jenny gasped, but didn't scream.

"He's telling you the truth," I said. "I'm here today to vouch for him, to tell you that he means everything he says, and that you can trust him, when he says he can save you."

"I'm here for that, too," Theo added.

Jenny looked over at him for the first time. Her eyes lingered on him, but I wasn't surprised. He was already dressed in his clothes for the Hallows party: all in black, his skintight T-shirt showing off his heavily muscled chest and his sculpted biceps. His jacket hung over one of the dining room chairs with his gun and holster, likely to save it from being covered in our son's tawny colored hair.

"Who are you?" Jenny said curiously.

Theo blushed. "I'm Sar's husband, Theo," he said with a friendly smile. "I work for Danial, doing his security. The baby cougar at your feet is our son, Devon."

Jenny looked down at Devon. Suddenly, he jumped on her. Though she caught him, the force of his jump almost knocked her back on the couch.

I went over and took him from her. "Sorry," I said, giving her an apologetic smile. "He's a handful."

"He's beautiful," she said appreciatively. "But did I hear you right? He's your son?"

"Theo is what is called a werecougar," I said patiently. "He can become a cougar at will. Devon was born a cougar, but he'll change form to human in a month or so."

Jenny looked at Theo, clearly awed. He looked away, blushing again. "This is a lot to take in," she said slowly. "Sar, are you supernatural too?"

"No," I said, giving her a smile. "I'm mortal—"

"Sar is what is called Oathed to me," Danial said, interrupting me. "She is mortal now, but that is only temporary, because of an illness she suffered. I intend to give her some of my blood soon, and she'll be as she was before, close to immortal, yet not vampire. You will be immortal too, Jenny, if I give you my blood, though you would not be as Sar will be. You would be vampire, as I am."

Theo was watching Danial, his eyes slightly narrowed. His thoughts were obvious.

"Would I need to drink blood if I became what you are?" Jenny asked. "To stay out of the sun?"

Danial nodded. "Yes to both, I'm afraid," he answered gently. "But I'd help you to procure the blood at first, and you'd be safe, living here at my estate. I'd ask in return to get your word that you'd work for me for a number of years, doing what your mother did for me. And I'd ask that you'd agree to swear an oath not to harm anyone else here and possibly to fight beside us if we were ever attacked—"

Jenny looked incredulous. "Do I have to decide today?"

Danial shook his head. "Not today, no. But by the end of this weekend, I want you to decide. You have to be strong enough to make the change successful, and I can tell from your heartbeat how weak you are, Jenny. I don't want to try it unless I'm sure you can make the change to vampire, that you have the strength to do it. So it has to be soon."

"I'll let you know by the end of the weekend," Jenny said slowly. "But I need to think about it. I'll come to you on Sunday night, and tell you my decision, if that's okay."

Danial nodded. "That is agreeable to me, Jenny. Go think on it. I'll talk to you tomorrow."

I showed her to the door. When she left, I went back in to see Danial sprawled on the couch looking exhausted, and Theo holding a sleeping Devon. I went to Danial, and put my hand on his shoulder.

He looked up at me, gently covering my hand with his. "I think that went well. I don't know whether to hope she agrees or declines."

"She'll say yes," I said, sitting down beside him. "She doesn't want to die, and there isn't another choice."

"That's true," Danial said, making a face. "I wish it weren't, but it is—"

"Sar, can you take Devon?" Theo interjected. "I need to get to the convention center and make sure everything's okay there."

"Sure." He gently placed Devon in my arms. I gave Theo a kiss goodbye. He kissed me back, then gave me a kiss on the forehead for good measure.

"What's the plan?" I asked.

"Titus will be here at six to teleport you, Danial, Elle, and T," Theo said authoritatively. "I know you could take yourself, but it's safer this way. Hans, Warren, Brian, and Aran are all working with me tonight, mostly watching things, but they'll be armed, too. Titus will be there, and Rip will be there on and off, too."

I nodded. "I've met him already."

"Rip is bringing Devon to Hayden right before we leave, where Serena is going to watch him," Theo said, malice coloring his words. "Lash is going to be guarding Venus and him with the other bears. I don't like it, but I admit he's safest there."

"I'll take him there," I said quickly. "All right?"

Theo turned suspicious. "Why, Sar?"

"I want to be there when he meets his twin again," I said happily. "I'm surprised you don't want to be there. They had to have missed one another."

"You know that I don't want him to go to Hayden at all," Theo growled, his eyes narrowing. "I want you to leave as soon as the ritual part of the party's over and bring him back here. Brian can come back with you and stay here until I get home. Tell Serena that Lash is not to get within ten feet of him, not ever. You make sure she understands that."

"I'll tell her," I concurred loudly. "Calm down."

"Sar, you need to get dressed," Danial said. "We need to leave soon, and you haven't showered yet."

He was making a point to say I smelled of snake. Thank God he attributed it to being around Theoron, who probably reeked of snake from all the tussling with Lash this morning.

"I'll go now," I said, nodding. "I'm going to put Devon on your bed, Danial. Can you make sure you don't let him out if he wakes up?"

"Sure," Danial said. "In fact, I'm going to have to shower with you or we'll be late—"

"I figured that was coming," Theo said, rolling his eyes in mock exasperation.

"Get out of here," Danial said, shooting a grin at Theo. "Don't you have work to do?"

"I'm going," Theo said, sliding his shoulder holster on, then his jacket. "I'll see you both later. Don't forget you do have a party to get to. I wouldn't want you to get sidetracked."

There was no jealousy behind his teasing. That was a big relief. Despite the bond between us being broken, Theo seemed to be really trying.

As Theo slammed out of the house, I went in Danial's room, setting down a sleepy Devon on the bed. He stretched out, uttering a soft purr. I petted him for a few moments, hoping he would fall asleep. He tried to resist me, purring louder, enjoying the attention. But soon his eyes grew heavy and his head swayed, setting down onto the comforter with a soft sigh. I gave him a quick kiss on the forehead, then got up carefully rom the bed.

By the time I joined Danial in the shower, he was done. He got out, flashing me a brief mock-interested look, then left. I rolled my eyes, then focused on getting ready. When I emerged, Danial was still absent.

I wrapped a towel around myself, another around my hair, and began to rub it dry. *Where had he gone?* I needed him to take off my fox choker; I couldn't wear both.

Just as I was finishing my hair, Danial came into the bathroom, a towel wrapped around his waist, carrying two garment bags in his hands. He hung them on the back of the door. "Here it is."

He unzipped the first bag. It contained his outfit: a pair of black jeans, and a red shirt in that swordsman's style he favored. The second one held mine, the red gown Tatiana had made. If I hadn't known it wasn't the original one, I'd have though it was my own red dress that I'd bought years ago. But touch showed the reality; this was silk. My other one had been cotton.

"It's beautiful," I said, admiring Tatiana's work. "I'll have to thank her tonight—"

"You're beautiful," Danial whispered in my ear. He embraced me, then pushed me gently backward, pressing me up against the wall. His ardent kisses became insistent, his hands reaching under my towel. It dropped to the floor, his towel following.

"I want you," Danial said hungrily, his erection becoming firmer with each passing second. He leaned into me, kissing down my neck, his delicate fangs brushing my soft skin. "Tell me you want me too, Love."

He was nervous about Jenny and the party tonight. *He needed comfort from me.* While I loved him enough to give him what he needed, I'd have to cheat a little. There wasn't time to let Danial spend an hour working up to sex. This needed to be fast.

I closed my eyes and imagined it was Lash in back of me, as he'd had me pressed against his truck that time, telling me he was going to have me right there.

I reached down and caressed his hard organ possessively. "I want you," I said roughly. "Take me right here."

Danial didn't need any other encouragement. He bent his legs, and with a clench of his buttocks, he pushed up into me, bringing a lustful cry from my lips and a loud moan from his.

"God, you're ready," he said huskily. "I wasn't sure you wanted me, darling."

I flushed, embarrassed about my thoughts of Lash, his words dissolving my fantasy. "I do."

"Then come for me, my love," he said lovingly, thrusting slowly.

I couldn't come for him with almost no foreplay, not with him being so gentle to me, so...so nice. I needed force, for him to take control utterly!

"Talk dirty to me," I growled gutturally. "Tell me you're going to have me, that I can't stop you, that you know I want it, and you're going to give it to me. Tell me you're going to make me scream for you!"

Chapter Seven

Danial paused for a heartbeat, then thrust himself in deeply. "I'm going to have you, right here like this," he hissed in my ear. "You can't stop me from doing it, Sar."

My head lolled, my eyes shut tight, imagining him to be Lash. "No...don't..."

Danial put his hands flat to the wall on either side of me, pumping his hips fast. "Yes. Tell me my dick feels good in your tight cunt, Sar. Tell me you want it deeper."

I cried out with each thrust of his body into mine. "It feels good. Please, please go deeper—"

"You've wanted this all morning," Danial whispered lustfully. "I've been aching to give it to you. My cock has been hard for hours, just waiting to sink into your soft, wet flesh—"

I was shaking hard, so aroused my knees were weak. Danial clasped me tightly in his arms, carefully lowering me onto the tile floor and following me.

"Please!" I whimpered. "Please, don't stop. Take me—"

"You fit me like a glove," Danial hissed in my ear. "Like a skillful, yielding hand stroking and teasing. You want me to spurt, to fill you with my come. Even if you don't, I'm surely going to in seconds—"

I felt the climax hit me, the waves arching my back as I drew breath to shriek.

Danial made a fist in my hair, yanking hard. "Scream!"

I convulsed in his arms, screaming at the top of my lungs: "God! Yes! Please! Please! Oh God! Yes! Yes! Yes!"

Danial shouted out his release in the midst of my screeching. After, we both went limp on the floor. My heart felt like it was coming out of my chest, it was beating so fast. Danial's was also beating fast against my back.

"Wow," Danial said, awed.

That pretty much covered it. I moved out from under him, as he rolled onto his back. "That was something."

Danial sat on the edge of the bathtub, still panting, then gave me a hand up to sit beside him. "I'm glad you enjoyed me so much," he murmured, kissing my throat. "Devlin had told me months ago to try talking coarsely to you, that you sometimes liked it a little rough now."

"Sometimes," I replied, feeling very guilty. *Had Devlin guessed why I liked a little roughness now? Probably.* I flushed.

"I'm glad you told me what you wanted," Danial said, giving me a relaxed smile. "I knew we had to hurry. We usually take a lot longer—"

"I'm glad you gave me my fantasy," I said quickly, giving him a peck on his cheek as I stood. "I've never asked you to say anything like that except when The Lust had me. I wasn't sure if you'd feel comfortable doing it."

"It matters that you enjoy our time together as much as possible," Danial said as he stood. He kissed my cheeks, my forehead, my chin, and even my nose. "If you want me to say certain things to you, or be a little rough sometimes, just tell me. I wouldn't want to do it every time with you, but sometimes, sure. I prefer being gentle when making love—"

"I know," I said, giving him a satisfied smile. "I always liked your gentleness—"

"Liked?" Danial said slowly, tilting his head, obviously irritated. "Past tense?"

"I like that you're gentle with me," I corrected quickly, beginning to dress. "I won't ask you to do what you just did very often. I'll leave that to Dev."

"Is he okay?" Danial said, picking up our discarded towels. "I'm surmising that because you asked me for this and not him, there's some problem. Are you fighting?"

He thought I'd asked him to be rough because I'd gotten to like Devlin's rougher style of making love, and wasn't getting any. That was a relief. Still, I had to be careful. "What did he tell you?" I asked, sliding into my dress.

"He's told me he healed the burns Ulysses gave him," Danial said, pulling on his jeans and shirt. "Is that true?"

I fixed my hair, debating what to tell him. "He's healed, but his new flesh is sensitive. I don't feel comfortable telling you more than that."

"I can guess the rest," Danial said, holding up his hand. "When you told me he gave you permission for Lash, I knew that he had to be hurt in some way."

Another flush immediately began creeping up my neck. "He'll be okay soon," I said confidently.

Danial hugged me tightly from behind. "I'm glad you love him, Sar," he murmured. "He needs a supportive woman now more than ever. This must have destroyed his ego—"

"Enough," I interjected. "He wouldn't want us talking about it, Danial. Don't let on that you know anything's wrong, either."

"I'll say nothing," Danial agreed, buckling on his sword. He came over and removed my choker with his symbol, stooping quickly down to fasten it at my ankle. While he didn't speak, his demeanor was grudging acceptance.

I fixed my hair, fluffing it up as Tatiana had taught me long ago, and turned to him. "I need to take Devon to Hayden. Wait for me?"

"Don't be long, or we'll be late," Danial replied. "Here, you'd better put on your cloak. Otherwise you're sure to rip your dress when Devon digs in his claws as you teleport."

Devon hated being teleported. He always screamed bloody murder as soon as he felt anyone doing it to him. We tried not to do it often, but it was so much easier than driving, sometimes we just had to grit our teeth and let him scream. Theo said he'd get used to it in time, but I wasn't so sure. And while Devon could sleep through just about anything else, my little furry angel would be sure to awaken caterwauling the moment he felt me teleporting him somewhere.

Danial threw a long cloak around my shoulders, fastening the clasp. It was heavy wool, with velvet lining, a perfect accent to the floor length silk red gown that clung to my curves, the scoop neckline just low enough to show the very tops of my breasts. "Thank you for the dress, and the cloak," I said politely as I turned back and forth before his mirror, admiring myself. Danial nodded. "You look beautiful in them," he said with approval. "Tell Titus to get moving. I'll go see where Elle and Theoron are."

I snatched up Devon and teleported to Hayden. He screeched immediately, digging in his claws as Danial had predicted. I held him tightly, my cloak taking the brunt of his tantrum. We appeared in the kitchen. Serena was there, having coffee with Nick. As I took them in at a glance, I knew suddenly he had to be the one she was falling for. It was in the way she rested her hand on his. What was dismaying was the lack of a signal from him that he was feeling anything more than friendly towards her.

"You're here." Serena stood up. "Hi, Devon. Aren't you handsome—"

Devon looked at her and hissed.

"Hush," I said sternly.

Devon stopped immediately, and looked up at me.

"This is Serena, Devon," I said calmly. "And this is Nick. They are friends, so you don't hiss at them."

"Hi, Sarelle," Nick said stiffly.

I expected him to be standoffish with me after that scene with Lash in the garage. "Hi."

"Get yourself to the gatehouse, Nick. Now," a cold hissing voice said.

I turned to see Lash in the doorway, looking intently at me.

Nick drank the rest of his coffee, and stood up. He gave Serena a last quick kiss, and then went for the door, grabbing his jacket from the chair.

Devon took one good look at Lash and hissed louder than I'd ever seen him hiss at anyone. He dug in his claws, too.

"Hush! Behave, Devon!"

Devon looked up at me and stopped. Then he looked back at Lash and growled again, lashing his tail.

"Just like your father, aren't you?" Lash hissed kindly. His look was gentle as he gazed at Devon in my arms. "You look just like him."

"Devon, this is Lash," I said calmly. "Your father wants you to stay away from him. But if he tells you to do something, you had better do it, or your father will be angry. Got it?"

Lash flicked his eyes to me, and nodded. "I'll watch him."

Devon growled grumpily, but I knew he'd do it. He always did what Theo told him, though he listened to me only about half the time.

"I'll take him, if he'll come to me," Serena offered, extending her arms.

I handed Devon to her. He didn't want to go, crying out and trying to hold onto me. I carefully unhooked his claws from me, and he cried out again, grabbing onto Serena, who winced as his claws sank into her arms.

"You are fine," I said calmly. "Shh."

"Does he need to eat anything?" Serena said, trying to hold a squirming Devon. "Can I give him some chicken?"

"It's better if you don't. As it is, I'll probably be coming back for him shortly. Theo's having a conniption about him being here. He probably doesn't want him to eat anything while he's here, either."

When Lash didn't offer up a sarcastic comment, I looked over to see why. He was gone.

"Titus should be here shortly," Devlin said, entering the kitchen with Venus in his arms. He put her on the floor carefully. She sat there, her golden eyes riveted on Devon. He began squirming all over, crying out plaintively. Serena let him down, and he bounded over to Venus, sniffing her. He began purring loudly, rubbing against her as she squeezed him tightly, kissing his face.

I swallowed hard, wiping at the sudden tears in my eyes as I watched the two of them hold each other, clearly overjoyed to be together again.

Lash came in the door, breaking the moment even in his silence.

"I'll go see what's keeping Titus," Devlin said, heading down the basement stairs. "We'll be late."

As Serena put the cups in the sink, Lash came over to me. "Having good times with Danial?" he hissed with a knowing look.

I went red, knowing he smelled Danial's scent on me, and what we'd been doing. Probably Serena could, too. "Um—"

"Don't be embarrassed," Lash hissed, giving me a faint smile. "I was just teasing. You're his Oathed One. It's right for you to be with him like that, just as you are with Dev."

Now Lash just had to convince Theo of that for me, and we'd all be fine. "He'll be a handful, but—"

"I'll make sure Devon's safe," Lash hissed. "You be safe too, Sar. Watch yourself, and stay close to Dev."

"I will."

His hand grasped mine, giving it a brief squeeze before he let go. "I've never seen you in a dress before," Lash hissed gently. "You look beautiful, Sar."

"Thanks," I said, flushing.

"We're ready," Titus rumbled, entering with a glower for Lash.

Lash hissed back at Titus, his eyes flat and narrowed. Titus glared back at him, blackness welling out of him in a cloud.

I'd had enough of macho bullshit, and the party hadn't even begun. I teleported myself back to Danial's house, Devlin and Titus arriving directly after me. Theoron and Elle were there waiting on the couch with Danial.

As they got to their feet, I took in their formal wear, my eyes focusing on Elle's dress first. She looked beautiful, but far too sexy for her tender age. Long, sensuous curls dangled artfully here and there from the crowning knot of her light blond hair. She had on a fair amount of makeup, but it wasn't done heavily. My guess was that Tatiana had likely helped her with it. Elle's deep red silk gown was still too low; the tops of her small breasts were bared and pushed up by the formed strapless bodice, almost threatening to spill out of her dress. The skirt at least was long, covering her to her ankles as mine did. But it was tight all the way down to her thighs, like a sheath. If she'd been another woman, I'd have been jealous of her young body while admiring it. Being my daughter, I was torn between pride in her looking so good, and wanting desperately to cover her with a tent-like garment so no men would be ogling my baby girl. Instead, I'd have to trust in her male relatives to watch over her tonight.

Theoron looked as tall, dark, and handsome as Danial. They were dressed identically, in the same red silk and black jeans, and those black thigh-high leather boots Danial had always favored. Theoron's hair had been done too, though his was shorter, and feathered back. He'd gotten the curliness of my hair, so his hair had a lot more wave to it than Danial's did.

"Aren't you going to look at me?" Devlin whispered seductively in my ear.

I turned to face him. He was also dressed in a red silk shirt, thigh high boots, and black pants, though as usual, he'd added his own flair. His pants were leather, their front laced up like a corset. They were so tight I could see his masculine package prominently displayed under the tight leather.

"You like?" he asked huskily.

I blushed.

He laughed, hugging me. "I guess the look on your face is answer enough."

"Let's go, Dev," Danial said in a clipped tone, obviously annoyed.

We joined hands and Titus teleported us to the convention center, where we ended up in a back dressing room. Danial led us out immediately, walking fast, the rest of us almost racing to match his long strides. Devlin and Danial took up positions beside me as we entered together.

"Devlin Dalcon and Danial Racklan, with Sarelle O'Connor," the loudspeaker intoned. "Theoron Racklan and Elle O'Connor."

I was glad there weren't many people there yet. I was still too shy for this, no matter that I'd played hostess to these huge parties more than a few times now. It didn't help that the guests I was dreading wouldn't be here for hours. Trepidatious, I pasted a smile in place, and began meeting and greeting.

* * * *

The early part of the night went well. After an hour went by, and more and more guests arrived, it was apparent that there were about four hundred people at the event instead of the usual two hundred. Likely, that was due to our boom in business this year. Devlin and Danial did most of the talking, as expected. True to what Lash had said, Devlin stayed by my side all through the evening, though Danial and Theoron left us to talk to clients after only a few minutes.

Danial stayed with Theoron for most of the early evening. I looked over at them often, enjoying seeing Danial and his son—our son—standing there so handsome and proud. Elle was slightly harder to spot, thronged as she was by single men. I didn't worry, though. Hans was with her, standing just to her left and behind. When my careful watching revealed that none of the men flirting with her or bringing her soft drinks were getting out of line, I stopped paying her close attention, and started to enjoy myself with Devlin.

Devlin had a lot more time to pay attention to me than Danial ever had. Most of the people he did business with weren't the kind who'd come to a party like this, and the business he handled wasn't the kind to be discussed once it was done. But Devlin did have to greet a few guests, among them the mobsters, Tony and Thane, who had made it this year. Tony looked the same as he had those years ago I'd seen him at Danial's: swarthy and solid, though he was more ruddy faced and on his second whisky at least. Thane I'd never met before, but he was just what I expected him to be: cold eyed, and powerfully built, his eyes clearly those of a predator. He was Italian, and he looked good with his black hair cut short, his Armani suit impeccably tailored, and his gold jewelry both thick and tastefully worn. But despite the air of menace about him, he was respectful toward me, calling me "Miss O'Connor." Was that out of respect for Theo, Danial, or Devlin? Maybe all three.

After speaking with Thane and Tony, I took a break to visit the tables. I grabbed a plate, and began loading it.

Elle sauntered up. "This is so much fun!" She looked over the table. "Can I have a drink?"

I was glad she hadn't been drinking yet. Danial had probably cautioned her about that. I let her have a sip of my Shiraz.

She grimaced. "I want something sweeter," she said, her tone wheedling.

While I was debating the ethics of letting her have one small drink, Devlin got her a Mudslide from the bar. She gave him a smile. I gave him a murderous look. Elle sipped it very slowly. Keeping one eye on her, I got myself some cake, and dug in.

"Now that you've indulged," Devlin said a few moments later. "Are you too full to dance?"

"I didn't eat that much," I said haughtily, putting aside my dirty plate before I went back for another piece.

Dev raised his eyebrows to say I clearly had.

"I'm expecting my period any time now," I said. "That's how it is. Get used to it."

He laughed, then offered his hand.

"Do you dance?" I said, giving him an inquiring look as I took it.

"You can decide for yourself," Devlin said, a sexy glint in his eyes. He led me to the dance floor, and signaled the band. "Lady in Red" started, making me giggle as we began to dance.

"I knew that would get Danial's attention," Devlin murmured with glee. "He's watching us with murder in his eyes, Sar."

"You couldn't have picked another song?" I teased, secretly pleased. As usual, Danial was completely engrossed in his business dealings. With Theoron beside him, he hadn't given me a second thought, other than to check that Devlin was watching me. That irritated me as much as it always had, being forgotten as soon as his business needed him.

"I wanted to dance with you to this one," Devlin purred, moving me expertly over the floor. "I wanted Danial to be jealous. I could smell he'd had you earlier, when you came to drop off Devon—"

I blushed. "Shh."

Devlin leaned in and kissed my cheek. "—and I was a little jealous then," he finished, turning me to promenade around him. "So this is only fair. He's lucky I didn't pick 'Set the Night to Music'. I checked, and the band knows that one."

I laughed aloud. Devlin joined in, pulling me close as the song ended.

"My Lady in Red, I love you," he said softly. His mouth covered mine swiftly, his openmouthed kiss shocking and all encompassing, lasting a full minute there on the dance floor, in front of everyone. By the time he released me, I was breathing hard, and so was he, his pants displaying the engorged length of him like a second skin.

Appalled, I pulled his tucked-in shirt out of his pants with a swift yank, covering him. Elle was not going to see this, even if Dev didn't care who else saw him. He'd worn those pants for this very reason. I should have known he'd have something over-the-top planned. He always did for any kind of party.

"You didn't have to cover me," Devlin purred, nibbling my ear as I pulled him off the dance floor by the hand, my face redder than my dress. "I want everyone to see what you do to me, Sar, how quickly you awaken me with just your kiss—"

"Shut up, Dev!" I hissed at him, smiling at guests as we passed them. "Shut up."

"I want them to imagine us together, to see the aroused length of me, and imagine me sinking it into you as you beg me to take you—"

"Stop talking to my wife like that, or I'll pretend my finger slipped, and I shot you by mistake," Theo growled, furious. He appeared behind Devlin, the muzzle of his gun pressed hard into Devlin's side.

Devlin looked at him, then laughed in his face. "You can't stop me, not with your threats, your bullets, or all the wishes of your pious heart. Not *ever*—"

Theo's eyes turned yellow. He was going to do it. Theo was pissed off enough to shoot Devlin, if I didn't stop him…

"Stop it!" Danial hissed, coming over and grabbing Theo's gun. "Put your gun away, and get back to your job, Theo. And Dev, knock off your shit! You're acting like you're at an orgy. What in God's name made you wear those pants tonight? This is a business party, *my* business party, and you will conduct yourself appropriately."

"Danial, the human guests are almost all gone," Devlin said, giving him a grin. "Most everyone left is faerie, vampire, or were."

Looking around, I perceived he was right. While we danced, most everyone had cleared out. It was nearly ten, time for the human guests to leave, and the supernatural ones to arrive. There were only a few here of the latter so far, maybe thirty of the hundred or so coming. The last human guests were already trickling out, their coats already in their hands.

"Everyone who is other than human expects this of me," Devlin continued, still grinning gleefully. "If you paid a little more attention to Sar, and a little less to your clients, you'd have a happier lover."

"Sar's still radiating satisfaction from the loving I gave her earlier," Danial said coolly, satisfaction dripping from his words. "She's always sated when *I*—"

I dug my fingers into Danial's side as subtly as I could. He smoothly switched words.

"—when *I* love her gently, and with respect. She doesn't want to be man-handled on the floor in front of everyone."

"I say she does, and I'm just the man to handle her," Devlin said, laughing. Theo growled again.

Enough machismo. "I'm heading to the bathroom for a minute," I said curtly. "Try not to kill one another until I get back."

Not all my grumpiness was at the men's antics; I'd felt slight cramping as we'd danced. My excuse for eating hadn't been a lie; I'd been expecting my period for days. It would be just my luck to get it now, here. I had put on a pad back in Danial's bathroom, in case having sex with him had started it, but it wouldn't hurt to check.

Devlin nodded, taking his arm off me. Theo tailed me to the bathroom, taking up position outside.

"Are you okay?" he said, taking my arm. "I've been keeping an eye on you. Until he grabbed you and kissed you, you look like you were having an okay time."

"I'm having a good time," I replied. "I was worried at first, but I think that this is possibly the best Hallows party I've been to. It's nice to be given some attention—" I trailed off, worried I'd offended him.

"I know Danial sometimes ignores you at these parties," Theo said grudgingly. "It's been worse this party, because it's all about Theoron, the father and son, the Solutions, Inc. Dynasty, blah, blah, blah. I'm glad you're not bored. I've got my hands full watching this many people, even with the other guards. I just didn't like Devlin saying those things to you."

"You know he's like that. Ignore him, Theo. I can handle it, even if it still embarrasses me sometimes. I don't know why it still does, actually. He's said enough things like that to me over the past months you'd think I'd be immune—"

"That's because you aren't one of his whores," Theo said flatly.

I gaped at him in shock, my mouth dropping open. "What?"

"Any decent woman would be embarrassed by him," Theo continued triumphantly. "It's a mark of your goodness that you find what he says so awful, and don't enjoy it."

Guilt flooded me. *What would Theo think of the things I'd asked Danial to say to me earlier?* I could guess. Worse, what Devlin had said to me earlier had made me a little hot. I'd been embarrassed he'd said the words to me where he had, but not that he'd said them. In fact, I'd be asking him to repeat them the next time I spent the night, and maybe wear those pants for me, too. I'd liked how they outlined the length of his erection—that engorged sweet hardness…

I fought down my rising desire. Theo would smell it on me, if I wasn't careful. It was clear he thought my lust inappropriate, and he was right; this wasn't the time to be thinking of sex. "I'll be right back, Theo."

I went into the bathroom and used the facilities. The mild cramping I'd felt minutes ago had vanished, and there was no sign of my monthly visitor, to my relief. Good. I'd be happier getting it any night but this one. While I'd been concerned my period was taking so long to come back this time, this was not the time for its return debut. Steven had said not to worry about it anyway.

Thinking of Steven reminded me that I needed to be checked for STDs. *What a waste of time.* Lash hadn't given me anything. Still, I'd go make sure, anyway. I owed Theo that.

Pasting on a smile, I came out of the bathroom to find Devlin waiting for me, grinning lecherously.

"Where'd Theo go?" I accused, suspicious.

Devlin grinned wider. "Perseus arrived a few minutes ago. Theo went to make sure Danial was safe with Titus. Zane, Samuel, and the rest should be arriving in a few moments. Rip is on his way, but he's not here yet—"

"So you volunteered to come watch me?" I finished skeptically.

Devlin pulled me close to him, rubbing our hips together suggestively. "I couldn't resist." He kissed my neck, then up my chin to my lips. Drawing his hips back from mine, he let his head fall back, a slight groan escaping his lips. I flushed, watching him fill out beneath his pants, his firming penis again stretching forth, pressing against the tight leather.

"I thought maybe I could get you to slip into one of these rooms with me," he purred seductively, pinning me against the wall, his body hard against mine. "And then I could slip into you. We have a few minutes—"

81

I ached for him, the rising need pushing aside everything but the wish to take him up on his offer. I slid my hand down over his lower body, pressing it tight over his bulging flesh, massaging and stroking. "Sounds good to me," I whispered.

Chapter Eight

Dev's eyes bugged out of his head, shock making his mouth drop open. "You're really, um, you want to—?"

He'd expected refusal, not to have his bluff called. But I was done playing; I wanted action, not teasing. "I love seeing how big you get for me," I said seductively. "Take me into the nearest room and sink yourself into me, Lover."

If he'd been his old confident self, my words would have compelled him to begin making love to me right here. Instead, Devlin looked down at me, his eyes hot, melting golden fire, and didn't move.

I took his hand, leading him into the nearest open doorway. The room contained only a small table, and a few chairs. "Do I need to seduce you?" I purred invitingly, leaning back on the small table. I lifted my dress hem, letting the silk slip through my fingers to bare my white legs, then the tops of my garters.

"I'm not going to tell you to stop," Devlin said huskily, his shining eyes riveted on me.

"Come here," I ordered, crooking a finger.

With a sultry smile, he walked over. I took his hand, then brought his fingers to my underwear, guiding his hand to slide inside the red lace.

"Stroke me," I breathed. "I want you inside me, Dev."

His control broke instantly, his strong arms lifting me onto the meeting table, shoving aside some chairs with a snarl. Dev kissed me hard, his tongue driving into my mouth, his left hand pulling down my panties as his right grasped my hip. Then his fingers were sliding inside, delving deep, my back arching as I cried out. Devlin cut off my cries with another kiss, then dipped his head to my throat, his fangs pressing gently.

"I want to be inside you," Dev whispered roughly. "Free me."

Breathing hard, I untied, then pulled the laces of his pants, loosening them. I peeled them down, then put my hands on him, loving how thick he was.

Devlin flexed for me, smiling impishly. Purposely licking my lips, I leaned forward, sucking the ripe head into my mouth, making him gasp, his hands clenching on my shoulders.

Devlin pushed me back on the table, spreading my legs wide as he took up position between them. Panting raggedly, Devlin slid his hands under my buttocks, tilting my pelvis up. Impatient, I pulled his rigid organ down from its erect position, making him jerk as a small drop of semen escaped. I rubbed the silky wet head on my clit, then pushed up, moaning. With a thrust of his hips and a very gratified sigh, Dev sheathed his length.

"Ooh," he groaned loudly, beginning to move. "You're so hot inside, I feel like you're burning me! I never dreamed you'd agree—"

"Deeper, Dev," I grunted. "Possess me."

Devlin, bared his fangs, snarling, his movements becoming purposeful as he thrust repeatedly, straining as he buried his firm flesh in mine. I whimpered in pleasure, the complete stimulation of his stroking making me shudder.

Devlin brought me against him hard, the sudden deep penetration bringing a scream from my lips. With a growl of satisfaction, he held me there, his head thrown back, his eyes closed and lips parted, his chest heaving as he moved.

It was almost too much, and yet my only desire was to be utterly filled by him, to have that wonderful stroking go on until I could stand it no longer. I wrapped my legs around him, pushing my hips tighter to his. His long length, already surely buried, slid in another inch, drawing a long moan of pleasure from my throat.

Devlin snapped his head down, his golden eyes almost glowing. "You see what you do to me?" he growled. "How much I love seeing you like this as I take you, Sar?"

"Go deeper," I moaned, clutching at him. "I want you deeper—"

Devlin bore down hard, his one last unsheathed inch sliding home. I let out another cry, jerking, as he bore down again and again, rubbing my clit with the top of his shaft, his long buried length massaging...

"You have me, all of me," he groaned, pushing in again. "I can't last, the warm wetness of you is too tempting, too good." He kissed my throat, then shuddered, driving faster.

With each word, my arousal had increased, the riskiness of being discovered—not to mention the ministrations of his body in mine—utterly compelling. As he bore down again, I felt the orgasm come over me. I was suddenly there in a flash of sweet release. Devlin covered my mouth with his, muffling my cries. As my orgasm ebbed, he drew back to watch me, continuing to slide himself into me to the hilt, again and again, making me cry out in pleasure until I was panting.

"Now me," he groaned, burying his face in my neck, his fangs pricking me as he kissed me. His breath came in quick pants on my throat as he drove in faster.

"Bite me, Dev," I whispered. "Can you feel how much I want you? How much I love you? Bite me—"

Devlin slid his fangs in, swallowing as he fed, his arms tightening around me. Another orgasm hit me, making me tense, my cries soft and languid as I clutched him close. Devlin sucked gently, then came a second later, pumping into me as he threw back his head to shout, "Sar! Sar! *Ahhhh!*"

They had to have heard that in the next county. So much for being discreet.

Dev contracted his muscles a few more times, letting out soft cries as he emptied the last of his semen. With a regretful sigh, he pulled out of me, still jerking slightly, breathing hard. He produced some tissues from somewhere, and cleaned himself off. He reached down and handed me my underwear. I quickly pulled them on, before smoothing my dress back down.

"It's good you were expecting your period," he said. "I gave you everything I had, Love. Danial would not be pleased if I ruined your new dress."

I flushed, my hands fumbling as I tied up Devlin's laces. "True."

Devlin gently helped me off the table, and gave me a lingering kiss. "I loved that, Sar," he said lovingly, his face both very happy and also peaceful, his golden eyes relaxed, yet still completely dominating. "I love how proper you seem to be, and how wild and naughty you get now sometimes when you think you won't get caught—"

"Shush," I said primly, putting my finger to his lips. "We have to get back to the others. Danial will be looking for us."

"No, he won't. He and the rest are all going to smell our sexual release as soon as we get in the room, even if they somehow missed my screams," Devlin remarked, utterly joyous.

I flushed red to my toes, realizing he was absolutely right. *Why hadn't I thought about that?*

"Don't be embarrassed," Devlin said in pure delight, opening the door for me. "I can't wait to see the look on Samuel's face. There is no better way to say to another man that a woman's yours than to have him smell the scent of your lovemaking all over her, the scent of her satiation wafting from every pore—"

That was true; Theo had been pissed off enough times about it over the years. But I needed to be claimed as Dev's in every way possible in front of Samuel and the rest of the Vampire Rulers. That mattered more than his jealousy right now.

Devlin slung his arm over my shoulder possessively, and we strolled into the main room together. Most of the other guests had arrived. Perseus, Zane, and Samuel were all standing together. A woman stood in their midst, flanked on all sides protectively. She was pregnant, showing only a little. That had to be Harriet. Danial and Theoron stood opposite their formation. Theo, Titus, and Rip were each ten feet back from father and son, positioned so they formed a protective triangle, but didn't encroach too close to Harriet.

Perseus turned immediately to face us. "Ah, Sarelle and Devlin," he spat sarcastically, baring his teeth. "Off for a quick interlude during the changing of guests? Or did we hear another man screaming Sar's name?"

"No, that was me, thanks for noticing," Devlin finished, flashing a triumphant smile. "I hope you didn't miss us too much."

Zane sniffed, and then rolled his eyes. "I'm glad to see you're still exercising your rights, Dev, even if she's barren," he said, an unfriendly expression on his face. "Humans need to remember their place."

"She is my Oathed One, and you will apologize to her immediately, Zane," Danial growled. "Right now."

"Danial is right," Samuel said with anger, looking down his nose at Zane. "You do not treat your host with such disrespect. Sarelle has given her all to our race. She's unable to have children now because of having first Theoron, and then Venus. She deserves your respect, not your sarcasm. Apologize now, and do it on your knees."

I expected Zane to refuse, or maybe strike Samuel. After all, he Ruled a territory that was vaster than Samuel's. But to my surprise, he got down on his knees, and looked up at me, a chastened look on his face. "I'm sorry, Lady," he said in a hushed, contrite voice. "Forgive me. I meant no disrespect."

"Apology accepted," Danial growled.

I kept my mouth shut, not liking him speaking for me, but knowing that I was better off saying nothing.

Zane got up, and resumed his position next to Samuel and Harriet. The tension evaporated somewhat, though I still felt very uneasy.

"Sarelle, it is good to see you," Samuel said, taking my hand and kissing it. I gave him a curtsey, and he smiled gently down at me. "You look well. Being Oathed to Devlin and Danial seems to agree with you."

Was that a dig at Theo? Probably. But it could be a reference to something else. I smiled in return, waiting.

"Do you have any pictures of Venus?" Samuel said eagerly to Devlin.

Devlin produced his cell phone, and pushed a few buttons. He handed it to Samuel. Perseus and Zane crowded in close to look.

"She's breathtaking," Samuel said, wistful. "She has your eyes, Dev."

"She is exquisite," Perseus said grudgingly.

"Very beautiful," Zane said jealously.

"Thank you," Devlin said proudly.

"May I look?" a gentle voice asked.

Samuel took the phone, and handed it to Harriet. "Harriet, this is Sarelle, Oathed One of Devlin and Danial. Sarelle, I'm sure you have heard of Harriet, my Oathed One, and also Oathed One to Perseus."

We curtseyed to each other. It was good to finally give a face to the name I'd heard for so many months. Harriet was beautiful, her dusky skin a light tanned color, like coffee with a lot of cream. Her hair was a rich brown color, and her eyes were bright blue. I wondered then if she was mulatto, or Creole, or perhaps half Spanish, half-white. She was certainly eye-catching, enough so that she could have easily been a model, if she'd not been otherwise…engaged.

"Her name is Venus?" Harriet asked. I nodded. "She's very beautiful. She looks a lot like you and Devlin, Sarelle."

"Thank you," I replied. She gave me a smile, then a shadow passed over her face, and she winced a little.

"What is it, dove?" Samuel said, holding her instantly. "Are you in pain?"

"I think the baby is kicking, maybe?" Harriet said, looking at Samuel nervously. Samuel was at a loss, looking at his cohorts. Finally, he turned to me, eyes questioning.

"How many months are you?" I said quickly.

Harriet replied, "Three to four."

"May I touch you?" I asked.

Harriet nodded. But I looked to Samuel, waiting until he nodded, too. I stepped closer, and put my hand on her belly. It took a few minutes to feel the slight movement, but I expected that.

"It's the baby kicking," I said comfortingly. "He's a strong one."

"I'm having twins, like you did," Harriet said happily. "Though we aren't sure of paternity yet, or the sex."

There was a groan behind me. I glanced over discreetly. Dev was rubbing his side, and Danial was glaring at him. Thank goodness he'd stopped Dev from saying whatever he'd begun to utter.

"Sarelle, I've heard from Samuel you had problems with a sort of lust," Harriet said.

I flushed. "It's true. In both pregnancies, I channeled the vampire blood lust into regular lust. It was not pretty, while it lasted."

"I haven't had anything like that," Harriet said worriedly.

"If you were going to, it would've ended by now anyway," I said reassuringly. "Count yourself lucky. But be prepared that you'll probably have the temperature regulation problem—"

"I've hired a demon to work for me," Samuel interrupted. "If we need heat, we'll have it. We're aware of the cooling Devlin and Danial did for you, too, Sarelle. But I thank you for your concern for Harriet."

I nodded. Samuel expected women to be quiet, unless he asked them a direct question. *Chauvinist Jerk.*

"We aren't staying long," Samuel said, giving Harriet a troubled look. "Harriet needs to keep off her feet. But she wanted very much to come tonight to meet both Sarelle and Theoron."

"He's very handsome, just like his father," Harriet said with a smile.

Theoron blushed, looking at his feet.

"Thank you, Harriet," Danial said kindly. "He is my greatest joy."

"As my son will be to me," Samuel said, his tone protective, possessive, and a touch emotional.

I was surprised at that, but told myself I shouldn't be. Despite what he'd tried to do to me, he clearly wanted a child as much as Danial and Devlin had. He probably would cherish it, and Harriet for giving him his dream. "I wish you the best," I said, meaning it.

Harriet gave me a mild smile. "Thank you, Sarelle. Would you mind if I asked you for your number? I had several questions I wanted to ask you, and now I find I can't remember them—"

She had to be pretty flaky for not writing them down if her memory was that bad. But who knew what Samuel allowed her to do? Maybe she couldn't write well. I knew almost nothing about her. I probably should be surprised she was able to hold a conversation after what Perseus had no doubt done to her. But maybe she was thinking the same thing about me and Devlin...I glanced at him, unsure what to say.

"You may call Sarelle at my house at any weekend," Devlin said quickly. "If she is not available when you call, she'll call you back at Samuel's within a few hours."

Good save, Dev. I nodded. "Yes."

"That will be fine," Samuel said, nodding back. "We have been staying at my estate in Manchester."

"I have the number," Devlin replied.

"Did you take care of Ulysses yet?" Perseus purred.

By the way he said it he both knew what had happened to Devlin, and that he hadn't taken care of him yet. *Asshole.*

"Not yet," Devlin said, tightening his arms around me possessively. "We've seen no sign of him at all, though all our guards have been keeping an eye out for him."

"He'll be back for your head this time," Zane said, his tone angry and forceful. "I missed the bastard by inches! He was in my sights, and he sacrificed a human, making her take the bullet for him."

"Devlin will end him," Samuel said confidently. "He's killed many would-be hunters over the years. And if he does not, his shadow man will. Lash even killed that one who almost staked you those decades ago—"

"Ramirez," Devlin said, spitting the name out with fury.

"—yes, even him who almost got you, Lash made an end of him. He took the stake for you that night, and even badly wounded, he still managed to kill Ramirez."

No wonder Devlin had given Lash his blood. He owed him his life. I understood better now what had happened all those years ago, even if I didn't understand why Ramirez had gone after him, or why Lash had risked his own life for Devlin on that long ago night.

"I owe Lash a lot," Devlin admitted with a sigh. "He is the most loyal friend I ever knew. He is watching Venus tonight for Sarelle and I."

He made no mention of Devon, to my relief. I didn't want these powerful men knowing Devon's name, much less where he was.

"You know I tried to get him to work for me soon after that?" Perseus remarked. "But he said he wouldn't take a stake for me."

"He told you to fuck off, as I recall," Devlin said snidely.

Perseus hissed at him, baring ivory fangs.

"We should be going," Samuel said, taking Harriet's arm in his. "I thank you for your hospitality, Devlin and Danial. Sarelle, it was good to see you. Theoron, I'm pleased to see you, grown into the spitting image of your father. Know you're welcome in Europe, should you ever be traveling there with your father, or Devlin."

"Thank you," Theoron said, nodding.

With a last nod, Samuel and Harriet left, Zane trailing along after them. To my annoyance, Perseus didn't follow.

"I'm glad to see your burns have healed, Devlin," Perseus said, his tone sarcastic and hateful.

"They were bad," Devlin said forcefully. "But I am myself again, thanks to the love of a good woman."

"I'd heard you were a eunuch now," Perseus said, each word cutting. "So badly burned you couldn't even get it up for your Oathed One. But I smell Sarelle's release on your body, and yours on hers. I'm relieved to see my information was only lies."

"Perhaps you should have just asked Sarelle, and not resorted to second-hand intelligence, Greek," Devlin said scathingly. "She is my only lover now."

"I heard that," Perseus said, disbelieving. "That is one of the reasons I thought you gelded."

"I have promised to only be with her until December," Devlin said lovingly. "We are renewing our vows then." His pleasant tone cracked in two, morphing to hateful. "I have revenge to focus on, Greek. Decadent pleasures will have to wait for the New Year."

"Despite our being enemies, I am pleased to see that you are yourself, the Devlin I always respected, even as I loathed him," Perseus said, his tone becoming earnest. "You were always the one who gave the hunters pause, who made them fear us Rulers. It is your reputation, the decades of your legendary cruelty and torture that keeps the hunters too afraid to come after us, fearing all Rulers are as dangerous as you are."

I shivered, telling myself it was a cool breeze.

"That is why you must end Ulysses," Perseus said urgently. "The longer he's at large, the more daring the hunters become. They must continue to fear us, and our wrath! Samuel said nothing to you, but I know there was an attack on his estate just this past week."

Danial and Devlin gasped in shock. I burrowed closer to Devlin, afraid too of the fear in those gasps.

"Who did it?" Danial said, letting out a breath. "Was anyone caught?"

"It was a younger hunter, cocksure, and he died quickly at Samuel's hands. Samuel sent his body back to the Van Helsing Group as a warning. They sent him an apology the next day. But just the fact that a hunter dared attack a Ruler—"

The "Van Helsing Group"? Shit, Stephen had been right. It seemed that vampire hunters these days had moved far beyond the traditional bag of stakes, flasks of holy water, and crosses. They probably were more like the superheroes portrayed in recent comic books and action movies. I'd never heard fear before in Danial's or Devlin's tone, not for anyone. And if I became part vampire again, something was telling me that the vampire hunters wouldn't think too kindly of me, either.

"It is very troubling," Danial said darkly. "There are easily enough hunters to take us, if they all came after us one at a time."

"It will never happen," Devlin said confidently, slipping an arm about my waist. "We've Ruled for centuries. This is how it's been for thousands of years, according to the histories."

"But times are changing fast now," Perseus said with unease. "The Internet is connecting the world. There are websites devoted to us, to how to kill us! You can buy a vampire staking kit for nineteen-ninety-five on E-bay! A hunter can be hired for a few thousand dollars."

"I don't think the humans will unite and destroy us," Danial said thoughtfully. "We are too valuable to too many men in power. They protect us because we're worth protecting, especially we Rulers."

With his words, I understood that Perseus and Samuel and Zane probably ran businesses much like Devlin did in their respective countries, arranging killings for money. There were always those men who needed other men out of their way for whatever reason. Or perhaps they had other dealings in the dark that netted them money, and the protection of daylight watchmen.

"But you're right, Perseus. Ulysses must be taken care of, as soon as possible," Danial finished. "He is a threat to us all."

"Thane has some men watching his parents, and his one surviving sister," Devlin said casually. "He hasn't contacted them. But if he fails to appear in the next month, I'll send Lash to kill his parents, and take his sister. That will make him emerge from wherever he's hidden himself."

I cringed at what he was saying, then told myself Devlin was right to take revenge. Ulysses had tortured him for hours in the sun. That Lash's hand would most likely be the one that hurt innocents wasn't any easier to take. But Theo would have done it for Danial. It made sense Lash would be the one to do it for Devlin.

"It may come to that," Danial said uncomfortably.

"He needs to be flushed from his hiding place, if we have to kill someone or several someones to do it," a venomous voice pronounced.

Michael, Vampire Ruler of Asia, had arrived. He was walking toward us, flanked by guards.

"Good evening," Devlin and I said together, echoed by Danial and Theoron.

"Good evening to you all: Sarelle, Danial, Devlin, and Perseus," Michael continued, bowing to each of us as he said our names. "Tell me that that young man beside you is not Theoron, Danial."

"It is," Danial said with a great deal of pride. "Theoron, this is Michael, Ruler of Asia."

"Good to meet you," Theoron said politely, shaking Michael's hand.

"You look just like your father," Michael said, his tone half pleasure, half disbelief. "I've been searching for a woman like Sarelle in my own domain, but so far have had no luck. But I'm not giving up. There are still many villages to scour."

That sounded bad. I made myself not think about it.

"Devlin, may I dance with your Oathed One?" Michael asked politely.

Chapter Nine

Devlin reluctantly handed my hand to Michael. "You are not to touch her skin, save her hands," he said flatly.

Michael nodded. "Come, Lady. I'll not hurt you."

He led me to the dance floor. As if on cue, the band began playing a haunting work called "Love Song for a Vampire." Michael swept me slowly across the floor. He was an excellent dancer, as Danial and Devlin were. Perhaps it was a prerequisite for being a Ruler.

"It is nice to dance with a woman wearing a choker, even if it's not my symbol at your throat," Michael said softly. "I was Oathed before, two decades ago. But I haven't found anyone since they turned that I cared for, though as I said, I have been looking."

"What is your symbol?" I asked, trying hard to think of something clever to say.

"The tiger," Michael said with a pleased smile.

I gave up on cleverness, instead blurting out my thoughts. "Why is it you Rulers all want children so badly? I understand Danial's love for me, and Dev's, but—"

Michael looked at me in surprise, then burst out laughing, still continuing to move me expertly. "When you live so long as us, life becomes boring. Though we Rulers can have almost anything we desire, children were always denied us. So it's natural to want what you can't have."

I understood that all too well.

"I adopted a human child a century ago," Michael continued. "I loved her very much, and I took much joy in watching her grow, and become a young woman. But as she aged, and married, I had to let her go. She knew what I was, and accepted it, but her husband turned suspicious of me as the years passed, and I remained the same. By the time he died, she was nearing sixty. She needed me then, and I took care of her until she took her last breath. It was agony watching her die over that next decade, knowing it was too late to make her a vampire, that I could do nothing to save her—"

What would have happened to Danial and I, if not for my resistance to the virus? I stopped dancing, blinking rapidly and wiping at my filling eyes. Michael produced a handkerchief, and gave it to me.

"I'm sorry for upsetting you," Michael said softly. "I did not mean to, Lady. I am surprised that what I said moved you thus."

"I'm sorry for your loss," I mumbled, trying to force a smile.

Michael considered me, then nodded. "You see now why it means so much to us?" he said, his brown eyes very alive with hope. "To have children of our own, ones that won't die, ones we won't have to let go after only a few short years pass…it's a miracle."

"I understand," I said, nodding. The sentiment was a mirror of how Danial felt about me.

The song ended. Michael led me back to Devlin. As I came again to stand beside him, Devlin slipped his arm about my waist, and gave me a kiss on my cheek. Perseus had gone, though Danial and Theoron were still standing nearby. Titus, Rip, and Theo were still in position around them.

"I must be leaving," Michael said. "I have another appointment tonight, I'm afraid." He paused. "Would it be remiss if I asked to hug Sarelle goodbye?"

Danial rolled his eyes.

"Sarelle, do you mind if he touches you?" Devlin said, his tone watchful and protective. "It's within his rights to ask, so long as he doesn't taste you or do anything sexual beyond embracing you. But I leave the choice to you."

I'd never thought of a hug as inherently sexual. Maybe it was to men. Theo wasn't going to approve, but I found myself liking Michael. Danial could use another ally, even if Devlin didn't seem to need one. If Michael stood with Devlin and Danial in regards to my welfare, then the next time those assholes Perseus, Zane, and Samuel attempted to take me for their own, that trio would be more than evenly matched. "Sure."

Michael stepped closer, holding me lightly in his arms. He did nothing out of turn, just held me gently, then let me go and stepped back.

He turned to Devlin. "Should you ever break your Oath to her, or perish, I would ask that you have someone notify me at once," Michael said. "I would not like to see her claimed by any of the other Rulers whom I know were here earlier tonight, as I'm sure you would not, either."

Danial hissed, his eyes going red in an instant.

Devlin gave Michael a considering look. "You would claim her if something happened to Danial and I? Keep her safe from the others, even though she's barren now?"

Michael nodded, his brown eyes hard. "Yes."

Devlin shook his head imperceptibly. "My answer is no. Though I appreciate your willingness to protect her, you don't have the power to keep her safe, Michael."

"I have the power," Michael uttered enigmatically. "I just lie low, only wielding it when there is something worth making enemies over. I have ties to the Yakuza, just as you do to the mafia, Devlin. I have informants in every camp, and I know everything almost as it happens. For example, I know you broke your Oath to her, that Sarelle is in truth Oathed to no one right now, not even Danial. I know she's been Lash's lover for the last nine months, during her pregnancy and after. I know what happened a month ago, why Sarelle needed demon blood to recover from her illness. And most important, I know she's barren by choice, not by accident."

"What?" Theoron gasped.

"Stop talking, Michael," Danial growled, taking a step forward. "Now."

"You're lucky my demon put a blocking wall about us," Devlin hissed, grabbing hold of Michael's arm. "No one around us heard what you just stupidly revealed."

Michael pushed him back, putting a few feet between them. "Listen to me," he said urgently. "I have no wish to take her from you. But you can't hide all of these things much longer, Dev. The other Rulers will find out soon, and they won't care that she loves you and your brother, that you love her, or that these were her choices. You will be blamed for losing us our miracle of the age! They'll want your head and your heart."

"What would you have me do, that you are telling me you know these things?" Devlin hissed, going after him. "And why? We aren't friends, Michael."

"I want you to Oath her by Christmas at the latest, or let me take her Oath myself," Michael said. "Give that doctor of hers a mind wipe, so he thinks the lie you spread about her womb being removed was truth. And keep your friend away from her, or include him in the Oath she gives you. They'll want his head, too, for what almost happened to her in Florida—"

"You'll Oath her over my dead body," Danial growled. "That you would even suggest—"

"You love her so much, you should have insisted!" Michael growled back. "You both haven't, clearly, and only a fool leaves himself open for his most prized possession to be claimed by someone else."

I fought the urge to open my mouth and chime in that all this was none of his business. But how far could Michael really be trusted? He hadn't taken sides when Samuel and the other Rulers had tried to take me for their own. But he hadn't lifted a finger to help us fight them either. It was better to listen silently for now, until I knew what his real motives were.

"Sarelle is mine," Devlin said, baring his fangs, his eyes red as hot coals. "I will Oath her soon, at our anniversary in December. I never want to hear another word about you Oathing her, Michael. Because I'd have to be dead for that to happen, and I know you aren't foolish enough to threaten me."

"You were almost dead when Lash saved you in September, and he nearly didn't make it in time," Michael stated, not backing down an inch. "I'm offering you a contingency plan, Dalcon. You're an idiot if you don't think you could ever perish at the hands of some hunter, an assassin, or even a lucky human sorcerer! If you really care for her, you'll agree."

There was dead silence. Danial and Theoron looked at Devlin, and then at me. Devlin looked only at Michael.

"I would not be looking for a lover, in Oathing Sar," Michael said very delicately. "Only protection for her."

"You would not force her to be your lover, or try to reverse her barren state, if she was yours?" Devlin scoffed. "I don't believe that."

"Devlin, you have surely heard the rumors about me," Michael said frankly.

"They are true, then?" Devlin asked, his tone weighty.

Michael nodded once. "My preferences for men would keep me from her bed. There could be no chance of a child. The surgery she had done isn't reversible, to my knowledge."

Thank God, I'd had that surgery. I should send Dr. Camlyn some flowers and a card tomorrow off the Internet.

"Barrenness does not indicate lack of desire, however," Devlin stated. "Besides protection, there is her happiness to consider. Would you let her have a lover of her own?"

Michael nodded. "Yes. I would have to approve the man, of course. I wouldn't want her hurt. But I'd want her for a companion, not a sexual partner." He flashed me a warm smile. "There is a kindness in her I find compelling."

"You got that from her in the space of a song?" Devlin said sarcastically. "How astute of you."

"I've heard you wanted her as soon as you tasted her, Dev," Michael said snidely. "That you fell in love with her the moment she finally gave in to your advances—"

"My son is present," I interjected forcefully, trying not to think how red my face was. "Please watch your words, Michael."

"You must have some power," Devlin said arrogantly, looking Michael up and down. "To bandy words with me at your young age." He smiled, but it did not reach his golden eyes, still cast with reddish tones. "But that doesn't mean that I could trust you with Sarelle, ever."

"Who can you trust, besides me?" Michael offered, a matching smile gracing his lips. "What other Ruler would you want to be Sarelle's keeper? Do you think she would fare better with Perseus, or Zane? Samuel would love to add her to his collection—"

That's it. I can't stay silent any longer. "Please stop this," I interrupted coldly. "I don't want to be discussed as a prized painting."

"That is all you are to them, and you know it," Michael said bluntly, his eyes staring into mine. "I know what evil would happen to you at their hands. I want to prevent that."

"You had an appointment, you said," Danial interjected harshly. "Leave now, and keep it. You've outstayed your welcome."

"I will leave," Michael said, baring his fangs. "Think on my offer." He turned and began walking away, his guards flanking him.

"Unbelievable," Danial muttered.

"It's probably a good plan," Devlin grumbled, rubbing his eyes.

"Are you crazy?" Danial said to him, incredulous.

"I almost died a month ago," Devlin said, his eyes fixed on Michael's retreating back. "I might not be his friend, but I know truth when I hear it. If he has the balls to stand there and look me in the eye when he's saying it, then he has enough guts to keep Sar safe if something happened to us." He paused. "Titus, bring him back."

* * * *

When Michael was once again within the boundaries of Titus's eavesdropping spell, Devlin began. "Michael, your proposal, though crudely made, has merit enough for me to consider it. But I warn you, do not act against Danial or me in order to bring about Sarelle's transition to you. You ever try to kill us to take her, and you'll be burnt ashes before the sun sets. Mark those words well, as I'll not say them again."

"I give you my word, Ruler to Ruler, I will not do that," Michael said, nodding absently as if Devlin hadn't just threatened him with a horrible death. "I'll let you know if I hear anything about Ulysses as well, though my U.S. network has been strangely silent about him."

"Sarelle, you heard Michael's offer," Devlin said. "While I don't like to think of the worst, I'm a practical man." He paused. "Go to Michael, if something ever happens to Danial and I. Give him your Oath. He'll protect you from the others."

96

"I will," I said quietly.

"Be careful, all of you," Michael said, looking at each one of us in turn. "Ulysses is reportedly furious that Devlin slipped out of his fingers. He knows Lash was the one that saved Devlin and Sarelle, so he'll probably be after him, too. But he may strike at all of you."

"We will be on guard," Devlin affirmed. "I thank you for your concern, even though I'm surprised that you would care."

"I don't align myself with other Rulers usually, or concern myself with their petty affairs," Michael replied seriously. "I prefer only to Rule my country, and contemplate the mysteries of various religions. But Ulysses is a threat to us all, Dalcon. He must be eliminated at all costs. I suggest torturing his remaining family to death. That should make him show himself." He shrugged. "But do as you will."

I kept my face passive with difficulty. Under his veneer of civility, Michael was as ruthless as Devlin. Something to keep in mind.

"A good night to you all," Michael said, and strode away once more, his guards flanking him.

Titus followed them, and Theo came over to us. Rip motioned to Theo, who nodded. Rip promptly disappeared.

"That's a relief," Danial said, turning to Devlin. "We have only to perform the rituals, and we're finished."

"Perseus didn't bring his usual guards tonight," Danial said musingly. "Zane was alone, too. Samuel's were the only ones. I wonder why?"

"It's good he left that fucking Cyrus at home. I was going to shoot him if I saw him, for his part in that spell Tasha cast on me," Theo growled. He looked over at me, and then away quickly.

He'd have some choice words later for my tryst with Dev. I grimaced, then pasted a smile back on, going with Danial and Devlin to the center of the dance floor.

The ritual went quickly. Devlin and Danial both tasted me, each taking a little of my blood in a kiss, and gave me a few drops of theirs. Afterwards, I stood near them as the various vampire guests rendered them their honor by bowing. Then we moved aside for Theoron, who took some blood from one of the women Danial had on hand for that purpose. He did it with as much skill as Danial did. Watching him, it seemed to me Theoron was Danial, or Danial how he'd been when he'd been a young vampire. He gave a soft smile to the girl, and thanked her for her blood politely. From her awestruck look, she was half in love with him just from being in his arms.

"He'll break some hearts, before he takes a mate," a courteous voice said.

Akira was standing next to me. He was half of a duo I'd seen each year at

Danial's parties. I wondered where his counterpart Chi was, but decided not to ask. What if she'd been killed by a vampire hunter, and wasn't just visiting the ladies room to freshen up?

"Thank you," I said pleasantly.

Akira bowed.

I seized on the sudden opportunity. "What does this symbol mean?" I said, taking out a pen from my bag, and sketching on a napkin the symbol from the etched knife Lash had given me. I'd looked at that knife a lot in the past month, enough so I knew the symbol by heart.

Akira studied it for a few moments. "It can mean several things. The order of the lines as they are drawn matters a lot in terms of what word is meant. I'm not certain what to tell you."

"What are the possible meanings?" I said, not to be deterred. Damn it, it had to look like at least a few words, if not a particular one. I should be able to reason out what word Lash had meant to write.

"If it is the word I believe it is, the meaning would be 'Partner', 'Lover', 'Mate', 'Companion', 'Friend', sometimes even 'Husband' or 'Wife'," Akira said. "But the most correct translation would probably be 'Beloved One'."

I'd suspected that Lash loved me. Here was the proof. But it was something to suspect it, and another to know it for a fact. I felt as if Titus had hugged me, my body heated up so much.

"Where did you see this word?" Akira said curiously, interrupting my thoughts. "It's not a common word in Japanese, Sarelle. This is an older version, almost ancient Japanese—"

"It was on a knife I found of Devlin's," I said vaguely. "I wondered what it meant. I think now the knife had to have been a gift from one of his former lovers."

My comment had the effect I knew it would. Akira shut right up about the knife, and changed the subject. "Elle looks very well. She's grown."

I craned my neck, looking for Elle. She was over near the bar, talking to Hans. They seemed to be discussing some couple they'd seen, by the motions they were making with their hands. "Yes, she's maturing nicely."

I felt cool arms take me around the waist. "Dance with me?" Danial said seductively in my ear.

"Good to see you, Akira," I said, then let Danial lead me to the dance floor.

The band began playing K. Loggins' "Meet Me Halfway (Across the Sky)".

"Remember that night?" Danial said with longing. "It was just you and I, and we danced for hours, Sar. That night was memorable."

I wanted to remind him he'd given me his full attention back then, but settled for flashing a smile. Danial was who he was, and he wasn't going to change. His ambition was admirable, even if it pissed me off sometimes.

He swept me around the dance floor proficiently, making me sigh at the romance of the moment as if it was my first time in his arms. Too soon, the song was ending, and he led me back to Devlin and Theo.

"Another hour, and we're done," Devlin said, looking at his watch.

Theo growled, looking at me pointedly. It was obvious what he wanted.

"Let me go get Elle. I'll teleport her home, and then go get Devon," I said quickly.

Theo nodded, then walked off, answering his ringing cell phone.

Devlin nodded reluctantly. "If you must." He leaned in close. "But I'd visit the ladies room first if I were you, Love."

Worried, I made a beeline to the bathroom. Indeed, my pad was soaked, but with semen, not blood. Muttering about the strange humor of men, I changed it, then hurried back towards the party. I was just heading in the double doors when I heard a low moan.

I'd moaned often enough like that to know it was a woman's moan, and what was being done to her. Worse, I thought I recognized the voice, though I hoped to God I was wrong.

I turned back and headed into the darkness, looking into each room. Another moan sounded close by. I eased to the door to my left, and looked in. My mouth dropped open.

Elle was on her back on the table, her dress pushed up and her underwear in a small discarded pile on the floor. Her top was pushed down, baring her breasts. Hans was there, partially on top of her, sucking her as she moaned under him. I thought at first he was having sex with her, but looking closer, his jeans were fully buttoned. His hand was moving between her legs, stroking her as she thrust her hips up to meet him, moaning over and over.

"Come for me, baby," Hans growled, moving his hand faster on her, his mouth taking her small breast deeply into his mouth, his white blond hair falling over his forehead as he moved on her. "Let me hear you."

"Please! Yes!" Elle breathed. "Just like that-oh! OH! OH!"

Hans kissed her hard as she shook in his arms. Then she was pushing him off, trying to get up. But he held her down on the table, his hands on hers.

"I want to be in you," Hans growled. "You'd like it a lot better than this, Elle. Trust me. I could make it so good for you."

"I can't," Elle said weakly. "I shouldn't be here with you like this."

"You love me touching you like this, you know it, and I know it," Hans said, kissing down her neck. "But this isn't enough for me. I'm a man, I've got needs, Elle. Say I can have you here, right now. Or I'm walking out that door, and I'll never touch you again. I'm tired of getting you off, and not getting any release myself."

"I'm afraid," Elle said in a small voice. "I've never done it before, gone all the way."

Hans switched tactics as soon as he saw her wavering. "You don't have to be afraid, baby," he said eagerly. "I'll be real gentle with you. I'm telling you, you'll love feeling me in you—"

"No. I can't," Elle said forcefully. "Get off me."

Hans backed off.

It was good I hadn't interfered. I'd prefer she told Hans no herself. I'd wait and kick his ass when he went to leave.

"Are you a woman or a little girl?" Hans jeered at her.

Elle growled at him.

"Sorry, I thought you were a woman," Hans said nastily. "But I see you're too young to really be with a man. You won't see me again, Elle. Don't come looking for me at the werecompound, saying you want to go for any more walks."

I took out the knife Lash had given me from my purse, waiting. Hans was going to get a gash for pressuring my baby like he had. But I was proud of Elle for saying no and sticking to her guns.

"Wait," Elle called.

Shit.

"I want you to…to make love to me," Elle said in a small voice. "But I don't want to get pregnant. You'll have to wear protection, Hans. I don't have any—"

Hans shut the door, the lock clicking instantly before I could grasp the handle. "I brought some, in case," Hans said from within eagerly. "Lay back for me, baby—"

I grasped the handle, taking a breath to yell.

Suddenly, Danial was there, spinning me around. "Where is—?"

"This is going to feel so good, Elle," Hans groaned. "Hold still, it will just hurt for a second—"

Danial eyes widened in shock. He let out a snarl, his eyes going completely red in a nanosecond, and then he was breaking through the door, me right after him. Danial pulled Hans off Elle, and threw him against the far wall with all his strength, cracking it on impact. Elle was trying to cover herself, screaming at her father to stop.

Hans got up, and drew his gun.

"You shoot me, you bastard, and you'll be dead a few seconds later,"

Danial growled. "I told all you foxes to stay away from her!"

"She wanted me, Danial," Hans said defensively. "She's been hanging around me for months, flirting and showing me herself! I'm not invulnerable to a female's touch! I'm were!"

"You should have resisted."

"*She* kissed *me*—!"

Danial punched Hans in the face, knocking him backward. Elle let out a shriek. I ran to her, grabbing hold of her. Hans looked up at Danial, sprawled on the floor, blood trickling from his mouth. Then he got to his feet, growling, his eyes bleeding to werefox as he partially changed.

"How long have you been fucking her?" Danial hissed. "How long?"

"I gave her the first orgasm of her life a week ago," Hans spat, his eyes golden brown. His fox fangs were bared at Danial, and his hands as he gripped his gun were clawed. "But your daughter's a tease. She never let me have her."

Danial went for Hans again. Hans eased the hammer back on his gun. Danial stopped, and hissed again at Hans, his eyes red, his fangs bared, and his hands taloned in his rage.

"Watch it, vampire," Hans growled. "I know you aren't wearing armor tonight."

"Stop it!" Elle cried.

"You're fired, you bastard!" Danial hissed. "Get to my estate, get your stuff, and get out. You have one hour. And then I'm telling Theo what I saw here, Hans."

Hans went white. He was out the door a second later, running fast.

"You always ruin everything!" Elle cried, sobbing in my arms. "He told me he loved me!"

"He didn't love you, he wanted to fuck you," Danial growled angrily. "There's a difference. You're too young to see it."

"He loved me!" Elle screamed.

Devlin came in the door, instantly taking in my attempts to pull Elle's dress down. His eyes tinged red. "Hans, I saw him running for the door. Did you stop them in time?"

I nodded.

"Why do you care?" Elle screamed at him. "You fuck almost anything that'll hold still for you! You had my mom earlier, I smell you on her!"

Devlin flushed, to my surprise.

"Take her home, Sar," Danial said tiredly. "I'll tell Theo what happened. Then go get Devon and wait at my house for us. We'll be there within a half hour. This party is over."

I nodded, teleporting Elle and myself in the next instant. We ended up in the great room.

I helped her to her room. Elle was crying, and very embarrassed.

I left her alone for a few minutes, waiting outside her door anxiously. When she called me, I came in to find her in bed, her eyes downcast.

"Do you want to talk about it?" I asked. "Or wait for your fathers?"

Elle said nothing. She wouldn't look at me.

I took her face in my hands and made her look at me. "I'm sorry this happened," I said, smoothing her hair back from her face.

She burst into fresh tears. I held her as she sobbed in my arms. As horrible as it had been, her crying jag didn't last long. "He lied to me, didn't he?" she said, wiping at her eyes with a tissue. "He didn't love me."

"If he'd have really loved you, he'd have stood his ground and faced your fathers, both of them," I said gently. "That he ran shows you he didn't. But that's his failing, not yours, Elle."

"I didn't want to give in to him," she said softly. "But when he touched me, he was able to make me feel something so good, Mom. I wanted to feel it again."

"He gave you an orgasm, honey," I said, blushing instantly. "It's normal for a woman to have one, when a man touches her intimately. And it's normal to want to have one, to want to feel that good—"

"Do you feel that, when you're with Dad, and Dev, and Theo?"

She would have to say all three. I flushed deeper and nodded. "Yes."

"I want to feel that again, Mom. It was the best thing I ever felt."

I didn't know what to say to her. There was no one I would trust with her, except Dev the sex master. He'd easily have taken care of her frustration while showing her the time of her life. But I couldn't share a lover with my daughter. It would be like something out of the National Enquirer. More importantly, I guessed she was maybe fifteen now in terms of maturity, and that was still too young to have sex. While I'd given into temptation that young, I didn't want that for her.

"You aren't ready for sex yet, Elle," I said finally. "But I'll tell you a secret. You don't need a man to feel that way."

"I don't?" Elle said, shocked.

I teleported quickly home, and grabbed a book from the shelf. Then I teleported back, and handed it to her.

"*The Claiming of Sleeping Beauty*?" she read, casting a confused look at me. "How is this going to help me?"

"See the folded down page?" I said, blushing hard, and hoping I wasn't making a terrible mistake. "Read these few paragraphs, Elle. Do as the book instructs. You can make yourself feel the way Hans made you feel."

"Mom, have you done this?" she asked.

I blushed ultra bright red, but nodded. "All women do at one time or another in their lives, though no one usually ever talks about it," I stammered, embarrassed. "I was alone for a year after my first husband died, Elle. I didn't want to be with another man, because I missed Brennan so much. But my body missed being with a man, and I did this, because I didn't want to have sex just to have sex, with someone I didn't love. And until you really love a man, you shouldn't have sex. Your virginity should be treated as something precious, Elle. You only have it to give away once. Make sure the man you give it to is worthy of the honor of taking it."

"Okay," Elle said dubiously. "I'll try it."

I hugged her. "Talk to me, if this doesn't work for you," I said seriously. "There are other books I can get for you that might be better than this one at explaining what to do. I'll be as honest as I can be with you, Elle. But you need to be honest with me, too. If you begin to feel that you love a man, and he loves you, you tell me, so we can get you on the pill. You are growing up fast. In another year, you probably will be ready to have a lover, and to take a mate, if you want one. But until you're mated, you should take precautions, so you don't get pregnant."

"I never thought I'd hear you say I was ready for anything more than sleepovers," Elle said softly, looking at me with tears in her eyes. "I'm sorry I didn't tell you, Mom. And I'm glad you stopped us tonight."

"It's okay," I said, hugging her. "That's what moms are for."

She hugged me back tightly, and then she went into the bathroom with the book. The bathtub began to run.

Hoping I'd solved the problem, I walked out, closing the door gently. Turning, I came face to face with Danial.

There was surprise, and also deep respect in his eyes. "You handled that well," he whispered under his breath. "Better than I was going to, anyway."

I took his arm, and led him back to the great room, so she wouldn't hear us. "Is Hans gone?"

Danial nodded. "Tell me everything."

I told Danial what I'd seen when I walked in on them.

He sighed. "I want so much for her, Sar. Perhaps we should send her away to college, when Ulysses is dead. She could take some dance instruction, and some classes. She's past a high school level already in reading and writing, and close to college level math—"

"That might be best. She's growing up fast, Danial."

"I don't want her to end up with one of the bodyguards," Danial said with disdain. "And if she doesn't leave, she will."

I gave him a narrow-eyed look. "I care most that she's happy."

"Don't you want more for her?" Danial snapped. "You know the life expectancy of one of the foxes who guard me? Five years, Sar. Dead by the time they're forty, usually, if they even make it past thirty. That's why they're all so young, save Warren. You usually don't get old in that business, unless you're very good, like Theo or Lash—"

"I get it!" I said stridently. "I just want her to be happy, Danial."

"So do I," he said, hugging me. "So do I, Sar."

"I better go get Devon," I said, yawning. "Serena is probably wondering where the hell I am."

Danial let me go. "Come back quickly."

I teleported to Hayden, ending up in the kitchen. Lash was there, reading a book, and eating what looked like the last of the cornbread. He looked up with a smile, then saw my face. The next thing I knew, he was holding me close to him, his arms tight around me.

"What happened?" he hissed loudly. "Are you okay? Rip said everything went well, the other Rulers had left. But you're really upset."

I hugged him, exhausted and glad to be in his arms. "Elle almost had sex with one of the guards who was supposed to be watching her," I said bluntly. "Danial stopped them in time. Danial fired the guard, but she was upset. Theo's probably going to go after him—"

"He should talk to Dev, and hold off," Lash hissed in a low voice.

"What do you mean?" I asked, apprehensive. "What do you know about this?"

Lash looked down at me, his eyes flat and unreadable. "Elle came on to Dev last week at her piano lesson," he hissed, hesitant.

I looked at him, my mouth open, my eyes blinking over and over.

"She was just touching his hand, and then all at once she grabbed his dick. He was shocked, and told her to stop, but she told him she knew he wanted her to touch him, that he wanted her."

"My God," I breathed. "Why didn't he say anything to me?"

"Elle said she'd say he was the one who tried to touch her, if he said anything to you or Danial about what happened. I told him to tell you, but he said he couldn't, that you might believe he'd done it."

"I don't believe it," I said flatly. "Dev's not the same as he used to be. Even then, he wouldn't have done that to Elle."

"She got his...him excited a little," Lash hissed softly. "You know Dev, how easy it is to get him going. He was embarrassed about that, too."

Suddenly, Dev's blushing made sense. He's been embarrassed because of what Elle had done to him. No wonder he hadn't gone near her all night, save to

The Eye of the Storm

get her that drink when she was with me. "Thank you for telling me," I said, embracing Lash again. "Tell him what I said, when he gets home, all right? I'll tell Theo to talk to Devlin before he goes after Hans."

Lash nodded, and let me go. "Devon's asleep," he said. "Come with me."

I followed him into the living room. Serena was sleeping on the couch, the remote near her hand where it had fallen. Venus was nestled in her arms. Devon was curled up near them, lying on Serena.

"I didn't want to disturb them while you were still gone," Lash hissed softly. "But I'll take Venus up to bed now. It's way past her bedtime."

I picked up Devon, who continued to sleep. Lash reached down and picked up Venus. She woke up, and smiled happily, putting her arms around him. I was surprised she liked him so much, but then, she was her father's daughter. Or maybe it was because she was her mother's daughter. *Sigh.*

"Goodnight, Sar," Lash hissed, giving me a tender look. As he turned away and walked off, Venus watched me over his shoulder, her golden eyes serious.

I teleported Devon to Danial's home. Theo was there, his eyes yellow, Danial and Devlin standing in front of him.

"I should go after him tonight," Theo growled. "His trail will be fresh. I can kill him before an hour's out—"

As usual, I was going to have to be the one to say something. *Might as well do it fast.* "Devlin, tell them what Elle tried with you."

Devlin went crimson. Theo looked over at him in horror. Danial just sighed.

"She grabbed me a few weeks ago," Devlin said haltingly. "I stopped her, but she had one thing on her mind, and it wasn't the song I was teaching her on the piano—"

Theo roared, and began pacing, his fists clenching and unclenching.

"You should have said something, Dev," Danial sighed, his face in his hands rubbing his eyes.

"Like you would have believed me without tonight to back me up," Devlin said sarcastically. "I know—"

"I believe you, Dev," I uttered, flopping down on the couch. "The question is what to do about it."

"I felt so dirty every time I thought about what happened," Devlin said, leaning against the wall. "She's like my niece, no matter that we aren't really blood-related. But what can we do, other than let her have a lover?"

"Danial, what are we going to do?" Theo growled. "I can't have my daughter acting this way."

"I've talked to her, and I think things will be okay now," I said firmly.

Theo looked at me. "What did you tell her; to abstain? Like that will work."

"Sar handled it, Theo," Danial said, rubbing his eyes. "We should call it a night. It's nearly dawn. Jenny will be here in mid-morning. I need to be rested, just in case."

* * * *

When Theo and I returned home with Devon, Theo put him to bed as I got the dogs and cats taken care of. Ghost and Darkness were both lonely from being on their own all night, and also overdue for going outside. I let them out, then got them settled in for sleep, then did a head count of the cats. Meanwhile, Theo made a fire for us. The wood stove had only dying embers left, and there was a chill in the air.

I undressed, put on pajamas, and crawled into bed. Theo came in a few minutes later, shutting off the light. He undressed, then got into bed and put his arms around me.

"When you got there, Devon wasn't anywhere near Lash, was he?"

Figures that would be the first thing he wanted to know. "Lash was in the kitchen, and Devon and Serena and Venus were in the living room. He was guarding them from a distance."

"Good," Theo said. "But I can smell he was near you. Very near you, Sar."

Here we go. "He took Venus, and put her to bed. I got Devon first, so he wasn't near him—"

"That doesn't tell me why he was so close to you," Theo said, his words dangerously soft. "Why you smell of him."

I resisted the urge to slap him. Instead, I pushed away from him, moving to my own side of the bed. "He saw I was upset as soon as I appeared, so he hugged me," I said. "Then he told me what happened with Elle and Devlin, when I told him how we found her. He wasn't trying anything."

"Don't let him hug you again," Theo said firmly. "I don't want you in his arms, even if it's just him trying to be nice. Okay?"

I thought for a split second of getting up and leaving Theo, and going tonight to Devlin, giving him my Oath, and then going to Lash and telling him I wanted him, that I was in love with him, that I'd had enough of all the bullshit, and denying my feelings, and being apart from him. Then I looked down at Devon sleeping beside our bed in his little bed, and let the fantasy go. I was an adult, and God damn it, I would act like one.

"I'll make him keep his distance," I forced out.

Theo brought me back into his arms. "I love you, Sar. Do you still love me?"

"You know I do," I said, irritated.

"I just want us to be happy, to have our family," Theo said persuasively. "I'm trying hard to make this work."

This wasn't his fault. He had every right to feel jealous. "So am I, Theo. Get some sleep. We're both exhausted."

I cried myself to sleep that night as I lay there beside him, tears silently sliding down my cheeks to wet my pillow.

* * * *

Jenny arrived about six the next afternoon. After I showed her in, the four of us again sat down together in the great room.

"What is your decision?" Danial said, very nervous underneath his smooth, confident tone.

"I thank you for your offer, Danial, but no," Jenny said.

The three of us all gaped at her in shock.

"Are you sure?" Danial said hesitantly. "You'll most likely die in the next two weeks, if you don't do this."

"I know," Jenny said, mustering a faint smile. "But I love the sun too much to just let it go. I want to spend my last days outside, eating French fries and pizza, and enjoying a few margaritas. I appreciate what you've offered me. I know you wouldn't have done this for just anybody. I'd make a lousy vampire. So there's no use in you putting yourself out trying to make me one."

"Very well," Danial said, getting to his feet with a shrug that said that was that. "I'll leave you now. Sar can show you out. I have business to attend to—"

"You have another choice, Jenny," Theo said softly.

Danial stopped cold, turning very slowly to look at Theo. Jenny looked at Theo, too, her eyes unsure. I looked at Theo in disbelief.

"Weres aren't just born, they're made, too," Theo said, his eyes holding Jenny's. "I was made were, not born this way. You could become werefox, werecougar, or werebear."

I waited to hear him say weresnake, then kicked myself. *Like he was going to say that.*

"Theo, that doesn't always cure cancer," Danial interjected. "The odds are fifty-fifty."

"Those are better odds than being dead in two weeks," Theo replied. "It's true neither Brian nor I have experience turning anyone. But I've read up on it."

I bit my lip so no sarcastic words came out of my mouth. I knew why he had read up on it. He'd been thinking of doing it to me back in the spring. For all I knew, maybe he still was.

"I'm willing to try, and Brian would be, too," Theo said earnestly. "Ivan has some experience turning humans, so he could also help, or be the one to turn you, if you felt safer being a werefox. It's fact that you wouldn't be hunted like Brian and I are, if a human sees us in animal form."

"Would I see the sun?" Jenny asked. "Or have to eat people, like in the movies?"

"Only evil creatures eat people," Theo said cuttingly.

I gritted my teeth, and stayed silent.

"I'm completely normal, save I sometimes eat raw meat, and I need to change form every few months to a cougar," Theo continued. "But I'm not immortal. I can heal fast, but not like Danial can. I age normally. My life span is that of a human."

Jenny was looking at Theo like he'd told her he was Christ Himself come to save her. "Would you try to make me a werecougar?" she said suddenly. "I couldn't live never seeing the sun, but I would like to try to be werecougar, if you'll help me."

There was something I didn't like about all of this, and it prompted me to speak. "It's going to hurt," I said darkly. "You'll feel your body dying before it's done."

Danial and Theo both turned and looked at me curiously. Perhaps they heard Lash's voice in my words. He'd been the one to say them, those weeks ago, when he'd talked to me about turning. I was betting no matter what kind of were did the deed, the dying feeling was the same.

"I can feel my body dying now around me," Jenny said bitterly, glancing at me. "I'll try this. Even if I don't make it, it's worth the chance."

"Go home then, and pack an overnight bag," Danial said to Jenny. "Come back here at dusk. Theo will try then to turn you—"

I looked at him, distressed. This was happening too fast.

"—Theo, you'd better prepare to spend the night here, too."

"I'll go speak to Ivan, and go over the process one more time," Theo said, nodding and also getting to his feet. "I already have a set of clothes here. Sarelle, please watch Devon?"

"Sure," I got out somehow, blinking my eyes, as both he and Jenny left, the front door slamming behind them.

Danial came over and sat next to me. "Are you okay? You look like you're in shock."

"I am in shock," I said slowly. "But I'm glad that Jenny chose to try to change. Mary's been a good friend. I didn't want her to lose her daughter."

"This may work out well," Danial said, nodding. "Jenny can still live a good life, and work for me, and all the hassles I would have had showing her how to walk in my world are not an issue. I'm very relieved not to have to turn her into a vampire."

I put my hand on his shoulder. "You'd better call Mary and tell her."

He nodded. "Do you want me to arrange one of the foxes to come home with you tonight?"

It hit me suddenly that Theo wouldn't be coming home tonight. He'd be spending the night with Jenny, turning her.

"You and Devon shouldn't be alone."

"No," I replied. "But I'll leave Devon here with you, Danial, if you don't mind. I'll go ask Elle to watch him tonight. It will be safer for him here with you. I'll be okay on my own; I can always teleport if there's anything the least bit out of the ordinary. Ghost and Darkness will warn me if anything seems wrong."

Danial regarded me as if he could see into my heart and knew why I needed the time alone. *Hell, he could likely smell I was upset.* "Very well," he said, kissing me on the forehead. "But call me before you go to bed. Theo's acting pretty confident, but there's a very real chance that this may not work. He's never tried this before, Sar."

"I have faith in him," I said, giving Danial a forced smile. "I'm sure he'll be fine."

After Danial left for his upstairs office, I played with Devon for a while. He was full of himself. As I rolled him over and over, he tried to bite me, growling and hissing.

"You're such a bad boy," I said, laughing. "Are you hungry?"

Devon bounded to the kitchen, putting his paw on the fridge handle, then looking at me meaningfully. As I was giving him some chicken, Elle came in.

I was fading fast, my exhaustion almost complete. "Can you watch over Devon tonight? He'll be sleeping here." I left Jenny out for now. If it didn't work, it might be better that Elle didn't know it. She might decide to turn a lover someday, as Aspen had, and I didn't want her to doubt that she could do it, even if Theo failed.

"Sure," she said, giving me a hug. "Come on, bro." She picked him up with ease—all sixty pounds of him—and carried him purring off to watch TV.

* * * *

As I walked the dogs that night, I prayed out loud to God, trying to decide what to do.

"Am I doing the right thing, God?" I asked aloud as I strolled. "Am I supposed to do something differently? I'm trying hard to do the right thing, but it feels like my heart's ripping out."

Ghost barked at something, and took off. I interrupted my conversation to yell at him to get back. He came bounding back, tongue lolling.

"I know I shouldn't love Lash," I went on sadly. "I know it was wrong to do what I did with him. Please God, take my love for him from me. And I pray for You to let him fall in love with someone else, God. Keep my resolve strong, like it is at this moment. And if there was some way for You to resolve the other three men I call my lovers, I'd be glad if You showed me how to do that, too. I can't do it without Your help, Lord. And I'm tired of trying to figure out the best thing to do. It's way past time I called on You for help. And maybe this hell I've been going through was Your way of telling me that."

I didn't know what else to say, but I figured God knew that. So I just said "Amen," and headed back to the house.

I called Danial later over my dinner of pasta. He reported that Theo would try to change Jenny shortly, and that Devon was already asleep. Uneasy, I wished him goodnight, and went to bed.

When I woke up in the darkness, I knew something was wrong immediately.

Chapter Ten

I felt sick to my stomach. I groaned, and lay there, not wanting to get up.

I shouldn't have eaten that plateful of pasta for dinner. It was too heavy, and then I'd felt so tired I went to bed...

I got up and used the facilities. But instead of feeling better, I felt worse. *Why am I so nauseous? Had the sauce been bad?*

The pain intensified. Soon I felt as if my insides were being ripped open. I swayed, and sat back on the toilet. I whimpered with pain, my vision going cloudy. My body broke out in a sweat.

I have to get up. I have to call someone...

I staggered to my feet, and took one step before I sank down onto the tiles beside the tub, catching myself with my arms so I didn't land too heavily. I rolled slowly on my back, and closed my eyes.

The tile floor was ice cold. *It feels so soothing...*

I don't know how long I lay there. It was long enough for my sweat to dry, my pain to ease, and my vision to clear. I was so tired. As I lay there, waiting for the pain to pass, I tried to think of what was wrong with me. *Did I have food poisoning? Had the beef been bad?* I lay there for a while, eventually falling asleep.

When I woke, I felt worse. I was chilled and clammy. What the hell?

I looked down at myself. In the gloom, there was blood soaking my thighs, a few spots crusted on the tile beneath me. My nightgown was soaked with it. I screamed, startling the dogs, who ran in the bathroom and sniffed me. But no one came to my rescue. No one would. I was alone.

I ripped the nightgown over my head and tossed it aside. I reached up and grabbed a robe from the back of the door, wrapped it around me, and teleported quickly, ending up in Stephen's office. After rifling through his desk, I finally found his number. I paged him from his office phone. He called back in five minutes, the longest five minutes of my life

"Who is this?" he said furiously. "Identify yourself immediately before I call the police."

"Stephen, it's Sar," I said quickly. "Come fast. I think I'm miscarrying again."

Stephen didn't waste a moment. "Go lay down in exam room three, Sar. Get undressed if you can. Ask whoever is with you to help you—"

"No one's with me, Stephen," I said quickly. "I teleported."

"Call Danial then, or Theo—"

"No. And don't you call anyone!" I said forcefully. "Just get here and take care of me."

"Sar—"

"Do it, Stephen!" I shouted. "God damn it, get here!"

"I'll be there in a half hour," Stephen said, annoyed. "You're probably going to be fine if you have the strength to yell like that."

He was right. This was nowhere near what I'd felt when I had miscarried Danial's child. Maybe I was just getting used to pain.

After hanging up on him, I went into exam room one. I undressed, and cleaned myself up as best I could. By the time I had, Stephen arrived.

He checked me over, then nodded. "Sar, I'd say the fetus you lost was only a month or so old. But I don't understand how you got pregnant in the first place."

"I must have healed what you did somehow," I said, rubbing my eyes.

"Sar, I cauterized your ovarian tubes. You don't have any of the virus in you anymore. That can't be it."

"The demon blood from Titus," I said wearily. "It must have healed the surgery."

"How much did he give you?" Stephen asked quickly. "When was this? When he healed you after Devlin took your blood?"

"Yes," I said as vaguely as I could. "But it was a fair amount that he gave me."

"Sar, I need to do another D and C on you," Stephen said, readying his tools. "But you should be fine. This won't hurt, like the other one did. Lay back and relax as much as you can."

He did what he needed to do, the procedure lasting a good hour. When it was over, I debated explaining to him in loud tones that the level of pain was comparative, and he hadn't been the one feeling it. But I was too worn out to make the effort.

"I'm done," he said, putting his tools down. "You'll be fine."

I would be fine, but I wasn't there yet. "Do the surgery again, please," I said, not moving.

"I can't," Stephen said, looking at me incredulously.

"You can and you will," I said harshly, glaring at him. "And then you are going to give me some kind of birth control besides. Maybe that stuff that's inserted in a woman's arm. I don't care what it's called, or how much it costs or how long it takes, Stephen, but you are going to do this for me, tonight! I am not leaving here without being protected, or as protected as I can be."

"I can't do the surgery now, Sar!" Stephen said forcefully. "You're mortal now, not partly turned. There's a limit to what your body can take, and you just had a serious incident. You'll need to schedule an appointment, though I can probably fit you in next week."

"Fine, then," I said angrily. "Give me some hormones to protect me until I can have it done. Something safe, but the most effective thing you have."

It took him only a few minutes to insert a hormone releasing stick into my left arm. I had him do it near an old scar of mine that was a little raised, so it wouldn't be too noticeable. It pinched a little, but I didn't care. Anything so I didn't have to worry about this ever again.

When it was done, I dressed quickly in my robe, then teleported home, and got out some cash from the safe that Theo and I always kept on hand. I teleported back. "How much?"

He gave me a shocked look. "Your insurance will cover—"

"I don't want there to be a record, Stephen," I said angrily. "Tell me your charge. I'll pay you, and you can forget this ever happened."

"Sar—"

"The other Rulers!" I hissed. "They need to keep thinking I got my womb removed! There can't be a record of this, or that I was able to get pregnant again. Now, how much?"

It was obvious that Stephen suspected that wasn't the only reason I wanted to keep what he had done for me tonight secret. He knew I couldn't be here alone here on accident. But he also wasn't eager to have Perseus or Samuel come back and see him again. "Two thousand. I'll have to replace the tools I used with you, and not have them sterilized, or the techs will ask questions. The tissue and other evidence I'll take now to the incinerator."

I handed him the cash. "I'm sorry to have gotten you out of bed so early."

"Sar, you shouldn't have sex with anyone for a week or so," Stephen counseled. "Call me if you have bleeding that won't stop. I can treat it under some other ailment."

"I will." I touched his arm gently. "And thank you."

"You're welcome." He turned away from me and began cleaning up. I teleported home, then sank down on the bathroom floor, exhausted.

I would just tell Theo and the rest that I had my period. They would leave me alone long enough for my body to heal. But I did have a problem. A big one.

Danial and Devlin hadn't made me pregnant; they had returned to their sterile state. Theo was still protecting himself, afraid of possible STDs. This all pointed to one hard fact.

Theo had thought I might have gotten something from Lash. I had, just not an STD.

I'd gotten a child.

It was the only possible explanation. Lash had been the last person I'd been with in the time frame Stephen was talking about. We hadn't used any birth control. I'd been fixed, so we'd both thought we hadn't needed any. But Titus's blood had healed me, including my reproductive system. And Lash's rejuvenated body had apparently been in full working order, too.

The only thing I wanted sitting on that cold tile floor was to call Lash, and tell him what had happened. He would come to me, comfort me. But he'd also tell Devlin, and I didn't know how Devlin would take the news. He might tell Danial. Danial would be wrecked to hear about another miscarriage, and furious at Lash. He'd unload on Theo. Then things would be much worse than they were already.

No. I would go home, and say nothing to anyone.

Besides, now that I'd dealt with this, I had another problem to resolve. Thinking of Theo and being in good old Exam Room 1 had reminded me that I had an appointment the next week with Stephen for a follow-up. It was going to be a tough sell, trying to make up a story about why I might need to be tested on top of tonight. So far, the explanation I was leaning heavily towards was that Devlin had asked me to be with one of his human friends, and I'd agreed. I couldn't face saying it had been Lash. Stephen would think I was an idiot after what had happened last time. Besides, a tryst with some unnamed potent human fit the facts well. The only thing I hated was it cast me as the oversexed nymphet.

I checked the answering machine. To my relief, I had no messages. *No one had noticed my brief middle of the night absence. Now to clean up the mess.*

There wasn't much blood on the bathroom floor, just a few spots here and there. I used a damp sponge to wipe up the tile floor where I had lain, then washed it. I threw the nightgown away. It upset me to do it, being one of the few clothes that Theo had gotten for me. But the bloodstain would never come out completely, and Theo might notice it.

I took the garbage bag with the nightgown out to the garage, and put it in the bottom of the can where Theo wouldn't scent it. It was a cold night. The moon was still high in the sky. The stars were out, shining still in the sky. Seeing them made me feel a little better, like things would be okay.

I went back inside and took a long, hot shower, washing my hair, and every trace of blood off me. Stephen hadn't said not to, and I wanted to feel clean. I put on some pajamas, and some underwear with a pad, just in case. There would be blood for several days, I knew from previous experience. But that would be good; it would make my lie believable.

God, I was tired of lies.

I lay down again, and tried to go back to sleep. But I couldn't stop thinking about what had happened. Was this a sign from God? And if so, what was He trying to tell me? What would have happened if I hadn't lost the baby? There was no scenario I could think of where I wouldn't lose Theo. Danial, I didn't know what he would think. He may have loved children, but he probably would have made an exception for Lash's, despite it was mine. Devlin, he would most likely be jealous, because it wasn't his child I was having. He would probably take it out on Lash, or me. Especially if it had been a son, like he had wanted for himself. And Lash, what would he think?

He was the only man of them that hadn't wanted a child. It was ironic that he had sired one on me in those few hours we had been together. The other times we'd had sex, I had been pregnant already. Devlin had said that Lash couldn't have children, back when he'd been taking the potion. But that was before I had renewed his body.

Oh, shit. Did Lash have any idea he'd gotten rejuvenated? His sex drive was strong now. What if he had thought he was safe, was with someone, and got her pregnant? I had to call him and make sure he knew, damn the cost. He was my friend. I didn't want him to be surprised, like I had been a few hours ago.

I dialed his cell. He didn't answer, as expected. I left him a message, asking him to call me, that it was urgent. The phone rang a half hour later.

"What is it?" Lash said, clearly worried.

"Look," I said hoarsely, blushing deep red, and very glad he couldn't see me. "I have to say something. You don't have to say anything to me back. But I have to say it, Lash."

"Then say it."

"I...um, you can, um...."

Lash waited silently.

"Please use protection," I said finally. "If you are with someone, use protection."

Lash said nothing for a long time. The longer the silence stretched, the dumber I felt for saying what I had, and not having thought of something more eloquent to say. But with only a half hour to prepare, this was the best I could do.

"That's all," I said haltingly, feeling stupid and lame. "I'm sorry for bothering you."

"Sar, why are you telling me this?" Lash hissed, irritated. "It's not your business anymore, what I do with my lovers. I don't tell you what to do with Theo."

"I'm sorry, about everything," I stammered. "I'll talk to you later."

"Are you afraid I'll catch something like before?" Lash hissed curiously. "Or do you just not like to think of me with someone like Cin without a glove on?"

I didn't like to think of him with anyone else, glove or no glove, but this was not the time to say that. "Please, just be careful. I've got to go, Lash—"

Lash lost his patience in point five seconds. "Sar, I'll fuck whomever I please, however I want to. Since you aren't my lover, you get no say."

I lost my patience and inhibitions. "Lash, you aren't shooting blanks anymore," I said bluntly. "Protect yourself."

There was a sharp intake of breath. I hung up.

Well, that had gone just about as bad as it possibly could have.

I went back to bed, lying awake in the dark. I'd done the right thing by calling him, stupid as I'd sounded. *He hadn't known.* He'd be safe now, and that's what mattered.

Stop lying to yourself. You called him because you're upset, and you wanted him to know, because there is no one else you can tell. And instead of just saying it, you handled it badly, just like you handle just about every single situation where he's involved. Why the hell can't you get a handle on your emotions, or at least for God's sake, your actions?

Full of self-recrimination, I was just finally dropping off to sleep when the dogs growled low from the other room.

Chapter Eleven

Something was wrong. I eased down under the edge of the bed, and grabbed my silenced pistol. Theo had given it to me for my birthday, telling me if I had to shoot someone in the house to use that, as it wouldn't deafen me like my .38 would in the enclosed space. I eased off the safety, thinking to myself that red is dead, and wishing I'd loaded it with explosive bullets instead of regular hollow points.

I didn't hear any more noises, but I got up anyway, going out to the window. I peered out the door. The shadowy form of a truck was parked in the driveway. The dogs were looking at it, growling softly.

There was movement behind me. I turned quickly, my hand instantly squeezing the trigger. Lash easily grabbed my hand, shoving the gun to the side as I fired. The bullet shot into the pile of wood next to the door with a soft "pfft," knocking several large chunks askew with the impact.

He took the gun away, prying it out of my hands gently.

I lost it. "Couldn't you knock at the door, like a normal person?"

The dogs hadn't heard him come up from behind. But at my yell, they'd turned, snarling to go after him. I grabbed them both by their collars, hanging on as I tried to calm them. Lash stood there, motionless.

"Hey! Ghost! Darkness! It's okay. Stop! It's okay!"

Both dogs thought it was definitely not okay that Lash was here, and kept growling at him. He remained still, his eyes staring at me.

"Time for a Cheweez?" I said in a high, offertory voice, moving toward the kitchen. Both dogs stopped growling, hurriedly following me. I gave them both the treat, and they settled down to munching.

I went back to Lash, who hadn't moved. "What are you doing here?"

Lash didn't reply, grasping my arm and pulling me into my bedroom. He shut the door, sat me down on the bed, and then leaned down in front of me, his shadow crouching so he could look in my eyes. "Are you pregnant?" he hissed softly.

"I was," I answered, not meeting his eyes. "I lost it this morning." I blinked my eyes, upset, and irrationally angry with myself for wanting to cry.

Lash hugged me tightly. For several minutes, we didn't speak.

Theo had asked me to never hug him again.

Fuck him, and his jealous cougar nature. I hugged Lash tighter, wrapping my arms around him as if I'd never let him go.

"You're sure it wasn't Theo's?" Lash hissed finally, upset. "Not to put too fine a point on it, but I smelled him on you the night you came to me in the Everglades. It's a reasonable guess that you've resumed husband and wife relations."

"He hasn't been with me without protection, since he found out what I did for you," I said, grimacing. "Stephen said the fetus was a month old. When I almost died, I was still fixed. It was only after Titus's blood healed me two days later that I was capable of conception. You said your sex drive had come back. Your fertility came back with it." I swallowed hard. "It had to be yours, Lash."

Lash was utterly still for a few moments. Then he reached out with his arms, and took my face in his hands. "Are you okay? Are you hurt inside?" he asked, his dark eyes worried. "I smell blood faintly, Sar. Your blood."

"I went to see Stephen a few hours ago. He checked me over. He said I would be okay."

Lash let out a breath, then exploded. "But you had surgery!" he hissed angrily, changing partly to snake. "Surgery to prevent you from having any more children. How could this have happened? I thought it was safe."

"So did I," I said gently, squeezing his hands. "But the demon blood healed me. Don't blame yourself for this. We didn't know. We couldn't have known."

"I do blame myself for this. I did this to you," Lash hissed sorrowfully, a good deal of guilt in his tone. "This is my fault."

He stood, then sat beside me, slipping one arm around my shoulders. His rough fingers grazed my neck, caressing gently. "I'm sorry. Why didn't you call me, and tell me what had happened? I would have come with you, been there with you at Camlyn's—"

"I wasn't sure how you would take the news," I said awkwardly. "We aren't a couple—"

Lash grabbed hold of my arms. "Anything happens like that again, you had better call me," he said in an emotionally charged tone. "I don't care that we aren't lovers anymore. You need someone, you call me. Understand?"

"Sure," I sighed, burrowing into him, and closing my eyes.

Lash grunted, and lay back on the bed, holding me close as he stroked my hair. "It had to be the demon blood. I'm back in my prime now." He paused. "Did Stephen say why you lost it?"

"No," I whispered. "When I miscarried before, my doctor then said it was a problem with the fetus; that it wasn't developing right. It's possible that while I was okay to get pregnant, I'm not strong enough to sustain a were child's needs."

"You're healthy enough," Lash replied. "It must have been a problem with the child. You'd just renewed me. My semen probably wasn't changed completely, or something. I guess it doesn't matter now." He paused again. "Do you mind if I tell Dev?" he asked hesitantly. "I'm fucked...um, messed up over this, Sar. I feel so many things, and I need to talk about them, or I'm going to lose it."

"Please don't tell him. I don't want Danial or Theo to know. Devlin won't be able to keep his mouth shut."

Lash let out a breath. "All right. I won't say anything."

"Talk to me, instead. I also need to talk about this. You're the only one I can tell."

"You first, then."

"I'm afraid. I feel powerless, and I hate that. I did everything I could to prevent having any more children. And it was all for nothing!" I rubbed at my filling eyes. "The worst of it is that I feel guilty, because part of me is relieved. You know the shitstorm that would have happened if Dev, Theo, and Danial..."

"You're talking about your cat, not the vampires," Lash hissed neutrally. "Theo would have been the most angry. It would have been the killing blow to your marriage."

I took a deep breath. "Yes, no question. Now everything is much easier, both for you and for me. But I'm still sad, because I hadn't even realized I was pregnant. I would have been so much more careful. I wouldn't have taken those drugs for my bronchitis, not without knowing if they could hurt the baby."

"Forget it," Lash said, kissing my forehead. "Those little pills wouldn't have caused you to miscarry. This isn't your fault, Sar. It didn't happen because of anything you did."

I took a deep, shuddering breath. "You and I made that life, and now it's gone, before it even got a chance to live." Tears came to my eyes again. I blinked them back, but they fell anyway, and then I was crying in his arms.

Lash held me, and stroked my hair until my sobs lessened. Eventually, I lay there exhausted and drained of emotion, hugging him.

"You would have told me, when you knew it was mine, if you hadn't lost it, right?" Lash hissed suddenly. He paused, his next words coming with effort.

"Even if you didn't know how I would react?"

"Of course," I answered. "You would have been the father. You would have had a right to know. You and I would have needed to make some hard decisions."

Lash was almost vibrating now, tremors running through him. "Would you have gotten Stephen to—" he hissed, and stopped.

I knew what he was asking, but I didn't speak, waiting for him to get it out. It took him a few tries, but he finally said it. "Would you have wanted Stephen to…to take care of it for you?" Lash hissed. "Once you knew for sure it was mine?"

He was asking if I would have aborted his child to hold onto Theo. "No," I said. "I might have if Stephen told me it would be too dangerous to carry your child, but—"

"Why not, Sar?" Lash hissed abruptly, still upset. "It would have been easier for you. Why would you brave Theo's wrath to have my baby, especially as you know he would never have stood for it? He would have left you the moment he knew. And you keep telling me how important he is to you, how much you love him."

There was so much bitterness and jealousy in his tone. I looked at his shadowy outline in my arms and almost told him I loved him, that I would have wanted his child just because I loved him. But I bit my tongue instead. I would not make this worse than it was already.

"It would have been a huge adjustment, and Theo might have left me over it. But it would have been my child. I couldn't just say, oops, sorry, I made a mistake, let's fix it—"

I stopped talking. Something had occurred to me that I hadn't thought of. I needed a minute to think of how to ask it. "Would you have asked me to go and get Stephen to take care of it when I told you I was pregnant?" I got out finally. "And that it was yours?"

Lash hugged me so tight I let out a little cry. He relaxed immediately. I took in a deep breath. "I'm sorry," he said. "I didn't mean to squeeze you so hard."

"It's fine. Now tell me the truth."

"No," he said lovingly. "I would have asked you to come and live at Hayden, where I knew you'd be safe. I wouldn't have trusted Theo not to do something to the baby, so that you would lose it—"

I went utterly still in his arms. *What if Theo had known? What if Theo had done something to make me lose the baby?* He could have easily slipped me a potion. He made dinner half the time, and I just ate it. *Oh, God…*

"Dev would have been upset about it," Lash continued. "But he would have been happy for me, too. He loves Venus to death."

Would Theo have killed a baby? He killed people all the time for Danial. What was the difference? It was my baby, was the difference. But it was Lash's baby, too. Theo hated Lash, and he knew we had been together. Maybe part of the reason he had worn protection with me was he was waiting to see if I would come up pregnant. If he knew that he hadn't been unprotected with me, he would know who the father had to be, long before any weresnake DNA showed up in my blood. *Then he would have told me to abort it...*

Lash was still talking. I forced myself to bring my attention back to him. Damn it, I owed him that much, just for agreeing not to tell Dev.

"—I had a girlfriend of mine get pregnant decades ago, Sar. But she didn't tell me, not until she'd terminated the pregnancy. She said she didn't want me stopping her from doing it. She was human—like you—and she said she wasn't having any slimy snake children—"

God, hadn't anyone but Dev ever treated Lash as a person? No wonder he was so hostile all the time. He kept expecting everyone to hate him and treat him badly, because that was all he'd known in his life.

"I couldn't stand the sight of her after that. To know I was fine to fuck, but too disgusting and repellent for her to want a child of mine. We'd been living together, and I was thinking...well, never mind, that's not important—"

Thinking he loved her? Was going to marry her? I couldn't ask.

"—I can still hear that bitch's voice. You'd think that after eighty years, some of the sting would be gone. But it feels just the same remembering her words as the day she said them."

"What did she say?"

Lash seemed not to hear me. "When I began taking the potion, Titus told me that I would lose the ability to make children. I resigned myself to it easily. He said there were things I could do—back at the beginning—so I still could. Kind of like what Dev did for you and him. But I didn't want children; I was done with that—"

*"Was" done? "*Did you ever want one?"

"Back when I was younger, I thought sometimes that I would like a child," Lash replied. "But the truth is I knew I would make a bad father. I'm too self-centered. My life is too dangerous to play the family man. Someone would always want to kidnap a child of mine, or hold it ransom. That's the price I paid, to be the best assassin and bodyguard there is. That doesn't seem to bother Theo, or Dev, at least not enough to stop them having children with you. But it would bother me that every second of every day I'd be worried someone was planning to hurt my child. I couldn't live like that, being that afraid all the time. I worry enough about you, Sar, when you aren't at Hayden."

I wanted to tell him that it didn't matter if you were in a dangerous line of work or not, any parent who loved their child at all worried like crazy anyway. "You do worry about them."

"But still...." Lash began, then stopped.

I wrapped my arms around him, and kissed his cheek gently. He tried several times to say what he wanted to, but he still couldn't get it out. "It's okay," I said gently. "I'm right here. Take your time."

He buried his face in my neck, and was quiet for a few minutes.

"Still, I wish you hadn't lost our baby," Lash whispered gently. "I would have liked the chance to share that with you, to know that we made something together. And to try to be a father, even if I wasn't as good at it as I might have liked to be."

There was such loss in his words, like an abyss of pain and suffering. I hugged him as hard as I could. "I'm sorry."

"I'm glad you told me, that you called me. It would have been easy not to, to just pretend that it never happened."

"Not for me," I said, tears again in my eyes. "I wanted to call you from Stephen's, to ask you to come. But I was afraid Dev would find out, or you would bring him, and I had enough to deal with—"

"He was with me, when you left the message for me," Lash nodded. "He would have come once he heard you were in trouble, and I wouldn't have been able to hide it from him. Though he's my best friend, he can be too much to take sometimes. It was better you did what you did, even though I should have been there with you."

"I'm glad you came," I whispered.

"I'll always come, Sar," he said tenderly. "Just call me, tell me you need me, and I'll come. Whatever it takes, and whatever I need to kill to get to you, I'll come."

"I need you now," I said softly, burying my face in his neck, breathing in his scent of soft musk, leaves, and earth. "Will you hold me for a while?"

"Of course," he said, covering me with a blanket. Cradled in his arms, I soon fell asleep.

Lash woke me up shortly, shaking me. "Wake up."

"What?" I grumbled.

"We can't stay here," Lash replied, standing up. "Theo will be back at dawn. That's only a few hours away. He can't find me like this with you, unless you want to lose him for good."

That was the understated truth. I rubbed my bleary eyes. "I know. I—"

"You need to come home with me. And we've waited too long to go as it is."

I blinked my eyes. *Had I heard him right?* "I can't leave my pets here. You should go home. I'll be okay—"

"No way in hell I'm leaving you here alone," Lash said, his dark eyes flashing, then going flat as he changed partway to snake. "What if you start to bleed again?"

"Stephen took care of me," I reassured him. "I'll be fine. There'll be a little blood, but that's normal."

"You are going to come with me if I have to drag you," Lash hissed firmly. "We are going to Hayden right now, tonight. Your pets can come, too."

I protested, but Lash wouldn't relent. Faced with being carried to his truck, I gave in, packing up the dogs and the cats. I moved slowly as I was still sore from the D and C.

"Is Devlin at Hayden now?" I asked, stacking cat food cans in a box.

Lash nodded.

Wonderful. "What is he going to say when you just show up with me and my pets?" I said heatedly. "He's not going to just say, 'Thanks for bringing her'. He's going to want to know why."

"I'll tell him you called me, and said there was someone at your house, that you were afraid, and since I was already out, I stopped by to check on you," Lash hissed. "Dev knows I was seeing Gina tonight. He's not going to think anything's going on."

I cringed inside, but admitted it was good news. At least Lash had a reason for being out my way. "Then we need to make it believable." I began grabbing clothes, and packing them in bags.

"What are you doing?" Lash asked, curious. "Are you really coming to Hayden to live?"

"If someone was really here, and I was afraid, I would pack everything precious to me," I explained. "That means my pets, a good amount of clothes, their food, my heirlooms, and other important things."

"Then tell me what to get, and I'll pack it in my truck," Lash said. "You shouldn't be lifting things, Sar. You've been walking around too much as it is."

"I'm not an invalid, I can walk around—" I said irritably, getting up.

Lash sat me back down firmly. "Stay put, or I'll tie you there," he hissed, flashing a smile.

I rolled my eyes at him, but I did stay put and tell him what needed to be packed.

It took more than an hour to get everything in his truck, even throwing things in bags and boxes as fast as he could. All the pets were panting and meowing loudly by the time he was done. But I'd gotten better at teleporting, and I took the truck and all its contents to the road outside of Hayden. In a second, we were at the gate, waiting for it to open.

"Let me do the talking," Lash said, fixing me with his dark eyes. "You just look afraid, and cry a little. Got it?"

"Got it," I said. I was afraid for real, so this should be easy. *Would Dev buy the story?*

Lash buzzed us through Hayden's gate with some code on a remote, and called Devlin from his cell as we traveled up the driveway.

"Dev, Sar's here with me, we're almost to the front door—" Pause. "She called me, said someone was at her house—" Pause. "No, I didn't see anyone, but I thought it best to bring her here, though she wanted to stay there alone—" Pause.

God, Dev wasn't letting him finish a sentence.

"Theo's out all night, changing that woman into a cougar, and Devon's at Danial's."

I hadn't told Lash any of that last bit, and he hadn't guessed, either. He'd been talking to Brian again.

"We'll meet you at the garage door." Lash hung up and grinned at me. "Piece of cake," he said easily.

"I thought you never lied to Dev," I said snottily, looking at Lash out of the corner of my eye.

"I never do," Lash hissed sharply, parking and shutting off the truck.

I gave him a sharp look back. "Then what—"

"Sar, there was someone who had been at your house tonight earlier," Lash hissed. "I saw fresh tire tracks in the snow. I didn't want to scare you."

"How could you not tell me?" I gasped, eyes wide.

"I needed to get you out of there," Lash explained, grabbing hold of me and making me look at him. "I wanted you to be calm, and not be upset, after what happened to you earlier tonight. Whomever it was had left by the time I got there, but I thought they might come back. I listened carefully the whole time I was there with you, and no one came back. I would've gotten you to safety, if anyone tried to hurt you."

"We have to call Theo," I said, panicked. "He might walk into an ambush."

"Dev is calling Danial now," Lash said, getting out of the truck. "Theo and Devon will stay at Danial's tonight, like they were planning to anyway. Theo won't go home without backup, unless he's an idiot. But he'll check it out first to make sure it's safe for you and Devon and your pets, before any of you go home." He slammed the truck door and came around to help me out.

"Sar?" Devlin said loudly. I turned, and was enveloped in his arms. "Are you okay?" he said, drawing back from me. "What happened?"

What should I say? Looking at Lash for help would be a dead giveaway.

"She heard a noise outside," Lash supplied. "She looked out and saw a vehicle. She called me. I was on my way back here from Gina's, so I stopped by to check it out—"

"Who was it?" Devlin growled, holding me tightly.

"I didn't see anyone," Lash said. "But from the tires, the vehicle was an SUV, heavily loaded."

"Any foot prints?" Devlin asked.

"No."

"Someone may have been just turning around in Sar's driveway," Devlin said, relaxing, drawing back from me to shoot a questioning look at Lash. "I'm glad you brought her here, but—"

"Dev, whoever was in that vehicle was there for at least an hour, watching her house," Lash said flatly. "They weren't professionals. They ran the heater to keep warm, and so they kept the SUV running. It melted a little of the ice under the engine, and the exhaust was visible."

Our fake/staged escape from someone meaning me harm had been real. I began shaking.

Devlin picked me up. "I'm taking you to bed," he said soothingly, "Relax, you're safe."

"Dev, I've got to put my pets in one of your spare rooms," I said, snapping out of my panic. "They're scared from the journey, from being packed up in the middle of the night."

"Let them out to roam the house," Devlin said, shrugging. "Phantom tolerates dogs, and he likes other cats, so there shouldn't be any fights."

"You sure?" I said, looking at him uneasily. "You'll have dog hair everywhere in a few hours."

"I'm sure," Devlin said, giving me a genuine smile. "Just don't let them on the bed with us."

"They won't do that, they're well trained," I said quickly, hoping Ghost wouldn't take this moment to prove me wrong.

When I let the dogs out of the truck, they came out warily, sniffing everything. I opened the garage door. Ghost and Darkness went outside quickly, and took care of business. The cats I was more worried about, so I put them together in one of the gray guest rooms I had painted, with their litter box and their water and food. Devlin helped with doling out food. I let him, feeling grateful.

"They'll be okay here tonight," he said, shutting the door with the two cats inside. "No one will bother them."

Lash had been busy unpacking his truck while we were taking care of the dogs and cats. He had carried most of the clothes and other things into the hallway, and piled the boxes and bags outside the kitchen, by the stairs to the second floor.

"Are you moving in?" Devlin said, eying the pile. There was sarcasm in his tone, but more than a little hope, too.

I flushed. "I tried to bring everything I valued most, except my tractor and truck. I brought some of Theo's stuff, too. I left most of my tools, books, and clothes, but I—"

"Don't worry about it, I was just teasing," Devlin replied quickly, as he opened his bedroom door and turned on the light. "Come in and make yourself at home. We'll unpack your things tomorrow."

There was a sense of disquiet to his grasping acceptance, but I let it slide without comment. Once Theo checked out everything, we could easily bring the boxes home, though I'd probably hear shit from Theo about how everything smelled of snake.

The dogs followed me inside Dev's bedroom. When I laid down their beds near the wall, they both curled up in them, panting.

"This is normal," I said to Dev, who was watching them as if he was waiting for them to chew something. "It's a new place. They'll go to sleep within the hour, once they understand I'm staying here with them." I sat down on the bed, and began pulling off my socks. "I'm ready to drop in my tracks, myself."

"You've had a rough night," Devlin comforted. "I was reading when you called. Do you want me to read you some of the poetry I was musing over, or would you rather sleep?"

"I'm exhausted," I said, flashing a smile. "But read if you like. I'll just curl up beside you and doze."

Devlin nodded, then undressed and slipped back into bed, picking up his book. I changed into one of the nightgowns I kept here, then crawled into bed beside him. When I snuggled next to him, he went completely still. "Sar, is it your time?" he asked quietly.

He'd scented the blood, just as Lash had. "Yes," I answered tersely. "I just started—"

"I just wanted to make sure you were okay," Devlin said quickly. "Please, just lie next to me and relax. No one will hurt you or your pets here."

I lay next to him, tense. But within a few moments, I was asleep.

* * * *

We were woken up at dawn by Lash pounding on the door as if he was going to break it down. "Dev! Dev! Wake the fuck up!"

126

"What the fuck?" Devlin swore. Stark naked, he stalked to the door, throwing it open. "Yes?"

Lash stood there, his eyes were full of sadness, as they had been last night. "Sar, I'm sorry," he hissed softly. "Your house burned to the ground early this morning."

Chapter Twelve

Horrified, I gaped at Lash as he regarded me miserably. Ghost and Darkness began growling at him, then tensed to spring. "Hey!" I said sharply. They both quieted, looking at me curiously.

I couldn't absorb Lash's words at first. Then in an instant, it all became clear as glass. If I hadn't miscarried, I would never have called Lash. He would never have come and seen the tracks, then got me out of there. My beloved animals and I would now be charred meat in the ashes of my house. Whomever had been lurking outside had done this. *Someone had been hoping to kill me last night.*

A scream worked its way out of my throat as the horror of burning to death crashed down on me, enveloping me in its smoky embrace. "Noooooooo!"

Devlin was by my side in a moment, holding me tightly as I began to shake. "Shh, Shh!" he consoled. "You're safe, Sar. It's okay—"

I screamed again shrilly, giving voice to all my rage and loss. It seemed to echo in the room. I wanted to keep screaming, but instead bit the inside of my lip hard, using the fresh pain to focus.

My beloved house. I'd done so much work there, fixing the place up when I'd first moved in. I'd painted, laid tile, redone the bathrooms, put on a new roof, and redone the skylights. Theo and I'd had done even more work that summer after he first moved in. I'd first made love with him there, just as I had with Danial, years ago. I had so many memories there of Brennan, and of Theo, Elle, and Devon, even of Devlin. There had been so much I hadn't taken with me. So much I would have taken, if I'd known I wasn't ever going to be able to go back. God, I should have packed my truck, and driven that. I could have brought twice as much.

"Sar, say something," Dev whispered.

"Did the garage burn too?" I finally got out.

"Yes," Lash replied softly. "But the fire department saved the barn, because it was so far from the house and garage. No trees caught on fire, either."

At least my John Deere tractor was safe, and most of my equipment. That was something.

"This had to be Ulysses," Lash hissed, his tone low and dangerous.

"Not necessarily," Devlin said forcefully. "Theo has many enemies. It's possible that this was aimed at him, not Sar—"

"You really believe that?" Lash said sarcastically. "If you do, I have a potion to sell you for a mil that will make you hard as a railroad spike—"

"Shut your fucking mouth," Devlin growled. "Sar's upset. She's just lost her home. She doesn't need to hear your forked tongue spouting shit."

Lash came over and sat on the bed, though he didn't touch me. "I'm sorry, Sar. I know you loved your home. I'm glad I got you out in time."

There was something in his voice that said he'd lost a home, too. He lived here with Devlin, not at his own place. Maybe there was a reason for that besides just guarding Devlin.

I moved back from Dev, then reached out for Lash, throwing my arms around him. "Thank you for saving me. I'd be dead if you hadn't insisted I come to Hayden with you last night. Thank you for saving my pets—"

"I'm grateful to you, also, Lash," Devlin said stiffly.

"Come have breakfast," Lash said, moving away from me and getting to his feet. "You need to eat something. Serena is making breakfast for Nick. She can make you some, too."

"It's okay, I can make it myself," I said hollowly, standing up and slipping on a robe.

"Come back after, Sar," Devlin said firmly. "You need to repose. You've been up with no real rest for the past thirty-six hours."

"I will," I agreed, rubbing at my gritty eyes. "But Lash is right, I need to eat something. I need to feed my pets, too."

I motioned to the dogs to come. They got up at once, tails wagging. I went downstairs with them, called for the cats to come eat, then proceeded to feed all responders. Phantom was there on the kitchen counter, meowing loudly for food.

"You don't need to feed him," Serena said, coming in from the dining room. She dished another pancake onto a plate. "Do you want anything?" she offered.

Her tone was cautious and sad. She'd heard about my house. Maybe everyone here at Hayden had. "No thanks."

"I'll make you a bagel," Lash said gently, coming into the kitchen. "You're going to eat something, Sar, and I know you like bagels. Sit down at the table."

I followed Serena back into the dining room. Nick was there, finishing the very end of what looked like a stack of pancakes. *Did she make him breakfast every morning now?*

Nick and Serena sipped their coffee, neither one of them saying a word. *Had I interrupted anything?* Watching Nick finish his pancake, I realized he had on a blue shirt. I'd never seen anyone here at Hayden dress in blue, except him. *Serena had been mending Nick's clothes that day I'd shown her how to sew. Why hadn't I put that together before now? Why did things seem so extra clear this morning?*

"Nick, don't you need to relieve Seth in a few minutes?" Lash said in a harsh tone, coming in with a bagel, a knife, and some butter on a tray. "Get going."

Nick got up instantly, kissed Serena good-bye, and a second later, he was out the door. Serena gave me a hug. "I'm sorry."

I murmured something in reply, I'm not sure what. Then Serena excused herself, leaving Lash and I alone.

I suddenly wanted some cocoa. I got up and went into the kitchen, Lash tailing me. I tried to make myself the cocoa, but my hands shook. The powder ended up going all over the counter. Lash took the spoon and whisk from me without a word. He cleaned up the spill, then got a cup ready, setting it in the microwave. "I'll take care of this. Go sit down."

Ghost whined at my hip, reminding me I hadn't let him out. I let Ghost and Darkness outside, then back inside when they were done. Afterwards I went back into the dining room, where Lash was waiting.

Lash had put my buttered bagel on a plate, the mug of steaming cocoa to the side. I waited for him to say something, like be strong, or that he was sorry my memories were now only comprised of what was in the boxes upstairs, but he didn't. I was grateful for that. I was consumed with images of everything that I hadn't been able to fit in his truck, so much that was ashes now, like the two chairs Theo had carved that we'd brought from Wyoming with us, and Brennan's wedding album with me, and my own albums of pictures.

I made myself visualize Devon's baby book, his toys, my pets, and all the rest I'd saved from burning. That was all that was left. It would have to be enough.

"Did you already eat?" I said hollowly to Lash, taking a bite of the now-cool bagel.

He nodded. "I usually get up early. I prefer the day shift, especially in winter. I like to be nice and warm under the covers when it gets dark, if I don't have to guard Dev, that is."

"Me, too," I replied softly.

Lash gave me a faint smile, his eyes still sad.

"How did you find out about the fire?" I said, after I'd eaten the bagel, and the cocoa had warmed me some.

"One of your neighbors called Danial's house. I think they were the ones who called in the fire. They called your house when they smelled smoke, but got no answer. Then they saw the fire through the trees and called the fire department. They didn't know where you were, but you'd given them Danial's number years back. Danial called Hayden, and got me."

"I'll need to go there later today, and get anything I can salvage," I said tiredly.

"The garage wasn't a total loss," Lash said. "There may be something salvageable there."

I doubted it, but I'd see when I got there. That could wait until sometime later. I sipped the cocoa. God, what a night…

There was a sudden commotion outside the front door. Someone began pounding on it. One of the bears went to the door, shouting, "Just a fucking minute! Hold on!"

"Excuse him," Lash hissed irritably. "That fucking Jerry is a foul-mouthed bastard."

There was a roar almost earth shattering in intensity. *"WHERE IS SHE? Where's my wife?"*

Theo.

My husband burst into the kitchen, saw us, and growled immediately at Lash. Lash just looked back at him calmly, his dark eyes cold. Theo grabbed me up out of the chair, hugging me desperately. "Sar, I'm so glad you're okay," Theo said passionately, kissing me all over my face. "I was so worried—"

"Were you?" Lash hissed sarcastically, his eyes flattening to snake. "Were you *really*, Cat?"

Theo looked up at him, his eyes yellowing instantly. "Why do you smell of him, Sar?" Theo growled, sitting me back down gently, his volume rising with every word. "I asked you not to let him touch you. I can smell his scent on your skin again—"

"You're one to talk, Cat! You've been doing more than hugging with some other female," Lash hissed scathingly.

Theo went crimson.

"I smell her on you, Cat," Lash hissed, his forked tongue flicking the air before disappearing back into his mouth. "You fucked her. Several times at least."

I held onto the back of the chair, blinking in disbelief at Theo. "Is what he said true?" I whispered.

Theo looked away from me and ran his hands though his hair. In that nervous movement, I had my answer, just as I was already sure the scent Lash smelled on him was Jenny's.

I would hold it together. I would not come apart at the seams no matter how much I wanted to. *Breathe, Sar, then think.*

The rest of this conversation needed *not* to happen in front of Lash. I had to talk to Theo privately, much as I wanted to tell him to just get out and not to come back. Theo had to have a good reason for what happened, not to mention that I'd done the same to him with the other man standing in this very room. I needed to deal with this like an adult. I needed to give him a chance to explain himself.

"I need to check on the cats," I said, trying not to let my pain and uncertainty show in my voice. "Theo, please come with me."

Theo followed me down the long hall leading to the ballroom and into the flame room. I shut the door behind us, then rounded on him. "It must have worked." My voice was a lot calmer than I felt, which was good.

"I changed her," Theo explained. "She's healed now, Sar. She even started to re-grow her hair, though it's very short, only stubble really—"

"I don't care about that," I said harshly. "Did you fuck her, like he said?"

"Yes," Theo said, looking at me stonily.

"How many times?"

"Four."

I shut my eyes, and sank down on the floor. The room still wasn't furnished. But I couldn't seem to find the time to go to a store and pick out anything. Things had been happening too fast since mid-summer. "Is this payback for what I did with Lash?" I asked finally.

Theo sat on the floor and hugged me. I wanted to slap him, but refrained.

"I'm sorry it happened like this," he began. "It had nothing to do with any kind of payback. I told you I forgave you for Lash, Sar. I would never try to hurt you like that, to use some other woman to hurt you—"

"Then what the hell happened?" I gasped, tears beginning to leak from my eyes.

"I helped her change for the first time, meaning just to run with her in Danial's woods, and help her adjust to walking on four legs. But when I saw her as a cougar, something came over me. I hadn't seen a female werecougar since Aspen, and the urge to mate with her was so strong—" Theo broke off, then began again. "The truth is I almost forced her, I wanted it so bad," he finished roughly. "She fought me at first, until her animal instincts took over."

Now for the hard question. I backed away, then faced him. "Are you going to be with her again?"

"If I say I need this, will you give me permission?" Theo asked.

I blinked at him, astounded. I'd expected him to declare his love for me, to tell me he only wanted me, as he always had in the past. But that was not what was happening.

"Sar, I know you don't want to hear this, but you need to. You have to! I needed to be with a werecougar female, to mate in animal form! I haven't been with anyone like that for over a year! I hadn't felt before how much I'd denied my animal nature! I feel like I've been sleepwalking for the last year and a half!"

Hearing his desperation and frustration, I knew suddenly that Titus had to have succeeded in breaking the last of our bond. Theo was now for the first time as he really was, without any magic to hold him to me. *Would Theo have picked me over Tawny all those years ago, or Aspen, if he'd been himself?* Something told me the decision would not have been so quickly made.

"It's normal to want to mate as soon as two weres of the opposite sex and same type meet," Theo went on. "I used to go with Danial to Europe almost every other month and see Tawny. I'd call her as soon as I got there, and she'd be ready, waiting near a phone for my call. It never took her more than a few minutes to get to the hotel. But sometimes it was still almost unbearable to wait for her to get to whatever hotel we were at," Theo finished, raking his hands through his hair for a second time. "I feel that same urgency again, like an irresistible pull inside."

Tawny's comment years ago of wanting to be ready for Theo took on a whole new meaning for me in that moment. It also brought up another question. *Would Theo have been only with Tawny, if there had been any other lions in the surrounding states, if he hadn't subverted his animal side for so many years?* Something told me he'd have had lovers in the high double digits, if he'd been a fox and not a cougar. Now I understood better why Ivan and Demetri and Suri had had all the trouble they did. *Jesus.*

"You said once you'd let me take a lover, if I needed one," Theo said. "I need to be with her in animal form. I want to stay married to you, but I need this, Sar."

"She's okay with you doing this? Being married to me, and going to her for sex, just as a were?" My words were harsh again, and this time I didn't even try to keep the judgmental tone out of my voice.

"She's upset that we had sex like we did, with me being married," Theo said. "So am I. It's not my style to cheat, or to do what I did to her. I apologized to her when we changed back. But the truth is we are the only cougars around here. It makes sense if we hook up, to take care of our animal needs. She's going to have the same kind of needs and urges that Elle is having, only stronger, because she's a full adult. And she's living at Danial's. She's going to scent me when I'm there, just like I can scent her—"

Christ! Why hadn't I protested more when he'd offered to change her? We didn't need any more complications. More ominous, had Theo changed her in part because he'd subconsciously wanted a cougar around to mate with? I couldn't bring myself to ask him. "Were you with her as a human?" I whispered.

Theo hugged me again. "No. This isn't about me caring for her. I barely know her, Sar—"

I resisted the urge to shove him away from me. *You're going to know her well, Theo, before too long, especially if you're fucking her every week.*

"—it's about sex, and only sex. I'm sorry that I even have to ask this. But I know if I'm cougar, and she changes with me, I'll probably mate with her again."

"You'll need to get tested, like me," I said flatly.

Theo nodded. "I know that."

Another question popped up, just like that. Frankly, with Theo having sex regularly outside the marriage, we'd be using condoms from now on, testing, or no testing. While I didn't like that idea, it would also make keeping my new fertility secret much easier. But Theo was my husband, and to know I'd never again feel him skin to skin with me made me feel unreasonably sad. It was like we'd lost something important.

I told myself it didn't matter. Lots of couples used condoms as their birth control. They didn't feel like they were missing out, so why should I? I'd still be able to be totally bare with Danial and Devlin, anyway. It would be an adjustment, but I could do it. After all, what choice did I have? "Okay, then."

"We'll go to Camlyn's right now if you want," he said quickly. "Danial gave me the morning off to come see you, when he heard what happened—"

The knowledge of my destroyed house came flooding back, making my shoulders slump. "I was able to save the most important of our things, when I left our home. I've got your woodcarving equipment, and the Woman and the Cougar."

Theo grabbed me, almost squeezing me too tight in his muscular arms. "I'm glad Lash got you out, that you weren't hurt," he said, fear of losing me in his tone. "It's good you called him, when you saw that strange SUV in the driveway. But I'm surprised he was close by—"

"He sees a woman a town over for sex. He was there last night," I said flatly.

Theo gave me a relieved smile.

He'd suspected Lash of being so close because he had been coming to see me, to meet me secretly for sex. I was furious with him suddenly, for fucking Jenny, and then having the balls to be so bent out of shape that Lash had hugged me, after our house had burned down and Lash had saved my life.

"There may be some additions to our new agreement," I said abruptly, and moved away from him again. "I'll need to think about this."

"Do you want to go and get tested now? I think we both should, Wife," Theo said bitterly. "We can pay extra and get the results immediately."

I took his hand, teleporting us there instantly.

* * * *

I'm not sure what Theo told Stephen about why we wanted the tests. Stephen gave me a sorry look when he came in to take my blood, and swabs. Despite Theo's blustering about immediate results, Stephen said he would call us later in the day with answers. He also gave me a quick check for curses, as he hadn't done that after the Hallow's party, and he usually did every year. His confirmation I had none did nothing to lift my spirits, yet I was relieved that he's remembered to check. I'd completely spaced on it. "I'll be at Hayden," I said coolly. "Please call me there, Stephen, when you have the test results."

Stephen nodded. "Sure. You can resume sexual activity now, just stay protected until I contact you with the results." He forced a smile. "I'm sorry to have to say that, but it's a new protocol we're being asked to follow after all STD tests we run. Some of these teenage weres think if they get the test, they're automatically negative."

Something was off with him. It was like he didn't remember last night at all. He wasn't acting furtive, hadn't given me any glances that were out of place, hadn't even asked me how I was doing this morning. He should have been acting weird, from what had happened last night and with Theo and I showing up here right afterwards. The only explanation was that Titus had given him a forgetting spell, like Michael had suggested. I'd have to ask my demon kin when I got back to Hayden. I wanted to know more about the bond breaking anyway.

I forced a smile myself. "Thanks again, Stephen, for everything."

* * * *

Theo embraced me again on Hayden's doorstep. "Stay here for now with Devlin, until I can find out if that fire was meant for me, or for you."

Was this just a ruse so he could stay with Jenny alone at Danial's and change with her every night and have her as a cougar?

"I'll grab my things you saved, and stay at Danial's," he continued. "Come in early tomorrow, Sar. Danial said he needs you badly to work this week, that things are way behind."

I rubbed my eyes. Where was I going to fit being secretary for Solutions, Inc. into all of this? Well, maybe it would get my mind off all the danger I was in. "Tell him I'll be there," I said, sighing. "And don't forget, we have therapy tomorrow."

"I'll meet you there," Theo said, nodding, his tone turning malicious. "Please tell me your answer then, Sar, about any additions you want to make."

I nodded, angry he couldn't give me a few days to think about it, when he'd taken more than a week last fall to consider Danial being with me, for much the same kind of reason he was asking to be with Jenny. And then he'd taken back his "yes" answer, anyway.

Perhaps it was time to let him know that there would be some conditions. "Theo, if we do this arrangement, you realize that you'll never have sex with me again without a condom, because you can't protect yourself when you're with her. I'm not going to be relying on testing every single week."

Theo looked at me and held my gaze. "I understand that," he said, clearly angry.

What the fuck did he have to be angry about? Jerk. "I just wanted to be sure. Goodbye."

Theo left without a reply. I shut the door behind him, and walked back to the kitchen. Lash was gone, our plates taken care of. I was glad of that, because in the mood I was in, I'd have told him I wanted him, and to have me on the kitchen table, and I knew he'd have done it in a heartbeat. I didn't want to use him like that just because I was angry. I'd fucked up his life enough.

Instead, I went back up to Devlin and slept next to him for the rest of the day. He was happy to hear I'd be staying for a while. I was happy too, for a few hours, because I dreamed no dreams.

* * * *

When I woke up about six p. m., I felt a bit better about everything. Devlin stirred, when he felt me move beside him, opening his molten gold eyes to blink at me. He pushed his delicious body up from the bed, then kissed his way up my body to my neck, pricking my skin gently with his fangs. I closed my eyes and relished his caress, running my hands over him. He sighed once, and then stopped kissing me.

"I love waking up with you. Are you staying the night?" he asked hopefully. "I need to feed, but after, we can rent a movie and have popcorn."

"Sounds great," I said provocatively, kissing him again.

He gave me a gleeful smile.

There was a knock at the door. Devlin made a face, then got up, and opened it.

Lash was standing there. "Candy's here," he said, shooting a look at me. "Want me to take her into the silver room?"

"The silver room?" I echoed inanely. "Candy?" Then it came to me that Lash meant the guest room I'd painted all silver, clearly. And that Candy had to be a blood donor of Devlin's.

"Please," Devlin said, nodding. "Tell her I'll be there shortly."

Lash nodded. Devlin shut the door, and began dressing.

"Is the silver room furnished?" I hadn't been in there since I'd finished it. But where else would Devlin have here that would give him the privacy to feed, besides his own bedroom? There wasn't a spare bedroom that was furnished yet. I hadn't even seen a couch in his study. *And who'd want to go down there by the dungeon to get romanced anyway? Ick.*

"Sar, I'll be a while, the good part of two hours at least," Devlin said, pulling on his shirt. "Candy's only my first. There will be several other women coming. Melissa's always late, getting in that last primp—"

I looked at him in surprise. "How many woman do you feed from usually?"

"Sar, I don't feed as often as Danial does," Devlin said patiently, buttoning his last buttons. "I take a lot more when I do though. I'll sleep for a while right after, to get my systems processing the nutrients from the blood, to renew my body. Danial prefers to feed a little at a time, because he says it makes him feel uncomfortable to feed that much at once. But it's what I've always done."

No wonder I'd never seen Devlin feed from a woman at Hayden before. He made it sound like it was only once every three weeks or so. "Why do you prefer this? I'm curious."

"Some of it is that I've been badly injured before, and had to, so I wouldn't die," Devlin said with gritted teeth, his eyes seeing some distant memory. "Danial has never really been close to dying, except that first time you saved him. He would've healed much faster if he drained you, and at least one other woman—"

"Get to the point," I said angrily, my good morning mood gone. Talk of draining me tended to make me irritable, especially when it was him doing the talking.

"The point is, this is more convenient for me, and probably easier for you to deal with," Devlin said, somehow keeping his patience. "You'll be staying with me some of the time from now on, no matter what Theo finds out—"

"Oh, really?" I said, raising my eyebrows.

"Yes, really," Devlin said, smiling permissively. "You can spend half your time at Danial's, and the other half here, at least until Ulysses is caught. If he was behind the attack on you, Sar, as Lash suspects, you'll be staying here until I can kill him. I want you where Titus, Lash, and I can guard you. Danial will not like it, but he'll agree it is best. He can come and spend some nights with us."

"You going to invite Theo, too?" I teased, smirking at him.

"Sure, if he wants to sleep with us," Devlin said easily. "I told you he was welcome to join us before in bed. But I probably wouldn't want Danial and he to be here with us at the same time." He shot me a devilish smile. "There is only so much of you to go around, Love."

Good to know you have some limits, Dev. I made a face at him.

"Ask him if you want, the next time you talk to him—"

"Theo doesn't want to be in bed with anyone but me," I said, laughing. Then I choked, because that might have been true yesterday, but it wasn't true now. I took a deep breath, and let it out.

Devlin came over and sat beside me. "I know about it," he said gently. "Danial told me, about what happened—"

"I don't want to talk about it," I said sharply.

"We don't have to, Sar. Just stay here and sleep some more," Devlin said, kissing me quickly. "I'll be back in a few hours."

Once he left, I lasted about ten seconds before thoughts of Theo and Jenny together began to swamp me. I bolted up, walking downstairs to the TV. Feeling blessed that no one was around, I turned it on and plopped down. Sadly, despite my searching, there was nothing on. It was what I referred to as the Black Zone of TV, that time between ten a.m. and four p.m. where there is nothing worth watching. I was mindlessly flipping channels looking for HBO or reruns of *The A-Team* when Lash came in and sat down next to me.

"I need to talk to you," he said quietly.

Chapter Thirteen

I didn't want to hear whatever he had to say. I had enough to deal with. I ignored him and kept flipping channels. Lash grabbed the remote from my hand in a lightning quick gesture, and turned the TV off. I thought about telling him to fuck off, but knew he was stubborn enough to just trail along even if I left the room. He'd follow me until I listened to what he had to say. He was that stubborn. *Just like me.*

"What?" I said, exasperated.

"Look, no one else is going to say this to you," Lash hissed. "But I'm your friend, and you need to hear it."

His tone said he was not happy to be here, talking to me. That probably meant I wasn't going to want to hear whatever it was he said. That alone made me curious. *How much worse could the day get?* I drew my knees up into my chest, folding my arms over them in a protective motion. "Say it."

"Understand, I'm not saying what he did was right," Lash said. "But you need to know that this is why weres usually stick to other weres—and even within the same type of animal, so they can mate. Like cougar and lion, boa and python, wolf and coyote—"

I closed my eyes, resisting the urge to put my hands over my ears.

Lash's hand touched my shoulder, resting there gently. "I thought you knew this, that you at least had an inkling. Theo needs to be with a female of his own kind, some kind of big cat. All weres feel the drive for sex strongly, but in animal form, it's almost undeniable. Some of that is that animals don't think sex is ever wrong, like sleeping and eating's not wrong. It's a physical need. He probably could resist it when there weren't any female cougars nearby except his daughter. But when you're animal and male, and see a female, it's—"

"You're saying I should let him go to her to slake his needs?" I said bluntly.

"That or ask Titus for a potion to change yourself into a cougar," Lash said, nonplused.

I looked at him in shock. *Why hadn't I thought of that?*

"There are potions that can do it," Lash said, nodding. "But they are expensive. Not ridiculously expensive, like the potion Devlin used to make you pregnant, or the one I used to use to stay alive, but still they're in the thousands of dollars. It's the damned demon blood—"

My shoulders slumped, dismayed. I—or rather, Theo and I—could afford to do it probably a few times, but I was betting it wouldn't be enough to keep Theo satisfied, not the way Lash was describing the need for weres to have sex. Not unless we did it once a month for twenty-four hours straight at a stretch. "How long do they last?"

"Only for a few hours," Lash said, looking at me strangely. "And even then, Devlin may not let you do it."

"Why?"

"Because Theo could hurt you easily, having sex with you like that," Lash said. "You're mortal now. Your regenerative powers wouldn't be were, they would be human. Theo's rough with you sometimes, or so I hear. Dev was pissed off about that before you and he even got together—"

Why the hell was Devlin confiding in Lash about my sex life? "Why are you telling me about this if it isn't a real option?" I said loudly, annoyed.

"Because you have choices, and I want you to know what they are. You think I can't tell how much you don't want him to go to her again for sex? For a woman who asks her mate— sorry, husband—to share her with two other men, you aren't understanding at all, Sar."

His bitter words stung me, mostly because they were true. "It's not that he needs to do it," I said tiredly. "I get what you're saying, and it makes sense. It's that I didn't know this before I married him. Theo's never mentioned this need of his before now. I feel a little blind-sided—"

That's not his fault, Sar. That was the fault of the bond, which you *put on* him, since that first time you kissed him. And *you* were the one to ask Titus to *break it. Don't bitch now, it's too late.*

Part of me had suspected what Lash was telling me, back when Theo'd had me in his cougar and liked it so much. Those times he'd been rough, I'd guessed that he needed that. That was why I'd let him do that to me, even though it hurt. But we hadn't done either act for the better part of a year. Even after our making up, Theo had only mentioned it to say he didn't want to attempt it, letting slip that he had found out from Tasha how painful it was to be on the receiving end. I'd been grateful not to do it, for the same reason. But biological needs didn't go away just because a person wanted them to, especially when they weren't being met anymore.

The Eye of the Storm

Lash interrupted my thoughts. "I can't speak to why the need is suddenly presenting itself, or why it hasn't been an issue until now, other than there just haven't been any female lions around here. I'm just telling you it's a true need, not something he's making up. If you love him, really love him, let him go to her. Don't hurt yourself trying to change for him—"

"I'll never be able to…it won't be the same," I blurted out.

"You're probably better off doing that," Lash said in a piercing tone. "It gives you an excuse to use birth control, Sar, a good one."

"It does," I said in a small voice.

"You don't want to be a cougar anyway," Lash said grimacing, with a full body shudder. "Too much fur, and claws."

I smiled in spite of the circumstances. "Thank you for telling me what you did, even if I didn't want to hear it. What you said made me feel better."

"Good," Lash said, squeezing my shoulder, and letting me go. "I wanted you to be okay with it."

Another conclusion dawned on me then. If I'd chosen Lash instead of Theo, would I have found myself on this same couch, hearing him saying the same things as he asked me for permission to bed a female snake? I didn't like the answer, but yes was probably the truth. Lash was were. He'd need to be with a female snake for sex, not just a human female.

"What?" Lash said, catching my odd look.

"Nothing," I said, blushing and averting my gaze.

Lash gave me a small rueful grin. "Yes, I feel those needs, too. It's why I said what I did to you that morning at Davy's. Back then, I felt the urges of my animal side all the time, because I was half changed. And for most weres, me included, having human sex usually brings the need to have sex in animal form."

"Why didn't you change me when you had the chance?" I said, my eyes locked on his.

Lash didn't brush me off with "We didn't have to," or "You didn't really want to be were", the pat responses I half expected. He answered me. "Because you were going to lose enough by giving me your blood, Sar. And no matter that he forgave me being with you, Dev was not going to forgive me changing your blood from summer to weresnake. He wants you to live forever, like him. You have a real chance to do that, to not die. I've been close to death, felt its icy hand reaching up to clutch my heart. I wasn't going to take that chance from you, just so we could be lovers and coil together. Not then." He clutched my hand in his. "Not ever."

I felt crushed. I was an idiot for not having seen it sooner. *Was I always going to be romanticizing the wrong man?* Lash had wanted to be my lover.

He'd wanted us to be able to have sex together. He'd never wanted me to be *just* his lover, for me to be his *only* lover. He'd wanted something casual, because he'd enjoyed being with me. There was a reason he hadn't told me he loved me. That was because he didn't want me getting the wrong idea about him. That was why he hadn't wanted to admit what the symbol on the knife said. Or maybe he'd meant only to write "lover."

So what if he'd given it to me? He'd thought he was dying. I'd probably be really meaningful, too, if I'd been dying. And I was old enough to know having a man love you didn't guarantee that you were the only woman he'd want to have sex with. *God, I was daft.* All the fantasies I'd been having, about coming to him and telling him I loved him! I'd almost thrown away my marriage on a good-timing man.

"Sar?" Lash said curiously. "What is it?"

"I'm okay," I said calmly, screaming inside. "But I should go and do a little work downstairs. Those files aren't going to finish themselves—"

"Screw that!" Lash said, looking at me as if I'd gone crazy. "You just had a horrible night and morning. Let me take you out for dinner. Dev will be busy for at least another two hours, probably."

I didn't want to be near him. I didn't want to talk to him. I wanted to get away from him, and nurse my feelings of self-pity. "Thanks, but I shouldn't," I said quickly, getting to my feet.

Lash got to his feet, and blocked me from leaving. "You're hurt," he said, flicking his tongue at me, scenting the air. "I smell it on you like a wound. Why are you hurt?"

Because I want you to be a man you aren't. A man you probably could never be. And I'm an idiot twice over for feeling sad that I lost a chance with you when we probably never had any real chance for anything except a steamy sex affair.

"Because I'm going to have to do it for him," I managed. "And it's going to drive me a little crazy thinking of them together. But maybe this is poetic justice."

"It's nothing but how things are," Lash said with a shrug. "Don't make more of it than it needs to be, Sar."

I'd heard that line from him before. Perhaps he used it with all his lovers. I did a slow burn, taking comfort in my anger. "Is sex ever more to you than need?" I said nastily, looking at him with slitted eyes. "Does it ever mean anything to you, besides that it feels good?"

Lash looked at me with flat eyes so long I dropped mine, and looked at the floor. "I'm not going to answer questions to which you already know the answer," he hissed, his tone that same dangerously low one he'd spoke to me in months ago. Then he stalked from the room.

* * * *

After lamenting my lack of a treadmill here, and the snowstorm outside, I had busied myself checking on all my pets. Everyone was adjusting to their new surroundings, something I could not comprehend.

Phantom seemed to like all his new housemates, dogs included. They all seemed to like him, too. Had the vampire blood Devlin had given Phantom to save him when he'd been hurt changed his scent when it healed him, so the other animals didn't see him as a cat? Maybe I'd discovered a new patent for vampire blood uses.

Next, I went downstairs to the filing room and tried to do a little work. Opening one of the white boxes, I looked through the contents. The files were from nineteen-sixty-two, the months of April to September. The organization was much like Danial's, with paperwork saying the client's name, and what Devlin had done for them, but the latter was in code. This document said Dev had arranged a person to paint a woman's house for her for a hundred thousand dollars. House painters didn't make that much, unless they were painting a house that was maybe the size of Hayden, it had a lot of trim work that needed specialized painting, and they'd used Sherman-William's best type of paint, the one that was guaranteed for fifty years.

The next files were the same. And the next. House painting, driveway blacktopping, garage building, excavating basements, and a hell of a lot of demolition work. I noticed then that a Mr. Lash was employed as the chief demolition expert on all of those files. Feeling a chill, I put them aside, then opened another box. These were from later that same year, through December. The codes were the same.

Lash had killed people; a lot of people. By these files, at least twenty-seven that summer alone, with another thirty in the last months of the year. Devlin arranged it, and took a cut. In addition, there were another seven men here who also took care of other kinds of business for Dev. All were named as Mr. So-and-so, with just one name.

That was enough of knowing Dev's business. I would file this by year, and leave it at that.

My work went faster after that. I just labeled the files with the month and year, and stuck them in a drawer, not looking at them other than to get the relevant data, and to group the jobs by type. Soon I had all of the sixties done, encompassing two boxes of files.

There had been a lot of demolition work in the sixties. At least a hundred jobs. How could I have feelings for a man who had done this, killed all these people?

I'd think about that another day.

I did the seventies, the eighties, and the nineties, the topmost white boxes. I stopped looking at the names, or the cases, and settled for grouping them by year. I didn't want to see Lash's name on any more files. It had been hard enough seeing all those from 1962.

When I got to the years 2000-2009, I began reading again, curious to know if Dev had arranged any jobs while he was in Rio. From the looks of this, he'd arranged a few by phone, but not many. *What had he been doing all that time, besides thinking of me, "wooing" me, and writing me that song? Taking a vacation? Oh, and doing fifty-plus women?*

I'd found a few pictures and love notes in with the files; not many, but a few. I found another one now, when I got the last file out of the box. It was tucked in the side. It was a picture of Dev, Lash, and a woman. They looked to be on a patio, with the ocean in the background, and the half moon shining down. The woman was behind Lash, leaning on his shoulder, smiling. She was darkly beautiful, her black hair long and wavy to her waist, her breasts easily D cups. But she wasn't really fat, just very curvy. In the picture, Lash was older, as he'd been when I first met him, but not scarred. The picture was dated December tenth.

Who was this woman? Why wasn't she here now? Had something happened to her? Lash hadn't been scarred on December tenth. But he'd been scarred by those last days of December.

Something bad had happened in those last days in Rio. What?

There was one thing I did know now for sure; while Devlin may have been lonely in Rio, Lash sure hadn't been. It was good Theo had dragged me to Camlyn's for testing. Lash had never used protection with Cin, or even offered to use it with me. He hadn't probably used any with this woman, either. *Who knew how many women he'd been with? Who knew if he really hadn't been with anyone else? He probably wasn't using anything with Gina, now…*

Suddenly disgusted with him—and myself for liking him—I shoved the picture in Devlin's memorabilia file, and pulled my hand out. My watch caught on a picture, almost tearing it as I jerked it out of the file. Letting out an exasperated breath, I picked it up off the floor. It was one of the first pictures I'd seen, the one of Devlin and the young man. There was something familiar, like a passing face you see in a restaurant that looks like one of your long-ago friends that turns out to just have a faint resemblance to the person you knew. But I couldn't think who this reminded me of. The easiest thing would be to think this was Lash. The date on the picture was right, for how old he probably was back in the nineteen-thirties. But this didn't look like Lash as he was now.

Lash was strikingly attractive now, to me at least. But I didn't find the man in the picture attractive in the slightest. His nose was too sharp, his eyes too squinty, his lips almost nonexistent, with a narrow face that resembled a rat's.

"Digging up old memories?" a hissing voice asked sarcastically.

"Must you always be lurking in the shadows?" I said, shooting him a smile.

"Sometimes," he replied, smiling. "What are you looking at so interestedly?"

"An old picture. The young man in it reminds me of someone, but I can't think who. I thought that the first time I saw it, months ago, but couldn't figure it out then, either."

"Let me see it."

I handed it to him. Lash took the picture in his hands, and looked at it.

"It was taken in New Orleans, near the Mississippi," he said after a minute, his tone heavy with memory. "It was a cool night, the breeze coming off the water smelling of fish, and the ocean. We were on a riverboat, partying. One of the better times."

"That's you?" I said, finally getting out the words.

"It's me," Lash said, handing me back the picture. "I know it doesn't look like me now, but that was me then. There's enough resemblance that your subconscious sees it."

"I don't understand," I said, trying to be delicate. "You must physically be the same age right now that you were then—"

"I am, but I don't understand any more than you do, Sar," Lash said with a shrug.

I furrowed my brow. "But you said you met Devlin when you were thirty seven—"

"Truthfully, I met him first when I was twenty one," Lash said, looking back at the picture. "The night that picture was taken. But we had a falling out, Sar, a bad one, after only spending a few days together. Some of that was my fault, and some of it was his. He didn't meet up with me again until two decades had passed, and I'd become the best assassin there was. That was when he said he wanted to hire me to be his personal bodyguard, and I accepted. I have been with him ever since, though it long ago stopped being about the money."

There was a lot of old pain and misery laced up in those casual words. There was a lot Lash was not saying, choosing to gloss it over instead. Although I was curious, I decided not to prod. My curiosity had gotten me in enough trouble with him lately.

"Your blood did something else to me besides heal me, and make me young," Lash said, looking up at me finally as he leaned against the filing cabinets. "It somehow changed my appearance, altered my bone structure. My face and lips are fuller now, my eyes seem wider apart, and I have visible cheekbones. I know I wasn't handsome back then. I looked dangerous and mean, like a born criminal. But I'm good looking now, or so Devlin tells me, anyway—"

I blushed, and dropped my eyes from his.

Lash stepped closer to me, until there wasn't an inch between us. "You like how I look now?" he whispered, giving me a penetrating look. His tongue flicked out to caress my earlobe.

"Stop that," I warned.

Lash's tongue traced its way down my throat, teasing me gently.

It would be so easy to reach out and touch him. To tell him I thought him very attractive, and kissable, and...*Sar, be an adult.* "Stop," I said harshly.

Lash drew his tongue back, smirking. "Answer my question, or I'll do more than lick you a little on your neck," he said huskily. "I can taste your arousal on your skin, Sar, no matter what I hear in your voice. Do you find me attractive now?"

Screw it; I'd wanted to say it anyway. "I find you very attractive, Lash," I said, rubbing my temple with my hand. "It was The Lust that made me want you first, no question. But I was attracted to you for yourself when we began to be good friends, even when you weren't handsome as you are now. I wasn't with you in the Everglades because of how you look now."

"Then why not be with me?" Lash hissed eagerly, licking me again. "It's not just meaningless sex with you, Sar. I was so pissed you would infer it even could be, after everything I told you that day in September. I thought I'd made my feelings clear. I told you I cared about you deeply—"

While I was dying to know what that actually meant, if I got him to tell me he loved me, my next words would likely be that I loved him back. Nakedness would quickly ensue. "Lash, you made it seem like sex for weres wasn't anything more than needing to come, and that once it was done, it was onto something else, or whomever else might be waiting in the nearby ferns to be noticed next. So why do you want so much to be my lover again?" I glanced over and held his eyes. "Or is this about hurting Theo?"

Lash leaned up against the filing cabinet, his hands on either side of me, trapping me as he leaned in close to my neck. "You want me to be blunt? Okay, how's this: I want to sheathe my body in yours, Sar," he breathed into my ear. "I want to thrust myself into you again and again, as deep as I can, to make love to you, and hear you scream my name in pleasure, like you did before. I want you because I care for you, because of the woman you are, not because of anything else."

God, all I had to do was hear his voice saying those words, and I wanted him so much…

"I was always attracted to you, like I'm attracted to most females, but that isn't why I want you like I do. It was so good between us that time in the Everglades—"

Wait a minute! He wanted to bed most females? OIY. That sure broke the spell. "I can't, Lash. Not now, of all times! Theo would take it as a revenge screw. And part of it would be. I'm not using you like that, or hurting him—"

"Theo doesn't have to know, Sar," Lash hissed seductively. "No one has to know. Dev doesn't care if we're lovers again. It'll be a secret, like it was the last time we were at Davy's. You and me, right here in this room, tonight. I'll do whatever you want me to—"

Waves of my teenage years washed over me. I wasn't some young girl to be seduced, today of all days! *"I* would know. I'm not doing that to Theo. While I don't regret being with you, Lash, it was wrong of me to betray the promise I made to him. I'm not going to make that mistake again. He was honest about what he did, much as I might have been hurt by it. Lastly, I'm not using you. You're my friend, and I respect you too much for that."

Lash nodded, and stepped away. "Understand, I want you very much, so I had to try," he hissed softly. "But I respect you more for telling me no, and honoring your promise you made. Mind you, I don't think less of you for giving into me when you did. We both saw the opportunity to be together and we took it. We care about one another. It wasn't just a fling; at least it wasn't to me—"

"It wasn't to me, either," I interrupted. "I care about you."

"I know that," Lash said. "I saw in your eyes then what I see in them now."

What did he see in my eyes that he was refusing to name? Could he see that I loved him?

"If you change your mind, or something else changes, you let me know," Lash said casually. "I won't bring it up again, or pressure you, though I might hug you from time to time. But know my offer doesn't expire." He shot me a smirk.

"All right," I said. "I can live with that."

"Come upstairs. You should eat something, and take it easy. Filing isn't hard, but you've been on your feet for hours. Your body should rest some; it's still healing."

He was right about that. I didn't need anything else to explain right now. "Sounds good," I said. "What's for dinner?"

Lash looked at me aghast, then breathed a sigh of relief when he saw I was kidding. "Shit, I can't cook! Well, unless you want another bagel or something I can microwave for you."

"I'll make something. There's got to be pasta or some ground beef in the kitchen."

"I've got T coming to train," Lash said regretfully. "I won't be done for an hour."

"Come in when you're done," I offered. "I'll make extra for you."

"You're on," Lash said eagerly.

* * * *

The evening was nice. I made pasta with ground beef for dinner. Lash came in as I was just dishing it out, and had some with me. We talked quietly about the newest movies slated for release this month. After, Lash went to check on the different guards, while Dev and I watched some bad horror film for an hour. But it was too bad—something about a killer mannequin—and we turned it off before it was over. Later, Lash came in to Dev's bedroom for a while, and had some scotch with him. I fell asleep listening to the two of them talking by the fire, sipping their Black Arts.

* * * *

The next day was another bad one. Devlin didn't want me to leave Hayden, worried I was going to be targeted by someone with a sniper rifle. He only let me leave on the condition that once he'd setup an office for me at Hayden I would agree to do the email and Internet work from his home. I thought it a little over the top, but agreed. I didn't have much choice. Dev was also unwilling to let me drive myself to Danial's house, even in one of the bulletproof Hummers. Since arriving with Lash would make Theo annoyed, I teleported to Danial's house instead.

There were piles of work. Theo, Danial, and Theoron had been busy, doing the meetings, and they were keeping up with the most urgent work. But the other emails and calls had gone unhandled, save for deleting the junk. I had thirty valid messages on voicemail and two hundred emails to sort through.

Danial came upstairs in the middle. "I'm sorry about what happened. You're welcome to stay here, if you want to."

I hugged him, and wanted to do more, not from lust but from a need for comfort. "Can you come to Hayden later tonight?"

Danial look surprised, but nodded. "I'll have Titus come and get me after my meetings." He kissed my hand. "I'm sorry not to stay, but I'm exhausted. The loss of Terian is taking its toll."

"How's that working? Business seems to be strong."

"Theo is attending meetings in the day, alone. He's the only company representative now that isn't a target of Ulysses. Theoron is also sleeping days this week, and I'm taking him to meetings, with Titus as transport to about half."

I guessed Danial was braving teaching Theoron how to drive en route to their other meetings, though I didn't ask. Hans had only given T the one lesson before he'd left. But maybe Warren had stepped in. "What about Brian?"

"T and I are taking Brian as backup to the meetings Titus can't attend. I want one of the two demon brothers with Elle and Devon at all times."

It made sense he was worried about Elle the most, as she was female. I wondered how Demi was handling Brian being in the line of fire again. He'd almost been killed before guarding me. But it wasn't really my business to ask. "How are Elle and Devon?"

"Elle is spending most mornings with Devon. She's trying with Bill to teach Devon some familiar spellings of words, shapes, and colors, so he will know enough words when he begins to speak to communicate with us."

That was great. I'd spent so much more time with Elle when she was young, nearly every waking moment those first few months. She had learned so fast to speak because I'd tried so hard to communicate with her, to make up for Theo not being there. With Devon, I'd relied more on Theo to translate for me Devon's needs and wants. I'd continued to work part-time, leaving him in Cia's care, or Elle's, sometimes. I hadn't thought it mattered at the time. But now realization made me feel guilty. "Good."

I walked downstairs with Danial. When he went to bed, I got a sandwich, then brought it upstairs, wolfing it down as I typed answers to e-mails.

When it was time to leave for my appointment with the marriage counselor, I called Theo on his cell, and told him I'd meet him there, to have the extra time to work. He said that was fine, and hung up without saying goodbye.

I was able to get most of the e-mail work finished by the time I needed to teleport. The filing there wasn't too bad. It could wait until tomorrow.

* * * *

Therapy with Theo was a debacle. Not only did we have to discuss our recent loss of the house, but also Theo talked to Carol and I about being with Jenny, about how he hadn't meant to be with her, but that he knew he needed that now. He was defensive, I was resentful, and the session ended with him storming out early, as he had last time. I didn't cry this time, though.

"Sar, something seems different," Carol said probingly.

I looked at her, trying to conceal my irritation. *You think?* Still, there was no point in being a bitch. "This is Theo as he really is, Carol. To be with a werecougar female was what he'd needed all along. The magic seems to have repressed his true feelings and needs, like I suspected it might be doing. Now it's broken."

"Sar, unless you let him be with her, there isn't much hope for your marriage," Carol interjected. "This is a common pitfall for were/non-were marriages, though I thought you two had somehow been spared that conflict, as it's never come up in the months you've been coming to see me. But you should know the statistics: almost all marriages with this issue break up within a few years, unless the non-were partner lets their husband or wife be with a lover for sex, or changes into a were of their partner's type themselves to save their marriage."

That was consoling. *Not.* "The second isn't an option for me, though I'm really considering the first."

"Sar, it's true that this might be better for Theo, for him to have a female he can be with in animal form. I don't know about Jenny, but for Theo, this would be fairer than him having to be just with you—"

Fair or not, I didn't want to hear it. I stood up. "Thank you for today. I'll be back next week."

Theo was waiting for me by his truck when I left Carol's office a few minutes later. "Sar, I need your answer," he said abruptly.

Chapter Fourteen

This was why he'd waited. *Bastard.* "Yes, do what you need to with her when you both change," I said tonelessly. "Please lay in a supply of protection for us."

Theo reached out and pulled me tightly to him, kissing my forehead. "Thank you," he said in relief. "I will. I'm glad you agreed—"

"Lash convinced me," I said, perversely glad at the way his face immediately closed down. "He said the urges you feel as an animal are strong, and that it's like breathing, to need that."

"I don't like him talking about that with you," Theo said, trying hard not to growl. "But I'm glad he explained it better than I did."

Why was I being such a bitch? We both needed to try harder. "Look, we need to go someplace and talk about things," I said, cutting him off. "There's a lot we haven't had time to discuss, that we can't talk about in front of Carol—"

"Get in the truck, and let's go see what's left of our house," Theo said, opening the door. "We can stop for lunch afterwards, for comfort food. I have a feeling we're going to need it."

* * * *

It was horrible seeing our house in ruins. My truck wasn't wrecked, at least. Theo checked it over, and pronounced it okay. "It's good you hadn't moved the tractor inside for the winter yet," he said bitterly. "Or it would be just burnt metal, like the lawnmower."

I nodded, but didn't speak.

Our chain saws, wood splitter, and garden tools were all okay. My birdfeeders hanging in the tree were also okay, though the paint on the metal had bubbled from the heat of the flames. It made me sad to think the birds this winter would be out of luck. I wouldn't be living here to put out food regularly. But I could take my feeders to Dev's for the winter, and nourish his wild birds.

With Theo's help, I removed them and put them in my truck.

I looked at the garage. With some repainting, the metal side that had been blackened would be okay. Morton buildings were made to last. While the backyard fence had burned, the garage was far enough from the house it had been protected. I mentally thanked God, my neighbors, and the volunteer firemen that there was this much left. It had been their fast response time that had saved the forest, and the garage.

We packed the various salvageable tools, extra birdseed, planting pots, extra potting soil, and peat moss into my truck bed. I left the garbage cans. We'd need to use them in the spring when we rebuilt…

My body broke out in sweat. Despite everything that had burned, my bloody clothes had not. They were still in the garbage bag, buried underneath the rest of the garbage from this week. Quickly, I put the two garbage cans in the truck along with the recycling bin, and ran them down to the curb. Garbage pickup was the next morning. I'd make a trip back tomorrow to get them, teleporting maybe. There wasn't another option.

Theo was where I had left him, looking into the wreckage of the collapsed house. What was left had all fallen into the basement. When the oil tank in the basement ignited, the foundation had cracked from the heat of the fire leading to that wall caving in. I wondered if the well was okay, then decided I'd probably need to have it checked. The pipes might have frozen at the surface.

"Henry's son said he would come back this week, and take care of the water," Theo said, kicking some debris. "We can rebuild, Sar. It was just a house."

"But it was my house," I said softly, beginning to cry again.

Theo came over and wrapped me in his arms, apologizing for being so thoughtless. "Don't cry, please don't cry," he murmured. "We'll start rebuilding in the spring, Sar. And we'll build a good house, for you and me and Devon. You can plant a new garden. I'll buy you a new lawn tractor."

I tried to smile, and wiped my eyes. "A John Deere?" I said hopefully.

"A top of the line John Deere," Theo said, smiling down at me. "With a padded seat, and everything."

"Are you sure you want to rebuild? It might be safer to stay with Danial, to build a home on his land."

"I want us to have our own home," Theo said. "I've enjoyed living here with you. Devon loves it here, Sar. And I want him to be here in the spring, so we can take walks with the dogs, and roast marshmallows over the fire, and look at the stars."

"Good," I said, hugging him. "I want to rebuild, too."

An expensive pickup pulled into the drive, and Theo turned with a growl.

"Relax," I said. "It's just Henry's son, Dave."

Henry had been a neighbor of mine who worked construction. He also had done snowplowing on the side, until a sudden heart attack had cut his life short one summer afternoon. I hadn't heard until the funeral was months old. His relative Dave had inherited the house and land, including the quarry. Dave was a good man, but his one passion in life was to hunt. Since he ate most everything he killed, and he obeyed the game laws to the letter, I didn't have a problem with it. Theo had felt uncomfortable around him since seeing the mounted elk and deer heads in his living room, and the black bear rug on the floor. But it had been the stuffed bobcat that he hadn't been able to take his eyes off of. That most of the mounted dead animals could be attributed to Henry—and that Dave only hunted for food, not trophies—made me feel easier about my new neighbor.

"Sar, Theo," Dave said gruffly. "I am sorry as hell this happened to you good people."

"Thank you for what you did," I said, nodding to him. "We have what we do because of your quick action."

Dave nodded. "If you want to rebuild in the spring, I can help. I can bulldoze some of the debris, and get it buried, or carted away."

"We'd appreciate it," Theo said, shaking his hand. "But we'll pay you for your time, Dave."

"We're neighbors," Dave said, shrugging. "Forget it."

"Thanks then," Theo said nodding. "And if you need some help with one of your construction jobs, let me know. I can lift and carry, if nothing else."

"Not necessary," Dave said gruffly. "It's the least I can do. I'll put the cans inside your garage tomorrow, after pickup, so you won't have to make a trip back here from wherever you're staying. Take care, Sar. Theo."

Dave got back in his truck, and pulled off, with a last wave.

"I'm always surprised how nice people are out here," Theo said, as we waved good-bye.

"That's country," I answered. "Dave is one of the best examples."

Theo and I got the last of the garage packed up and into my truck. "Should I come back for anything else?" I asked Theo.

"Probably. I can check into storage, if you want. There's not room at Danial's. Hans left with his vehicle, but Danial bought a Land Rover for Theoron, so the spot's already taken."

Danial was spoiling him. I was betting it wasn't a used Land Rover. But at least he'd be safe. "Let me ask Dev about it. He has more room at Hayden. The tractor is going to take up a lot of room."

"Fine," Theo said, though I could tell he wasn't happy.

A battered SUV came down the driveway. Theo turned with a growl again. "Hush, its just Mark," I said. "I recognize the vehicle."

"Why's he here?"

"Probably driving by, and saw our truck," I said. "He lives a few streets over. News like this travels fast, Theo. Everyone in town knows by now."

Mark pulled up, and got out. "How're you doing?" he asked, concerned.

Mark was about my age, with a wife and a house full of kids, mostly boys. I'd been working with him when I'd first met Danial, at the metal fabrication shop in the town just north of my house. He was a good worker, and we got along fine. The only thing I had against him was he was an avid snowmobiler.

"We've been better," Theo said, looking at the ruins.

"I got something to help you," Mark said, his tone both secretive and angry.

I looked at him in confusion. "What?"

"I was out last night at about four a.m., with my brother, riding—"

Snowmobiling was what he meant.

"—we were heading back from a long ride, and his sled broke down. It was hours fixing the damn thing. And then we saw a white Explorer barreling out of your driveway, as we were riding by. I knew it wasn't you guys, and then we saw the flames—"

"You called the fire department!" I exclaimed.

Mark nodded. "My cousin and my uncle are on the volunteer squad. I called them on my cell phone, and they got here fast. They would have been here sooner, but there was some ice on the roads—"

There had been ice. That had been one of the reasons Lash had asked me to teleport his truck. He'd worried about us sliding into a ditch on the way to Hayden.

"What did the vehicle look like? Who was driving?" Theo growled.

I put my hand on his arm. I didn't want him changing in front of Mark. "Can you give us any details?"

"I saw two men, but no one else," Mark said. "Probably a '10 model, or maybe an '11. It wasn't a new Expedition. There was rust on it." He pulled a slip of paper from his pocket. "I got the license plate," he said, his eyes glinting. "New York numbers."

"Thanks," Theo said, both eager and grateful.

Mark handed it him. "I know you deal in some darker stuff. Get the motherfuckers. The police won't do shit. Word around town is they think it was kids playing around. But I saw the men, and this was arson. This kind of shit shouldn't be allowed to slide."

"They'll be dealt with," Theo said darkly. "I'll be calling today to follow up on this. We owe you—"

"You don't owe me. Just get the fuckers, Theo," Mark said flatly, climbing back into his SUV. "They tried to kill her and you. It was just luck you weren't home, and you aren't both dead. Watch your asses." With a wave, Mark drove away.

I got on my cell, and called Devlin immediately. He answered on the first ring. "How's it going?" he said carefully.

"Two things," I said quickly. "First, a friend of mine saw the men who torched the house. They got the license plate—"

"Give it to me," Devlin said, cutting me off. "Lash, pick up the kitchen extension."

"I'm here," Lash hissed. "Go ahead."

Theo gave me the paper. I read the plate number to Devlin.

"New York plates," Lash hissed.

He could tell that from the number? "Yes."

"I'll get on this," Devlin said with authority. "What else?"

"My barn is okay, but we've got a lot of equipment. I don't want to leave it here, in case it gets burned some other night. Can you arrange for a tractor-trailer to come here, and pick it up? I'm not good enough to bring it all by teleportation, and I wouldn't know where to teleport it to anyway, or if you have room enough at Hayden—"

"Titus could usually teleport it, but he's exhausted from working with Terian while still trying to take Danial and Theo where they need to go." Devlin sighed. "I've got plenty of room, an extra four car garage that's mostly empty. I'll arrange for it to be done later this week, Sar."

"Thanks," I said.

"When are you coming home?" Devlin asked. "It's already four."

Kind of late for Theo's proposed lunch. It would have to be dinner. "I'll be home by dusk. We're exhausted, but my truck is okay, and we salvaged everything we could from the garage—"

"Sar, your truck wasn't torched?" Lash asked.

"No—"

"Is your transmitter still there in your truck for the front gate, and garage at Hayden?"

"Yes, it's still there."

"Ulysses's men should have taken it, to get the signals. That they didn't means they were very stupid to have missed it, or very smart, bringing what they needed to get the signal so they could make it look like they missed it. We'll recode everything this afternoon to be safe," Lash hissed. "Come and see me when you get home. I'll give you a new transmitter for your truck. They'll patch you through at the gate manually tonight."

"All right." I looked over at Theo. He was busy dialing his own mobile. "I'm going to go eat something," I said wearily. "See you both soon."

Theo was already in conversation with Danial when I turned around again. He hung up after giving him a minute-long synopsis of what had happened. "Let's go eat," he said, taking my hand.

I followed him to one restaurant we both favored, remembering almost nothing about the ride except for the relentless banging of tools in the back of my vehicle. I was too numb right then to care anymore about much of anything, least of all scenery.

We got a table, and our regular waitress came over to serve us with her friendly smile. "You guys are early tonight," she said pleasantly. "What sounds good to you?"

Theo ordered a steak, and I ordered fettuccini with ham. Comfort food was good. I was really going to have to ask Devlin for that treadmill. My jeans were beginning to groan. Usually that fact would have been something that made me pause, and call back my order in favor of a healthier choice. But tonight I was too tired to care.

We had a pleasant dinner. It was over dessert that things went south, when Theo started in out of nowhere. "I don't want you to give another Oath to Devlin. You don't need to be with him anymore to live, and you can't have children, either. There's no reason for you to go to him, or to do what he wants you to do. It's the same for Danial, though I understand if you want to give him an Oath, or spend time with him. He'd be devastated to lose you. But I'll agree only on the condition that he not give you any of his blood, so you become dependent on him again to live—"

"Don't you think that's my decision to make, Theo?" I said bluntly.

"No, because you're my wife," Theo said carefully. "It's our decision."

I didn't think this was "our" decision. It was my life, and that made it my decision. But Theo's tone held conviction; he really believed he had the right to tell me what to do. At that moment, I realized suddenly that sometime in the last year, Theo had stopped asking me what I wanted, and started telling me what I should want and what I was going to do. I'd gone along with it, because I'd thought that was right, that a wife should listen to her husband. But there was a difference between giving him a say in my actions, and having him dictate them to me.

I already had another man who also believed he had the right to tell me what to do. Him I usually listened to, even when I didn't want to. But with Theo, those days were over. "Dev's not going to go for it," I said, eating the last forkful of my pie. "He already wants me to live with him half the time—"

"You didn't tell me that," Theo said loudly.

Several diners turned around to look at us.

"Lower your voice," I said coldly.

Theo glared at me, and said nothing.

"You need to stop living in Theo-land, and get back in the real world with the rest of us," I said bluntly. "Devlin is not going to give me up, not ever. He said nothing was coming between us, when I asked him to consider me not giving him another promise. His exact words were 'nothing, not even death'. If you try to keep me from him, he'll kill you."

"Fine, stay with him for now," Theo snapped. "You're safest there while I'm working, anyway. But spend time with Danial, too, and don't let either of them take your blood again—"

"They aren't going to until it goes back to normal."

"—and don't take any of their blood, not even to heal a wound—"

His voice was almost strident. *Why was he so upset?* This was more than jealousy. "Theo, what's gotten into you?"

"I almost lost you before to Dev, and I'm not doing it again," Theo growled. "You're my wife, not his; no matter that he wears that gold band like it means something—"

"We've been over this a thousand times—"

"—and I wonder if Devlin knows as much as he says he does," Theo added darkly. "What if he's just hoping, and it's in vain? What if your blood doesn't revert? Devlin will only wait so long before he takes your blood again. He's not famous for his patience. If he gives you his blood, and you aren't resistant to it anymore—"

I shifted uneasily in my chair. Theo was right, Dev wouldn't wait forever.

"—stay away from Lash, too," Theo growled. "You living there, I know he'll be hanging around you, hoping to get back into your pants, so make sure he keeps his distance—"

"Any other commands or duties, general?" I said sarcastically.

Theo glared at me, but at least he shut up.

We ate in silence for a few minutes.

"Terian is doing better," Theo offered. "That's some good news. I'll be so relieved when he's back at Danial's. I never worried about Devon or Elle when he was around—"

"Rip's around."

"Rip spends most of the time guarding Danial, wherever he is," Theo said bluntly. "And Danial is out a lot at night doing business meetings. We figure he's going to be Ulysses's prime target. But I have other enemies. As a father, I worry."

His heartfelt words were really a snide remark that my mothering instinct was lacking because I wasn't frantic with worry. That brought to mind a nice little question for him that I'd been meaning to ask for a few days now. "Theo, did you tell Terian about us having sex? About what I'd do to you sometimes? Because when he said things to me that night he turned demon, he pretty much said you gave him a blow-by-blow description. And I mean blow, Theo."

Theo went beet red. "I never told him details," he whispered. "I just said you were amazing at it, that I loved that you liked oral sex, that you'd do that for me. None of the other women I was ever with acted like they wanted to at all. And even when Tasha did it for me one time, she wouldn't—"

"Stop, I get the picture," I said, closing my eyes. "How did you think that was not giving details?"

"I'm sorry I bragged about how good you were at it," Theo said, shamed. "It was just obvious Terian envied me having a woman who liked to do that."

"Theo, Terian envied you *me*," I said deliberately. "Hearing about our sex life might have been something that added to him losing control. And did it occur to you how I'd feel, when I learned you told him graphic details about us?"

"I know that now," Theo said, guilty. "I'm sorry, too, for not considering how you would feel. I won't ever say anything again about it, I promise."

I wanted to ask him if that included Jenny, too, but felt too disgusted just thinking about it. "Thank you."

"Come on, it will be dark soon," Theo said, getting to his feet. "I want you behind locked doors, where you're safe."

His possessive words made me wince. But while I was still annoyed at him telling Terian about our sex life, I gave him a kiss good-bye at the restaurant, anyway.

Theo insisted on waiting until I was within Hayden's gates before he drove off. As I drove up to the garage, the door opened as if by magic, Lash's form framed in my headlights, waiting for me. He moved over as I pulled my truck inside, then shut the door behind me. I shut off the engine, manually rolling down the window so I could give him my transmitter.

He handed a new one back through the window. "I'm glad you're home," Lash hissed, opening the truck door for me. "Devlin confirmed that was Ulysses's truck that was at your house. He was behind the fire."

It had been strange when Devlin asked me about coming home earlier. It was doubly odd to hear it from Lash. But Hayden was going to be home for a while. Danial's house had been a home for me once, but with Jenny there now, it couldn't be home to me anymore, no matter what Danial might want. That made me sad, because that was just another thing I'd lost.

"Sar, what is it?" Lash asked, touching my arm. "You smell of sadness again."

"Did Dev locate Ulysses?" I asked. "Give me some good news."

"No," Lash said. "But Michael already jumped the gun. He heard about your house burning from his spy network and sent a man to kill Ulysses's parents, and grab his sister. He dropped her off here earlier. The death of his parents will make Ulysses act, if anything is going to. But until he does, I want you safe, Sar, which means close to me."

I left my truck as it was. There was nothing that needed dealing with tonight, except the bird feeders. I got them out of the cab, and put them by the door, to give me a visual reminder to fix them the next day.

"You are moving in with Dev and me," Lash said happily. "You like birdwatching?"

"I need to clean these up, but they should still work," I said, ignoring his words. "Do you have any metal paint?"

"Sure. I've got spray paint," Lash said easily, eyeing me. "What color you want?"

Spray paint? Did he do graffiti? He was the type for sure. "Good, I'll need to borrow some. Color doesn't matter. I just need to fix where the paint bubbled up—"

"Devlin would be glad to buy you some new ones," Lash said curiously. "You don't have to fix these, Sar—"

Just like that, I lost it.

Chapter Fifteen

Tears formed, even as I tried to blink them back. "I don't want new ones. These were mine," I said, beginning to cry again.

Lash took me in his arms, and hugged me tightly. "Shh, Sar, don't cry—"

The dam I'd been holding back so long burst wide open. "I lost all my things, Lash! All I have are a few boxes! Everything else is ashes! My books, my DVD collection, most of my clothes! And I'm losing Theo, and T's growing up so fast, and I'll probably lose Devon, too—"

"I can't speak for your cat," Lash hissed softly. "But you aren't going to lose T. He loves you and you're his Mom. Devon loves you, too. I could see it when you were holding him, and he didn't want to leave you."

"But he'll love her more, because she's cougar!" I wailed, mortified to be losing control this badly when I'd held it together all day. "She'll be his Mom!"

"Shh," Lash said. He kissed me very, very lightly on the lips, then applied more pressure. The sensation wasn't sexy, it was reassuring and comforting. I was so shocked, I stopped crying.

Lash ended the kiss, then looked down at me with his dark eyes. "You have your memories, Sar. Your pets are alive. We'll get you more clothes, and replace your books."

"I'm sorry," I said, beginning to tear up again. "I don't mean to be one of those weak hysterical women, falling apart all the time."

"You're stronger than most men," Lash said affectionately. "What you lost wasn't insignificant. Everyone needs to cry sometimes. Even me, much as I hate doing it."

I wasn't sure what to say to that, so I kept quiet, taking comfort from him.

When I had calmed down a few moments later, he released me. "Come inside," Lash said, opening the garage door. "Dev's waiting for you with Venus."

We went into the kitchen. Devlin was feeding our daughter. His stubble was back, and he was also almost glowing, his skin was so luminous. It was good to see he was revitalized, even if his appearance was rough. Venus held a tiny cup to her mouth, and was sipping from it daintily. Its contents looked a little like blood, but it was probably liquefied steak.

"Lash told me Theoron liked this," Devlin said, smoothing Venus's golden curls. "She likes it, too."

Venus looked up at me. She waited a full moment, then triumphantly said, "Mommy."

I didn't need to look at Devlin to know he was beaming. I gave her a big smile, and crouched in front of her. "That's right. Now can you give me a hug?"

She hugged me around the neck tightly. The breath went out of me in a whoosh from her strength.

"Not so hard," Devlin said gently. "Mommy's mortal. You can't hug her as hard as you hug Lash and I and Serena."

"Is that why she smells like food?" Venus said.

I gaped at her. "She's clearly inherited my bluntness."

"She's a prodigy," Devlin said, so prideful I was swimming in it. "She's saying full sentences at only a month and a half."

"Probably, Venus," Lash said gently, sitting down at the table. He put down a cup of his own.

I pulled up a chair and sat down myself. "So did everyone have dinner?"

"Yes. Can I have popcorn?" Venus asked winsomely.

I marveled sometimes that she was my daughter. She was so unearthly beautiful. But most of that spectacular beauty she got from her father. "Sure, after you finish your drink."

V gulped it down, then belched loudly. Lash burst out laughing, but Devlin looked appalled. "You are not to do that!" he said in a strangled voice. "Young ladies don't do that, Venus."

"Uncle Lash does it," Venus said petulantly.

Lash colored, and looked at the wall.

"Uncle Lash?" I teased.

"Lash is not a young lady, despite his pretty appearance now," Devlin said in a lilting tone. "You are not to do that. If you must, you say 'excuse me' after. Understand?"

"Yes," Venus said with a shrug. "Excuse me."

"Sar, there's sushi for you in the fridge," Lash said, apologetic. "I was going to wait, but I realized you might not be hungry after eating lunch so late, so I ended up eating without you."

"Thanks, I'm full. I'll have some with you tomorrow."

"Good," Lash said. "I saved some of mine for tomorrow, too."

I looked at him oddly, then at his drink of liquefied steak. "But if you aren't hungry—"

"This is just an after-dinner snack," he supplied. "Like dessert."

I wisely kept my thoughts to myself, and began making popcorn. Lash and Venus ate the first batch entirely before I got any, so I made another. Later, the four of us watched a movie. Devlin and Lash enjoyed it, though I thought it was a little too graphic and grim for Venus. But for the most part she wasn't watching it, she was sleeping near to Lash in the crook of his legs. Devlin was spooning me, so I too ended up missing much of it from my exhaustion. As the movie finished, I realized belatedly with some worry that Danial hadn't · appeared.

Devlin noticed I was distracted, and guessed the reason. "Danial is coming on Friday. He's doing his best to both keep up with his business, and to monitor for any sign of Ulysses. He is meeting with Michael tonight to try to get some more information from his spy network. This has gone on far too long already."

"It has," Lash hissed, suddenly furious. "Is he going to call once he talks to Michael?"

"Yes," Devlin said, getting to his feet, then helping me up. "But you and I'll talk to him. Sar, you are going to bed. I don't want you to get sick again, and you're clearly worn out. Hold still, so I can pick you up."

Devlin acted like I was going to protest, but I just nodded, holding out my arms expectantly. Devlin carried me up to bed, and Lash carried Venus, who was still sleeping. I was beginning to think he put her to bed most nights. Devlin helped me take off my clothes, and get into my nightgown.

"The computer system is set up, Sar," he said as he took my dirty clothes into the bathroom. "You can do your work for Danial from here tomorrow."

"Dev, I need to go see Devon. I miss him—"

"You know if you go to Danial's you may run into Jenny," he cautioned.

I nodded. "I know. But I can't avoid her, either. It's better if I face her, anyway. I need to know woman to woman what she feels for Theo, and what she might be expecting from the relationship they have now. I don't want any more surprises."

Devlin sat beside me. "Sar, you need to remember something, too. Theo isn't using anything with her. She may already be pregnant. It's true she'll lose it if she shifts form, but if she got pregnant as cougar, and stayed cougar—"

I hadn't thought of that. "I need to ask her that, too," I said, feeling overwhelmed. "It will be just my luck to find out she always wanted to be a mother."

"Some women are like that," Devlin commented. "You aren't, but a lot of women are, Sar. It's normal to feel that way—"

"Not with my husband, it's not."

Devlin seemed about to say something in reply, then wisely closed his mouth. "Get some rest. I'll be in later. I'll tell you in the morning what Danial found out."

"Will Titus be here tomorrow?" I asked, yawning. "I need to talk to him."

"He'll be here at least in the afternoon, to help guard you and Venus," Devlin said, nodding. "I have a few jobs to arrange."

"More house painting?" I said, trying to smile but grimacing instead.

"Demolitions, à la Lash," Devlin said, smiling with his mouth and not his eyes. "Not a lot, but these particular jobs called for his expertise. Two of the clients asked for him specifically by name—"

"Does he like it?" I said abruptly. "Tell me the truth, Dev."

Devlin looked at me a moment, as if searching for how to phrase his reply. "He used to. In his youth, he loved to kill. But you should know it was always men, Sar. He never would kill a woman, or a child. He refused to, though he never gave a reason."

"And now?"

"After coming back from Rio, Lash told me he needed a vacation. He didn't give a reason, though I can guess his reason now: his regenerative system was failing. So he wasn't doing any jobs then. Very soon after our return from the Gathering, I needed him to stay here to watch you, because of The Lust. He also took last summer off, too, for the most part." He paused. "After he got back from the Everglades, he said that he was ready to go back to work. So he's been doing some of my arrangements for me. The money's not as good for him just doing security for me or making arrangements, but it's still twice what Theo makes doing what he does for Danial."

"But he's not happy staying out of the action, is what you're saying?"

"He's not likely happy missing out on easy money," Devlin corrected. "These two jobs are a half million each, and shouldn't be very hard for him. Though to be honest, Lash never truly cared about money anyway, so long as he had a woman to share his bed, and some alcohol to drink."

The way he said it made me think that those were both commodities to Lash. "Didn't he ever have a girlfriend? Someone who cared for him?"

"There were women that liked him, over the years," Devlin said, eyeing me carefully. "But Lash never seemed to care for them, beyond having a favorite woman to have sex with. And he preferred to pay them for their time, though I don't know if that was because it made it easier to leave them when I moved operations, or because down deep, he felt like a woman wouldn't want to be with him if he didn't pay her—"

"Stop, this is too awful," I said in a tortured whisper. "No one should feel like that."

"Sar, don't feel sorry for him," Devlin said, smiling faintly. "Lash hasn't been lonely for female attention, even though he wasn't conventionally handsome. He didn't get the kind of attention I did, but he didn't go without often. And remember, he wasn't looking for love. Not all men are. I sure wasn't when I bedded you."

"Weren't you?" I contended. "Down deep, I think that was exactly what you were looking for."

Devlin regarded me for a long moment, then he took off his clothes. He got in bed, gathering me close so we were again spooning. "Maybe I was," he said finally. "But sometimes men just like sex, Sar. Look at the men that go to Serena. And she doesn't love them—"

I became very, very quiet, stilling my movements.

Devlin rolled his eyes, because he understood at once why I'd frozen up. "It's Nick, isn't it?" he asked with a sigh, moving slightly so I lay on my back as he leaned over me. "Serena has feelings for him?"

"I think so, yes," I said reluctantly, hating to betray Serena's confidence. "How did you know it was him?"

"I was afraid of this," Devlin stated, ignoring my question. "Why do women always need sex to be more than release? Why does there always have to be emotion tied up in it?"

"Women aren't the only ones," I said, my tone so cool it had ice in it. "I seem to recall a man who said he only wanted sex, and then told me he loved me after—"

"Hush," Devlin said gently. "I'm not so much angry, Sar, as irritated. Serena was doing a good job keeping the single males calm. It was a good arrangement. Now, no matter how this love affair of hers turns out, that arrangement is most likely going to end."

"I know," I persisted. "But doesn't she deserve to be happy, too?"

"Everyone deserves to be happy," Devlin said firmly. "I just wish this didn't have to happen now."

While I couldn't get Devlin to help, maybe I could get his aid in minimizing the damage to my friend. "I told her not to say anything to him about her feelings. I saw them together, and I don't think he loves her."

"I know he doesn't," Devlin said flatly. "Nick sees another woman in town on weekends, a kind of girlfriend. Klara is werebear, like him. He uses protection with her, on my insistence, and gets checked out each time after he's with her as bear."

Why are so many handsome men always jerks? "This is awful. I know it's not really two-timing, but still, Serena doesn't know. She's pinned her hopes on him. What should we do?"

"Nothing," Devlin replied. "We have enough to deal with. Serena and Nick will have to sort it out on their own, or wait until we have some time after Ulysses is caught. And it's really not our business, it's between Serena and Nick. If she wants him to stop coming to her, that's fine. I'll only say something to her if she stops servicing the other males."

"I don't know if I can *not* tell her he's seeing someone else," I said uncertainly. "I know how I felt, when I was in her shoes."

"Serena was warned to say nothing to you, if she wanted to keep her job. As for Lash, he's my best friend, and best friends are supposed to keep that kind of thing secret," Devlin said, rolling his eyes. "Besides, he made it very clear to me how much he disapproved of what I was doing every single time I talked to him that week. He was on your side even then, Sar."

I didn't reply. I was not going to discuss his treachery with his old lover Catherine. It would surely lead to a fight.

Devlin looked down at me. "Are you still nursing a grudge over that?" His words were hesitant, but underneath was a dangerous current.

Same old Dev. "No. She's dead, and you said you wouldn't do that to me again."

"I won't," Devlin said softly, kissing my head. "I gave you my word, Sar."

We would see. "It's late, Dev." I nestled close to him. "Goodnight."

* * * *

The next morning, I awoke to find Devlin sleeping next to me, but not on my chest. It was so odd I woke him, to make sure he was okay.

"I'm okay," Devlin said, smirking at my curious expression. "I like to sleep on my side, too, and spoon you. I didn't see you that often before, so I wanted to always sleep in your arms. But I don't have to clutch you so hard to me, Sar, now that you're here with me willingly, and you're staying for the next few weeks, at least."

Theo was not going to go with that. No way. In fact, I had to get to work right away, before he called and asked me why I hadn't done e-mail yet. And I was going to have to go to Danial's every week for a few hours just to file. I couldn't do that from here, much as it might have been easier.

"I need to shower," I said, yawning. "Danial said he had a lot of work for me to do."

"Let's shower, and then I'll show you the set up," Devlin said, offering me his hand.

I let him lead me to the bathroom, happy in the knowledge he was comfortable in his own skin again.

* * * *

Devlin had done an excellent job. The computer set up was state of the art, and also easy to use, much as Danial's office space for me had been. There was only one thing off-putting: he'd set up my new office within his own study, near the dungeon. Right now, the dungeon was occupied. In fact, a woman was screaming loudly.

"Is that Ulysses's sister?" I asked pensively.

Devlin rolled his eyes. "I knew I'd have to help him," he muttered. "Almost always, when it's a woman." He stormed off.

I followed him, the desire to see my enemy's sister compelling. As I walked down the hall, the light grew fainter; the bright electric lights, drywall, and trim abruptly changed to dimly lit recessed lights in cold stone walls that were sweating moisture. Then I walked past empty cells with metal bars that resembled an underground jail.

Devlin strode to the next-to-last cell. A woman was there, cringing on the floor. Lash was before her, crouching down in front of her, baring his fangs. He took no notice of us, though the woman looked at us pleadingly, especially me. She had Ulysses's bone structure, brown hair, and green eyes.

"Help me!" she screamed. "He's going to bite me!"

"I will bite you," Lash hissed. "Tell me what you know of your brother's plans, or I'll pump enough venom into you to stop your heart, Diana—"

"I don't know anything!" she screamed, cringing back against the bars. "Please, I swear, I don't know anything!" She looked at Devlin desperately, reaching through the bars with grasping hands. "Please! Don't let him hurt me. Save me! Don't let him kill me! I graduate next spring, I'm going to be a nurse! Please, I only ever wanted to help people—"

I closed my eyes, leaning back against the far wall. Everything in my nature told me she was innocent, and I should help her. But Lash's interrogation might be the only thing keeping my loved ones from a terrible death. Devlin might deserve punishment for all his crimes, but Danial and my children did not. I had to let this play out without interfering.

Devlin opened the cell door with a metal clang, making my eyes snap open. He crouched near her, then glared at Lash. "Get out of here, you." Lash hissed at him ferociously, then exited, taking a stance over near me. Devlin sat beside Diana. "Come here, child," he crooned softly.

Dev is playing the "good vampire" to Lash's menacing monster in an effort to find out how much Diana knows of her brother's plans. Would it avail us?

Diana tried to burrow into his arms, beginning to cry. "Hush," Devlin said softly. "I won't let anyone hurt you. You're safe. But what this man said to you is true. Your brother plans to hurt my brother—"

"Devlin?" Diana blurted, then clapped her hand over her mouth.

Ulysses knows of Danial, of Devlin's relationship to him…one small fact making everyone I love in danger. But he had not shared with his sister physical descriptions…something Devlin would undoubtedly exploit.

Devlin nodded. "Yes, and I love him like you love your brother, Diana. So I need to know everything you know, so I can stop your brother from killing him."

"You promise you won't hurt him?" Diana said, looking up at Devlin with wide eyes. "I can't lose him. I just lost my parents in a terrible fire."

I closed my eyes. The act of arson that had claimed Diana's parents had been Michael's work. He was taking an eye for an eye.

"I promise," Devlin lied smoothly. "I'm sure if I sat your brother down and talked to him, explained things to him, I could get him to change his mind."

"No, you won't," Diana said unhappily. "I've tried for the last four years to get him to let go. Heather was always a loose cannon. She liked men who weren't good for her. It was only a matter of time before one of them got her into something that was going to hurt her—"

"Your sister was twenty-five," Devlin said. "Old enough to make up her own mind about what she wanted out of life. She was the age you are now, correct?"

Diana nodded, wiping her tears from her eyes. "She was going to go to Africa, work with the doctors there. She wanted to help people."

"You became a nurse for her, to honor her memory?"

Diana nodded, smiling through her tears.

I wanted to throw up. Devlin was playing her like an instrument.

Devlin tilted her head up, and then kissed her passionately. Diana stiffened, then melted in his arms, groaning as her mouth moved insistently on his, her body pressing and rubbing against him. Devlin drew back from her. "Do you want me to kiss you again?" he said lustily.

I saw in her besotted eyes that she was lost: he was all she saw, all she wanted. Dev had given her some of his blood, enough to enthrall her. I'd always wondered how quick that worked with a normal woman, a.k.a., one whose blood wasn't resistant like mine. Now I knew. *Shudder.*

"Please," Diana whispered. "You taste so good, like nothing I've ever tasted before."

"Tell me what you know, all of it," Devlin said softly, brushing his lips on hers lightly. "And I'll kiss you again, Diana."

"I don't know much," she said quickly, looking up at Devlin pleadingly. "Only that Ulysses came for a visit in September. He told my parents he'd finally found Devlin's weak spot, that there was a woman who was vampire that was going to help him. He said that he'd finish Devlin for good. But something happened. He called later that week, and said his revenge was going to have to wait, that he was leaving the country, to be careful, and not to worry—"

"We know that," Devlin said softly. "When he returned, what was his plan?"

"He didn't tell me," Diana responded, just softly. "He called me last week. I hadn't heard from him since he'd left. He said he'd found out that Devlin had a brother, Danial. He'd hypnotized some woman, Carol—"

Oh, shit.

"—she'd told him that there was a woman Devlin loved, really loved, named Sar, that Danial loved, too. This woman had helped Devlin escape last time, with the help of a man called Lash. And that Sar had children with Danial, a girl named Elle, and a boy called Theoron, and also a child with Devlin, a girl called Venus—"

Lash let out a loud, angry hiss. Diana shrank into Devlin's embrace, looking at Lash with horror.

"Go on," Dev said softly, giving Diana another gentle kiss on the lips. Diana tried to kiss him again, but he held her back.

"That's it," Diana said half-heartedly. "My brother said he was going to tear down Devlin's world stone by stone, and that the next time Sar was in his grasp, he would kill her. That they were all going to pay for Heather, and for Devlin getting away."

I leaned back into the wall, my legs going weak. Lash put an arm around my waist, propping me up against him. "I won't let anyone hurt you," he hissed in my ear. "You're safe."

I clutched Lash like a life rope with my hands, my eyes riveted on Devlin and Diana.

Devlin kissed Diana again deeply. She practically orgasmed in his arms, shuddering and moaning. He pulled back from her and watched her blissful, eager face as if savoring it. Then he bared his teeth, and sank them into her throat. Diana let out a loud cry, clutching him close, and jerking in his arms. Devlin drank for about three minutes, his throat working as he swallowed down her life, sighing softly. Diana stroked his hair and cried out over and over, as if she couldn't get enough of the feeling of him drinking her down.

Dev drew back again to behold his victim, his expression again savoring. Diana's skin was faintly luminous, as mine had been that night Danial had given me a little too much of his blood. Her incisors were longer, too. "Diana, you love me, don't you?" he whispered, his golden eyes almost glowing in the gloom of the cell.

"I love you with everything I am," she whispered, lolling in his arms. "Will you make love to me, Danial? I've never been with a man before. I wanted to be in love, and I hadn't ever fallen for the boys I knew in college. But I want you like I've never wanted anything, ever—"

"I know you do, Diana," Devlin said softly, getting to his feet, then helping her stand. "But I have to go see my brother, and make sure he knows what you told me—"

"I'm glad I told you," she said, hugging him hard. "If Devlin's as wonderful as you are, I don't want him hurt, or killed."

Devlin tilted Diana's head up, so she could look him full in the eyes. "Diana, *I am Devlin*," he said, pronouncing each word slowly, absolute glee in his tone. "And you love me anyway, don't you?"

Fear flooded Diana's eyes, and she cringed back from him. But as she held Devlin's gaze, she trembled, then embraced him. "Yes, I love you! I don't want my brother to hurt you, it's not true what he said about you, it can't be—"

Devlin looked up, his pleased golden eyes meeting mine, his predatory smile both knowing and triumphant.

Dev loved bending her to his will with so little effort. It was horrible and terrible, and I hated that he was enjoying it this much. But I told myself it was necessary, and looked away.

"Come upstairs," Devlin said softly, swinging open the cell door. "You can stay in my guest room, Diana. Since you love me, I'm sure you wouldn't hurt anyone here in my home—"

"I swear it!" she said vehemently.

"—and I trust you won't try to escape—"

"Never! I only want to be with you, for the rest of my life! Please let me stay here with you!"

Jesus. That blood of Dev's was powerful stuff. I silently thanked God for letting me be born with resistance to it as Lash and I followed Devlin and Diana up from the basement.

Devlin led Diana to Titus's old room. It was nicely furnished, though it was done all in black, and shades of dull red, like blood. Titus's favorite colors, no doubt. *Why didn't Devlin come here with his women to feed, if the room was free and nearby?*

Lash went in and disconnected the phone, taking the whole thing out a second later and heading downstairs with it.

"Stay here, Diana," Devlin said softly, sitting her on the bed. "I'll be back later tonight, and bring you some food, if you wish it. There's a robe on the back of the door, would you please wear it for me?"

Diana nodded, then threw her arms around Devlin again.

He gently pushed her back on the bed. "Promise me you'll stay here," he said sternly.

She nodded fast, her eyes wide and hopeful.

Devlin locked her in, and then turned to me. "No more therapy, Sar," he growled.

I nodded. That went without saying. "I'm sorry for that. Carol said it was confidential."

"She didn't have a choice. What Ulysses did to her was probably magical," Lash hissed, rubbing his eyes. "There's no defense against that, Sar. She probably doesn't even realize she even said anything to anyone—"

"Doesn't matter," Devlin said, grinding his fangs together. "Ulysses would have found out what he wanted to know another way. At least he's not targeting Theo or Devon."

That was something, at least.

Devlin called Danial, reporting that I'd be staying there today, and everything Diana had told him. After listening for a bit in silence, he hung up. "Sar, Danial asks you teleport tonight, to visit with Devon, Theo, and him for a few hours. He wants to see you, but he said he wouldn't come here tonight, that it's too risky. Michael had no news of Ulysses for him, nothing. Also, Theo and Devon are going to stay with him until Ulysses is caught, in the upstairs bedroom at Danial's—"

"Good," I interjected.

"He said Elle isn't happy, but she'll be staying on the premises, though Theoron will continue to go out with him and Rip or Titus to meetings. He asked that you teleport Theoron every day for training with Lash for as many hours as Lash will teach him." Devlin's gaze flicked from me to Lash, expectant.

"Max is probably five hours," Lash said, shrugging. "There is only so much damage his body can heal. But that means we can finish this week, if T pays attention, and can learn fast—"

"T?" Devlin said, wrinkling his brow.

"He wants to be called 'T', not 'Theoron'," Lash said, shrugging again. "I respect that."

"I'm not surprised," Devlin said snidely.

Lash shot him a dirty look.

Whatever that was about, it could wait. "Dev, what are you going to do with Diana? I heard that bit about putting on a robe. Are you going to take her virginity, turn her, or both?"

Chapter Sixteen

Devlin's eyes were hard, his smile sinister. "I'm going to do neither, Sar. As she is now, she'll be loyal to me for another week, until the blood I gave her wears off. She can return to human if I don't take any more, or give her any more of my blood. But she's right at the point of turning. I'll wait to hear from Ulysses. Then I'll tell him he has one family member left, that I'll let her go unharmed, if he'll give himself to me in trade."

"Will he fall for that bullshit?" I said with raised brows.

"I'll really do it," Devlin said, slightly annoyed. "She's a decent girl, and not part of my quarrel with him. I don't want to have to hurt her. But if he refuses, I'll most likely turn her, and send her out to kill him."

I cringed, horrified at his casual cruelty and ruthlessness.

"But I don't want to have to do that. No one should have to die a virgin," Devlin said regretfully. "He'll kill her for sure. And I can't be with her; I'm Oathed to you—"

"That's what bothers you? You could always send one of your men to her, and have Titus make them look like you," I said sarcastically.

"Ah," Devlin said, grinning ear to ear. "Good idea. I'll think on that, Sar." He smiled again. "It's nice to know I haven't lost my power."

"You wanted me to be like her, those years ago when I first met you, when you gave me your blood," I whispered, appalled. "This is the real reason Danial was so pissed off when he'd found out you'd given me some of your blood in your kiss. You wanted me to be falling all over myself, in love with you and not Danial—"

"So what if I did?" Devlin said with no guilt and a lot of defiance. "It didn't work. You resisted me like no one ever had before, except for Annabelle. Most women aren't like Diana anyway. They take a little longer to feel the effects of my blood. But when my blood had no effect at all on you that night, I knew you were something special, something to be *savored*—"

My eyes narrowed. "Haven't I asked you repeatedly not to be creepy?"

Devlin stared at me and let loose a low laugh that started out soft, then grew loud and gleefully malicious. It raised all the hair on my arms, making me shiver. When I finally averted my eyes, he turned his attention from me with a last grin.

"Lash, can you bring Sar to Titus's shop?" Dev said, yawning again. "I need to get some sleep. Then you should get some sleep yourself. It's bound to be an eventful night. Titus will be here today working, he can keep an eye on Sar." He cut eyes to me. "You are welcome to stay, also, if you wish."

Lash nodded. "Sure."

Devlin kissed me, and then went into his bedroom, closing the door.

I was not joining him in there after his little display. Instead, Lash and I wandered downstairs. "Are you hungry?" I asked. "I'm going to make something to eat. We'll have the sushi for dinner."

"Eggs?" Lash hissed hopefully. "Bacon? Sausage?"

"Eggs, bacon, and sausage it is," I said, mustering a smile. "Get out the pans."

* * * *

Halfway through breakfast, the phone rang. Lash answered, then handed me the phone. "Stephen for you," he said, his voice carefully neutral.

I took the phone from him. "Hello?"

"Sar, you didn't contract anything from Theo," Stephen said without preamble. "I've told him, and he's asked to be tested every week. He asked me to tell you."

"Thank you," I said, not sure how to feel about what Theo was trying to do. Because it was clear he was trying to be with Jenny, and test himself, so that sometimes we could be together without worrying. But I found the idea repellent, anyway. I knew it wasn't fair after all the things I'd done, but there it was.

Lash noticed I was subdued after the phone call, but he said nothing about it.

Titus walked in just as we were finishing up. Lash gave him a smirk, then got up. He bent, and whispered in my ear, "Thanks for lunch, Sar." With a gentle trailing touch of his hand across my shoulders, he swaggered out of the kitchen. Titus glared at Lash, a little black evilness oozing out of him.

"Want some raw bacon?" I offered, my tone a little forced.

Titus smiled, and shook his head. "Thanks, I've already eaten." He came over and sat at the table, pulling up a chair across from me. "I have good news to share with you. Terian is recovering faster than I expected. I think two more weeks should do it."

Finally, some good news without a bloody underside. "That's great. Can he talk to you yet? Can he see anyone?"

"Sometimes. It's still touch and go on which half is in control at any given moment. But we're getting there. And no, he still shouldn't see you, Sar, not until he's completely back in control. But I'll tell you when it's safe for you to see him." Titus reached for my hand, and then he squeezed it. "I'm sorry about your home," he said sadly. "Will you be staying here at Hayden?"

There was a lot of unspoken question in his words regarding Theo and I. Was he worried I'd blame him? "I know you broke the rest of the bond. It's okay, I asked you to do that."

"The bond isn't completely broken yet, Sar," Titus amended. "I've tried several things, trying to break that first layer of it, but still nothing even seems to make a dent. But I have a few things left to try. And if nothing else works, Hellfire is sure to—"

Hellfire? I tried not to squirm in the chair.

"—don't worry," Titus finished, in what was probably meant to be a reassuring tone. "I'll take care of it."

"Did you wipe Stephen's memory of my surgery?" I asked directly. "He seemed…a little distant on Monday."

Titus nodded. "He will be. All he has is a cloudy blankness where his memory of you was. Devlin asked me to wipe out all memories Stephen had of you for the last month. He'll remember the birth, but vaguely. Nothing about what he did, or after, when he saw you, though he will remember that Devlin drank your blood, and that I gave you some of mine, and that is why your blood is different now. Stephen just dabbles in magic. Most of what he knows is healing magic, so it wasn't difficult to take his memories, especially for just that brief time. But I can't do this again to him for a while, Sar, without damaging his mind. So my advice to you is to make sure that nothing happens that you might need me to take his memories of you again. Don't slip and say something, because he'll be suspicious if there is anything to give him cause to wonder why his memory isn't clear, as it should be. He has to have knowledge of the spell I used, and he'll guess what was done, and who ordered it, which means soon after he'll be guessing why. Devlin would rather have him killed than have to worry about you being taken by another vampire. So be very careful of your words around him."

Guess I wouldn't be getting that surgery from Stephen now. In fact, how was I going to get more chemical protection? The stick in my arm was only for one month, as Stephen had thought I'd be back the following week to get my tubes tied again. That meant I had another three weeks at most. And Theo was not cooperating; he wanted to be with me without condoms. If I refused he'd be suspicious, especially if he brought me proof he was safe, as I was betting he would. *Shit.*

Well, I had someone I could ask to help me who could most likely get me some birth control pills. If he was in the mood to help me, that was.

But there was a darker current here that needed my concentration. Was Titus saying he'd seen some of the memories he'd taken from Steven, as Terian had viewed mine months ago? Did he know I miscarried? Or was he just taking another opportunity to warn me away from Lash? Better to be brave and know for certain. "Titus, what exactly are you worried about?"

Titus's voice was as if the earth itself cracked open, and erupted. He was clearly worried, irritated, and more than a little annoyed. "If you're living here, Lash is going to keep trying to get you between the sheets, Sar. Or anywhere else he can have you. I've seen how he watches you, and waits to catch you alone. I'm surprised he hasn't asked Devlin to share you—"

"He wouldn't get very far," I said, giving Titus a cold expression. "Just leave it at that, Titus."

"Okay, then," Titus said curtly, nodding. "But it's normal to worry about you. You're like my daughter."

"Do you know if my blood will change back soon?" I said hesitantly, desperate for a different subject. Every time he talked about being like a father to me, I was both touched and weirded out. Some of that was Titus appeared about forty-something, not that much older than I was. Some of it was he was demon. And some of that was that he was Terian's father, which made Terian and I kind of like siblings, which then made me feel even more repelled by what Terian had tried to do to me.

When I thought of all the therapy I needed and wasn't going to be getting at this point, I decided to load up on self-help books the next time I had a chance. Maybe Amazon.com had a supernatural self-help section.

Titus considered my question. "I can't say," he said finally. "I'd guess it would be a few months, give or take. But Devlin's right, it will go back to how it was before. You have lost none of your resistance to the virus he carries in his blood, just by losing a great amount of it. Don't worry. You will never be like that young girl upstairs."

I heaved a sigh of relief. *Whew.*

Titus got to his feet stiffly. "I need to get back to work. I'll be in the basement."

"I'll join you," I said, taking my plates and Lash's to the sink. "I have a lot of work to do, too."

I spent the rest of the afternoon and early evening working on e-mail. There were more than fifty to answer, but I managed to deal with all the new business by the time six p.m. rolled around. It felt very odd to be there, to be sending cases to Danial's personal e-mail address with a number, and printing off Devlin's to leave on his desk. But I got into the swing of things by the end of the first hour. And I still sent on praise to Danial as well, though my smiley faces were not drawn as they always had been before, but instead the emoticon in typeset forty-eight Times New Roman, colored bold red.

I was just turning off the computer, when Lash came and got me. He scared me when he suddenly rested his hands on my shoulders. I jumped, and let out a gasp, as I hadn't heard him approach.

"Shh, it's just me," he said softly, rubbing my shoulders. "It's dinner time, Sar."

"Ah, please push down on my shoulders a little," I sighed, stretching. "I'm so stiff, from sitting here so long."

Lash kneaded my shoulders as I stretched happily beneath his hands, sighing gently. "Better?" he hissed.

Shit, he was aroused. I shouldn't have asked him to touch me. "Much better, thanks," I answered, uneasily.

He leaned down and kissed me lightly on the forehead. "Come on," he said, grinning down at me. "Theo and Danial will expect you in an hour, Sar. You need to eat before you leave. And I'm starving."

Damn it, I'd forgotten all about seeing Danial and Theo. And that there was any sushi, for that matter. "Let's go."

I had an enjoyable dinner with Lash, talking about another author we shared in common, William Johnstone. Lash had read his westerns, and also some of his military/action books, just as I had.

"I'm surprised you liked his writing," I said, eating some vegetables dipped in tamari sauce. "I would have thought you'd had enough excitement in your own life."

Lash let out a loud guffaw at my choice of words. "I like that the assholes always get what's coming to them," he said seriously. "And that the author thinks that killing a person isn't necessarily a bad thing, that sometimes it's exactly what's needed. His heroes never take any shit from anybody, either."

I was not surprised to hear Lash voice that opinion. I was surprised to find myself nodding and agreeing. "Yes, I like that, too."

"Do you like the horror stories he wrote earlier in his career?" Lash said, giving me a penetrating look. "You may not have read them; they're mostly out of print now—"

"I liked *Wolfsbane*," I said thoughtfully. "But I haven't read too many of the others. They were hard for me to afford, being out of print, though I looked for them in my local used paperback store. I had others of his later books, but—"

"I have them all, if you want to borrow any of them," Lash said, after a moment. "Everything he's ever written."

"I may take you up on that," I said with affection and gratefulness. "I still can't believe mine are gone."

Lash ate another piece of salmon. "If there's some you like in particular, Sar, keep them," he said gently. "I can always get another copy for myself."

"Thanks but you're being too nice," I said with a laugh. "It's enough that you'll let me read them. It's like my own personal library."

"You say it like that, maybe I should make you pay dues," Lash said, giving me a leer.

I rolled my eyes at him, making him laugh louder.

Devlin joined us with Venus mid-meal. She adventurously tried a few pieces of my eel, though she didn't like it. After, I gave Devlin a kiss goodbye, and teleported to Danial's.

Theo was there with Devon, both of them in lion form. They were playing gently, while Danial read on the couch. As soon as he saw me, Theo bounded up the stairs to the extra bedroom to change forms, with Devon in hot pursuit.

"Sar," Danial said eagerly as he got up, tossing his book aside. He grabbed me and kissed me hungrily, pressing his body to mine. He drew back from me in the next moment. "I smell that snake on you," he said, giving me a sideways glance. "But just on your shoulders?"

"I was working all day, doing e-mail," I explained, snuggling into him. "Lash eased some of the tension—"

"What?" Theo said angrily, coming down the stairs in his jeans with no shirt, or shoes.

"Relax!" I said, instantly irritated. "I was stiff, from doing e-mail all day."

"I don't want him touching you, Sarelle," Theo growled. "I'm not going to say it again—"

"Well, I guess you'd better just get used to it," I said flatly.

Theo gaped at me in shock. Danial did, too.

"What are you saying?" Theo said loudly.

"I'm saying that I live with him and Dev now, and he's going to touch me occasionally in a non-sexual way."

"Have you forgotten Carol's—?"

"Fuck Carol!" I hissed.

Theo and Danial's jaws dropped. Danial backed away from me a few steps. As I watched him do it, I wondered if he thought I was somehow not Sar, but some sort of an impostor.

Theo came over to me slowly. "Sar, is this about Jenny?"

"No," I said, letting out a breath. "This is about you and me. Look, Carol might not have endangered you and Devon, but she endangered the rest of us, whether she meant to or not. And if I hadn't called Lash that night, I'd be dead, Theo. I owe Lash my life. So if he wants to hug me, or touch my hand once in a while, I'm going to let him. It's not going to go farther than that. And you are going to relax about him touching me, because you are getting what you need from Jenny. I'm not putting any limits on what you do with her, as lions, time-wise, or anything else. So knock off your jealousy, already."

Theo looked at me for a long moment, then nodded. "All right."

"But I do need to speak to Jenny tonight," I said. "Right now."

Theo looked nervous. So did Danial, for that matter. Maybe they were remembering what had happened to Monica. I felt a little nasty happiness at that, and then let it go reluctantly.

"Jenny doesn't want to see you," Danial said firmly. "She asked that I tell her, whenever I know you are coming here, and she'll stay away, until you leave. I think that's best. Theo and she might need to be together as lions, but this is your home, Sar. And I want you to stay here with me some nights every week. Theo, you and I can sleep together as we did before, with Devon in his bed close to us—"

"I need to see her, tonight," I said resolutely. "I need to talk to her, woman to woman. Call her, and ask her to come, or tell me where she is, Danial. And I'll decide after I talk to her if I'm going to be spending any nights here from now on."

Theo looked at me like he didn't know me. "How can you say this to me?" he whispered. "Do you not love me anymore?"

I looked at him squarely. How long had this been coming? The last nine months at least. But maybe Theo hadn't been the only one affected by the bond we shared; maybe it had affected me too, I just hadn't seen it. Looking back, I was surprised I'd acted so compliant all last fall, and this spring. Theo had told me to do something, and I'd just done it, regardless of how I'd felt about it.

But that time was over. I wasn't doing anything else just because he told me to. "Theo, this isn't about love. This is about who I am. It's about what I need from my relationship with you, and from my life. It's about what I can and will do, and what I can't and won't. And if Jenny tells me she wants a child, your child, I'm sorry, but I'm not going to stand for it."

"That's not fair," Danial said fractiously, baring his fangs. "It's not fair to Theo! You've had a child with Devlin—"

"I don't *care* if it's fair," I yelled bitterly. "You hear me, Mr. Racklan? Life isn't fair, and I'm tired of trying to make things fair between you three. Because they aren't. And the truth is, they never will be, just like life. And it's not my job in life to make you all feel good about yourselves!"

Danial stared at me, then nodded. Theo just looked at me warily. "Very well, Sarelle," Danial said, "She's at the werecompound."

I teleported instantly, and found myself in the common room. Cia was there, with Janice, and Jenny, all talking together like the best of friends. They all looked up when I arrived. Jenny went red, and Janice looked nervous. Cia just looked angry. Understandable; she still hadn't really forgiven me for that episode with Serena back in the summer.

"Sarelle," Cia said stiffly. "Do you need something?"

"Yes, to talk to Jenny," I said politely, but commandingly. "Alone."

Janice got up, nodding to me. Cia stood by Jenny, and didn't move.

"You try anything—" Cia growled.

"Cia, if I wanted Jenny dead, she'd be dead, and so would you—" I said easily.

Cia snarled at me. Jenny was white now, her eyes wide and afraid.

"—and it wouldn't be by my hand."

"So it's true, what Aran overheard?" Cia said. "I didn't want to believe it of you, Sar, that you'd let Lash have you willingly—"

Aran? It had been Aran who'd told Terian? As much as I didn't want to believe it, I guess I had to. At least I could tell Dev, and he could have Titus or Rip take care of it.

"How could you?" Janice said accusingly. "Theo loves you so much, Sar."

"Does he?" I grated out, looking hard at Jenny.

She looked at the floor.

Why am I doing this? I was making things worse. I hadn't come here to play the vengeful wronged wife. Even I saw the hypocrisy there. "Look, Jenny, this isn't your fault, none of it. I came to tell you I know that, okay?"

"Okay," she whispered, her eyes still averted.

"But I need to know if you plan on trying to get pregnant in lion form," I added. "I have a right to know that, as his wife."

All three of them gasped.

"We haven't talked about it," Jenny whispered.

"Do you want a child of your own?" I said abruptly. "If you do, it's most likely going to have to be his, unless you take a lover besides him, and don't change form for the duration of your pregnancy. Even then, you might need another werelion. I'm not sure—?"

"Yes," Janice said quietly. "Sar's right. It would have to be another were, not a human."

I didn't get why a baby of Jenny's couldn't have a human father, but that didn't matter.

"I am just happy to feel healthy again," Jenny interjected. "I didn't become were to take Theo from you, Sarelle, or even to be intimate with him."

"I know that," I said wearily. "But all the same, I want to know beforehand if you are thinking of getting pregnant, Jenny. I don't have a right to tell you what to do. But I do have the right to decide what I can handle, and what I can't. So I need you to be truthful with me."

"That's fair," she replied. "I'm not pregnant now. I was tested yesterday. I want you to know I'm on the pill. I started two days ago. I'm not going to be with Theo again until it takes effect. Then I won't conceive, though Dr. Camlyn said with my body as weak as it was when Theo changed me, it probably will be unlikely anyway for another month or so. I'm not planning on getting pregnant, Sarelle. I've got enough to adjust to as things are."

Now that the sordid details had been worked out, I just wanted to leave. "All right," I said. "I'm leaving now. Sorry for interrupting."

Cia was still glaring at me.

"You got something to say, say it Cia," I said harshly. "And while you're at it, stop being an ass about Serena. She became what she became because she had to, and you have no right to judge her for what she chooses to do for Devlin. She would much rather be a werebear than a coyote, I know that for a fact. And she had nothing to do with killing your parents."

Cia's look of resolute hate lessened, then faded away. "Sarelle, you've changed so much from how you were," she said, her eyes looking over my form as if she couldn't recognize me as the friend she'd known, the woman who'd helped her win her mate, and taught her to bake. "Do you even know who you are anymore?"

"Yes I do, though it's true I don't always like myself," I said. "Be happy you have your uncomplicated life, Cia, that you have only one male to please, that you never had to walk in my shoes. This past year has been hell for me."

Cia's shoulders sagged a little. "I'm sorry," she said, coming over and hugging me. "I know you didn't go to Devlin willingly. But Danial was so upset last fall, missing you. He was so happy, when you were Oathed to him again. Now he's overwrought with the business and Theo is upset because you're staying with Devlin. When I'd heard you'd been with Lash, Aran, and I, well...we just didn't know what to think."

"No matter what you think of Lash, he's a good friend of mine, Cia. He saved my life a few nights ago. I haven't forgotten what Devlin did to you years ago, but he's also saved my life several times over. And despite that he's a bit much to take sometimes, he's not the monster that I thought him to be. Neither of them are."

Well, Devlin was sometimes, like earlier today. And Lash, he sometimes could be very, very bad, but most of the time I liked that...*Stop.*

Focus.

The three of them looked at the floor, guilt on their faces. "We were just talking about that," Janice said, blushing.

Get three women in a room together, and sex always came up, at the latest, in about four minutes. And what better thing to gossip over than a woman who'd had four lovers in the same time period? "And?"

"And...we were wondering who was the best of the four men," Janice said, coloring.

I rolled my eyes. Best at what, I didn't have to ask. Had Jenny had been putting in her two cents about Theo's abilities. *OIY.*

"You don't have to answer; it's not our business—"

"Is Sundown here?"

"No," Janice said. "She went to visit Terian. But she'll be back shortly. Her room is the second on the left, down the stairs."

I walked away, resisting the urge to speak. At the last moment, I gave in, and turned back. "Janice?"

She looked up.

"Dev, hands down," I said with a grin. "But Lash is a very close second. It's the tongue." She gaped, and colored, the other women choking and sputtering. I walked away laughing, feeling very naughty myself.

* * * *

Sundown appeared about ten minutes later, near her room with Titus. Titus hugged her quickly, and then disappeared. Sun looked the worse for her ordeal with Terian. She had cut her hair shorter, so it was just to her shoulders, and gained a little weight since I'd seen her last. She'd been thinner than I was since I'd first known her. Now we were about the same size. Well, truthfully, she was still thinner. "Sun?"

She turned. "Hey, Sar. Are you okay? You look a little weary."

You and me both. "I've been better," I said, giving her a hug. "How is Tears?"

"He looks like his old self," she said with relief. "I missed him so much, and I was so worried. But he's like he used to be. He apologized over and over for what he did to me."

I looked at her, holding my breath.

"I forgave him," she said.

I let it out, breathing in deeply. "I'm glad. He loves you."

"He's loved you far longer," she replied. "He still does. But I'm okay with that now, Sar. I knew it the first time he talked about you. It was hard for me to deal with for a long time. It was the reason I refused to marry him the first time he asked me."

Christ. How to apologize for something like that? "I'm sorry—"

"For what? It's not like you asked him to love you," she said, her blue-green eyes locked on mine. "You told him the truth about how you felt." She seemed to decide something, her face softening into a smile. "I'm pregnant. Titus confirmed it tonight. When it's part demon, it's easy to tell, apparently."

I shivered, and quickly tried to make it look like I was just stretching. "Congrats."

"When I told Terian, he proposed immediately. We're going to get married," she said, still smiling happily. "January eighth. The anniversary of the day I called him, and asked him to see me again. He said he can't wait to be a father. Titus said not to worry; he could make sure I wasn't hurt during the delivery. The baby will only be a quarter-demon anyway—"

I'd be damn worried in her shoes, and I'd had two half-vampire children. "Congratulations," I said, hugging her. "Please invite me to the wedding."

"Be my matron of honor?" she asked. "Theo is going to be Terian's best man."

"Sure," I said, nodding and smiling. "Just tell me when to start going for fittings, and if I need to arrange anything. It's been a long time since I was in a wedding, since I was a maid of honor. Getting Oathed just isn't the same."

We laughed, and hugged once more. Then I teleported back to Theo and Danial.

Theo was pacing, and Danial was yelling at him to sit down and knock it off.

"Theo, she's not going to hurt Jenny—"

"Sar is a lot more violent than she used to be—"

"Thanks for your kind words," I said sarcastically. "I talked to Jenny. She said that she's using protection. So I'll do my best to deal with my feelings."

"Are you going to come and sleep with us?" Danial said, his tone swimming with a deep undercurrent of wanting underneath his soft words. "I want time with you, Sarelle."

I knew what he was after. He was still hoping for Theo, me, and him to get together. Theo heard it too, because he gave Danial an uneasy look.

"I'll come on Monday," I said. "I'll stay a few days."

"Good," Theo said, and Danial echoed him. Both of them looked unhappy I'd not said tonight.

Devon bounded up to me, and began purring. With difficulty, I lifted him into my arms. He was close to sixty-five pounds now, I guessed. Theo would be helping him change form to human for the first time very soon. "Are you my big baby?" I said lovingly, hugging, and then petting him. "What kind of mischief have you been getting up to?"

"Ripping up the sofa, chasing Briar, and getting up on the counter where he was trying to eat my dinner," Theo said, coming over to slip his arms around both of us. I leaned into him, feeling the familiar strength of him. At that moment, I noticed someone was missing.

"Where's Rip?" I asked, worried.

"He took Theoron to Lash for training tonight," Danial said. "He'll be back soon, Sar. But T will be staying with you at Hayden for the next few days, until the end of the weekend, so he can learn as much as he can. Dev said Lash will be finished training him by then anyway."

Theo looked like he wanted to growl, but he didn't. Good for him.

"Good," I said, stroking Devon as he purred loudly.

"Have you eaten?" Theo said, hugging the two of us. "I was going to ask Rip to get us some Chinese food."

"I ate, but I could always go for Chinese food," I said smiling up at him.

Theo kissed me gently. "I get that you're upset," he said in my ear. "And I get why, too. I'll bring you proof this weekend from Stephen that I'm safe, Sar."

Guess I'd better have that conversation with Lash sooner, rather than later. I nodded, because I didn't know what to say to Theo. "Good" sounded mean. "Okay" sounded like I didn't care, and I did care. And "Thanks" was more generous than I wanted to be.

The rest of the night went nicely. Rip showed up bearing Chinese food. I had some shrimp fried rice, and a few egg rolls. Theo had a lot of chicken, three quarts worth, which he shared with Devon. I gave Devon some of my shrimp, too, which he seemed to like a lot. He even ate the tails, which made me grimace a bit when he crunched them down. Danial mostly read, and watched Theo and I play with Devon. I wondered that he wasn't clinging to me more, after the way he'd acted after finding out I was mortal, but maybe he was feeling more secure now that I was marked? Maybe he was irritated at me, for insisting on seeing Jenny? Hard to say. For all that Danial could always read me, I often couldn't do the same to him, not since I'd stopped living with him. He kept his feelings too close now.

Around ten, Theo took a sleeping Devon from my side, startling me out of my doze. "I'll put him to bed," Theo said, giving me a kiss. "Goodnight, Sar. Please be safe, and think about coming to meet Devon and I for lunch every other day. I have meetings tomorrow, but Friday and Sunday would be okay."

I knew damn well that Theo wouldn't have a meeting on Saturday. So what else did he have planned? I tried to cover my suspicion quickly, but Theo was getting better at reading me.

"I have to fit in target practice on Saturday," Theo continued carefully. "Too many of the foxes have been using my increased absence during the days to let their practice slide. So I need to evaluate everyone, and get them practicing again. Which by the way, you need to consider doing more often, too."

"You're right," I said, meaning "I'm sorry." He nodded, his blue eyes looking troubled. Then he was gone, taking our sleeping son upstairs.

Maybe I should do more target practice. I hadn't done any in a long while. I probably couldn't hit the broad side of the barn anymore if it was more than fifteen feet away.

"Teleport back, Sar," Danial said affectionately, coming closer. "I'll be seeing you soon, darling."

I gave him a hug and a kiss, and teleported back to Hayden. Devlin, Lash, and a sleeping Venus were waiting for me on the couch. The surrealism of going from one vampire lover, their best friend who I'd also been intimate with, and a child of mine to another set of the same was so intense for a moment I couldn't move.

"Come sit!" Devlin said excitedly, beckoning to me. "You're missing the best part."

They were watching one of the *Saw* movies. "Thanks, I'll pass," I said, yawning. "It's been a long day."

"You're right," Devlin said, taking Venus from Lash as he untangled her arms from his legs and whip. "We should all head to bed."

I gave him a funny look. Since when did Dev think bed was good at this hour?

"Sar, I don't have any 'arrangements' to make this week," Devlin said carefully. "I plan on keeping your hours, to a great extent. Venus also needs to be up in the day, and I want to spend time with her. So even though it goes against my nature, I'm going to try sleeping most of the nights, and being awake for a good part of the days."

"Me, too," Lash said, nodding. "I can't guard you both if I'm sleeping. And it makes sense if there is an attack on Devlin or Hayden, it will happen during the day."

"Because Ulysses will figure him asleep?"

"That, and in daytime, he only needs to get Devlin outside Hayden's walls to burn him in the sun," Lash said grimly. "But don't worry. Titus and Rip have erected a magical barrier around Hayden, reinforcing the stone and mortar. It would take a nuke to crack her walls, Sar, and barring that, someone would have to get in here to place an explosive, to bring down the roof or the walls. And no one is getting in here past me, or Titus."

Reassured by his words, I relaxed a little. "Bring her to me, Dev."

Devlin came to me, Venus in his arms. I kissed Venus softly on her forehead. She didn't even stir in Devlin's arms. "Have only good dreams, daughter dear," I said fondly. "Know you are loved very much."

Devlin gave me a soft look, and then headed upstairs. I went first to grab a cold glass of water before following them to bed. I'd gotten in the habit here at Hayden, but it had been hard to remember at first. Ghost and Darkness were passed out on the kitchen floor. I woke them up, and let them outside. As I waited for them to finish, Lash came up behind me, wrapping his arms around my waist as he rested his chin on my shoulder.

"Did things go well at Danial's?" he hissed softly in my ear. "You seem much calmer than I thought you would be. Did you talk to the female cougar?"

How did he know that I'd planned on talking to her? Did he know me that well? *Maybe.*

"Jenny doesn't want to have his child, so I'm doing better," I replied. "But I learned Sundown is pregnant. Terian's going to marry her, so it's good, but I'm worried for her."

Lash was quiet for a few minutes. I watched the dogs and gave them a few moments to play. They hadn't had anyone to walk them that day, and I reminded myself that here, there was no one who'd do that for me. *Maybe I could convince Serena to go with me on walks...*

When Lash spoke, the words out of his mouth were the last ones I expected him to utter. "Would it have bothered you to have a child out of wedlock? You were married to Theo, and Oathed to Danial and Devlin, when you had their children."

In Dev's case, that wasn't technically true, but I got what he was saying, that all three fathers had been very involved in the pregnancies, and in their children's lives. Besides, what Lash was really asking didn't have to do with any of that. He was asking if I'd have been upset if I hadn't miscarried our baby; to be pregnant by him and living here with him while having no real lasting commitment from him.

Should I tell him I loved him, that because of that it wouldn't have been like it had been with Devlin, where I'd been for all intents and purposes forced into it? No, because I wanted to tell him very much, and I was just looking for an excuse to tell him, hoping for some stupid romantic fantasy. It'd just make things more complicated. The truth was if Theo had left me, and I'd been having Lash's child, it would have bothered me to be pregnant and not married. I knew women did it all the time, but I remembered growing up without a father, and it still made me sad, to think that I had never seen him smile, that I had no memories of him. Being pregnant and living with Lash here at Hayden would not have been the same as being pregnant and married to him. But the idea of being married to him, a man like him, was another whole separate issue, one I didn't want to get into at that moment. *What in hell should I say?* There were so many things I could say that sounded judgmental, or too personal.

Lash was still holding me, but he hadn't moved, waiting for my answer.

Tell him the truth; just say it agreeably and very briefly. "I think like you do," I said finally. "A child needs both their mother and father. Terian's marriage to Sundown is a commitment to both her and his child."

"I've never been married," Lash hissed. "I've had women who I've known for years, some I fu...was intimate with for years, but it's not the same thing. I was never going to marry any of them, or commit to them."

I let the dogs in, mentally scrambling to find some words to say back to him.

"But not all women want that," I said, shrugging. "Some just want a good time, the same as some men—"

Lash let out an angry hiss. I looked up at him in confusion.

"Sorry, I thought you meant that as an insult to me," Lash replied. "But I can see you didn't. And it's fair, anyway. It's true that I wasn't looking for romance with any of my former lovers, just sex. But I was always clear about that with them—that I never wanted more than that."

His cold cut-and-dry attitude was repellent, to say the least. Not only had I heard enough, it was time to change the subject. "Is anyone listening?" I said softly as I could, interrupting him.

Lash took me outside quickly, and closed the door almost all the way behind us. "No one will hear us, over the wind," he hissed. "But hurry up and talk, as I'm freezing my balls off out here. What do you have to tell me that can't be overheard?"

"Look," I said uneasily. "I need some help, if you'll give it to me."

"Who?" Lash said.

By his eyes and the stance he immediately slipped into, he thought I wanted him to go after someone. "Not that kind of help," I whispered. "But I can't get the surgery, Lash. Titus gave Stephen that forgetting spell, and I can't wreck it, or Dev might hurt him. And Theo's not cooperating—"

"You want me to get you protection?" Lash said, to my relief not laughing or rolling his eyes. "Birth control pills?"

"I'm sorry to ask, but—"

"I'll pick some up tomorrow," Lash said, nodding. "Do you have any allergies? Is there a particular brand?"

I wondered how and where he was going to get them and then decided it was better not to know. "No and no. And I'm sorry to ask—"

Lash led me inside, and shut the door behind us. "Sar, I told you I'd help you. And even if I didn't owe you my life, I'd still help you with this. Though I don't understand why you just don't say something to Theo. Surely if you told him, he'd help you? For that matter, so would others we both know. I'm not the only one you could ask for this, so I'm naturally wondering, why are you asking me?" Lash stared at me hard.

"For the same reason I don't say anything to someone else, either of them," I said quietly. "I don't want any more. They do. And even if I did, this is the worst time with Ulysses looking for vengeance. I have enough to worry about, without one that can't defend itself."

"I understand. Say no more," Lash said, nodding once. "I'll meet up with you tomorrow. Now I've got to go check on Theoron before I turn in. He is learning fast, Sar, but he was badly hurt by what we worked on earlier, and I want to make sure he healed okay."

When he mentioned Theoron's injuries, I immediately wanted to go myself to see him. But it was better to wait until morning, when T would be healed. I knew if I saw him hurt, I'd tell him to stop training. My son needed this, maybe more now than ever before. Lash's training hadn't seemed that important, back a few weeks ago. Now, it might save T's life.

"Good night, then," I said gratefully, giving Lash a light kiss on the right cheek.

"Good night," he said seriously, "and next time you want to aim more to the left, and down a little."

I looked at him in confusion for a minute, and then we both cracked up laughing.

Walking upstairs, still chuckling, I found Devlin in bed waiting for me, annoyed. "No more kissing, or anything else with him, Sar," he said in a dangerous tone. "He has Gina, and you have Theo, Danial, and I. I am recovered enough to take care of your desires, to say nothing of Danial or Theo."

I was very, very glad we'd gone outside to talk. Clearly, Devlin had been listening to us.

"Sure," I said, taking off my clothes, and sliding in beside him.

"Just 'sure'?'" Devlin said searchingly. "You aren't going to protest?"

"Why? You're right. It's probably better for both of us, anyway, if we don't touch or kiss. I just miss —"

I clamped my lips tight together. *Shit.* At least no more sentiments had slipped out.

"What is it exactly you are missing?" Devlin said, his tone dripping jealousy.

Chapter Seventeen

I stayed quiet, my mind racing for a non-offensive answer.

"Sar, tell me what you miss, and I'll provide it for you. As I told you before, I can be anything you want me to be."

I thought about leaving, but for where? He'd come after me, anyway. I didn't speak.

"If you are embarrassed to say it, I can surmise it. Titus can give me a potion that will make my tongue as his is," Devlin said delicately. "I can—"

I should've known he'd think that it had to do with sex. "I am sexually sated with what you do already," I said, trying not to smile. "You don't have to do—"

"What do you miss, then?"

Devlin was not going to be put off. I'd better think of something quick. He was getting angry.

"Answer me, Sar. Right now."

"It's not sex," I blurted out. "It's always about sex with you. I'm not missing sex!"

Well, I was a little, as Lash had been so very *good* at it, but for the most part that really wasn't it. I missed being with Lash himself. I was missing being intimate with him, being close to him, and sharing quiet banter with casual touches that were both comforting and still erotic as hell. I missed his sense of humor. And that was much, much more important to me than just good sex. But I could not admit that, not without starting one hell of a fight.

"I'll ask you one last time. What are you missing with him?"

I had to say something that was true, and yet not so revealing.

"I miss the easier times from the last part of the summer. I miss the sun, and laying with him on the rock, and feeling it warm on my skin—"

"Ah," Devlin said, mollified. "I know what you mean. I miss the warmth

189

of Rio myself. This winter has set in faster than any I can remember, and I remember a good few." He held me closer. "I'm sorry I can't take you to a warmer climate for the winter," he said, kissing my brow. "But it's too risky. We will go next year though, if you like."

I looked at him, hesitantly euphoric. "You mean it? I wouldn't have to be here, with the snow, and the ice, and everything?"

"Of course not, if you didn't want to be," Devlin said, giving me a generous smile. "Venus would love the beach, I'm sure. I know Lash would like spending the winters in a warmer climate."

"But he said here was home that night you marked me, that he didn't want to leave—"

"Why are you always interested in him, in how he feels?" Devlin said, angry again. "Why aren't you interested in pleasing me?"

I didn't reply. There was nothing safe I could think of to say.

"I am sorry," Devlin said finally. "I know you must have questions about some things that you heard us say that night, Sar. Excuse my ill temper. I'm feeling overwrought from Diana—"

"Did you turn her?" I asked, even though I didn't really want to know if he had.

"I kissed her at length, but didn't take any of her blood," Devlin said, holding me about the waist as he eased his blond curls down on my breasts. "She'll sleep until dusk tomorrow, being partly turned as she is. Ulysses has until Sunday night to come to me. Michael was able to locate me a cell phone number for Ulysses, and I left him a clear message, on what I expected, and what would happen to Diana if he didn't agree."

I caressed him gently, and he sighed under my ministrations.

"I don't want to hurt her," Devlin said, kissing my fingertips as they passed close to his face. "But I'm probably going to have to. Heather was a featherbrain, but she was a good girl at heart. She just didn't think things through, and it led to her death. But I made her a vampire because she wanted it and I liked her, not to punish her. Diana won't feel the same, when my blood wears off her, no matter that she pleaded with me over and over tonight to make her my 'immortal bride'."

"It's such a waste," I said with disgust. "She never asked for this."

"No one ever does," Devlin said ominously. "But often, misfortune strikes anyway."

* * * *

The next morning, I discovered that Devlin and I were not alone in bed. Danial had joined us sometime in the night. I awoke in his arms, and he awoke with me, as he usually did. Danial was at my back, and Devlin was still in my arms, cradled against my chest.

"Good morning, Love," Danial said softly, running a fang tip down the side of my neck.

"Stop that," I said, giving him a smile.

"Kiss me, then," Danial said, hungrily. "It was all I could do to give you time with Theo last night. I wanted to have you to myself."

I looked over at Devlin's sleeping form lying half on me, and then pointedly back at Danial, saying with my eyes that he didn't have me all to himself.

"Dev's going to sleep for a while yet," Danial said, helping me move Devlin off me gently. "Why don't you and I go get you some breakfast? I hear T downstairs in the kitchen, getting some cereal for himself."

If so, that meant it was about eight, and T wouldn't be alone down there. But I was hungry enough that didn't matter. I put on my robe, and Danial put on Devlin's. I mused if he'd done that to ensure Dev would stay upstairs, but decided he knew Devlin better than that. Being naked wouldn't stop Devlin from coming downstairs, if he wanted to.

We went downstairs to find T eating some cereal alone in the kitchen. He was surprised to see his father, but happy, too. I was just glad to see he was uninjured. I got a bagel toasting, and some fruit out for myself, and Danial pulled out a chair and sat down and began talking to T. Business quickly turned to training.

"Dad, do you want to come and watch Lash and I spar? I'm getting better every day."

"I need to sleep, my son," Danial said, putting his hand on T's shoulder. "But I would like to see you demonstrate what you are learning later, if you wouldn't mind. Maybe against Theo—"

"T is not to teach your cat anything he learns from me," an angry hissing voice said. "It was a condition of my agreeing to teach him."

I turned to see Lash in the doorway, baring his hooked snake fangs at Danial.

"I did promise," T said, nodding. "But come watch us, Dad—"

Danial opened his mouth, baring his own fangs at Lash. "I will do what I—"

"Lash, would you mind, if Danial and I came to watch you and T, just for a few minutes?" I interjected. "We won't stay long. I understand that you want to keep your secrets, and Danial and I are grateful to you, for teaching our son."

Lash looked over at me, his eyes snake eyes, unreadable. "If you like, Sar," he hissed finally. "But hurry, as we have a lot to do, and I'd prefer you only stayed for the very first part."

"We'll all come," Devlin said, striding into the kitchen fully dressed. "I would like to see how my nephew is progressing. Sar, why don't you and Danial get dressed, and meet us there?"

Lash nodded. "We'll wait."

Danial and I headed upstairs. Danial tossed on some clothes of Devlin's. They fit, the brothers being close to the same size. Just as we were opening the bedroom door to go back downstairs, Devlin shouted, "God damn him!"

Danial and I ran downstairs to see Devlin looking lividly into a square foot box. Lash was sipping some water in a chair, looking thoughtful.

T looked a little confused. "But Dad's here—?"

"What is that—ugh!" Danial said, stopping in his tracks as he looked into the box.

T handed me a piece of paper. "Look."

Dalcon,
It was quick for him, compared to what it will be like for you. Set my sister free, unharmed, or the next ashes you get will be Danial's.
Ulysses

I looked in the box. There were ashes, and bits of burnt bone: the remains of a vampire.

"Who is that?" Danial said softly, peering into the box and wrinkling his nose.

"Probably one of my constituents," Devlin said with a sigh. "At best, one of yours. Either way, one of us will be getting calls, as soon as whoever this is gets missed."

Danial sighed and sat back down wearily. "I always envied you your power as Ruler, Dev. But it's so much more trouble than it's worth. Someone always wants something from you, or expects something."

"Power always is," Devlin said, shrugging. "But to be without it when you need it is much worse, Danial. Just ask Sarelle."

"Nice, Dev." I grimaced at him.

He ignored me, instead turning to T and Lash. "Lead on, T—"

"Devlin, there's a call for you on line one, no name," Keith said, interrupting from the doorway, Jerry peering over his shoulder. "And Danial, you have a call on line two from Theo."

Danial and Devlin exchanged looks, and then Danial picked up the kitchen phone, and Dev went downstairs to his study to take his call.

"C'mon." Lash motioned to T, and they both headed to the basement gym.

I followed.

Lash pushed open the doors, and walked to the mat. Then he surveyed Theoron, and gave him an irritated look. "Go get your loose jeans on," he said. "I told you, you have to wear looser clothes if you want to be able to fight, so you have freedom of movement. For example, your mother couldn't fight anyone dressed in those jeans she's wearing; they are way too tight—"

"Watch it," I said sharply. Lash shot me a grin. T was already off to the shower room to change, the door swinging shut behind him.

I was annoyed as hell. These were once my loosest pair of jeans. And Lash was right, they were skintight now. Worse, I couldn't even say I was pregnant as an excuse. "I can fight well enough to knock you on your ass," I said with narrowed eyes.

Lash raised his eyebrows at me and grinned. "Come on, then," he said, moving backward onto the mat and beckoning to me. "I'll be gentle, when I knock you on yours."

I faced him, and two seconds later, he had both my arms behind my back, and I was struggling, but to no avail. "You were saying?" he said, grinning down at me.

I began kissing him lightly up the side of his neck. Lash went rigid, though he didn't let me go. I kept kissing him, but I also slid my right foot behind his right leg, which was the one he was balancing most of his weight on. Lash was hissing now, but he still didn't release me. Without pausing in my kissing, I swiped my leg behind his, and pushed into him fast. Lash went down, and I landed on top of him. He let out a loud aggravated hiss, but he was laughing, too.

"I told you!" I crowed, pleased with myself. "Right on your ass! Ha ha ha ha ha ha!"

I grinned at him, then raised my body off his. "I can't believe you didn't see that coming," I said, getting to my feet. "I mean, really—"

Lash grabbed my leg, and I went back down with an "Oof!" He pulled me beneath him, and put one hand on each of my wrists. He eased himself between my legs, and I felt his erection pressing against me, flexing through his jeans. "Did you see this coming?" he said with a grin, looking down at me with his dark eyes. He kissed me, his tongue gently stroking my closed lips. I pushed up feebly with my upper body but Lash held me right where I was, still kissing me. This wasn't the rough, forceful kiss he'd always given me before. It was filled with longing, and wanting, and good old-fashioned lust. God, I wanted him. This was what I'd been missing, this kind of loveplay, this kind of seduction. In a second, I gave in completely, opening my mouth to let his tongue taste mine, wishing I could devour him. Lash let go of my hands, our arms wrapping around one another, both of us shaking as we tried to push our bodies as close as possible. My hands found his shirt bottom, sliding up underneath, my hands moving up over his muscular back. He groaned, then began to press down with his hips in rhythm, his hard penis pressing through the soft cloth, thick and firm.

It would feel so good to make love with him again. All I had to tell him was yes.

Sar, don't do this. Theo will...

Oh, Fuck Theo, and his constant bitching! I loved Lash! What about what I wanted? I wanted Lash with everything I was. Absolutely everything.

I thrust up against him, rubbing against his hardness as I grabbed his ass, pushing his erection tight to my crotch.

Lash let out another hiss, this one eager. He pulled back from me, breathing fast. "Did you change your mind?" he said ardently, giving me an intent look. "I can tell T we'll be back in a while. You could teleport us—"

Shit. What are you *doing*, Sar? Where is your brain? You can't do this!

"No," I panted, moving out from under him. "I'm sorry for doing this. Dev read me the riot act for just kissing you on the cheek last night, and told me I had to stay away from you."

"Jealous bastard," Lash hissed grumpily, rolling onto his back and reaching into his pants. "Sorry, I'm twisted up."

I resisted the urge to watch, averting my eyes. "It doesn't matter anyway. It's only been a few days since I...since—"

Lash dropped his eyes, his smile vanishing as he remembered our shared loss. "Don't speak of it." He stood up, then helped me to my feet.

"I'm sorry," I said, putting my hand in his and squeezing. "I'm giving you mixed signals."

"Sar, it's enough for me that you want me as bad as you do," Lash said, smiling faintly. "I'm getting by, seeing Gina. I should apologize for starting this with you, and then offering you more. I heard Dev being a...I heard what he said to you last night. But if you give Dev your Oath in a month or so, he'll change his mind. I can wait until then to be with you—"

"Good, because you are not to touch her again until she gives it," Danial growled.

Lash and I turned to see him coming toward us, his eyes red as blood. Lash slipped his arms around my waist, and hugged me.

"Don't, you're making it worse—" I gasped, but he didn't let me go.

"It really gets under your skin, doesn't it, vampire, that she wants me and cares for me?" Lash hissed at Danial, his chin resting on my shoulder. "That you with your pretty face and your tall model's body aren't enough for her?

That when she was mortal, and no longer felt the pull of your blood making her want you, she chose me—"

"You are loathsome," Danial said, wrinkling his nose in disgust, as he had with the box of ashes. "I still find it hard to believe my Sar would ever let you touch her. I am beginning to think you used some kind of compulsion spell on her. Why would any non-weresnake want someone like you?"

Lash looked at Danial as he hugged me gently, and then released me. "I'll say only this, out of respect for Sar," he hissed meaningfully. "The Lust she had when she was pregnant is long gone. There is no spell on her, vampire, to make her desire me, nor was there two months ago. And you know it well!"

"Enough!" Devlin snarled, striding into the room. "Lash, you are not to kiss Sar, or do anything else with her, no matter what you or she desires, until I say otherwise. Is that clear?"

Lash looked with flat eyes to Devlin and nodded. "Crystal," he hissed coldly. "T, get into position."

T came up, his eyes all for Lash. By his expression, he'd seen at least Danial's entrance, if not more. *Just great.*

Lash and T began to spar. It was obvious in a few moments that Theoron had vastly improved. He was quite good, compared to how he had been just a few weeks ago. Lash still beat him, but it was not over nearly so quickly. Lash also didn't beat on him, as he had the first time I'd watched them.

"Time for you to leave, audience," Lash said, letting T up for the third time. "We need to work on other things, and they are not for your eyes."

"I've seen enough, anyway. There are other things on my agenda this morning," Danial said pointedly, walking out.

"You're getting good, T," I said, giving an encouraging smile to Theoron, who beamed. I shot a last smile at Lash, who gave me one for a second before he turned back to T.

I followed Danial back up to Dev's room, where Devlin was waiting. As they both began to undress, I got an inkling of what they thought was going to happen. Danial had meant something by his remark to Lash.

"Join us, Sar," Danial said seductively, getting into bed. "I would like to have you with Devlin, as we did before in the spring."

While the offer would have been tempting a few hours ago, my interest in a threesome right now was nada. "Danial, I can't. It's my time—"

"It won't hurt you, to be intimate with us during your time," Devlin said, looking at me with half lidded eyes. "We both want you, Sar. Now go in the bathroom, and prepare."

"No," I said, pronouncing each word with emphasis. "Not until my time is over."

They both gaped at me. It was almost comical.

"You were eager enough for Lash," Danial said icily, his eyes tinting red.

"I told him the same thing I just told you, actually—"

"You were aroused enough for him—" Danial began scathingly.

That was it. I gave Danial a cool smile. "And I'm not for you, so I guess you'll have to find something else to do with your morning."

Devlin looked disbelieving, then anger replaced his shock. "Come to us," Devlin ordered. "Now, Sar."

"No," I said simply, leaving the room.

I was halfway down the stairs when Danial's arms encircled me. "Come back to bed," he said, trailing kisses up my neck. "I want to make love to you, sweetheart."

I turned and gave him a kiss full of longing. Danial groaned, thinking I was agreeing, then tried to lead me back upstairs.

I pulled back. "No. I meant what I said, that I don't want to right now. But I promise I'll come to you and Theo on Monday, Danial, and we can be together then. Or if you would prefer, you and Dev. The latter is probably better. You know Theo is not going to go for a threesome, anyway."

"I know," Danial said regretfully. "Monday it is, then, and Dev will join us instead of Theo. But come back to us now and sleep—"

"You know your brother," I said. "He's in one of his moods where he's not going to take 'no' for an answer. I'm not going to fend off his advances for the next hour, or wake up to find him having me anyway. I'm done with feeling like a sex slave."

Danial looked at me cautiously, but when I didn't pull away from him, he gave a last hug, and released me. "I'll tell him to get up then, if he wants to spend time with you. I need to sleep for a few hours, though. I've got meetings for most of tonight—"

That was a given.

"—but I'll be up around two or so. Maybe I can join you for a late lunch?"

"That would be nice," I said, giving him another kiss on the cheek. "I'll be taking the dogs for a long walk this afternoon. They missed their walk yesterday, and the day before, I think."

"Devlin said he was getting you a treadmill," Danial said, curious. "Are you training for some reason?"

I laughed. "Trying to get into shape," I said, looking down at my body. "I still haven't lost those last ten pounds from the babies, Danial. I've gained another five at least in the last two weeks."

"I think you look fine as you are, but I know you well, and I'll say nothing more," Danial said, hugging me. "Feel free to use my gym at the fox compound if you want to. If you are worried about running into Jenny—"

"I've made my peace with her, for now," I said, pushing my hair back from my face. "But I'll let you know if that changes."

"So what are you going to do with your morning?" Danial asked.

"I'd brought my sewing machine, and a lot of the material I had a week ago to Dev's, because he asked me to make him a quilt," I said, excited. "I'm glad I did now. I just put the boxes in the room, and did nothing since then. I've got to set things up, so when he gives me the material, I can start making squares, and laying them out. Plus, I've really got to make a list of furnishings I need for those guest rooms—"

"Go work then," Danial said indulgently, letting me go. "Passions need to be enjoyed not only in bed, but out of it, too. Please keep your cell handy. Even here inside Hayden, it's good to be careful."

"I will," I agreed.

The rest of the morning went quickly, but I enjoyed it a lot. It had been a long time since I sewed, and it was good to work with cloth again. I set up my machine on a long folding table I'd brought, and got a chair from the kitchen to use for now. I looked through my material. I would need to go and buy some velvet for the one side of the quilt, but I had enough black velvet for the edging. I also had a little velvet left over from the quilt I had made those years ago for my mother. I decided on 5 x 5 squares, and spent the next hour cutting them out.

I had also brought an old, worn king size quilt that had been on my bed at my old home years ago—before Danial had come into my life—to use as the filler for Dev's quilt. It seemed odd to still have this, and to know that the new mattress, and fine linen sheets he'd bought for us were gone. The ones we had made love on the first time, all those years ago, when we'd first met, and I'd first loved him, and so many other memories...

Leave it alone, Sar. Think about something else for a little while.

I spread the old quilt out on the floor. I ripped the seams, and another hour later, I had the batting laid out, and some of the squares on it. I wouldn't be able to decide on a pattern until I found out how much velvet Dev was going to give me, or what colors the old clothing was. But this was a very good start.

About ten-thirty, Devlin came in to see what I was up to, Venus in tow.

"Hey," I said, giving them a smile. "What have you been doing, angel?"

Venus came over and looked at the material, touching it. "It's so soft," she said in her tiny yet melodious voice.

"It's velvet," I said. "This is satin, and this is silk." I handed her a few scraps.

"Can I have some to play with?" she asked winsomely, her golden eyes doing their best to charm me out of some material.

"Depends," I said mock seriously. "What are you going to do with it?"

"I want to make some clothes for my dolls," Venus said to me seriously. "Party clothes."

"Tell you what," I said seriously back to her. "Bring me some of your dolls, and I'll make you a few dresses for them. But I'll give you some scraps to play with in the meantime, too."

"Thanks, Mom," she said happily. I gave her a big hug. She remembered this time not to squeeze me too hard back. I handed her a few pieces of silk and satin, and then she was out the door, running.

Devlin came inside the sewing room, and looked at the beginning of the quilt to be.

"I can see you are going to need a lot of velvet."

"It looks like a lot, but not too much. Remember, they do sell it in stores. You don't have to give me all I'll need. I don't want to cut up clothes you might wear again—"

"If you want to come with me, I'll show you some of the velvet I was going to give you now," Devlin offered. "Serena is watching Venus, and they're playing in the ballroom. I think that's her favorite room."

I looked at him and decided he must be over his irritation at my refusal of him this morning. At least, he was behaving normally again. Maybe Danial had talked to him.

I followed him down to the basement, and into one of the storage rooms. I looked around in shock. There had to be at least fifty plastic tubs here. "Is this all clothes?"

"I like clothes," Devlin said defensively. He opened a few tubs, and closed them. "These are all beach clothes. Hold on, let me move a few of these."

That a vampire had beach clothes was hilarious, but I held in my laughter, my face twitching. Devlin moved a few more tubs, and then opened some others.

"Here we are," he said, pulling out a long tunic in raspberry velvet. "This can go."

"Should I make a pile, or—?"

"Let me go through two containers worth, and then I'll help you take some upstairs," he said, offering me a smile. "I'll try to go through a few tubs every day, until I've gone through them all."

It was a velvet windfall. "Sounds good."

Devlin went through two tubs, declaring that everything inside could be used for the quilt. There were a lot of colors, though predominantly they were red, purple, gold, white, gray, silver, and black. We each took an armload, and ascended the stairs. As he carried them in, and I discovered that Venus had been back, and left me a pile of at least ten Barbie dolls.

I'd expected two or three. "How many did you buy her?" I asked Devlin.

He looked embarrassed. "One of each kind. Was that wrong?"

I thought of how many kinds of Barbie were out at any given time. Thirty? Forty? More? OIY. And I thought Danial had spoiled Elle.

But Ulysses wanted to kill Dev, and he'd almost succeeded. Venus had almost had to grow up like me, without a father. Even if this turned out okay, Devlin might still get killed by someone else out to get him. He had a lot of enemies. Given that, I didn't care if he bought her a hundred Barbies.

"It's okay, she's your little girl," I said kindly. "Just don't give her everything she ever wants."

"Why not?" Devlin said, moving closer to take me in his arms. "I want her to be happy. Just as I want you to be happy."

"Happiness doesn't come from being given things, or having things. It comes from liking who you are, and loving others," I said as gently as I could. "Having it all leaves you nothing to wish for. And having nothing to wish for leads to boredom."

Devlin hugged me to him. "I understand that better than I used to," he said contentedly. "But it helps also to have the power to have whatever you want, even if you don't indulge yourself in everything. And I enjoy giving you and Venus everything you could want." He pulled back. "Speaking of which, they delivered your treadmill an hour ago, Sar. I had them put it in the gym. Why don't you come and try it?"

"Lead on," I said, pleased.

The treadmill was a nice one, top of the line, of course. There were so many buttons and settings I had a hard time finding the switch to turn it on. I walked for a half hour, and decided I was very out of shape. Devlin watched me nervously, as if he expected me to fall off. Or maybe it was that I was huffing and puffing a great deal.

"It's great, thanks," I gasped, stepping off. "I'll get in shape in no time with this."

"Don't lose too much weight, Love. I do not want you to be a thin stick like so many woman of this time period are."

I looked at Devlin. He was serious. I remembered Catherine's body and flushed. I'd prided myself that I was thinner than she was. I'd never thought that maybe Devlin preferred bigger women. Anna also had been plump, by her portrait.

"I'm just saying I like your curves," Devlin said, obvious worry in his voice that maybe he'd offended me. "I—"

"You remember what I looked like when you first saw me?" I interrupted.

"Of course," he replied with a leer. "I remember wanting to know what you looked like under that sea green dress, and wishing it had ripped in another place that night—"

"I'm not going to get any thinner than that," I said. "I like to eat too much to be a size four, or even a six."

"Speaking of that, I ordered you some more chocolate," Devlin said, smiling wickedly. "It came today, too. Come up and have lunch."

I took his hand, and we went into the kitchen. Theoron was there, eating some sandwiches with Lash, and Danial was listening to them talking.

"I'm telling you, you should travel, T. I saw a lot of the world in my youth, and—"

"I don't know, Lash. It seems like too much trouble. I can see everything I need to about the world on the Internet—"

"But you feel differently, being there," Lash hissed, his tone almost emotional. "You can't look at a picture, and smell a river, or a city, or hear the sounds that the people make as they pass by in the streets—"

"It's too dangerous right now—" Danial interjected.

"I'm not saying right now, Danny Boy," Lash hissed in irritation. "I'm saying in a few years—"

"Don't call me Danny," Danial said angrily, "or I'll call you—"

Lash let out a loud hiss, reaching for his knife.

"Stop and be nice, children," Devlin said teasingly. "Lash, leave the knife in its sheath."

Lash gave Danial a dark look, but left his knife alone. He gave me an angry look, and then got up and left. By the set of his shoulders, he was still annoyed. Why was he mad this time?

I wanted to go after him, but knew it was better not to.

Moving to the fridge, I opened the door, looking at what fixings were available. The refrigerator was almost completely empty.

"Where is Robin?" I said aloud. "She usually keeps the fridge stocked—"

"Shit!" Devlin swore, jumping to his feet. A second later, he had taken off down the hall, his feet running up the stairs, then his fist pounding on Serena's door.

He was back in a moment, looking a little frantic. "Serena said Robin went out late this morning for groceries. She's not back yet."

I didn't need to hear the rest of what he had to say to be worried. I took off after Lash walking fast, and caught up to him near the gym.

"Lash!" I called frantically.

Lash not only stopped, he immediately turned, running back to me. "What is it—"

"Robin went this morning for groceries, and she's not back."

"God damn it!" Lash snarled, his eyes going flat instantly. "I told her not to go alone, to come and get me or one of the bears if she was going out—"

"She did," Devlin said, running up with Danial in tow. "Keith said that John went with her."

"He's no bodyguard, he's just young muscle," Lash hissed angrily. "Damn it!"

"Something's happened," I said, putting my hand on his arm. "We all know it. The question is, what do we do now?"

"First, tighten security," Lash replied. "As of now, Sar, you don't go anywhere without two guards, and preferably one of them either myself or Titus. Dev, you're going to have to do your 'arranging' from home for the next month, or until Ulysses is caught—"

"I can do that," Devlin said reluctantly, "But Rip could—"

"Ulysses wants you bad enough, Dev, he'll find a way to get you. The only place you are truly safe is here at Hayden. The same goes for Sar—"

"She is safe at my house too, with Theo and I—" Danial started.

"You want to risk her life, just so you can bed her?" Lash hissed venomously. "You and your kittycat?"

Danial recoiled, and didn't reply.

"Lash, I do need to go out once in a while, like to see Dr. Camlyn. I can teleport—"

"Then Titus or I will go with you," Lash said. "I'll keep you safe, Sar. But you can't do as Robin did, and go off alone with someone who can't protect you. Promise me now."

He meant anyone besides Titus and him. Knowing how he felt about demons, he really meant only himself. "I promise I won't."

"Good." Lash said, then turned to face Danial. "I can't tell you what to do. But Dev cares about you, so I'll give you this advice. Cancel your meetings and stay home. Keep your son and daughter close to you, and have both Rip and Theo around you at all times—"

"Theo and I both have to keep doing what we've been doing, and T needs to, also," Danial said smoothly. "Or everything I've worked for is going to collapse into ashes."

"You want to be ashes instead?" Devlin said angrily. "Listen to Lash!"

"Dev, Ulysses wants you and Lash, and maybe Sar. This vendetta of his has nothing to do with me, Theoron, or Theo."

Devlin was undeterred. "Danial, I heard this right from Diana's lips, Ulysses is after you!"

"Leave it, Dev," Lash hissed. "Danial's old enough to choose his own life, and his own death. You can't choose it for him."

"I'll tighten security," Danial relented. "But until I know for sure he's gunning for me—"

"He said the next ashes I got would be yours!" Devlin grated. "How can you think he means otherwise? What reason do you have to not take this seriously?"

"Because Ulysses is human, and as far as we know, he's working with some mercenary werebears, and that's it! This is pure scare tactics, Dev! You killed his one vampire connection, and he knows only a little magic! We have two centuries-old demons watching our backs, not to mention the two best bodyguards in the world, and even more men besides! You know demons are very hard to kill—"

"But not impossible," Lash hissed ominously. "Watch your back, T. Depend on yourself and no one else, if something happens. Don't be a hero. Got it?"

"I will," T replied, his tone serious—but astonishingly enough—not afraid.

"Second, Venus must have someone with her at all times, even when she's sleeping," Lash said. "Serena can do nights; we'll put a bed in the nursery for her. She's a light sleeper—"

How in hell did he know that? Had Serena reconsidered for real and bedded him in the last few weeks? I didn't want to know.

"—Titus, Sar, and I can switch off with you to guard her in the daytime, Dev. Venus is not to go outside, not for any reason, and she shouldn't even teleport anywhere else. And no inhabitant of Hayden is to go anywhere, even inside the walls, without a charged phone on their person, both to warn of attack, and to call, if they notice anything out of the ordinary."

Devlin nodded. "That's doable. Anything else?"

Lash paused, thinking.

"Danial, call Rip to teleport you home. Theo needs to know all this," Devlin said. "And Titus will need to come here, so Lash can go try to find Robin's trail—"

Danial looked annoyed about being told what to do, but he went to the phone, and called Rip. To say we were all worried and scared wasn't an understatement. I was afraid, terrified actually, but I put my faith in Lash, trusting him to protect us all.

Lash went upstairs for a while to his room. Rip appeared, and teleported Danial home with T, after he hugged me good-bye. Devlin got me my phone from my purse in the hallway, and made sure it was charged and clipped to my belt, before going in search of Venus and Serena in the ballroom, saying he would give her one of the spare phones, as she didn't have one.

I sat and looked forlornly at my large basket of Godiva chocolate, which I'd longed to try only a few minutes ago, and now it seemed my urge to taste it had evaporated. I put my hands down on my arms, and felt sorry for myself. I'd liked Robin, just from meeting her that once. Now she probably wasn't going to be coming back. The odds were she was dead, and we'd never get that chance to bake together as she'd wanted to. Any recipes she'd had to pass down to me were lost. I wanted to cry, but too much had happened in the last few days. I just didn't have any tears left.

"Sar," a hissing voice said. "I have to go find her."

I looked up into Lash's reptilian eyes. He was dressed in his black, heavy wool clothes. Made sense, with it only about twenty degrees outside. His tone said he didn't expect to find Robin alive.

I got up and went to him. "I'm sorry."

He nodded. "I liked her very much. She was kind to me. Whatever bastard did this is going to rue it."

I just hugged him tighter, hearing his pain. Robin had been a friend to him, and he didn't have that many friends.

"Here are your pills," Lash hissed quietly in my ear. "Don't move; I'm putting them in your pocket. I got you a three month supply, but tell me when you need more."

"Thanks. Will a hundred cover it?"

"No, but some cornbread might," Lash hissed. "If you'll make some more for me."

"I'll make it tomorrow," I said gratefully. "I've been meaning to ask you, should you show me some escaping techniques maybe, like you showed T?"

Lash pulled back from me slowly, his eyes showing his confusion. "Escaping techniques?"

"When Ulysses had me, I tried to think of ways to get free. But I couldn't think of anything to use in the room. There was nothing—"

"Shh," Lash said. "I saw the room, Sar. There wasn't anything you could've done, unless you had a grenade, explosives, or a semiautomatic gun with a few clips. What happened before isn't going to happen again. You have a tracking spell on you, and Titus is going to recharge it tonight, so it's at full strength. If you somehow get captured again, you just sit tight, and I'll be along shortly to get you. Okay?"

"Okay," I said, blinking back tears.

"You get some sleep," Lash said, kissing my forehead. "I won't be back until dawn, probably."

"You be careful," I whispered, holding him close. "I don't want anything to happen to you. I've lost enough this week."

"I'll be okay," Lash said reassuringly. "Now kiss me for luck, before I go."

Right or wrong, I gave him a long loving kiss full of passion and love. Then Lash was out the door, driving one of the Hummers into the swirling snow.

I went back and ate a piece of chocolate. It should've tasted sweet, but it seemed to have no taste at all.

* * * *

Later, I read in bed, relieved that Titus had fully recharged the tracking spell on me earlier. Even with Lash still not back, I felt a lot safer knowing I could be found in the event I got taken prisoner. Titus had reaffirmed that he would be able to get to me in a matter of seconds, once he knew something was wrong. That's what the phone I would be carrying constantly from now on was for: a swift warning.

Theo had called about nine to say everything was fine at Danial's, that the male fox guards were all patrolling, and several were staying in the main house with Danial, along with Rip, and Theo, and Theoron. He also said Devon missed me, and asked whether I was still coming for lunch tomorrow.

"Let me call you tomorrow morning," I'd replied. "Frankly, I'm not sure how this is going to work. Danial thinks it's nothing, but he didn't see how angry Ulysses was that night he ambushed us, or hear Devlin screaming when he was tortured. I've met Ulysses, and he's serious about making Dev pay, and now me, too. This guy is not just some amateur with a stake and some holy water, Theo. He's a planner, and he has something up his sleeve."

"Call me tomorrow, then, and tell me," Theo said gently. "I miss you, Sar."

"I miss you, too," I'd answered. As I hung up, I realized I didn't feel anything. I'd just replied automatically to Theo's words. I was wound tight as a spring, emotionally walled off.

I'd taken a long shower before bed, washing my hair, and dressing in a simple nightgown. I had stopped spotting this afternoon, raising the issue of Devlin possibly looking for action later, especially after my denial this morning. But maybe release was what I needed. Something had to break, and soon.

When Devlin came to bed at midnight, sex was the furthest thing from his mind.

"I just got a call from Lash," he said bleakly. "He's been arrested, Sar. They've got him for murder."

Chapter Eighteen

"Murder? Who? Robin?"

"Lash called at ten and said he found Robin's car. She never even got to the store. Someone shot out her rear left tire, and the car crashed near the bank of the river. You know the bridge, right before you reach the center of town? With the trees near the far riverbank, it's an isolated enough spot, plus her car was white. It was hidden just off the road, in some pines and a drift of snow."

I wiped at my eyes, and tried to listen.

"Lash found a little blood, and tire tracks. He followed them under the bridge, where he found her body. Her guard John was there, too."

Devlin handed me some tissues, and I wiped my eyes again.

"Their attackers skinned them both," Devlin added softly. "You may not know this, but werepelts are worth big money to sorcerers—"

"I know it," I whispered, remembering Cia's parents, and the bounty hunter who had taken their pelts. "Did they…torture her?"

Dev shook his head. "Lash said it was done execution style. She didn't suffer. But Ulysses will have funds now, from selling the two pelts. Likely it was to a private buyer, one I won't be able to trace, even with my black market network. Michael has touched base with me, and he had no news either."

This was horrible. I had to think of something else, anything else. "How did Lash get arrested?"

"He tracked the vehicle to a local bar, waited, and confronted the owner as he went to leave. The man pulled his gun. Lash broke his neck in retaliation, then killed him with his own skinning knife for vengeance. An off-duty cop there with his friends witnessed it, and tried to apprehend Lash with a gun. Lash thought it was another assassin, and he punched the cop hard enough to break his jaw in two places. The cop's buddies pulled their guns, announcing they were police. Lash gave himself up, because by then a crowd had gathered. They found the weapons on Lash when they searched him, and arrested him right there for assault with intent to kill." Devlin forced a smile. "Don't worry. My lawyer is already on it, Sar. He assures me they can't prove a thing."

This was just what we didn't need. "Can't Titus get him out?"

"No," Devlin said wearily. "The whole killing was a setup, designed to lure Lash out, to get him out of the way. Ulysses knows I can't get Lash out of jail except through legal channels, and that it will take some time."

"How long?"

"Long enough," Devlin said cryptically. "But you need to sleep, Sar—"

"How can I fucking sleep now?! Things are so awful—"

"Take this," Devlin said, handing me a pill. "You'll sleep, and dream no dreams."

I should've asked what it was, but I just took the pill and swallowed it down.

"He asked if you'd come and visit him tomorrow. Visiting hours are two until three."

"Okay," I said sleepily.

* * * *

The next morning I was groggy, but rested. I didn't want to get up. Everything was falling apart. But I made myself get up, and take care of the dogs and cats. I also made Lash his cornbread, hoping I'd be allowed to give it to him. I cut it up into squares, so the officers would know there wasn't a knife hidden in it, or some other weapon.

Devlin came down just as I was finishing, hugging me from behind as I worked. "Are you feeling well enough to go out?" Devlin said with concern. "You'll be safe enough with Titus, especially with your own teleportation powers, but you don't have to go. I can have anything you want delivered—"

I had been stuck at Hayden under threat from Ulysses for so long, there was no way I was going to miss this chance to escape for a day. "Yes," I said, iron beneath my tired tone. "I'll be safe with Titus."

"Yes, you will," Devlin said, rubbing his smooth cheek on mine. "I'll want you to call me, when you stop for lunch to check in with me. Titus is not to leave your side, Sar, not for any reason. You go to the bathroom, he's going with you."

I cracked a brief smile. "I'll be ready to leave in a half hour. Is Titus here?"

"I'm to call him at the last minute," Devlin said. "He's working with Terian this morning, because he knows he's got to get Terian back into play ASAP, with this new threat. And Rip can't help as much, because he's guarding Danial."

I nodded, packing the cornbread into a container. "That truck is also coming today to bring my equipment here from home. I don't want to put it off, and risk Ulysses torching it."

"I'll call the trucking company, tell them to make it after three," Devlin said. "Lay in food for a siege, Sar. Things are going to get worse, before they get better."

* * * *

The day went pretty well. Titus was very helpful, though even in his loose shirt, John Deere cap, and jeans he still looked supernatural, especially with the heat coming off him. But his blackness wasn't too bad, and I wondered if he'd done some sort of spell to dampen it a little. But I didn't spend too long thinking on it. I was too emotionally dried out, like a husk of myself.

We went to the store first, loading up on cases of food of all kinds, and bottled water. Except for the fruit, I thought everything I'd picked should last, and there was enough for a month. I didn't want to think this nightmare could go on longer than that.

The Hummer held it all, and there was even some room left over. So the next hour I spent at the mall, getting some fold-away beds ordered, and also two full beds, a nice chair for my sewing room as I hadn't brought mine from home, and some end tables, floor lamps, and table lamps. I didn't order a lot, just enough so that there would be beds enough if Theoron, Theo, and Devon had to come and stay at Hayden. Danial would sleep with Dev and I, so I didn't worry about a bed for him.

I hoped that when this ordeal was over, I might have some time to go to a few garage sales and maybe get some furniture to refinish. I'd done that, years ago when I was in college for a hobby, but found it too time consuming in the years since. But I longed to lose myself in a project, to take my mind off of all the bad things that had happened. And it made me feel a little like myself, to think that I could maybe still do that someday.

Titus reminded me at noon we should eat, so I stopped with him, and we shared a pizza. Actually, I had a pizza, and he did something magical to make it seem as if he was eating that, but instead, he just drank from a flask. I knew it was blood, and that it was likely human. But I was past caring, and didn't even flinch at the thought.

I called Devlin and checked in, when we were waiting for the bill, only to be upset again when I found out that Hayden had been attacked by a vampire hunter in the last hour.

"He wasn't experienced," Devlin said candidly. "He went into the basement through a window, and Seth caught him coming up the cellar stairs. I have him in a cell, waiting for Rip to come to test his blood. Usually I would have drained him on sight, but this seems too easy, that Ulysses didn't send a better hunter. He may have poisoned the hunter, expecting him to be caught, and for me to indulge myself. Either way, I'll question him later, and find out if it was his handiwork that did in the late William."

I surmised William had been the dead vampire/ash pile in the box yesterday. "Ah."

"Give the phone to Titus," Devlin said. "And make sure when you are out to get some takeout for you and Venus. You may not be getting any more for a good while, Sar."

Cringe. I handed the phone to Titus, and he talked to Devlin for a bit before hanging up, and handing me the phone back.

We lingered over lunch, Titus telling me about the little house that he lived in with Leri, and how happy he was they were back together. He seemed happy enough with her, and I was happy he was happy, even if I still didn't trust her. I had to admit, even though Leri was a bitch, she was right there in the trenches, fighting for her son. And she had covered for me when I'd needed her help. Maybe I'd forgive her, in a few more years.

Titus was also ecstatic to be a future grandfather. He couldn't talk enough about how he hoped the child of Terian and Sundown was a girl, and how much he wanted to spoil her. I was surprised, but didn't say anything. I thought it was nice to hear a male parent-to-be say he wanted a girl child, instead of always harping on about how a son was what he wanted.

Finally, in my fog, I remembered I had something to tell him. "Titus, it was Aran who told Terian about Lash and I, and what really happened. At least, I think it was."

My voice sounded a little off, even to me. But I couldn't seem to be focused. Titus was immediately alert, looking directly at me. "Someone told you something they shouldn't have known?"

I nodded. "Cia. She said Aran, her mate, told her Lash and I had been together again, that he had overheard something."

"I'll take his memories, and hers. I'll also look at them, to see what they remember. I'll find out the truth, Sar, whether they heard it or were only told about it. Don't worry."

I was frankly worried about too many other things to even be concerned by that anymore, but I wasn't going to tell Titus that. It was important that he find out, and after this latest crisis was over, I would most likely care very much that no one knew I could save an ancient dying being with only my blood.

"Terian said that a werefox told him, but not which one did it. Maybe it was Aran."

I'd forgotten someone had told Terian everything, and so far no one seemed to know who. "Thanks," I said. "Let's find a hair salon, since we're out anyway."

Titus looked at me strangely.

"I need to get my hair cut. The ends are ragged, and I need to have them trimmed."

"Sure," Titus said. "We should do any errands for the next few months today, if possible."

I didn't like the sound of that but conceded he was probably right.

We found a place that accepted walk-ins, and I got about three inches taken off the ends, and a few layers put in as well, so it wasn't so straight, but more flowing. I wanted badly to cut it short, but decided not to for the moment. I might regret it, if I did it on a whim. And it was nice enough to see some bounce in my hair, some of the curl coming back as the weight of it lessened.

When we were done, Titus said we'd best get visiting, if we were going. As it was it was almost two-thirty. He drove to the jail, and I shuddered, just looking at the cold, concrete building. What if Lash was cold in there? Cells were concrete. It was winter. It might not be cold for a human, but he wasn't human. Then I remembered Lash could come all the way back to human form now, and he should be warm enough.

Titus parked, and looked over at me. "I can't go in with you," he said neutrally "They'll see me as a threat for sure, especially with the blackness that I can't completely conceal. I've had people shoot at me before for that reason alone, and police are human, in spite of their training. And you need to appear innocent, so you can do what needs to be done."

I didn't understand that, but Titus said nothing more. I thought it was probably just that he didn't want to see Lash, but who could say?

I got out of the car, and began the walk to the door. It was only fifty feet, but it felt longer. As I walked, I thought to myself: I really didn't want to be here. Jails creeped me out worse than hospitals, and that was saying something. But I'd promised Dev that I'd come see Lash when he'd told me about how Lash had used his one phone call to talk to Dev. Besides, I owed him the cornbread.

I'd left the knife Lash had given me in the car, along with my other pocketknife. I didn't want any trouble with the police. The piece of steel I always carried in my purse was there, too.

I went in, and signed in at the desk as a visitor. I also wrote in that I was there to visit Lash, and the policeman at the desk gave me a visitor's pass. Then he looked at the clipboard, and back up at me. "Is this some kind of a joke?" he said, his voice gruff.

"I'm sorry?" I said respectfully. "I don't understand."

"There's no prisoner called 'Lash' here. You need a last name and a first name, Ma'am."

I blushed, silently calling myself an idiot. Had I thought that his real name? Lash couldn't have been born with the name I knew him as. But what could I do? I only knew him as 'Lash'. And I felt a jolt of fear, too, that I'd maybe let out a secret. Lash had to have a lot of enemies too. What if they found out he was here and defenseless? My fear for him bathed me in sweat, and I bit my lip hard, using the pain to focus. And I made up the best lie I could. "I'm sorry," I said quickly. "I only know him by that um…nickname. I just met him a few nights ago at a bar, and I called him that, because of his whip. But I don't know his real name. You just arrested him last night. He's a shorter man, mid-twenties, looks Spanish, black hair and dark eyes-"

The cop rolled his eyes, and frowned at me, and I knew by his expression he knew who I was talking about. Disapproval was heavy on his face. He scribbled out "Lash" with a black felt tip pen, and wrote another name beside it. "I know who you're talking about," he said in his smoker's voice. "Man by the name of Tristan Valeras."

I opened my mouth, but nothing came out. "Tristan" was Lash's real name? "Tristan"?

"You look like a nice girl," the policeman said gruffly. "You shouldn't be wasting your time with a man like that—"

"Please—"

"—you should go home to your husband, Miss, before you make a big mistake—"

"—please, just bring me to him," I said nicely, but with cold steel behind my words.

The cop glared at me, but he buzzed me through the door. "Go through those doors. Talk to the policeman at the desk. He'll get Mr. Valeras, and bring him out to talk to you."

I nodded, and went through the doors, feeling nervous. I spoke to the policeman at the desk, and told him I'd brought some cornbread for Mr. Valeras. It was odd saying the name, and I ended up getting the accent wrong on the end of it. He made me remove the cornbread from the container, and put it in a plastic one that he handed me, and gave me my container back. I didn't see the point, but said nothing. The policeman searched me, and then he pointed me toward a little cubicle sort of area. There was a chair, and a glass partition, with a few holes in it so the person visiting could speak to the person behind the glass.

I wouldn't even be able to touch him. Jesus.

I went and sat in the chair, and a minute later, a policeman brought out Lash. He was handcuffed, but at least he was wearing his own clothes. His whip and knife were missing, of course. I realized it was the first time I had ever seen him dressed and without them. They seemed so much a part of him he looked half-naked to me without them. I was betting he felt the same way.

He saw me at once, and his dark eyes held mine as the policeman walked him over to the chair, and sat him down. They were carefully neutral, but I found them just as beautiful as I always had.

"Call me when you're ready, Ma'am," the police officer said. "You have five minutes, but I wouldn't want to spend more than two talking to this character."

I waited for Lash to say something cutting, because I knew he wanted to. But he said nothing. His eyes were all for me.

"I'll call you when I'm done, officer," I said, looking back at Lash.

"She brought you something to eat, though you don't deserve it," the police office said gruffly. He placed the cornbread in its container in front of Lash, who gave me a fleeting smile. Then the officer walked back to his desk, leaving Lash and I as alone as we were going to get.

"I wasn't sure you would come," Lash said softly, looking at me. He shifted a little, his handcuffs making a clinking sound.

"I said I would," I replied. "I try to always do what I say I'm going to."

Lash took a piece of cornbread and ate it slowly, relishing it. "It's very good. Thanks, Sar."

I looked Lash over. He was subdued, but unhurt.

"Sar, I want you to take my whip, my gun, and my knife," Lash said. "I've signed a paper that releases them to you."

"Won't they need them as, um, evidence?" I said, grimacing.

"They only have me on assaulting a police officer," Lash said roughly. "They can't keep my weapons, since I didn't use of any of them to hurt anyone. But they are trying to get a court order to test them for blood."

I nodded. There had to be enough blood traces on them to keep Lash in here for the rest of his life.

"I'll take them to Hayden, and keep them safe," I said, making Lash visibly relax. Likely he felt for his weapons what I felt for my favorite tools. That's what they were, in a way.

"I'm glad they let you wear your own clothes."

He let out a breath, and smiled. "This isn't maximum security, Sar. I haven't been sentenced yet. You don't have to wear a jumpsuit until you're sentenced. Though I'll be wearing one soon enough."

Lash was talking like this was something he was very familiar with.

"You've been in jail before," I stated.

"Not for a long time," Lash replied. "I served a few years for killing a man back when I was twenty-six. It was hard labor, back when they didn't worry so much about prisoner's rights. This is nothing compared to how that was. I shouldn't be in here for more than a month or two --"

"A MONTH or TWO?" I said loudly, upset.

"Sar, I killed a man in front of a cop," Lash said in exasperation. "They believe he was trying to kill me, and they have the weapon he was trying to hurt me with, so it will probably be ruled self-defense. But it's still assault, because I hit that other man, not knowing he was a policeman. I shouldn't have punched him so hard, but I thought he was going to try to kill me, too. There's no way I'm beating the 'assaulting an officer' charge."

"But I…we need you," I said, glad I hadn't blurted out that I needed him. "Ulysses tried again to get Devlin, this time through a hunter."

"I know, Dev got a message to me via lawyer this morning," Lash replied angrily, shifting in his seat. "Seth stopped the hunter in time, but I'm not happy he even got as far as the cellar stairs. There isn't anything I can do, Sar. Ulysses set me up! He arranged for the police to get there just in time to see me kill that man. He wanted me out of the way, and he planned this well."

"Can't Devlin pay someone off to get you out of here?" I asked, desperate. "I'm scared without you at Hayden to protect Venus and me. I'm fucking terrified."

Lash shifted again in his chair restlessly. "Don't be afraid. No one's going to hurt you. Ulysses is after Devlin, that's his true target, not you. Stay near Titus, and inside Hayden's walls, and you'll be safe."

I reached out, and put my hand up against the glass, wanting so badly to be in his arms, the one place where I knew I was truly safe. Lash hissed, and looked away from me.

"Sar, things are going to be okay. Because of what you did for me, my body's slightly altered. Ulysses didn't know that; he thought as soon as they fingerprinted me, I'd be locked in here for years. And he'd have been right. But my fingerprints are different than they used to be, not a lot, but enough so it looks like I don't have a record. I checked it the day after we got back from Florida, when I saw how I didn't look the way I used to when I was younger. I've even been using my real name, because it's safe to—"

"I was shocked to hear it, Tristan," I said, smirking.

Lash gave me a dour look. "You see why I go by 'Lash'? People would laugh their asses off if they knew my real name."

"I like it. It's a noble name."

Lash reached up his cuffed hands to put them up against the glass on the other side of mine. "Sar, I'll be out of here in a month or so. Don't come back to see me. I'll call you, when I get released."

I was crushed. "Why don't you want to see me?"

"Because I see your eyes, I see how much you need me, and I think how easy it would be for me to break these cuffs, and smash this glass between us. And I want so badly to hold you, I might give in and do it. I've got to stay here, and serve my time, because we don't need the police after me on top of everything else! What goes on in secret out in the world has to stay hidden, you know that from Danial by now. Dev might be a Ruler, but even he has to follow some laws. And one of them is that when you're caught with your dick out by the law, you have to give yourself up, and let the lawyers fight it out."

"I'll think of you every day," I blurted out.

Lash looked at me quickly, his eyes full of emotion. "Thoughts of you, memories of us together, will keep me sane in here. Now go, before I say fuck it, and fight my way to you."

"Please be safe," I said, giving him a last look. I got up, went to the door, and called for the guard.

He came and let me out. I asked him for directions to the place where I could pick up Lash's personal belongings. He looked at me with a little anger, but he pointed me to the right place. I went there, and signed about twenty papers, taking the time to read them. I had to show them my pistol permit, and pay some money to get Lash's gun added to my permit, before they would let me take possession of it. It took about an hour, all told.

Finally they brought out Lash's weapons, including his gun, his jacket, his wallet, some change, and a little leather bag. What was in there? I knew I'd better wait until later to see, when eyes weren't watching me.

I went to put the weapons on my belt, but the policeman stopped me, and said I couldn't wear them. I put them inside Lash's coat instead, and the wallet and other stuff in my purse.

I walked out with a police escort, and put the items in my car, showing the officer that I unloaded the gun, and put the ammunition clip in the glove compartment, and the gun itself in the trunk with the knife and whip, as the law required. He left when he saw I had done everything as I should, though he kept his hand on his gun at his waist the whole time.

Titus had seen me coming out, or been warned somehow, and he'd not been anywhere in sight when I came outside with my escort. But I felt him, the blackness of his presence for the first time comforting. I knew that was why the police officer was so on edge. Titus had been right not to come in with me.

As soon as the police officer was back inside the building, and out of sight, Titus materialized beside me in the passenger seat. "Did you get the weapons?

All of them?"

"Yes," I said.

"Stay here in the SUV. I need to report in to Devlin, before we head to your house."

"Sure," I said, and Titus got out of the truck.

I lasted about ten seconds, and then gave in to my curiosity. I looked at Lash's wallet first.

There was his ID/driver's license that read Tristan Valeras, and a picture of him, as he looked now. There was some loose cash, and his one black credit card. And there were a couple of condoms as well, tucked in the side pocket. I felt a little odd looking at them. Then I noticed something strange. They were expired by more than a year.

Why weren't they new ones? Lash had been seeing Gina for a month now. I blushed red when I concluded maybe she was the one who was protecting herself against pregnancy. Lash seemed to prefer not using anything, from what I knew of him. At least, he'd never used anything with me. Maybe that was why it had been so easy for him to get the birth control pills for me, because he'd gotten some for her as well. It was so none of my business. I put them back as I found them.

Next I took a look at the little bag. What was in here? Did Lash chew tobacco? I looked inside, and pulled out a familiar braid. It was my hair, the braid that Lash had cut that day back in the Everglades. I'd wondered what had happened to it, and figured he'd just thrown it away. But I told myself I should have known that he'd kept it. Apparently, he carried it with him always, just like his weapons. I held it in my hands and felt a rush of feeling for him.

I had a brief fantasy of going back inside and breaking him out of jail with his own gun, and then taking him to the nearest hotel…

Forget it, Sar. You'd never make it. You're still mortal. And you'd need a hell of a lot more guns.

But I could teleport him, if he smashed the glass. He could be free in moments…

I sighed and let the fantasy go. Lash was right. He needed to stay here, because we had enough trouble. We couldn't fight the police, too.

I took his coat, and held it to my face, inhaling the scent of him: leaves, earth, musk, and leather. It comforted me, and I stayed there a while, just breathing in the scent of him, and telling myself to be calm, that at least I didn't have to worry about something happening to him now. He'd be safe where he was, even if he was unhappy.

Titus came back in then, and sat down. "We're ready," he said, looking at me curiously. I'd tried to blank my expression, but I could tell Titus had seen

I'd been upset.

I started the car, and put it in drive. It was past time to get moving. We still also had to go to my burnt house.

Before we stopped there, I took a quick detour to the post office. I filled out a change of address card for myself, asking for all mail to be sent onto Devlin's house, to my attention. Theo never got any mail, so that shouldn't be a problem.

I was very happy to see the tractor-trailer waiting for me when we arrived at my home. Titus scanned it, verifying there was no one in it except the driver, and that the barn was also unoccupied. I opened the barn, very glad I'd always carried the barn key and tractor key on my main key chain. Otherwise, they would be useless, burnt metal in the ruins of the house, as all my other keys were. I started the tractor, and used it to load the other equipment into the back of the huge truck with Titus's help. In two hours, we had everything loaded. Which was good, as the sun was already fading, some storm clouds moving in.

Another storm? I thought wearily. We'd had one every few days, it seemed like.

Titus gave the big-rig driver directions to Hayden, and he left with a squeal of hydraulic power as he downshifted, going down the steep hill towards Devlin's home.

"What about the wood?" Titus said. "You want me to teleport it?"

I looked at the wood. Theo had cut and split most of it himself, when I'd been pregnant. But the far greater part was the wood I had cut with the werebears and Lash, that last week in September. I'd been so happy that day, so proud of myself...

"Sar?" Titus said, putting his hand on my shoulder. "What is it?"

"Can you hide it? Devlin won't use much in his fireplace, so there's no point taking it. Just make it look like the shed's empty?"

Titus made a few gestures and sounds, and the wood disappeared.

"If someone tries to back in there, they'll crash into it," Titus said. "But it will stay hidden, even if they do."

We got into the Hummer, and drove to Hayden, arriving right behind the truck. The bears at the gate were just coming out to check it over.

"Wait right here, Sar," Titus growled suddenly, tensing up. Heat broiled off him. "Duck down, and stay down, no matter what you hear." He got out of the Hummer, speed dialing his phone.

Chapter Nineteen

Everything happened at once.

The back of the truck burst open, and a man wielding an Uzi stepped out. He fired a clip into the Hummer, but none of the bullets got through the glass. I shrieked, crouching on the floor behind the dashboard. There was more gunfire, and then wet ripping noises.

The wet noises went on for a while, and then became eating noises. I stayed right where I was, ignoring the cramps in my legs. I knew I didn't want to see what was happening.

Minutes later, Titus came back, and got inside the SUV. There was no blood, but the scent of blood and meat surrounded him. "You can sit up. The men who were waiting inside that truck are all dead."

I said nothing, just got my seat belt back on, and drove us up to the house, then back around to another four-car garage. The sun had set by now, and Devlin was there standing in the open bay. Titus got out with me.

"Trouble?" Devlin said to Titus, as I hugged him tightly.

"Ulysses got men into the truck as it was moving," Titus said, clearly surprised. "But I sensed them, and killed them. No one got hurt."

None of us said it, but I knew he'd eaten them, too, and then probably burned what was left with some of that blue fire. I thought with a little hysteria that at least they hadn't gone to waste, that their deaths meant something. A giggle rose in my throat, but I stifled it, not wanting to appear crazy even if I was heading that way fast.

"Sar, go ahead inside," Devlin said. "Seth, Keith, and Nick can began unpacking the groceries—"

"I need them to help me with my tools, to unload them," I said, giving myself a mental shake. "Then if they'd just carry everything in the Hummer to the kitchen, I'll only need one of them to help carry things downstairs. The furniture I ordered will be coming to us in a day or so."

"Then I'll help, too," Devlin said. I nodded, surprised but grateful.

With everyone's assistance, my tools and the rest were unloaded in a half hour. But after backing down the tractor, the only truly heavy thing left was the log splitter, which weighed about two thousand pounds. I lifted that down with the tractor loader, and towed it inside. I wondered as I looked at the machine if I'd ever use it again. A week ago that would have seemed ludicrous. But now my future seemed so uncertain.

Titus teleported the tractor-trailer back to the company, and left it there, making it seem that the driver had returned it. Devlin said he had paid by credit card, so the company would have no reason to suspect him. I didn't need to ask to know why. We didn't need any cops knocking on Hayden's front door, asking about missing drivers.

Everyone carried in groceries, and I spent the next hour putting them away. I realized then I'd forgotten to order any takeout. I made some quick soup from a can for Venus and I, and some toasted cheese sandwiches. Devlin sat with her as she ate, and I ate while I unpacked, not wanting to stop until I was done.

"Sorry honey," I said, to Venus. "Mommy forgot to get you any Chinese food."

"Tomorrow I need to go down to town anyway," Nick said from the doorway. "I can pick up something then for everyone from the Chinese place there. They know me, and I trust them. Besides, Lance and I, we can eat a little first of everything, and if there's a problem, like poison, Titus can heal us."

"Thank you both," I said warmly. Nick gave me a quick smile, then dropped his eyes.

I felt suddenly awkward, realizing the reason he was going to be going to town was he was going to see Klara. Perhaps Lance was, too. How could I out him to Serena now, when he'd just offered to do me a favor? But how could I call myself her friend if I didn't?

I blushed, and busied myself putting bacon in the freezer, deciding to wait another day to deal with that issue. The extra cold stuff I had the guys take downstairs, and then I collapsed in the chair. Venus crawled on my lap, and I hugged her.

"I'm glad you're here, Mom," she said in her sweet voice, looking at me with her golden eyes. "Are you going to live here now?"

Devlin was staring at me, the same question in his eyes. I didn't know what to say, so I just hugged Venus, and said nothing.

"Let's go in on the couch," Devlin said reaching out to touch my hand. "You've got to be exhausted, Sar."

"I'm too tired to move," I groaned.

"Then don't. Just hold still." Devlin picked both Venus and I up, and carried us into the couch. Happily, we snuggled into him. "There's my girls," Devlin said lovingly, giving us each a kiss. "Relax. Shall we watch a movie? I think *Poltergeist* is on."

The phone rang, but none of us moved to get it. Keith brought it in a second later, and handed it to me. "Theo for you," he said quietly. "He's called five times today."

Shit. I'd never called him about lunch. Why hadn't Dev said anything? I looked over at Dev, but he averted his eyes to the TV. It was clear that he'd not wanted me to talk to Theo, or to even know he'd called. More jealousy, even when I was here with him, and not with Theo? That had to be it. Sigh.

I swallowed hard, and said "Hello?"

"About *fucking time*!" Theo roared loudly. "Where have you been? You never called me, Sar! We were supposed to have lunch!"

Devlin's lip curled up immediately, and he took the phone from me. "Listen, you shmuck!" he hissed. "My best man is in jail, a vampire hunter attacked today, and Sar's been out all day running herself ragged. We just had another attack when she got home. So either be loving to her, or I guarantee that you won't talk to her again until you are. Maybe not even then."

Devlin smiled sweetly at me, then handed the phone back.

"Sar, are you okay?" Theo said worriedly, all traces of anger gone. "You aren't hurt?"

"I'm not hurt," I said tiredly. "I'm sorry I forgot to call. I'll try to teleport tomorrow to see you and Devon for lunch, with Titus."

"That would be fine. Or I could come with Devon there, if Titus will come and get us."

A shard of anger pierced me. Theo was only offering to come NOW, because Lash was in jail. How many times had I asked him to let me bring Devon here to see his twin sister? Fifty? A hundred? *Prick*. I said nothing, not trusting myself to talk.

Devlin moved to take the phone from me, but I held up my hand, and he stopped.

"No," I said, trying to not be testy. "I'll come to you. Is Theoron there?"

"Yes, he's home, and Danial is too, though he has a meeting he said he can't cancel tomorrow—"

Danial was going to die for his damned business. "Theo, don't let him go—"

"Sar, he's not just my friend, he's also my boss, and at four hundred plus, he's old enough to do what he wants."

It was true that you couldn't protect people who didn't want protection. But I'd try one more time anyway. "Can you put him on?"

Theo growled something in a low voice. A few minutes later, Danial came on.

"Hello, my Sweetheart," Danial said gently. "Devlin has told me how things are going—"

"Danial, don't go to your meeting tomorrow! Come to me here, instead." I took a deep breath. "Come and be with Dev and I."

There was silence. But I'd never flat out asked Danial not to go to a meeting, though I'd implied often through the years that I'd prefer he'd stayed home on occasion.

"Please," I whispered, "for me. Please don't go."

There was more silence. I waited.

"I'll be there, at sundown," Danial said finally. "But I'll have to go the next night, Sarelle. The client is too important to not take the job."

Same old Danial. Well, at least one night might make a difference.

"Tell Devlin I'll be there, if he isn't listening in already," Danial said. "I'm looking forward to seeing you. Now I'm going to put Theo back on."

By his tone, Theo was upset. I braced myself, waiting.

"You want to see him, for him to come there for sex, but not me and your child?" Theo growled, hurt. "What is wrong with you? Who are you, Sar?"

"Danial has always come here willingly," I grated. "You were the one who protested. And frankly, I'm very glad you did. I prefer Devon not come to Hayden, Theo. I don't want Ulysses knowing he's my child, for fear he'll try to hurt him." I swallowed hard. "Spend time with Jenny and he in lion form," I said, feeling like each word was ripping out pieces of my heart. "Do it outside, as soon as you can. If we're lucky, anyone watching will think Devon is her child, not mine, and then he'll be a lot safer. His safety matters more than me getting to see him."

Theo said nothing for several minutes. "I know what it cost you to say that," he said finally, his voice breaking. "I'll do it tonight, Sar. But I'm coming to Hayden myself next week, to spend the night with you. I'll make sure Devon's safe, and Rip's here to guard them both, but I need to see you, to be with you."

Would that work? Maybe. "Sounds good."

"I love you," Theo said.

Hearing the conviction in his voice, I softened. "I love you too. Take care."

I put down the phone, then snuggled into Dev's arms again, closing my eyes.

"I never thought Theo'd want to sleep with us," he teased.

I opened one eye and looked at him. He couldn't be serious. "You know that wasn't what Theo meant."

"You sleep with me, in my bed," Devlin said arrogantly. "He thinks he's kicking me out for the night, or taking you to another bed so he can have you alone, he's in for a surprise."

Did he have to be so deviant and jealous when I was so tired? "Why don't we all go to bed now?" I said with a sigh. "I'm exhausted."

"Good idea," Devlin said. "I need to talk to you privately anyway, before you're too tired to listen."

That didn't sound good.

I put Venus to bed, and saw Serena was there, asleep already. She awoke when I came in the nursery, even though I was as quiet as I could be. "Sar, I'm sorry about everything," Serena said, hugging me. "I'm glad you're staying here, where you're safe."

I wanted to tell her about Nick, but this was so not the time. I'd do it tomorrow.

"Sar, come to bed," Devlin called from his room. I gave Serena a last smile, and went to him.

As Devlin and I undressed, I worried for a moment that he was going to make a move. But he just put on pajama bottoms, and got in bed. I went in the bathroom, and dressed myself, putting in a small tampon so it looked like I was still menstruating. As it was I was pushing it by a night, saying I'd be with them both tomorrow. But one night shouldn't matter. I wasn't going to be trying for another child anytime soon, if ever again.

Devlin waited until I was settled in bed before he spoke. "Sar, Danial is taking this more seriously, but still not serious enough. So first off, thank you for convincing him to come tomorrow. I'll try to talk some sense into him." He paused. "Second, Lash is going to have to be in jail until probably mid-December—"

I went tense as a clothesline in an ice storm. "*Mid December!*"

"—he'll be acquitted of everything except punching that police officer. My lawyer is certain of it, and he's the best there is at this kind of thing. We've got Lash's weapons, and Titus also brought back Lash's truck from where he'd left it in town, so there are no traces of blood to find anywhere. I've also bribed the guards at the prison. Lash can call at least once a day here, and receive calls from Hayden at all times—"

I breathed a sigh of relief, relaxing.

"—but you are not to call him, or talk to him when he calls—"

Annoyance was rapidly becoming fury. "What? Why?"

"—because he asked that you not call him. Not because he doesn't miss you, but because he misses you so much. Those were his words. But Gina will go to him every week for conjugal visits, or as much as he needs her to. I've had my lawyer forge papers saying she's his wife. At least he can get a little relief, even if he can't drink—"

I felt tears threatening, I was so frustrated, worried and jealous. Devlin noticed, took on a reassuring tone. "Lash is going to be stressed out in prison. First off, it's loud and noisy, and he's quiet. Second, he'll be with people a lot, and you know as well as I that Lash prefers to be alone. I got him a private cell, and other perks, like his own TV, but he'll still have to eat with everyone else, and shower with them, etc.—"

Shower scenes from a ton of prison movies filled my mind, making me queasy.

"—And third, he can't change form. If his sentence was any longer, I'd have Titus break him out, and substitute someone else, making them look like him. But that's risky, and if we were discovered, Lash would have to go into hiding for the next sixty years or so. You remember all the trouble Theo had in that small town, the first time I saved your life? There are always some officers who can't be bought for any price. And their memories are usually very, very long, even if their lives are short human ones. And killing them never works, it always causes more problems."

I nodded. I remembered too well. We were in this ordeal because of a vendetta. The last thing we needed was to create new ones.

"Lash is going to come back different, more tense," Devlin said, regretful. "But he'll be okay in time. And he won't have a record. My lawyer is going to have the case sealed, and the papers misfiled. All Lash has to do is serve the time. Besides, there's really no way to get around it. He's got to walk out of there, not break out, or it won't matter he has a new face and fingerprints. He'll be wanted, and restricted to the grounds of Hayden for the next twenty years, if not longer. And it will also screw up his jobs, too, those ones he has to do in December."

Wouldn't want to fuck up any assassinations, no sir...*Don't say that aloud, Sar.*

"I've killed that hunter, drained him completely, so I won't need to feed for at least a few weeks. He was responsible for killing William, so I am sending the remains of the hunter, and William's ashes to his best friend, a not un-influential vampire in Quebec. That solves that problem at least."

"Good," I said, not knowing what else to say.

221

"On a happy note, Theoron is staying the weekend, even with Lash not able to give him any more training. I thought you'd like to know, so you can spend time with him."

That was good news. "I'll worry about him a lot less here."

Devlin ran his hand along my cheek and neck, stroking gently. "You know, you could bring Devon here, if you wanted to—"

"Theo would never go for it, not if he wasn't here too," I said, trying to be gentle. "But it's okay. Devon is safer where he is."

At least, that was what I was hoping.

* * * *

The next day went fast.

I took the dogs for a long walk. Devlin had let them out for me yesterday, but they were crawling up the walls, looking for some exercise. And a promise was a promise. Titus went with us, and in front, so he melted the snow for us a little with his body heat. It was slushy, but I wasn't complaining. It was a hell of a lot easier walking in slush, as the drifts we walked through were five feet high in places, and I no longer had any snowshoes to wear.

I also walked on the treadmill a little later, and practically died after forty minutes. But I was making progress. My jeans felt looser, or so I told myself anyway.

I made some good lunch for Venus and teleported to see Theo. It was a disaster. Devon was in one of his moods where he thought it was cute to try and trip me. Theo told him to knock it off with growls three separate times, but he merely waited until Theo left the room to talk to T to start in again with his winding around my feet. Finally, he did trip me, and I dropped the entire lunch I was making—our grilled cheese sandwiches, on the floor, and the pan hit my foot. I cried out in pain, cursing, and fell against the stove, and the tomato soup in the pot fell off, a wave of it going over a shocked Devon, coating him from head to foot.

"What the hell?" Theo roared from the doorway. "God Damn it, Devon!"

Devon put his tail between his legs, and tried to run, but Theo grabbed him by the scruff of his neck, and held him up in the air, roaring at him loudly, over and over. Devon howled loudly at whatever Theo was saying to him, shivering in Theo's grasp, and I felt immediately bad for him. I went to take him from Theo, but he gently pushed me back, and roared again, one last time. Devon's eyes went huge, and then he began to bawl, and Theo set him back on the floor, glaring down at him. Devon shook under his father's gaze, and then he made a puddle on the floor.

I looked at him in shock, and then gathered him up in my arms, grunting under the weight of him. He was still shaking, and crying loudly, and he tried to burrow into me.

"Devon, it's okay!" I said, hugging him, but he just cried harder, still burrowing into me.

"What did you say to him?" I said in a low voice, but there were razors in my words.

"Sar, I'm sorry, I—"

"*What* did you say to our son?"

"I told him that he'd better behave from now on," Theo said gruffly. "That I would spank him until his bottom was raw if he ever did anything like this again. That he was a bad son, and I was ashamed of him."

Theo stopped.

"And what else?" I said in a dangerous voice.

"I told him that unless he started being the son I knew he could be, you wouldn't be seeing him again. That you wouldn't come visit him again. That you wouldn't want to."

Devon began to cry again loudly, and it was in the moment I finally understood that he could really understand what was being said around him, when people spoke to one another. Because he was being hurt all over again, hearing the words in English a second time.

"How dare you?" I hissed at him. "How dare you say such a thing to my son! I will always love him, always want him, always come to see him, even if he doesn't behave—!"

"I said I was sorry, I'm just on edge! And he's *our* son—!"

"It was *you* I didn't want to see!" I hissed at him. "You with your judgments, your selfishness, your endless wanting of all my affection—!"

"I'm your *fucking husband*, and I *deserve all your affection*! I—"

I pushed past him, not listening, and went into Danial's bathroom, putting Devon down on the floor, and shutting the door behind me.

"Devon, I need to wash the soup off you," I said tiredly. "Cooperate. Got it?"

Devon looked at me and nodded.

"Get into the tub," I said, and he jumped in, grimacing a little.

I washed him off with shampoo, and he cried a little, when it got in his eyes, but I looked at him sternly, and he stayed there, under the water. When it was all off, I dried him off, and then told him to stay there on the towel, and wait for me. I got some clothes from Danial's room, and dressed. Then I washed off the speckles of soup on my arms and face, and the ones here and there all over the bathroom. Devon was good, staying there, and watching me.

After I was done, I gathered Devon into my arms, even though he was so heavy it was like lifting Ghost, and brought him into Danial's bedroom, staggering a little under his weight.

"You know I love you," I said, kissing him gently. He purred for me, and nodded, but his long tufted tail was still tucked between his legs, not held in his normal relaxed-happy question mark position.

Seeing how upset he still was, I wondered seriously if it might be better to take him to Hayden with me, to live with me, and not Theo. Theo was trying to deal with Jenny, and helping Theoron and Danial run the business, while still doing his own job of security. Maybe it was too much, to have him be the sole parent of Devon, too, even though I knew Elle, Cia, and the other foxes were helping out.

But was I any better? Could I give him that much more attention than Theo did? Venus was watched a lot by Serena, and now Titus. She ate more meals with them than me, though that was going to change, if I was under house arrest from now on.

But Devon needed me. The time I was spending with him clearly wasn't enough. He wanted more of my attention, just as his father did. That was why he'd acted out as he had.

I wondered also how much of Theo's anger was due to my refusing him sex earlier. When I'd teleported to Danial's, Theo had been waiting for me, and he'd clearly wanted to be intimate. He'd kissed me hard, and been backing me toward the basement bedroom when I'd told him to knock it off. I'd been upset from Lash going to jail, and finding out Robin had died, and I hadn't been in the mood for sex, I'd wanted to see Devon. Theo had been angry, accusing me of always being in the mood for Devlin, but never for him.

I'd glared at him, and opened my mouth to say something probably better not said, but then Devon had come running out, purring, and Theo had relented. Elle had visited for a while, but she'd left when Violet called to talk to her. Theo assured me she'd been meeting Violet at the mall once a week, but he'd tailed her himself the first time, and she'd behaved herself, seeing a movie, and then having dinner at the food court. I had given Theo a hug, and told him I thought he was a great father, and he'd beamed under my praise like a schoolboy. Now I wasn't so sure.

After thinking everything through, I relented, and decided to leave Devon where he was. Ulysses didn't know about him. It was better for him to be here, and be a little miserable for a while longer, instead of being dead. He meant the world to me, and I couldn't risk him being hurt. Here he was safe. If he came to Hayden, Ulysses would know he was my child. I couldn't risk that.

I cleaned up the kitchen, with Devon's help, and then I told him I had to get home, but I'd be back again. Elle was off the phone, and she said she'd look after him until Theo got back from wherever he'd gone. Devon looked sad to see me go, but when I promised him I'd see him that weekend, he purred again. Theo hadn't been around when I'd emerged with Devon from the bathroom. So I left without saying good-bye to him.

Chapter Twenty

Late that afternoon, I decided to hang up the birdfeeders, and got a surprise. Lash had fixed them both for me. He'd sanded the bubbled and blistered paint down to the bare metal, and repainted them a forest green, with gold trim.

I cried for a while, holding them, wishing he were here so I could thank him.

I hung them from the front tree, in front of the largest kitchen window that faced the forest in back of Hayden. I filled them with seed, then sprinkled some on the ground. I knew it would take the birds a few days to find them. As I looked up, I saw on the bottom of the bigger feeder, Lash had written something. There, where only the person filling it would see, if they were shorter as I or he was, was "Sar + Lash" in gold paint. I laughed seeing that, and for the first time that day, I wore a real smile. There was some good still in the world, in spite of all the bad things. But it was getting dark, and colder as night fell, and I slowly trudged inside, feeling tired.

Devlin came down later, as I was eating some bologna cheese sandwiches and soup with Serena and Venus and said he was going to get an update to Lash via his lawyer. "I'll say hi for you."

"Tell him thanks, for fixing my bird feeders. I liked the green and gold very much."

Devlin looked at me a little strangely, and said he'd pass on the message.

Soon, it was night, and an hour after dusk fell, Danial arrived. He came and sat with Venus and I and Serena, and talked with us, as we finished up the cake Serena had made with Venus earlier. And then, he took me by the hand, and led me upstairs to Devlin, who was waiting for us both.

I felt a little scared, as I took off my clothes. I worried that I'd be hurt, or just too frigid, with all that had happened to enjoy making love with anyone. I sure hadn't felt like it with Theo earlier, and part of his anger had been about that. But when I felt the brush of their fangs on my bare skin, I forgot my fear, and embraced them with longing and passion.

Devlin had prepared me this time before Danial had arrived, so my body was ready to receive them both. Devlin entered me first, as we lay on our sides kissing. But before long, I felt Danial easing inside me as well, moaning softly as he held my body still for him.

"I love the feel of you squeezing me, holding me so tightly, my love," Danial said raggedly. "Dev, I can't wait—"

"Don't then," Devlin said eagerly, and they began to move as one inside me. My eyes closed and I gasped, and Devlin chuckled low, as he kissed my throat.

"Sigh for me, Sar," he whispered, pricking me with his fangs. "There's a sigh for yes and a sigh for no and a sigh for I can't bear it. Tell us how good we're making you feel, that you can't bear for us to stop!"

Wave after wave of pleasure hit me, and I cried out again and again. "Please, please don't stop…it feels so good…you feel so good!"

Danial and Devlin didn't draw it out, as we all needed release badly, and soon, I was screaming for them, as they bit down together into my neck.

"Danial! Devlin! *Please*! *Oh*! *Oh*!"

Danial shuddered once, pushing himself deeply into me, and I felt him filling me, as he drew his fangs out of my skin and cried out wordlessly, louder than I'd ever heard him. "*Ahhh!!*"

He slipped out of me, as his orgasm ebbed, and Devlin rolled on his back so I was astride his sitting form, still feeding from me as he moved his hips rhythmically under mine. Devlin was drinking me down, still thrusting, but he came a moment later, pushing my hips down on his to receive all of him as he came. "*Sar!*"

Then he was easing me down on him, to hold me close, the both of us panting. We didn't say anything for some moments, just breathing and trying to get enough air into our lungs to slow our racing hearts.

"I could do that every night with you, Sar, and it would feel just as incredible," Danial moaned. "God, I can't get over how good it feels, being in you like that."

I was glad I felt so good to him, but equally glad that he didn't sleep with me every night, because while I might not mind all the prep work for this once in a while, I would for sure mind doing it every night. A lot. As in, I wouldn't do it.

"It's so good to be with you and she like this," Devlin said with pleasure, looking over at Danial with me in his arms. "I love hearing you scream as you have her, to feel us coming together within her."

I thought that a little weird, but then I guessed Devlin had to be a voyeur. I wasn't surprised, to find that out about him. Danial was too, at least a little, or he wouldn't have been so interested in having a threesome with Theo. He knew Theo was were, and would go on making love to me long after he was through. But maybe Danial would get some of that demon blood. Then he might give Theo a run for his money.

I shivered a little, and Devlin laughed a little, thinking it the remnants of my orgasm.

Danial and Devlin hugged me gently, and were quiet. But I had a question. Two actually.

"Who said that quote, Dev?" I said with interest, running my hands over his golden chest hair. "This isn't the first time you've quoted me that."

"Keats," Devlin said, brushing my neck with his lips. "And I knew you would remember I had quoted it to you before, my Darling Sar. I knew you would remember *when...*"

There was so much affection in his voice I found it hard to think about much else, despite he was being a little creepy again. But I had one other question. "Is my blood nearer summer?"

They were both quiet for a full minute, and I was dismayed, knowing what their silence meant.

"It's the same," Devlin said finally. "The first thaw of winter, Sar. But it's going to take time. Titus said probably in December, it would be like summer again."

Danial clutched me tight to him, and I felt his fear again, that he would lose me. I opened my mouth to ask them if I smelled different too, but left the words unspoken. Danial was upset enough as things were. I didn't need to rub it in. Besides, neither Danial nor Devlin had ever spoken of my scent to me. For all I knew, I only smelled like a partly turned human. And after lovemaking, I was drowning in their scents anyway, their sweetness and spice engulfing me completely.

"Dev, I want you to remove Sar's choker," Danial said in an emotional voice. "I brought mine with me, and I would like her to wear it for a while. We'll trade off, every other week."

I expected Dev to sneer, and refuse, or just flatly say "no," as he had the one time I'd asked him to remove the choker, right after the Hallows party. But he didn't speak, just reached his hand to my neck, and undid it. A second later, Danial had fastened his choker with the fox head about my neck. He hugged me tightly to him, and then Devlin reached his arms around both of us and hugged us. "I love you both," Devlin said softly. "Sleep. We'll find a way clear of all this. The worst is over."

I fell asleep, wanting to believe him, and dreamed no dreams.

* * * *

In the morning, things went to hell again. A frantic Serena awakened us at six a.m., as she pounded on the door. "Nick never came back last night from town," she said, her eyes tearful. "No one's heard anything—!"

Shit! That was right! Nick was going to bring us takeout! "Has he called in?"

"Damn it! I told him not to go alone!" Devlin roared, getting out of bed wearing only his skin. I flushed, then remembered Serena had seen him naked before, and blushed harder. Danial put on a robe, and handed me mine.

"Is Titus here?" Devlin said as he pulled on his jeans from the day before, and Serena nodded.

Poor Titus was getting a workout. But he'd been ready to let Lash die, so he'd kind of had this coming. I sure as hell wasn't feeling bad for him. Well, maybe a little.

Devlin threw on some jeans, and went downstairs. Danial, Serena and I followed him. Titus was at the kitchen table, looking at a map of some kind. Devlin went to him.

Titus looked up at him, and he looked bone weary. "Nick's by this bridge," he said sadly in a rumbling tone. "The tracking spell on him says he's alive—"

That was smart, putting tracking spells on all of us, not just me.

"—but he's very weak. I'm going to teleport him back, but..."

"Do it," Devlin said, nodding. "Is everyone else accounted for?"

"Yes," Titus said. "But Lance is dead, Dev. We are down two guards now. Rip is with Terian. He's close to normal, but it's probably going to be another few days at least, even if we push it, Devlin—"

"Don't push it," Devlin said, sitting down. "We need him on our side, not Hell's."

What did that mean? Did I want to know? *Probably not.*

Titus nodded, and disappeared. Venus came in looking sleepy, and I hugged her wordlessly. Devlin saw how upset I was, and he hugged the both of us. I motioned to Serena, and she came, and embraced us too. Devlin looked a little uncomfortable when she did, but I figured he could suck it up, just this once. After all, if he hadn't always been bedding so many women, he wouldn't always be finding himself in uncomfortable positions.

Titus was back in a few seconds with a man that looked like...just muscle. I ran to the bathroom when I realized Nick had been skinned, dragging an interested Venus along with me by the hand. She was too young to see this, though she kept looking back with curiosity. I shut the door behind us, and locked it. I felt bad I wasn't out there helping, but I just couldn't take anymore. My mind felt like it was going to snap.

"Mom?"

"Shush," I said, trying like hell to be calm. "We need to wait in here a little bit. Be good, and wait with me. Your father has to do what he can, and we need to be in here, until he's done."

Venus was irritated, but she listened to me, and sat down quietly on my lap. A little while later, Danial knocked on the door. "Sar, can I come in?"

I opened it, and he came in and shut it behind him.

"Is he dead?" I whispered. I'd liked Nick, and even if I hadn't, for Serena's sake, I didn't want him to die. She'd already lost one lover this year, and she hadn't loved him the way she loved Nick.

"No," Danial said. "But he's very weak. Titus is doing something, with Serena's help. He said it would save him, though he'll need bed rest for a week. If Serena hadn't been waiting for him this morning, and raised the alarm that he and Lance were missing, he'd be dead. As it was he was just lucky that Ulysses's men did him second. Lance died from blood loss, Sar. They—"

I put my finger to my lips, and Danial cut off his words. Venus didn't need it spelled out for her that this time, the werebears had been skinned alive.

I hugged him, and Venus, not to be left out, hugged us both. Danial gave her a gentle smile, and pulled her between us, where she smiled up at us happily. "That female werebear he was seeing in town was dead, skinned too," Danial said, speaking carefully. "Werewolf pelts are worth the most, because they're so rare. But even a werebear pelt of a kind that's common, like grizzly, is about a hundred K on the black market, Sar. Ulysses has even more funds now to draw on."

I looked up at Danial. "Don't go home, please," I pleaded. "Come here to Hayden, stay with us—!"

"And leave my home?" Danial said in surprise. "Elle and Theoron call that their home too, and Theo—"

"You're a prime target, like me," I said, tears forming. "I don't want to see your ashes in a box!"

"You won't, I promise you," Danial said reassuringly, kissing me. "Now come back to bed with me, and sleep. Devlin is busy working, trying to locate Ulysses with Michael's help. Devlin's going to leave him a message tomorrow, but—"

"Can I come too?" Venus asked, looking a little lost.

"Of course you can, Princess," Danial said with a loving smile, lifting her in his arms. "I'll even carry you. Your mom has to feed the pets, though, before she can join us."

Danial left the bathroom with her, and I stayed behind to feed the dogs. Someone had let them out, probably Serena, but they ate, and went out again. I called them with me as I went upstairs, and they followed reluctantly. The cats Serena had already fed, and they were all sleeping together—Phantom and Cavity, and Jessica piled into one, large, pillowy cat bed. I looked at them lovingly, and was happy again they were getting along so well.

Soon, Danial and I were settled back under the covers, Venus between us, the dogs in their own beds. Venus fell asleep quickly, and Danial kissed her lightly, stroking her hair. It reminded me so much of he and Elle that for a moment, I couldn't say anything.

"It makes me wish we'd had a girl, too," Danial said, looking over and caressing me with his eyes. "She's so beautiful, Sar."

"She is," I said, laying my head on his shoulder. "Just like her father."

"Things are going to be okay," Danial said, kissing me. "Believe me."

"I do," I said, but I think both of us heard the lie in my voice.

* * * *

Later that afternoon, I awoke to find only Venus beside me, nudging me. "The door's locked," she said, petulantly. "Open it, Mom. I want to play with my dolls. I can't sleep anymore!"

I got up, and tried the door. It was indeed locked. I looked over and saw the spare key on the mantle, but I waited to unlock the door, as Danial would not have locked it and left silently without a good reason. First, I helped her take a bath, and get dressed again. After, I made her wait for me, as I showered, and then, after dressing her in fresh clothes from her room, we went downstairs, hand in hand, the two dogs in tow.

The kitchen was empty. I looked down at Venus. I needed some normalcy. "Want to bake some cookies with me?"

Her face lit up. "We've never done that!" Venus said with excitement. "How do we do it?"

For the first time, I was glad that I was living here. If everything hadn't happened, I'd be missing out on this time with my daughter. And I didn't want to screw up again.

"Come on," I said, laughing, "I'll show you."

We made chocolate chip cookies, and oatmeal raisin cookies, and brownies too. Titus came in partway through our baking session, and inhaled, looking envious. Devlin was with him

"This might be worth a spell, so I could eat one of those brownies," Titus said longingly.

Devlin looked at him in utter amazement, then craftiness. "Make one for me and Danial and yourself," he said, hugging me. "I've long wanted to taste Sar's cooking, whatever it costs."

"It wouldn't be expensive," Titus said. "I just have to set something up to teleport the food out of you and me after we'd swallowed it, before our bodies process it."

This sounded like a magical sort of eating sickness. I made a face, but made sure they couldn't see it.

"Isn't there some spell so I could actually digest it?" Devlin said hopefully.

"Dev, you're vampire," Titus said in a droll voice. "You can't digest anything but blood, as you well know after you drink wine."

I carefully concentrated on getting the cookies off the rack, because I didn't want to think too much about what he was saying. Way too much information.

"Fine," Devlin said with a little regret. "It's enough to taste it."

"It will take five minutes for me to whip up," Titus said. "I'll be right back."

Sure enough, Titus was back in five minutes, and they both drank down a potion. Then they grabbed one of each kind of dessert, and sat at the table.

Devlin seemed nervous and hesitant, but Titus bit into his brownie without preamble.

"These are very good, Sar," Titus said, groaning a little in his bass voice. "Moist and gooey! Give me the recipe, and I'll give it to Leri. She'll like these very much, she's a chocoholic. And if you don't mind, I'll take a few to Terian, too."

"Please do," I said, and I handed him a cookbook. "There's the recipe."

Titus tucked it under his arm, and gathered up his two other cookies, and about five brownies. Devlin was still looking longingly at his own plate of baked treats.

"Dev, you had five minutes," Titus said in exasperation. "Now you have four. Eat already! Once it wears off, that's it for a few days. I can't give you another one. And don't be taking the one you got for Danial, it'll make you sick if you take them both."

Titus disappeared, leaving Devlin still looking at the brownies. "It's been four hundred years since I had anything but blood, water, and wine," he whispered, looking scared. "Since I ate anything solid, any kind of real food."

I put my hand on his shoulder. "Try one," I said, my voice encouraging.

Devlin took a cookie, and hesitantly bit into it. Then he was stuffing his face, eating brownies and cookies one after the other, grinning, and making a mess of crumbs all over himself, the table, and the floor. But four minutes later, he stopped. I was happy but also relieved, as he'd eaten six brownies, and five of each type of cookie.

"They were delicious," Devlin said, hugging me, his golden curls nestled against my stomach. "I've had a kind of cake before, but not like those brownies. We didn't have chocolate back then. And I've never had cookies before, ever. At least, not that tasted that good."

"I'm glad you liked them," I said, ruffling his hair. Venus ate a few too and pronounced them good, as she watched me get out the last batch.

"I have a favor to ask," I said. "Can you ask Rip or Titus to teleport these to Gina, so she can take some to Lash, when she visits him?"

Devlin looked at me curiously. "You know she's going there to lay him, and you still want to make him things to comfort him?" he said in surprise. "Danial was right, you do love—"

"Will you do it?" I said sharply, cutting him off.

"Yes, I will," Devlin said, giving me a very calculating look. "It will be good for his sanity and morale, to eat your cooking. Though I suggest you make meat loaf or something with meat in it next week, because he's probably needing protein a lot more than sugar."

Ah. Why hadn't I thought of that? "Ask her to ask him what he'd like," I said. "And also what they'll allow. There might be restrictions. I don't want to send something, and then have them say he can't have it."

Devlin nodded, his eyes still on me, a thoughtful yet calculating expression on his face. Then he walked out of the room.

* * * *

Later that night, we watched an old eighties movie, *About Last Night?* Venus was playing quietly on the floor, coloring in some coloring books. She could do that for hours. Dev and I had each colored a picture with her, but after completing one, my hands were tired. I rarely held a writing instrument these days. All my work was done on computer. Which reminded me, I needed to get back into doing some work tomorrow.

I turned to Dev in shock only ten minutes into the movie.

"What?" he said, noticing my expression.

"I knew you reminded me of someone, back when I first met you," I said, studying him.

Devlin rolled his eyes a little. "I thought when the twentieth century was over, I was done with that—"

"You have his eyes," I said, more than a little lust in my words. "Rob Lowe's—"

"Stop," Devlin said, acting grumpy, though I could see he liked me lusting after him. "There isn't that much resemblance. You can just say I have sexy eyes."

"Okay, you have sexy eyes. Very sexy eyes."

"Well, thank you, my darling," Devlin purred. "Perhaps it's time for bed?"

"Not just yet," I said with a smile. "I haven't had time to see T all weekend, and he's heading back tomorrow morning, early."

"Tonight, actually," T corrected, coming into the room with an easy smile. "Dad and I have a meeting tonight at midnight, and I said I'd be back. But I wanted to spend some time with you, Mom. What movie is this?"

I knew just by looking at him that something was different. "Something's different about you," I said, looking at him. "What is it?"

T looked at me and flushed a deep purple. I flushed a little myself, as I couldn't believe that Devlin had taught him so fast. Because that was what this had to be. No wonder he'd come for the weekend!

"Did things go well?" I said softly. When had Serena had time?

T nodded.

"T was very good," Devlin said. "Diana was very pleased with his performance. All three times."

"Diana"? I looked at Devlin in shock. T blushed deeper. Then it hit me; Dev had let my son have sex with Ulysses's virgin sister, under the influence of his blood!

"What?" Devlin said with a shrug. "I just let her know that it was what I wanted her to do, and she did it happily, Sar. She was willing enough."

I stared at him, my mouth open, letting him know I was appalled, and disgusted, because with his blood, there was no way she could have resisted being willing. But I said nothing. T didn't need the guilt, and it wasn't his fault. But I was going to break it down real well for Dev later.

Dev caught my look, and sighed. "Sar, I'm going to let her go, if Ulysses does what he's promised, and gives me himself," Dev said slowly. "But I have my reputation to think of. And there was no way I was letting her go still a virgin, especially when that is the best thing a young man out for first time instruction can have."

"*Why* is that?" I choked out. "I'd think an experienced woman—"

"Because she didn't know what to ask for, or do, and T's lessons are not about just his own pleasure, but how to give it too. He needed to know how to take a woman's virginity, so as not to hurt her, and how to move her, how to position her, where and how to kiss her, when to move very slowly, and when to move fast—"

"All right!" I get it!" I said loudly. T was almost purple again, and I was red myself.

Devlin wasn't embarrassed at all. "Your son is much as you are, Sar," he said, a gentle smile on his face as he ruffled T's hair. "He's adventurous in bed, despite that he's so young, and he has some natural skill, as I do. He needs no more instruction from me. Half the fun of bedding women is learning new things! But after you take him home, I'll be needing your presence. Come to me in the Jacuzzi."

Lust was strong in his words, and I knew for a fact then that he'd been in the room with Theoron and Diana, instructing them both, probably, and watching them. But I'd known he was a voyeur from before. A romp in the tub could wait, though, and so could he. My interest in the movie was forgotten, and my interest in joining him in the Jacuzzi was nil.

I got up from the couch, and teleported T home immediately. We arrived to see Danial there waiting for him on the great room sofa, looking a little nervous. He rocketed to his feet as we appeared. "How did it go, T?" Danial said, his words very careful.

Clearly, I was the only one not in the know about why T was spending the weekend. But maybe I was just trying to turn a blind eye. With Lash in jail, what other reason would T have had to be at Hayden?

"Fine," T said, casting an embarrassed look at me. "I had read a lot, to prepare myself, so nothing was a surprise, except that she wanted me to drink from her, Dad, once she felt me biting her during the love play."

"You are surprised because of your mom, because you know it hurts her? But you've drunk from many women, T; you know most women don't feel pain, just a rush of pleasure, if they notice at all."

"This one was different. She noticed as soon as Devlin had me open a shallow cut, when I was kissing her. She almost liked the biting more than...than the sex. And she didn't want me to stop biting her and taking her blood, not even when she was beginning to get weak—"

"Who were you with?" Danial said, furrowing his brow. "Serena is not like that, Dev would've told me when he first had her, back in Rio. He's always liked those types of women best—"

Big surprise. Ugh.

"Diana, Ulysses's sister."

Danial's face drained of blood, and then he looked a little sick. He cut his eyes to me, and then back to T. He took a deep breath. "There are very few women who are as you describe. They are very sensitive to the healing component in our saliva, so sensitive that what they feel when bitten is close to climax, at least as one woman described it thus to me."

I remembered Jeannette, the woman in Europe Danial had fed from. I understood now why Devlin had picked Diana. It wasn't just that she was a virgin.

"You have that component in your saliva too, because your body renews itself with blood, T. And you have to be very careful with women like that, or you can kill them easily, or turn them. You will often have to pry them off you, when you feed off such a woman, and you must be very careful when healing them, before you leave them."

"I healed her wounds just enough to stop the bleeding, under Devlin's careful instruction," T said. "But there was still a wound."

"Probably best," Danial nodded. "We don't know yet if your blood can also turn a human, if you give them enough. You should be very careful, until you know for sure."

"I'll be careful," T nodded. "Dev said I also might not have the vampire immunity to disease, though he thought I probably did. I'm going to be very careful, even if I know that I'm with a woman who is, um,…safe."

It was in his words that he was going to be seeing someone soon for sex, and I looked at him in shock and then at Danial, telling the latter he'd better say or do something.

"T, who is it you are going to be bedding?" Danial said. "I understand if you don't want to tell me, but—"

It couldn't be any of the women on the grounds. They were all spoken for. Then I had a horrible thought. There was one who wasn't, and she wasn't related to him by blood…

"Serena," T said. Danial and I immediately let out a relieved sigh.

For a moment, no one said anything. Then T began speaking. "Devlin said to go to her as much as I wanted to for the rest of the year, that it was his gift to me for becoming a man."

It was more than that. He was hoping T's good looks and kindness would get Serena's mind off Nick. And it was true, it might. Nick was by far more muscular, but bigger muscles wasn't always what a woman hungered for…

Stop right there, Sar.

"—and so I spoke to her, and Serena said it was okay if I came to her with Mom, when she went back to Hayden after visiting you during the week."

Danial hugged T to him. "I'm glad it went well for you. My first time did not, and I wanted you to have no bad memories, as I did. Go take a long shower, and get some rest. I need to talk to your mom a minute, before she goes back to Hayden."

T nodded, and after hugging me, he left. Danial waited until he was out of earshot, and then he turned to me. I didn't have to say a word, it was all on my face.

"Sar, Devlin was going to do something like this, no matter what," Danial sighed. "But in spite of the fact that it worked out well for both he and Diana, Ulysses now has a reason to hate T specifically, where he didn't before."

"I know!" I said, shaking my head. "I can't believe he did this! I'm going to put his balls through the wringer when I go back tonight, Danial, that he—"

"—but it's true, women like that are rare, and it's good that T had his first time with one," Danial said quickly, as if making himself say the words. "If he hadn't, he might have been with one someday and killed her, or turned her, if it's possible he can. It's easy to do, with a woman like that, and I'm saying this from experience, Sar. And I don't want T to be a killer."

Another dig at Lash. Wasn't it enough he was in jail? Then I saw Danial's face and understood he'd killed a woman, drained her. This hadn't been a dig at Lash after all. It had been a confession.

I went to him and hugged him, saying nothing. After a moment, he hugged me back, and then we separated. "Go home," Danial said, kissing me. "I'll call and let you know if anything happens."

"Here," I said, offering him the potion and a plate of cookies and brownies. "These are for you. Titus said you only have five minutes, from the time you take the potion."

Danial looked at me questioningly.

"You can eat these, if you drink this first," I said, some of my joy for him coming through to my voice. "Devlin tried it earlier, and it worked, he didn't get sick."

Danial pulled me to him so fast I almost dropped everything. The potion and the plate of cookies clattered down on the nearby coffee table as he kissed me with enough tenderness and love that I swooned in his arms, and my legs went weak. Danial pushed me gently back and in the next second I was on the couch, and he was laying his body on top of mine as he had those years ago, the night we had first kissed. He kissed me for a long, long time, and I held him to me, running my hands though his glossy hair, and over his wide shoulders. I inhaled the scent that was his and his alone, that mix of cedar and nutmeg, spice and allure.

"Take me, please, Danial," I whispered gently. "Right here, the way I wanted you to that first night we kissed on my couch—"

Danial let out a groan, and then he kissed me harder, slipping off my jeans, and then his own. He thrust hard into me, and then he was crying out softly in pleasure, as we moved in rhythm together. He pushed my top up, and in a moment, his lips were fastened on my breast. I let out a long moan of pleasure. I ran my hands over his chest, over his wide shoulders. I remembered that long ago night like it was yesterday, and too soon, I was climaxing hard, Danial coming a second later as he bore down with his hips in a frenzied motion, moaning loudly as he jetted into me.

"I wanted you so much that night," he whispered, kissing my throat, my face, my lips. "It had been years since I'd really desired a woman, since I'd even lain with one..."

I looked at him in shock. I hadn't known it had been that long. "I knew there was a reason you were so into me," I said teasingly, kissing his neck tenderly.

"You are my reason for everything I do," he whispered softly in my ear. "My reason for being so happy. I'm so glad I met you, that we're together. Tell me you feel it for me too, Love. That you don't regret everything that's happened, saving me, loving me, having a child with me—"

"Danial, I could never think that, any of it—!"

"I brought you into this world, and made you my own. You are in danger and have been these past years because I didn't leave you alone, as I knew I should."

"We're all in danger because of Dev! Not you, Danial! All of this is Dev's fault, because he can't control his behavior! And I'm going to give him a piece of my mind tonight—!" *If not a sharp pointy object, too.*

"Sar," Danial said soothingly, hugging me. "Dev's not going to change. There's no point in yelling at him. And it is fact that Diana is probably going to die as collateral damage. It's not pretty or fair, or anything but sickening, but Devlin can't afford to be soft now. The other Rulers are watching, the vampire hunters are watching, Ulysses is watching. They see a moment's weakness, and they'll descend one after another. Then even with Titus's help, and Lash's, if he were here, Dev wouldn't stand a chance. Neither would you or I. Devlin must be almost legendary in his cruelty, as he always has been, or the blood that will be spilled will be yours, and mine, and your children's. I'd spill Diana's blood myself to stave off that. So would you."

I took a deep breath, and put my anger aside. But just for now.

"Come," Danial said, taking my hand, and helping me up. "I want you to be here when I eat these. I'll need to leave within the hour. I'll be gone until tomorrow night, but I'll call when I get home."

We got into our clothes. Danial drank the potion right after, and hesitantly bit into the cookies. He ate the first one slowly and delicately, but when I told him he only had three minutes left, he began to devour them as Devlin had, though he was neat and didn't get crumbs everywhere. He closed his eyes, and savored the taste, chewing with relish, and making little "Ahh" noises. After he was done, he hugged me. "Tell Dev thanks for me," he said with a smile. "I've wanted to eat your baking for a long time, my Sweetheart. Have him tell me how often we can do this, too. I'm sure he's already asked, and Titus can make him and me potions regularly, so we can do this again. I'd love to try that pumpkin pie Theo was always going on about—"

"How is Theo?"

Danial was quiet, and I could see by his face he was wondering how much to tell me.

"Don't hold back like you did with Tasha, Danial. Tell me, and tell me all of it. Right now."

Danial sighed. "Theo's overwrought from trying to watch everyone, and also manage the business with me. He hates that you're with Devlin at Hayden, even though Lash isn't there, even though he knows it's the safest place for you to be. If anything, his jealousy seems to be worse now than it ever was. He's been changing every night, and mating with Jenny in lion form. That seems to be keeping him from losing it, but I don't know how much longer he can keep it together. He misses you, and he's going crazy here with no one to strike out at. But we're all tense, Sar; the foxes, the bears, all of us, even the demons with all their power. Everyone is at each other's throats. Aran and Brian were fighting today over a TV show! Everyone seems to be at their breaking point."

"I thought so! I knew it! I knew he was!"

"Don't be too hard on him, Sar. He's trying hard to do everything he should."

"I want to know right now, Danial, if you've heard him yelling at Devon, if you've heard Devon crying after Theo's been with him!"

Danial looked at me strangely, hearing the anger in my voice, and so I explained the scene that had happened with the lunch, the last time I'd seen Theo.

"No," Danial said finally, rubbing his eyes and sighing. "I've never seen him even raise his voice, Sar. Devon usually listens to him the first time he growls at him."

I breathed a sigh of relief.

"Go back to Hayden," Danial said, hugging me. "I'll call you tomorrow."

I gave him a last kiss, and then, I teleported back.

I sat for a while at the kitchen table reading my *Vampire Hunter D* novel, putting off facing Devlin. I didn't want to get in the Jacuzzi with him, but I also didn't want to fight with him. I was furious with him over what he'd done, and knew I was going to say something to him, if I saw him in my current mood. I wished Lash was here to talk it over with, but...

The phone rang, and I was so startled I dropped my book. The phone rang again.

Could it be him? God, please! I dove for the phone, and said, "Hello?"

"Sarelle?" a voice answered. A very calm, almost drugged-calm voice.

"Yes," I said quietly. "This is she. Who is this?"

"It's Harriet."

"Sorry, Harriet, I didn't recognize your voice. How is everything?"

"Good." That told me nothing. She seemed to have no inflection, no emphasis in her speech pattern. How could that be?

"Was there something you wanted to ask me about?"

"Yes. Let me think a moment."

I read a page of my book before she spoke again.

"Sarelle, I wanted to ask you, did you get any cravings for blood? For flesh?"

I felt a chill down my spine, and I swallowed very hard. My throat was suddenly dry as a desert.

"No," I got out finally. "But you must be channeling The Lust that way, Harriet. It's maybe specific to the bloodline? My advice would be to sate it, because trying to fight my own just made it worse. And you should know, your body will change from having a vampire's child. Your blood work will show that you are vampire, for all intents and purposes."

"We know that Sarelle, thank you," Samuel inserted coldly, and I shivered. I hadn't known he was listening in, though I should have expected it. "Harriet's blood shows she should be turned, but she has not so far—"

How long would that last? How much had Titus been able to change her? He'd had my blood to help him, and time to study it. Maybe it had been enough? I hoped so.

"—other than that, she is having your symptoms, Sarelle. She has been too warm this past week, and we've been using ice, which is working well."

I needed Dev here to help me. There might be something I hadn't thought through.

"We also called to ask you if you know what exactly made you unable to have children. Perseus is adamant that it not happen to Harriet. The first time, you healed because of the blood Danial had given you, from being partly turned in situ. But the second time, it didn't work, despite you having a Caesarian section—"

Shit!

"—were you told what made it different? If so, please tell us."

"She was not told," Devlin's voice purred into my ear. "She was asleep, for the surgery. The cougar came out first, but as before, the dhamphir was born with its vampire nature present. And the best way I can describe it was that my child fought being born that way. It didn't help that the dhamphir was moved into position to be born the normal way. And when the anesthetic took effect and the contractions stopped, it began to try to tear its way out of her."

240

I gasped at the horror of the picture he was painting, even though Dev was lying though his teeth.

"—Camlyn did the best he could, but it tore her up badly before he was able to get it out of her. And he took me aside, after he'd gotten the babies out, and Sar stable, and said it would be best that we remove her womb—"

"Couldn't he have done something, used some of your blood? She healed the last time."

"My advice would be to let Harriet deliver naturally," Devlin lied smoothly. "She'll be hurt, but she'll heal in time. Sar would have healed the damage in time from Venus, but Stephen said there was no time, she was bleeding to death. As it was, I had to use some of my blood to heal her, as Danial used some of his when she had Theoron. Sar isn't full vampire, and her healing abilities are not ours. There is only so much she can regenerate, Samuel, even with vampire blood."

"Mores the pity. But I'll take it under advisement, Dalcon. Now we've got to get to our doctor's appointment. As always, Sarelle, it has been a pleasure. Take good care of her, Dalcon."

It occurred to me that he was on Europe time, not USA time. Wasn't it day over there now? But then he'd said he had a demon working for him, so maybe they were teleporting in?

"Our best to you and to Harriet," Dev said smoothly, and we all hung up.

I sat back down, and then heard Dev's footsteps on the stairs. I stashed my book, though I was tempted to let him catch me reading it. Devlin came in a moment later in his robe, and sat down next to me. I thought he might want to talk about Harriet, or what might be wrong with her, as I was wondering if there was something wrong, if she was turning for real. It sounded like it, from what she had said.

But Devlin of course wasn't concerned with anyone but himself. "Why haven't you come upstairs?" His voice was a little annoyed. "I've been waiting for you in the Jacuzzi."

"Because I knew we were going to fight, and I didn't want to," I said honestly, not looking at him. "I've got enough to think about, without sleeping next to you, angry."

Devlin sat back in his chair, and looked at me. "I know you're angry because of Theoron being with Diana. Know this as well: Ulysses has not responded to me, and he was not at the door of Hayden tonight. He has until midnight to show himself, or I'm going to turn her."

"She's done nothing, Dev! Don't punish her for her brother's actions—"

"Sar, this is how war is waged—!"

"This isn't a *war*! This is a blood feud you caused, with your endless lust,

241

and irresponsible behavior! And you are just making things worse! Now T will be in danger, too! How many more people have to die? Robin, Seth, all the deaths, they are all on your head!"

Devlin got up, but he didn't seem angry, or as angry as I expected him to be. "I acted as I always have, Sarelle, to protect what matters to me! This is who I am, who I've always been! Now do you want to share my bed tonight or not?"

"Like I have a choice—!"

"You have a choice," Devlin said, his burning eyes slitted. "The furniture you ordered was delivered earlier today. Make yourself up one of the guest beds, and sleep there in a guest room, if you've a mind to. I don't care, so long as I know where to find you if the mood strikes me—!"

"I will then. Goodnight." My tone was pure malice. I got up, and turned to go, utterly furious with him.

But he wasn't done. "Fine," Devlin hissed furiously. "I'll be at your door in an hour, and I expect to find you both waiting and willing. But when I'm done with you, I'll leave you alone, to think over your ill-thought idealistic principles."

I was so furious at that moment that I debated getting my gun, and killing him. Ulysses could thank me, and maybe this would all be over, if I killed him. Then I remembered my explosive bullets gun was twisted burnt metal. I'd forgotten it that night at my house along with Theo's extra guns. I'd have forgotten the shotgun too, if Lash hadn't noticed it, and grabbed it. And my regular .38 and .22 would have no effect on Devlin.

"I can see in your eyes you're thinking about denying me—"

I'm thinking about killing you, you bastard! "How could you do it?" I whispered. "How could you force her—?"

"She liked me watching her, as T gave her her first orgasm. She said so as she cried out—"

"You disgust me! How could you force a woman like that, Dev? You know she would never have done it, if you hadn't given her your blood!"

"What I did to her wasn't forced. Neither was our first time together, or any of what happened after! You haven't seen real force," Devlin sneered, his eyes angry, but still that beautiful melting gold. "I was very gentle with you in that hotel that day, Sweet Sar. But I'm not going to be gentle with you tonight. And you can fight me if you want this time, but I'll have you just the same as I did then."

"You fucking no good son-of-a-bitch bastard! Maybe I should let Ulysses inside Hayden to finish you once and for all! Perseus couldn't be more despicable! No one could!"

Devlin stalked toward me, until he had me against the wall, his hands on either side. His eyes were red tinged now, and angry. "Shut your mouth!" he hissed. "You depend on me for your safety, and you dare to judge my actions? I didn't see you crying for Catherine, when Lash slit her throat, or Tasha, when I drained her! But maybe if you'd been the one tortured by Ulysses, you'll be a little less sanctimonious!"

"Lash told me the truth, that he drained her," I said, my eyes shut as the tears trickled out of them. "And I suspect he maybe ate her too. You don't have to lie for him, to protect me. I know what he—"

"Stop talking about *him*!" Devlin shouted. "I hate you, you bitch! I hate that I love you, that I keep wanting you, and you never want me!"

"How can I want you?" I screamed back at him. "When you do these things that are so monstrous! I told you that you could change, that you didn't have to be this way! But now, after all this time, it's obvious! No one ever made you be this way. You *like* being a monster! You love it! You love hurting people! You are evil, right to the core of your black heart!"

Devlin looked so angry that I thought he might strike me, but as before, he did nothing, just walked away. I heard his feet going up the stairs, and wondered if he was going to Diana's room, to either have her or kill her. I decided it didn't matter, not right now, because no matter which it was, I couldn't save her, or stop him. I'd be lucky if I could save myself.

I got up, and went to the green and gold room. I'd have gone to the flame room, but that was my sewing room now, and I didn't want to sleep on the floor, no matter that I wanted to feel close to Lash. And I knew the door to his room would be locked. It had been when I'd tried it yesterday, anyway.

I turned on the ceiling light, and saw the bed had been set up, and the mattresses were there too. I went downstairs to the laundry room/linen closet, got a sheet set and matching blanket, and made up the bed. They were plain cotton with a rosebud pattern, and I liked that suddenly, as they reminded me of sheets I'd once had years before. The comforter was soft, and I felt a little better. I could pretend I was home maybe, really home, even if just for tonight. I put my book on the nightstand, and plugged in the floor lamp. The nightstand lamp was already plugged in.

I thought about taking a shower, but knew I had no shampoo, or soap. I traipsed back to the supply closet, and got some regular soap. I wasn't going to Devlin's room to get my shampoo, or leave-in conditioner. Then I realized that in the midst of everything, I'd forgotten my dogs. I'd seen them earlier, but where were they now? They must already be in their beds. I couldn't be here, and leave them alone in Devlin's room with him. I wouldn't.

Fuck it. I would have to go and get them. I could get my shampoo while I was there.

I went to the door, and opened it, to see Devlin standing there, his eyes golden, and filled with desire. He wore only jeans. I backed up without a word, and he advanced, slamming the door behind him, and breaking the lock, so the door couldn't be opened.

"Get on the bed. Now." His voice was menacing, low, and filled with anger.

I thought about fighting him, but knew there was no point. I got on the bed, and without a word, Devlin stripped off his jeans, and began tearing my clothes off, literally ripping them into pieces when they wouldn't come off fast enough for him. Soon, I was naked, and Devlin flipped me over face down on the bed. With no warning, he thrust the whole length of himself inside me, and I cried out in pain. Devlin groaned in pleasure, but even in that sound, his anger was still present. He began thrusting hard, making me take all of him, as he growled over and over. I wasn't ready, or wet enough, and every thrust brought pain.

"Please stop!" I gasped out. "I won't fight you, Dev! Please, don't hurt me anymore!"

Devlin stopped at once, and withdrew from me, rolling on his back. For a long time he just lay beside me, and said nothing. I rolled over with effort and a small hiss of pain to lie on my back, but I said nothing either. I reached out to him, and grabbed his hand, holding it.

It was true he was awful, was terrible, and he'd just hurt me. But I needed his protection. And more than that, Venus did. We all did. With Lash in jail, it was only him who stood between Ulysses, the vampire hunters, the other Rulers, and me. Theo couldn't do it, much as I wished he could. Danial, much as I might love him, was just not ruthless or cruel enough. Devlin was in spades, but that savageness came with a price, and that was being with someone like him was hard, because his ruthlessness and cruelty were a large part of him, and not something he could just take out of storage and dust off when he needed to defend me, just as Lash wasn't any less a brutal killer just because he'd been a gentle lover and good friend. But I made myself hold on to the fact that although Devlin had said horrible things to me and he'd made me cower, in the end, he'd never struck me. And when I'd asked him to stop, told him he was hurting me, he'd stopped immediately.

I knew Theo wouldn't agree that I still needed to be with Dev for protection. But I had thought about that a lot earlier tonight, and I'd decided he was wrong to assume my mortality would mean anything. I might be human now, but all that was needed to change that was some vampire blood. I wasn't stupid enough to think that Samuel or Perseus, or now even Michael wouldn't want me to be bound to them as I had been to Dev and Danial, or that they wouldn't do exactly that, if they were given a chance. Especially if they found out I could bear children again, or that I was no longer under Devlin's protection.

This wasn't all his fault either, even though it was easy for me to blame this all on him, as I had with Danial earlier, and with Dev himself in Hayden's kitchen. Remembering what had happened, I felt the kind of shame I hadn't felt in a long time, for what I'd said to him. We were all on edge because of the attacks, and the constant tension. I had just as bad a temper as he did. And he always seemed to bring out the worst in me, just as I brought out the worst in him.

"I'm sorry," I said quietly. "I shouldn't have said those things I said to you. It's true, I've never fought a war. Ulysses tortured you as painfully as he could, and he meant to kill you. I remember well how severe your wounds were that night. And I am thankful to you, for protecting me and our daughter. I'm just not used to seeing innocents hurt in the crossfire. Guards, sure, but not a girl who just wanted to be a nurse, who never wanted to hurt anyone." I paused and swallowed. "You aren't evil, Dev. And I'm sorry I said you were. And the...the stuff, too."

Devlin squeezed my hand, and then he pulled me into his embrace. I felt him crying, and soon we were both weeping, sobbing together, holding each other tightly. After a while, our tears lessened, and Devlin drew back to look at me. He looked as weary and worn out as I knew I had to look. But some of our tension had eased, flowing out of us in our tears. "I'm sorry for what I did to you," he said quietly. "If you'll let me, I'll heal you, Sar."

I nodded, and he moved himself lower on the bed, hesitantly touching me. I closed my eyes, and lay back. Soon, I felt him kissing me intimately. In a few minutes, the pain eased, and then stopped all together.

Devlin crawled back up beside me, and cradled me in his arms, looking down at me. "It's true, what you said. I enjoy having power over people. I enjoy bending them to my will. I always have, even when I was mortal. It wasn't something I became. The vampire blood just seemed to make the desire stronger, my need for it worse..." He swallowed. "And there is evil in that, that I like it, that I desire it, that I didn't have to force myself to do what I did to Diana, like Danial would have had to, if he'd done it. I knew she was innocent, and I loved taking that innocence from her, in just the way I took it."

He bent in to kiss me gently, and I let him. "I understand, if you don't want to stay here at Hayden with me now, or Oath to me. But I ask you to stay at Hayden, at least for now, where I can protect you, Sar. And if you leave to go to Danial's, I ask you to not distance yourself from Venus because of me. Don't stay away for days and weeks like you did before, just to avoid me. I can not be here, when you come to see her, if it will help—"

"I'll stay for now."

Devlin hugged me tightly, and said nothing for a while. "Part of the reason I did what I did was because I didn't want T to fall in love with Serena," he said finally. "A man always remembers his first. And he might decide he needed to save her from her current profession. But there was no one else, Sar! I would not trust just some woman that we picked up in a bar like Davy's, or one of my blood donors, or Danial's! And the rest of the reason was that Diana also needed someone to take her virginity, to be tender and careful with her, the way one of my men would not have been. I didn't want to break my promise to you, and do it myself. Despite that a grim fate most likely lies in store for her, I wouldn't have her tortured, or hurt...like I just hurt you."

"I can forgive you hurting me," I said softly. "You stopped, when I asked you to. But do you understand that I'm probably not going to Oath to you again, because of what you just did to me? I can't be with a man I can't trust not to hurt me. And I can't trust you, Dev. If I give you an opening, you'll hurt me again, sure as you are sorry about it now. It's not 'if', it's 'when.' And it's way past time I faced that, and stopped making excuses for you."

"Do you still love me?" There were tears in his voice.

But when I answered him, there were none in mine.

"I'll always love you. But that's not enough. And when Ulysses is dead, I'm going to go and live with Danial and Theo. Theo and I'll rebuild my house in the spring, and then I'll live just with him. But I'll come to see Venus every other day. And it's fine, if you're here when I visit her. It's maybe the best thing to come out of all of this, that I'm spending time with her, and getting to know her. I wouldn't have otherwise, not like this, and that would have been something I would come to regret, when she was older. "

We said nothing for many minutes. Devlin just held me, and I held him too.

"I want to stay here with you for a while, to sleep. Will you let me stay here with you?"

"Of course. But I'm going to read my book, if you don't mind."

Devlin grimaced a little but nodded. He held me, and laid his head on my chest, and was asleep in moments. I rolled my eyes, but let myself get engrossed in my reading.

I was finishing the last page of *Vampire Hunter D* when my fox head choker fell off my neck with a soft clink.

Chapter Twenty-One

I stared at the shining gold choker for a split second in confusion, then a horrified scream built up inside me and raggedly burst free. "Devlin!" I screamed at the top of my lungs. "Devlin!"

Devlin woke with a start, sitting up at once and reaching for me. "What is it?" he said, his faintly shining eyes worried at my panic. "Sar, say something!"

I bit my lip hard enough to draw blood, fighting for control to get the words out, my shaking hands fumbling at the choker, trying desperately to clasp it around my neck. Yet the links wouldn't join together no matter what I visualized in my head. "The choker!" I stammered. "Danial's choker! It fell off! It fell off!"

Devlin stared at me, then down at the choker in my hands, his expression more scared then I'd even seen him. "You must have brushed it, Sar," he said quickly, "Try to refasten it!"

"I tried already!" I shouted, frantically trying again. "It won't fasten! The links aren't moving at all!"

There was the sound of booted feet running down the corridor toward us. Several guards burst through the door, guns drawn. "What is it?" one of them asked. "Boss?"

Devlin yanked me into his arms, holding me so tightly I couldn't breathe. "Call Danial! Find out where he was tonight, Keith, immediately," he shouted. "There's been an attack! Get Titus! Get him here at once!"

Keith was already at the doorway when Jazz slammed into him trying to get into the room. The guard's normally easygoing expression was horrified. "Devlin!" he said hastily. "A van just dropped a body by the front gate, with a note on it."

"Take us there, Sar," Devlin ordered, tossing me a robe as he shrugged one on himself and belted it. I slid the robe around my shoulder, grabbed his hand, and teleported us, the bitterly cold ground making me stagger as we materialized near Hayden's front gate.

Nick, Seth, Del, and a few other bears were there standing in a half circle, a crumpled body lying at their feet.

What I had feared most had happened. "Danial!" I screamed, releasing Devlin's hand and setting off at a run. Devlin also ran to Danial, his vampiric speed letting him arrive first. He knelt at his brother's side, turning him over. Danial was ash pale, paler than he had been that night years ago when I had first discovered him. His dark hair was limp and caked with dirt. A huge, ragged, bloodless wound covered his throat. His eyes were closed.

I knelt beside him in the snow, grasping his hand in mine, looking for a heartbeat. There was none I could detect, but I told myself that didn't mean anything. *Danial can slow his heart when he's injured or cold. That's all it is, his self-preservation kicking in. He's going to be fine. He's going to be fine!*

"Ulysses drained him," Devlin said brokenly, hugging his brother's body to his chest. A second later he leaped to his feet, Danial in his arms. "Take us to Titus's basement lab," Devlin yelled to me, extending his right hand from beneath Danial's back. I grasped it, and teleported us back, with difficulty. Titus was waiting there almost if he expected us, Keith and Jerry with him. Together, they cleared a section of the floor and helped lay Danial down on some blankets.

"They didn't take his heart," Devlin murmured, tears running down his face. "There's hope."

"Not much," Titus said slowly. "He doesn't have a heartbeat, Devlin."

"I'll give him my blood," Devlin said, rolling up his sleeve. "But you'll have to pull him off me, or he'll kill me."

"Don't do it," Titus cautioned, evoking my horrified stare. "This is what Ulysses wants, to tempt you into making yourself feeble and weak by trying to save your brother. You give him enough of your blood, Dev, you'll lose all your strength."

"I don't give it to him, he dies!" Devlin shouted back at him. "Sar's blood isn't back to normal yet, and demon blood or were won't do it, Titus! He needs my blood."

"Dev!" Titus shouted, his bass voice cracking and rumbling with sheer power. "Listen to me. You are going to need to defend not only your territory now, but his, too! Give him only a little. You can feed extensively, and give him a little every day."

"*It won't be enough!*" Devlin screamed frantically, flinging his arm dramatically, his nails grown to talons in his fury. "We've got to get an older vampire, someone like Catherine."

"You have any other old lovers willing to give you their immortality?" Titus said sarcastically. "You'd need a vampire that was at least a few hundred years old. There are none in this state, save you and your brother. There are only a few on this continent! They are too well protected now for me to kidnap one of them, after it got out what happened to Ebediah and Sola!"

Devlin didn't respond, he just bit his wrist, and held it over Danial's mouth, prying open Danial's mouth with his other hand. The wound closed within a minute, and Devlin reopened it, snarling in his fear and worry. Devlin's blood dripped into Danial's mouth, but he didn't respond. Devlin did this repeatedly for the next ten minutes, as I paced back and forth beside him, wanting to help but not knowing how. Keith and Jerry leaned against the door, watchful while trying not to stare. Titus sat in one of his leather chairs, paging though a tome as though this sort of thing happened every day. Danial's body didn't change, or show any signs of life with Dev's repeated donations of blood. The hole in his throat remained ragged and bloodless, the grey tint to his skin unchanged.

"Fight," Devlin snarled down at Danial, pausing in his efforts. "Damn it, fight!"

"Devlin, you are going to have to—" Titus began gently.

"No!" Devlin shrieked at him, his face a mask of blood, his golden eyes solid red and glowing with rage. "I am not letting him go! Not now, not when we are finally true brothers again, after spending hundreds of years back stabbing one another! It's not going to end like this!"

Devlin staggered to his feet, then grabbed a serrated knife from a nearby shelf. He turned back to Danial and in one quick motion, he cut his own throat. I screamed, and Titus started forward, but Devlin had already sunk to his knees beside Danial, leaning over him, the old blood pouring from the grievous wound into Danial's mouth. And beyond all hope, Danial reacted, his hand reaching up to clamp Devlin's wound to his lips as his throat worked to swallow the life-giving blood. Titus and I froze in our tracks, watching and waiting.

Within a minute, the wound had closed around Danial's teeth, but Danial was still drinking. Devlin was swaying on his knees, his normal color turning to ash pale as Danial drained him. His eyes flickered to me, the light in them faltering.

Titus acted, yanking Devlin away from Danial. Blood spurted from Devlin's throat as they both fell to the floor, Devlin on top of Titus.

Danial was no longer gray, but he was still very pale, and his arm had fallen by his side, in its original position.

"I…I can't give him any more," Devlin said weakly. His throat had healed, though the flesh looked raw. "Not and still be able to recover with only human blood. I—"

"Stay here and don't move," Titus instructed, dragging Devlin another few feet from Danial. The evil feeling was suddenly pouring off him, permeating me to the point I shivered. It was an indication to me of how worried he was, that he had released his hold on it so completely. "I'll call, and arrange for some of your regulars."

Titus got to his feet, and yelled for Seth to "start calling the list."

"Ten, at least," Devlin called weakly, staying where he was on the floor.

Titus looked to the door suddenly, and motioned to Jerry and Keith. They both nodded. In a flash they were gone out the door, their feet pounding up the cellar stairs.

"I had better go now," Titus rumbled, looking a little put out. "Teleporting would be fastest. Devlin can't go long without replenishing himself, or he may lose consciousness, too."

Devlin's response was to lie back slowly so he was spread-eagled on the floor.

"Sar, stay away from them both," Titus intoned in a cautionary manner. "They are both near death, and weak. I shouldn't leave you here with them alone, but—"

"Let me get dressed, and I'll help you bring the women here," I offered quickly. "Another person teleporting will make it go faster."

Titus looked surprised, but nodded. "Yes, it will. Dress and return to me." We ascended the stairs together quickly. As he went into the kitchen, I ran up to Devlin's bedroom, and pulled on some clothes. I raced back down the stairs, then sought out Titus, who was just hanging up the phone.

He teleported me to the first girl's house, and left me there to bring her back to Hayden. We worked in tandem this way, until there were nine girls in the living room. All were larger women, yet more unneeded proof that Devlin preferred women blessed with larger breasts and hips. All women, including Catherine and Anna, that I had ever seen him feed from or be with had been at least a size twelve or fourteen, with a C-cup or greater. He had meant what he said, when he'd told me I was getting too thin for him. I felt a little odd thinking of that at a time like this, so I let it go, telling myself to worry about being jealous later.

Keith and Jerry had been busy while we'd been gone, as all the women had been ready "for pickup." Nick was also present, getting information from the girls as they appeared and taking it down on a clipboard. He looked the same as he had before Ulysses had skinned him alive. I was very glad to see him with skin on again, and looking none the worse for wear.

The first girl I'd brought to Hayden opened the cellar door, looking weak and pale. Nick took her arm and motioned to me. I hurried to her side and supported her, as he motioned to the next woman to come with him downstairs. I teleported Devlin's donor back to her home, and helped her lay down on her couch while I got her a glass of water.

"Who are you?" she said softly. "Are you Titus's Leri?"

I tried not to grin at that, and mostly succeeded. "I'm Sarelle, Devlin's Oathed One."

Her expression became surprised. "You don't have his symbol. Aren't you supposed to have some kind of necklace?"

How did this woman know all this? "Who are you?"

"I'm Rebecca," she said softly, blushing a deep red. "I feed Mr. Dalcon sometimes."

At her admission, I wondered instantly if she got paid or she did it because Devlin was so attractive. But it wasn't the kind of thing I could ask, and it really wasn't my business anyway. She was willing, which was all that mattered to me.

"Do you live with him, there at his house?" she said hesitantly. "I know he takes us to the Silver guest room now usually, because he said he'd given his word not to have any woman save one in his bedroom."

That was touching, that Devlin had said that, and meant it. Too bad he was such a royal bastard some of the time. "Yes," I said, nodding. "I live at Hayden with him." *For now.*

"You can go ahead home," Rebecca said, offering a tentative smile. "I'll be okay. He took more than he usually does, but I feel fine, and I don't have to work tomorrow."

"You're sure?" I said with concern. "I don't want you to faint."

"I'll sleep here for a while, and be just fine," Rebecca she assured me. "But Devlin's weaker than I've ever seen him. You should go back to him. He needs you."

I nodded, and with a last good-bye, teleported back to Hayden.

That same scene repeated the rest of the night. The girls changed in coloring and beauty, but all of them seemed to adore Devlin, to actually be concerned for him. I was surprised but pleased at that, to know they both liked and cared about him. I finally reappeared after getting the last girl home.

Titus was waiting for me in the living room, sitting on the couch, watching the end of some bad Sci-Fi movie about a ghost ship. I eased down beside him, and he gave me a warm hug.

"Devlin's fine," Titus said, his tone an odd mix of relief and sadness. "He is almost back to full strength, though he'll have to sleep for a good while tonight and tomorrow."

"What's wrong?" I asked pointedly. "You're upset about something."

"Rip was guarding Danial and Theoron when they were attacked."

I felt another scream building and rose off the couch to teleport. Titus grabbed my wrist, stopping me from disappearing.

"Your son is okay," Titus said quickly. "Ulysses's men beat him badly, but he managed to get away before they could kill him. He said they thought he was dead."

Tears began to leak out of my eyes, making my vision heavily blurred. But for Lash's training, T would probably be dead. *God, what I wouldn't do to have him here with me, in my arms.* "Where is Theoron?"

"He's recovering back at his house. He'll sleep through the night, I gave him one of my potions to help him heal faster—"

I drew a long shuddering breath of relief.

"—but Rip they banished back to Hell," Titus said, agonized. "I have to get him out of there, Sar. He's probably being tortured right now."

I looked at him fearfully, because from his voice, he was asking for my help. "I don't need to sell my soul or anything, do I?" I said hesitantly. "I want to help, but I can't do that."

"No," Titus said, his smile forced. "I wouldn't let you do that, anyway. But I will need your son's presence and some of your blood to help break my brother free."

"Of course, we'll help," I said, nodding

Titus patted my arm, for the first time losing his worried expression and looking resolute. "We'll do it tomorrow night. Dev needs to be at full strength before I'd want to leave him unguarded, and he'll be recovered by then, hopefully. With his help, it will go more smoothly."

What? Rescuing Rip from Hell? In what world can that go smoothly?

Titus got up, and held out his clawed hand. "I'll take you up to Devlin. You should get some sleep, too. It's nearly dawn, and tomorrow night's already looking busy."

I was exhausted and moving on will alone, I was so tired. Titus led me upstairs, and left me at Devlin's door. I entered. My handsome vampire was asleep in bed, lying on his side as he liked to when he was alone. He didn't stir when I entered, leaving me to conclude that he was renewing himself with blood and he'd be unconscious for a while.

Even in my state of fatigue, I stood there for a few minutes, studying him. It felt odd to be here back in this bedroom with him, after what had happened earlier between us. I'd pretty much told him I was leaving, and going to live with Danial. Now here I was, getting ready to climb into bed with him after helping him to regain his strength. But what else was there for me to do? Where else could I go? Theo was probably enraged after hearing what happened to

Danial, and most likely was with Jenny right now, working out the kinks. He wouldn't welcome me showing up and saying I needed him to hold me. Lash was in prison, though most likely someone had called him to let him know what had happened. Sure, I could go to Theoron and spend the night watching over him, but I had noticed tonight that Serena was nowhere in evidence, which made me think that Titus had left T in capable hands, ones he might welcome more than my own. Sure, I could go to Danial's house, and spend the night in his bed, and be alone with my thoughts. But was it right to be selfish and leave now like I'd planned? Devlin needed me here now, maybe more than he ever had.

Think about this in the morning. Tomorrow things would be clearer, with a good night's sleep, or at least something resembling one.

I let out a resigned sigh. I'd made this bed my own, and chosen this man, even if I'd second-guessed that decision more than a few times to date. I'd lie in it with him for now. But I was going to shower first.

After cleaning up and dressing in a simple cotton nightgown, I climbed into bed beside Devlin, and fell asleep, though I didn't touch him.

* * * *

What felt like a minute later, but in reality it was likely more like six hours passed before there was a knock at the door. I went to get up to answer it, but Devlin roused himself instead. He looked completely recovered, if a little sleepy, as he walked to the door and opened it.

Titus was there, waiting. "Danial's in my old room, lying on the bed. There's no change, Devlin."

The demon said the words as gently as possible, but Devlin still bowed under them, the weight of his grief a heavy burden. And I blanched, wondering where Diana was now, if Titus had acted on his own to destroy her in retaliation for Ulysses's draining of Danial. I said a quick prayer for her, and let it go. I still hadn't wished her harm, but I had my own wounds to nurse right now.

"But his heart is beating again," Devlin said quietly. "That's something." He shut the door, and came back to the bed, taking me in his arms.

"What are we going to do?" I whispered, clutching him to me.

"I will go to war," Devlin said darkly, his arms tightening around me. "It will not be pretty, Sarelle. A good deal more blood will be shed before this ends. But I promise you, I will protect you, and the life we have. I will find a way to bring Danial back to us, whatever the cost. This terror will end with Ulysses's death." He kissed my forehead. "I give you my word, my Oathed One."

I held him tight against me, tears leaking from my eyes, and prayed he was right. And I gave no voice to correct him.

About the Author

Tara Fox Hall's writing credits include nonfiction, horror, suspense, action-adventure, erotica, and contemporary and historical paranormal romance. She is the author of the paranormal action-adventure *Lash* series and the vampire romantic suspense *Promise Me* series. Tara divides her free time unequally between writing novels and short stories, chainsawing firewood, caring for stray animals, sewing cat and dog beds for donation to animal shelters, and target practice.

Other works by the author with Melange Books, LLC

Return To Me
Surrender to Me
The Origin of Fear in Spellbound 2011 Anthology
Night Music in Midnight Thirsts II Anthology
Partners in Midnight Thirsts II Anthology
Kink in Wicked Christmas Wishes Anthology
The Oath in Wicked Christmas Wishes Anthology
Bedtime Shadows Anthology
Make Me Behave Anthology
Latham's Landing, An Anthology

The Promise Me Series
Promise Me, Book 1
Broken Promise, Book 2
Taken in the Night, Book 3
Taken for his Own, Book 4
Promise Me Anthology, Book 4.5
Immortal Confessions, Book 5
Her Secret, Book 6
Point of No Return, Book 7
Lost Paradise, Book 8
Dark Solace, Book 9

Coming Soon
Tempest of Vengeance-Promise Me, Book 11

www.ingramcontent.com/pod-product-compliance
Lightning Source LLC
Chambersburg PA
CBHW050459260626
47157CB00004B/1115